Sordaak quickly withdrew his blade as the man dropped his weapon and began clawing at the small hole that had appeared in his neck. The farmer sagged to his knees and slumped forward. He ended up face down on the hard-packed dirt floor, where he lay still.

With no small effort, Sordaak forced down his rage, bent and wiped his blade clean on the dead man's tunic and glanced around, looking for possible threats. The thief had one farmer under control, and the only other discernible adversary was scrambling through the door into the night, his pockets jingling with coin.

Sordaak made his decision. He leapt after the fleeing figure with the words to yet another spell forming in his mind. He brushed aside the curtain that led out to the now darkened boardwalk and stepped into the gloom beyond. As his eyes adjusted, he spotted his quarry scurrying down the center of the street, oblivious to the fact he was being followed.

The words sprang to the sorcerer's lips, and he pointed his forefinger at the man, who stopped abruptly as if waiting for someone to catch up....

DRAGMA'S KEEP

VANCE PUMPHREY

Kellie,

Thank you SO much for your continued
support - It makes writing easier. I hope
you enjoy this the 2ⁿᵈ version of Book One
even more than the last. As Always
Thanks for reading!

LEAPING WIZARD PRESS

Vance L Pumphrey

Dragma's Keep
Book One in the Valdaar's Fist Series

Copyright © 2015 by Vance Pumphrey

Cover Art © 2015 Joe Calkins
Sword Logo Design © 2015 Joe Calkins

Published by Leaping Wizard Press

ISBN-10: 0988740532
ISBN-13: 978-0988740532

This book is also available in digital formats.

Discover other titles by the author at
VancePumphrey.com

I'd like to dedicate this book to my family—immediate and otherwise.

First, to my wife for holding our family together
(the really hard work) while I wandered the oceans
beneath the waves in the U.S. Submarine Force.

To my two sons, their wives, and my granddaughter,
who are really my pride and joy—
they are all doing so well and I am so, so proud of them.

My mother and father, without whom I would not be the person I am today.

My brothers and sisters (four of each) who,
through the tried and true method of punch first and ask questions later,
helped shape my personae in a manner
that can be seen in the words, thoughts, and actions
within the pages of this book.

And to my extended family for their love and support.

Thank you all.

Valdaar's Fist

What has Gone Before

Forged by mortals. … Enchanted by Drow. …
Wielded by a God. …. Lost by man…

Or was it?

The legend of *Valdaar's Fist* survived for many years even after it was reported destroyed with the god Valdaar in ages long since passed. But eventually even the legends were forgotten. However, since the purported reappearance of this ancient foe of chaos and good, many a sorcerer and high priest have been found poring over ancient tomes and moldy manuscripts.

Though it has been several millennia since the powerful sword last wielded its terrible might, the legends and stories should not have been forgotten. For during the time of its reign it was common knowledge that the blade, and the life force within, could not be destroyed. Now much time has been wasted and many lives lost. *Valdaar's Fist* is once again in position to wreak its evil.

Most accounts of the sword's power and might are forever lost, but a few have surfaced—enough to instill fear in the hearts of even the most fearless of men.

The blade was commissioned to be forged by Praxaar in an age when he was not yet a great god. A council of the highest of all the Dwarf clans in the land convened to determine which metals were to be used. Much arguing ensued, until Praxaar stepped in and appointed one master metalsmith from each clan to enter the mines of Tressgaard and forge the blade from the strongest metals known to men or gods. It was a time when the lore of metal was at its peak—indeed a time when artifacts and Vorpal weapons were abundant. A lore now mostly forgotten by mortals.

Several years passed before a suitable alloy was found. An alloy lighter by half than iron, as hard as the purest of diamonds and able to hold an edge better than even Mithryl. An alloy now known as Adamantine, the metal of the gods.

On the day the forging was completed, a full legion under the command of Valdaar (Praxaar's twin brother) attacked the commission and wiped it out. The sword was stolen and all but one of the dwarves responsible for its creation were hunted down and killed. That lone dwarf escaped, going into hiding. He used the lore gleaned from their efforts only sparingly. It was thought that he carried to his unmarked grave the knowledge of how to make—and to unmake—the metal. But he, Forrin Shieldsmasher, lived a long, long life as dwarves sometimes do. And during that time he formed a secret sect that continued to work with the metal formula that only they knew. But that is another story for a different tale.

Valdaar turned the blade over to the Drow (dark) elves for its enchantment. In return for the most powerful sword known to man or the gods, Valdaar promised to deliver them from their self-inflicted exile beneath the mountains of Tressgaard, into a position to once again rule the destiny of the land.

Valdaar's Fist, as it was now becoming known, made the descent into those depths, where it remained for almost a decade. What happened to the blade during those years is not recorded anywhere. However, the emergence of the sword is marked clearly in any text dating back that far.

While waiting on his sword, Valdaar was not idle. He assembled under his command the largest army ever known. Orcs, Half-Orcs, Goblins, Men, and even Drow Elves had united under his leadership.

Finally, one spring morning in the year Praxaar was crowned Lord of All the Land, Valdaar called together his vast army and was presented his new sword.

The sheath was of the purest Mithryl with a single large red ruby on its side—said to be the eye of the sword when sheathed—that was mounted just below the braided Mithryl tie string. The pommel, chipped from a single piece of pure obsidian, was wrapped in the same Mithryl braid as a grip and had an intricately carved skull affixed to the end, a skull fashioned from a huge black diamond almost as large as a fist. When drawn, the eyes of the skull emitted a deep blood red glow, and it is said that the horrid mouth moved when the sword chose to speak—an occurrence known to be seldom.

Valdaar signaled for and received silence. Such a hush spread over the gathered throng that even the birds in the trees stopped singing and the insects ceased buzzing. He raised the sheathed sword at arm's length above his head. Slowly and with definite purpose, he withdrew the blade. An even deeper silence spread over the land for miles as the power of blade was unleashed.

When fully drawn, it writhed and seethed with black flames. Not glowing, the flames instead seemed to pull the light out of the air around the sword, giving the edges an indistinct appearance, making it hard to look at for any period of time. Through the flames, runes danced and glowed golden upon its blackened surface, shimmering as if seen through a haze.

The dark force grew until it engulfed Valdaar, and he seemed to physically grow with the power, until all in the army could see and hear him clearly. "I name you *The Fist of Valdaar!*" he said, his voice rising with each word until, at the end, he spoke clearly to even the farthest divisions of the army.

Here the ancient texts disagree. Some say the sword spoke next, others Valdaar. But all agree as to what was said: "Make preparation for war. We march in a fortnight. By the time winter comes all of the Land will be ours!" The last word echoed for several moments in the sudden silence that followed. Then a cheer erupted, one that within the space of a single heartbeat grew to deafening proportions.

By late fall, Praxaar and the tattered remains of his army were besieged within the walls of the once fair city of Urendale. They managed to hold out for several weeks, but the city was doomed to fall. Praxaar and the members of his High Council were secreted out under the cover of darkness and managed to escape. He vowed to one day return and avenge the deaths of those who sacrificed their lives to guarantee his passage.

Valdaar was crowned king with his brother's crown and the dark ages settled upon the land.

The tales that emerged from that six-month war cast fear and doubt into hearts of even the gods. The Blade was known to speak several languages and was able to disguise itself at will. Worse yet, any servant of Chaos and Good that was so much as to be scratched by the sword disintegrated, leaving just a burnt patch where he or she once stood.

The texts get very indistinct as to which were the powers of the sword and which belonged to Valdaar, as little was known about either prior to the war. During the ensuing years, as many records as could be found concerning the blade were destroyed in an attempt to continue the confusion and to ensure there was no knowledge passed that could lead to the sword's unmaking.

Through the power of *Valdaar's Fist*, The Dark King, as he was now beginning to be known, grew in strength and stature. His council consisted of dark Lords of the Drow, several high priests and powerful sorcerers. He seemed to never age and his wisdom surpassed all. Thus his reign lasted for more than a hundred years without opposition.

But Praxaar's vow also kept him young. He amassed his army in secret. Finally, however, fearing they would soon be discovered, he attacked. Once again the might of *Valdaar's Fist* was called upon. It is said that without its support, Valdaar would have never lasted even a year, so vast was the army of Praxaar. But such was their combined lore that the battle dragged on for nearly a century. In the end, Valdaar was betrayed and defeated.

The great hall where Valdaar and the remnants of his Council made their final stand was littered with hundreds of dead and dying. When the blade in Praxaar's hand, said to be fashioned from a piece of the sun (yet another story), pierced Valdaar's heart, he sank slowly into a heap in a corner, his eyes still open, hatred spewing from them.

When they finally glazed over, his entire body seemed to collapse, leaving nothing more than his armor, helm, gauntlets, and, of course, the sword. The sword spoke then, its evil stare piercing into Praxaar's eyes, holding him momentarily powerless. "We are vanquished now. But, when the time is once again right—when a suitable vassal walks the land—I will return. Together we will rule all there is to rule, and even the gods will be at our mercy." With that, the sheath appeared around the sword and it fell silent.

Praxaar and his forces secreted the sword and other artifacts away, fearing his brother would find a way to make true on his promise. After a millennia or so, the worry subsided, and the good times that had settled into the hearts of his host pushed aside the fear of those last words. Praxaar began to believe the sword had indeed been merely boastful.

Now, almost two millennia after its reported demise, the blade has returned.

Chapter One

A Chance Encounter

Sordaak glared at the others in the tavern. The stench of unwashed bodies and stale smoke only added coals to his mood.

"Fools," Sordaak muttered under his breath as his gaze fell upon some of the locals at a nearby table who were losing badly in a game of chance to a man who was an obvious thief.

Then Sordaak chuckled as a glimmer of an idea began to work its way through the haze of ale that clouded his mind. *Yes, maybe this will be just what I need to ease the boredom,* he thought as he stroked the few scraggly hairs on his chin.

Sordaak mumbled the words to the spell quietly so that no one would hear and made the required arcane gestures within the folds of the voluminous robe that hid his slight frame.

As he felt the force of the spell build around him, the mage closed his eyes and forced his thoughts into the mind of the farmer across from the thief, who had his back to the caster. Sordaak sensed the confusion of the man, but he pushed that aside to insert his message.

"You are being cheated," Sordaak projected. The farmer's shoulders tensed and he glared around suddenly, looking for the source of the whisper. Failing to see anyone close enough, he turned back to the game.

"That man across from you," Sordaak projected, "watch his hands closely." The man looked right and left. Again seeing no one in the immediate vicinity, he shifted nervously in his chair. But now his eyes locked on the thief's hands.

The opportunity Sordaak was waiting for came soon enough when the rogue's right hand moved to straighten his tunic under his cloak.

"There! See!" Sordaak hissed.

It mattered not whether the rogue was trying to cheat. The farmer surged to his feet, sending his chair skittering backward, where it crashed into Sordaak's right shin.

"Cheat!" the farmer shouted. "Thief!" he spat as his hand dove toward the knife at his belt.

"I saw it, too!" said one of the others who had been losing just as badly, his hand also flashing for his blade. A third followed suit, while the remaining farmer who had been losing the worst of all reached for the pile of coins in the center of the table.

The thief's hand appeared out from his tunic in a flash with a long, thin dagger. In a blur, he pinned the greedy farmer's hand to the table, the blade passing cleanly through the back of his hand and deep into the wood. The farmer screamed as two more daggers appeared as if by magic, one in each of the rogue's hands. He bent into a crouch to deal with the remaining farmers. Both men's eyes bulged out of their sockets as they stared at the hand pinned to the table.

Sordaak neither heard nor saw any of it. A red haze blurred his vision of everything but the insolent farmer who had struck him with the chair. As the mage kicked the offending piece of furniture aside, he spat several arcane words, jumped a step in the direction of the unwary farmer and backhanded him from behind atop his ear.

A loud crack was heard at the point of impact, and the man's head snapped over, his neck clearly broken. The farmer's body stiffened and he fell over with a crash, the side of his head around his ear charred and smoking.

The farmer on Sordaak's right shouted, "Accomplice!" He swung his short-sword in a vicious arc that would have decapitated the spell-caster—or at the very least made breathing a bit more difficult—had the mage not seen it coming and thrown himself to the floor, his hand reaching for a dagger at his belt.

Unaccustomed to the sword, the farmer recovered slowly. He kicked a chair out of the way just as Sordaak came off of the floor in a lunge. The farmer struggled to get the sword back around in a futile attempt to block Sordaak's flashing blade. Sick realization clouded the man's eyes as the dagger sank to the hilt in his throat.

Sordaak quickly withdrew his blade as the man dropped his weapon and began clawing at the small hole in his neck. He sagged to his knees and slowly slumped forward. He ended up face down on the hard-packed floor, where he lay still.

With no small effort, Sordaak forced his rage down, bent and wiped his blade clean on the dead man's tunic and glanced around, looking for possible threats. The thief had one farmer under control, and the only other was scrambling through the door into the night, his pockets jingling with coin.

Sordaak made his decision. He leapt after the fleeing figure with the words to yet another spell forming in his mind. He brushed aside the curtain that led out to the now darkened boardwalk and stepped into the gloom beyond. As his eyes adjusted, he spotted his quarry scurrying down the center of the street, oblivious to the fact he was being followed.

The words sprang to the sorcerer's lips, and he pointed his forefinger at the man, who stopped abruptly as if waiting for someone to catch up.

Sordaak hustled up to the farmer and emptied the man's pockets into a small bag that he pulled from under his cloak. The mage then stepped back and swung the heavy bag, clouting the man behind his ear with a thud that caused the coins inside to clank together in a most satisfactory fashion.

The farmer sank to the ground with a sigh just as the rogue came running up, stuffing coins into various folds in his tunic—obviously taken from the unfortunates he'd left behind in the tavern. They would not need them anymore, he reasoned.

"Thanks for the help," the thief said quickly, looking over his shoulder toward the still covered tavern door.

Unwilling to let his part in starting the fracas be known just yet, Sordaak said, "An innocent bystander who saw an opportunity to make some coin, that's all."

The thief squinted as he looked a little closer at the robed figure next to him. "Thanks all the same. They don't take kindly to those of The Profession around these parts—spell-casters, either, for that matter." After another quick glance in the direction from which they had come, he said, "I think we had better make ourselves scarce."

Sordaak turned to also look in the direction of the tavern, which was decidedly more active now. Several loud voices could be heard from within, although no one had stepped through the door. "Any thought as to which direction?" the caster asked after a moment's consideration.

The thief paused a moment to ponder the question. "The local guild will put us up until things have cooled off a bit," he said. "Of course they will want a cut…"

"No, thanks," the mage answered. "If it's just the same to you, I would rather not get myself associated with your associates, if you know what I mean." He glanced at the thief. "No offense intended, of course."

"None taken, at least not at this point," the rogue said with a grin.

"Well," Sordaak said after another glance toward the inn, "let's get out of town. Right now might be a good time." The curtain to the inn moved, but still no one appeared. "I have a friend north of town—"

"With a temper like yours," the thief interrupted, "you still manage to make friends?" After a sharp glance from the caster he went on quickly. "North it is!"

Just then the curtain separating the tavern from the boardwalk was pushed aside, spilling light from the doorway into the dusty road. "Now *does* look like a very good time to get started," the rogue said. He darted to their left between two buildings, with Sordaak close on his heels.

"There they go!" shouted a man from the doorway. "After them!" The speaker ran toward the man left lying in the street, several others not far behind.

A few minutes and many twists and turns later found the pair in an alleyway behind the Trails End Inn, the site of their escapades.

"I've got a horse and a couple of pack animals in the stable here," the thief gasped between breaths, pointing to a large building looming out of the darkness. "By the way," he wheezed, "my name is Savinhand. Most just call me Savin, or Thumbs. What do I call you?"

"Sordaak. Just call me Sordaak," the sorcerer puffed as he peered into the darkness, looking for pursuers.

"Don't worry about them," the rogue said, "I'm pretty sure we lost 'em."

"I'm not so sure," Sordaak said as he approached the partially open stable door. "Thumbs? How did you get a nickname like that?"

"Just a moniker someone once saddled me with that stuck," he said, flashing a smile of white, even teeth. "Actually, as you may have noticed I am pretty good with my hands." Turning toward the stable door, he lowered his voice. "Do you suppose word has made it this far? I would hate to wander into a welcoming committee."

"Agreed." Sordaak dropped his voice to a whisper as well. "However, I hear nothing from within." He didn't really sound all that convinced as he started around the corner.

"Just the same," Savin said, stopping the mage by putting a hand on his shoulder, "better let me go first." He noted a dim light emanating from behind the stalls that probably spelled trouble. The rogue stepped into the doorway first. "I know how to handle these types of situations," he said without looking back. Indeed, he seemed to disappear into the darkness without a sound, leaving Sordaak staring intently after him, mumbling to himself and trying to figure out where his new companion had gone so quickly.

Shortly, a muffled thud came from within. A moment or so after that a whisper at Sordaak's elbow nearly caused him to jump out of his skin. "Don't *do* that!" hissed the spell-caster, his heart in his throat.

"Sorry," said Savinhand, stifling a chuckle. "Come on. It's clear now." Once again he disappeared into the open doorway, Sordaak a short distance behind.

After a few steps they approached the light and came upon a man slumped over a small table strewn with a deck of filthy, dog-eared cards.

"I thought you said these animals were yours," said Sordaak, a bit of not-too-veiled sarcasm creeping into his voice.

"They are," Thumbs said in a tone that managed to sound both hurt and amused. "He'd had some visitors not long before we got here." He waved a casual hand in the direction of footprints in the dirt floor of the stable. "So I figured a little additional caution wouldn't hurt."

"Not you, anyway," muttered the spell-caster, shaking his head.

"Huh?" said the rogue with a confused look on his face. "But I thought…"

"Never mind," said the caster. "Let's get on with it before he comes to or his friend returns."

Deciding to let it go, the thief led the way into the gloomy darkness, heading in the direction of the stalls.

Still muttering, Sordaak yanked a second lantern, lit it from the first and followed. He watched closely where he stepped, as it was obvious that cleanliness was not an amenity this hostelry offered.

The mage stood and looked on silently while Thumbs threw a saddle on his horse and began tightening the straps. "I only have the one horse," Savin said, smiling. "But I do have two pack mules, either of which you are welcome to…"

"Oh no," said the caster, "I'm not riding any raw-boned jackass! I'll just have a look around." Sordaak walked away and was soon out of the thief's line of sight as the rogue continued readying his mount.

"You mean *steal* one?" asked Savinhand, a hint of mockery in his voice. "Tsk-tsk."

"Shut it!" snapped Sordaak. "Anyway," he said over his shoulder as he stepped up to an occupied stall, "you have no room to talk—robbing those poor dirt farmers of their hard-earned income!" The mage eyed a huge black horse two stalls over from where his companion was working. "I think this one will do," he muttered, more to himself than anyone. He looked around for a saddle.

"Yeah, I noticed how nice you were to those 'poor dirt farmers,'" Thumbs said. "Easing two of them from their obviously miserable lives and still another from his heavy burden of coin!" He snickered. "A real gentlemen, you are."

"Enough!" Sordaak said, struggling to get the saddle onto the big black, cursing under his breath. He was unaccustomed to being gotten the better of in a battle of wits. *I must be out of practice*, he reasoned. The horse turned to watch and rolled his eyes in apparent amusement.

"Not you, too!" muttered the flustered spell-caster.

"What?"

"Nothing! I wasn't talking to you!"

Just as the mage tightened the last strap, he heard footsteps retreating into the night. He jumped out of the stall but was too late. The stable hand was gone.

The thief was already leading his horse and pack animals out of their respective stalls. "I thought you said you took care of him?" accused Sordaak as he raced back into the stall and snatched up the reins of his mount.

Savinhand started to open his mouth in protest, but Sordaak cut him off. "Never mind!" he said, pleased at regaining the upper hand. Both could hear voices rapidly approaching. "I think we're going to have company," the mage hissed as he vaulted nimbly up onto the huge horse's back.

The big black, startled by the sudden movement, bolted for the door with Sordaak struggling mightily to hang on.

"Hey!" the rogue called after the rapidly disappearing horse. "Wait for me!" He jumped onto his horse's back and kicking the animal hard in the ribs. The animal took off after the caster's mount, the pack mules trailing on their tethers. On his way past, he slapped at the oil lamp with his reins, sending it flying across the aisle and crashing into the wall, spilling oil and flames over the aging wood.

"That should keep them busy," Savin said as he ducked under the door frame.

A man with a knife and strong misconceptions of his ability to stop the charging mount rounded the corner. The shoulder of Savinhand's horse caught him squarely in the chest, and the air left his lungs in a *whoosh* as the would-be assailant was knocked sprawling. There were others behind the unfortunate townsman, but they scattered before the charging horse. One tried to reach up to grab the thief's tunic as he swept by, but a sharp whip of the reins across his face drew a yelp and caused him to fall back, his hand going to his bleeding cheek. Savinhand raced off in the direction the sorcerer had gone.

There was much cursing and even more shouts behind the fleeing pair. Someone had finally noticed the flames and was yelling for help.

Savinhand smiled, pleased with himself at the distraction. He bent lower over his mount's neck. A glance behind showed the mules were keeping up nicely. A good mule could really run when it was of a mind to, as these certainly were.

He spotted the spell-caster just ahead, still having trouble with the big horse. Sordaak had one hand tightly gripping the reins and the other knotted in the beast's mane, both holding on for dear life as he bounced all over the horse's back. Thumbs thought he heard curses intermingled with a painful yelp now and again, but he couldn't be sure because of the pounding hooves of his own animals.

Finally Sordaak's horse slowed, indicating the mage was gaining control. He got situated in the saddle and slowed the beast to a gallop as he waited for the rogue to catch up.

"Having problems with your mount?" Thumbs asked as he pulled even with the caster, a smirk crossing his lips.

Sordaak turned and glared at the rogue for a moment and then his eyes swiveled back to the road ahead.

"I thought you said your friend was north of town?" Savin said, still grinning.

Sordaak gave the rogue a confused look and then glanced around to get his bearings. It was dark, but the road had many markings. "Damn!" he spat. He raised his hand as if to cuff the horse on the ear but thought better of it. "We'll have to circle the village. Probably just as well. No sense in giving them an idea as to which direction we went. I hope they're not too persistent."

"Oh," said the thief, "I don't believe we'll have to worry about them for a while." He turned and looked back over his shoulder toward the town.

Sordaak looked at the thief to see if he could figure out what he was talking about. Then, following the rogue's line of sight, he turned in the saddle and looked back as well. By now the flames lit up the horizon behind them.

"What—" he began. "Oh, never mind." He shook his head. "I probably don't want to know anyway!" He turned his horse off the trail.

Thumbs turned his animals and followed, the grin still on his face.

Chapter Two

Recompense

Sordaak rose reluctantly from the depths of a blissful slumber. It had been an escape from the pain that now flooded into his wine-addled head.

The night before must have been a good one. The last thing he remembered was performing various magiks for the farmer and his wife, of whom he and Savinhand were guests. But somewhere along there things just faded out. The copious amounts of wine probably had something to do with it.

Slowly, painfully, he became aware of the reason for the rude intrusion into his sleep. A hand was shaking him none-to-gently by the shoulder. A voice penetrated the pounding of drums that engulfed his mind.

"Sordaak!" the voice said through the haze. It sounded urgent. "Sordaak! Wake up!" Even more violent shaking accompanied the persistent words. "There's someone here that wants to talk to you!"

Sordaak tried to form the words of a curse, but his mouth seemed to be lined with cotton and his tongue a stick.

Savinhand, sensing success at last, stepped back in the event his friend's nasty temper came into play.

The mage swallowed a few times, almost gagging. Finally he managed to croak out, "Wha-?" Speaking made his head throb even more. "What?" his voice cracked. He was determined to be rid of this fool.

"There's someone out front who wants to see you," Savin repeated, stepping back even farther. "I think it's the owner of that big black you 'borrowed' last night."

"What?" Sordaak began again. Slowly his mind, which seemed to be swimming in molasses, ground into motion. Sudden realization popped his eyes open. They had been tightly shut because any light only added to the pain, not that opening them helped much.

"I said," repeated the rogue, who glanced nervously around, looking for any possible avenue of escape should that become necessary, "someone out front wants to talk to you. I think—"

"Shut up!" hissed the caster. Where he was and how he had arrived there came back to him in a rush. Sordaak sat up quickly—too quickly. A blinding flash pierced his skull, forcing him to sink back down to his cloak which was doubling as a pillow.

"Damn," the sorcerer whispered softly. "Son-of-a-bitch!" A little louder this time. "Let me think," he finally managed to get out as he sat back up, more slowly this time. "Stall him. I've got to find a place to hide," he said as he swung his legs around and put his feet on the cool, rough-hewn floor.

The thief cocked his head sideways as if trying to listen to something just out of earshot.

Catching the motion out of the corner of his eye, Sordaak said, "What?"

"Shhhh," Savinhand hissed while holding up his hand.

Sordaak started to protest further, but the rogue jumped aside. There was a splintering crash as the door swung inward, slamming into the wall.

The thunderous noise set the tiny men with the rather large hammers back to pounding away with a renewed sense of purpose inside Sordaak's skull.

"You son of a—" the caster began, his temper flaring.

"So, you are the swine that stole my mount," a voice boomed into room, which now seemed much smaller. The words reverberated off the walls most unpleasantly.

Sordaak's vision slowly began to clear. What he saw standing in the doorway did not please him.

The man—the caster was pretty sure it was a man—filled the door frame. He was taller than any human Sordaak had ever seen. His shoulders were so wide they seemed to brush against both door jambs.

"Ugh-oh," Sordaak groaned.

"That is right, little man," thundered the voice as a meaty fist attached to a ham-like forearm reached for the caster. "You are in trouble. A whole lot of trouble!"

Sordaak quickly mumbled a few arcane words and made the required gesture in the direction of this threat.

The big man seemed to hesitate, but then he smiled as he grasped a handful of tunic and easily picked Sordaak up off the cot where he'd been sleeping. "A spell-caster, huh? So you are the one that killed all those farmers. I know some townsfolk back in the village that would like to get their hands on you." His smile broadened. "Well, they can have what is left of you when I am finished!" Still smiling, he added, "Assuming there *is* anything left!"

Sordaak hung limply in the man's grasp, his feet dangling two feet off the floor. He tried to straighten. "That's right," Sordaak said, summoning his best nasty disposition, "I'm a powerful wizard!"

The mage had completed his apprenticeship only a couple of years earlier, but this big oaf didn't know that. Besides, unless he figured a way to bluff his way out of this one, he might not *get* the chance to become a powerful wizard. "You'd better—"

"*You* had better *shut up!*" the man boomed. "I have not yet decided just what to do with you." He appeared to ponder this for a bit before continuing. "However, I am certain I can able to come up with something suitable." Now the smile was most definitely sinister in nature.

Savinhand, who had been hiding in the shadows, leapt at the back of the huge man, a knife in his hand. The big man sidestepped and ducked under the onrushing thief's blade. He then smacked the rogue with the back of his free hand, sending Savin smashing into the wall, where he hit his head with a thud. The thief's eyes glazed over and he slid slowly to the floor.

"I figured he was in on it," said the big man in a voice that was way too loud, affixing his glare on the thief supine on the floor. He turned his attention back to Sordaak, whose feet still dangled in mid-air. "Now to take care of you," he said as he drew back his fist.

"Wait!" stammered the caster. "Maybe we can be of use to one other."

The big man raised an eyebrow. "Of what possible use can you be to me?" he asked.

"I've been working that village for over a week trying to gather a suitable group to make a raid on Dragma's Keep," the caster said, his eyes never leaving the fist. He sensed a possible opening.

"Dragma's Keep?" The man's voice remained dubious.

"Put me down and I will tell you more," insisted Sordaak.

"That keep has been lost for more than a thousand years," spat the big man, doubt in his voice. "I think I will hold you up here just a bit longer." However, he lowered his fist ever so slightly. "You are going to have to do better than that."

"It's not lost anymore!" announced the caster. "I have been researching that keep for over a year, and now I'm fairly certain I've located it." He paused. "Now, put me down if you want to hear the rest."

The big man hesitated. "All right," he said grudgingly. "But just you try to get away and I will break that scrawny little neck of yours."

He set Sordaak on his feet and stepped back warily, keeping his big body between the caster and the door. The significance of which did not escape the sorcerer.

Sordaak made a show of straightening his tunic while attempting to gather his dignity, *and* his thoughts. "Don't you worry!" he said looking up into the darkness hiding the big man's face, "I have plans for this neck—and *for you!*" His anger was returning in the place of the fear, but he forced that down and worked to remain calm. This brute could really be of some use if Sordaak could win him over. "About two days' ride to the east, there is an old outcropping of buildings," he continued after giving some thought as to just how much he needed to reveal to this man, who despite his size was certainly human. "I found a reference that indicates there is a hidden entrance to Dragma's Keep there. It's said to be the final resting place of the old sorcerer and his fabled jewels."

"The Dragma jewels?" the fighter said, suspicion deep in his voice. "Now I *know* you are just making this up. They have been lost for even longer than the Keep! Surely you can do better than that."

Sordaak cocked one eyebrow and gave the big man an impudent stare. "They are not lost. Dragma has—had—them. Hence the name, the Dragma jewels. I found another reference that places him in this region before he disappeared, and I'm certain he had the jewels with him." He hesitated. "And now I have found the keep. At least I think I have." He took in a shaky breath. "All we have to do is find the entrance from the upper, much newer, section."

"Right," countered the big man. "If it is that easy, why has this entrance not been found before?"

"Good question," said Sordaak, knowing he now had the big man hooked. "However, I never said it was *easy*. As I mentioned, I have been researching this for a long time and..." Again the dramatic pause.

"Go on," urged the big man.

"Are you with us or not?" queried the wizard-wannabe, now eyeing the big man with his best suspicious gaze. "I mean, how do I know you won't kill me after I give you the story?"

"You do not," said the big man flatly. "However, if you do not tell me, you are dead meat anyway. There is still the matter of my stolen mount."

"Again with the stupid horse!" retorted Sordaak. "Will you let that go already? I had every intention of returning your mangy flea bag. What possible use could I have for a horse that big? After all, the damn thing nearly killed me just getting out of the stable!"

The big man chuckled.

"I just needed a fast horse fast, and yours happened to be the first I came upon," the spell-caster continued. "I do apologize for taking the beast without asking. But I hope you can understand there was an angry mob nipping at my heels at the time!"

"Very well," stated the big man. "I will withhold judgment until your tale is told." A pause for effect. Apparently the big man was not above a bit of drama as well. "However, this had *better* be good," he added as he pulled up a chair. He straddled the back of the seat and sat down, his wary eyes still on the caster.

Sordaak sat down slowly on the edge of his cot as Savinhand began to stir.

"Ugh," the rogue said as he shook his head slowly from side to side. "What in the name of the seven hells hit me?" Sordaak moved to help him sit up.

Sight of the big man in front of him refreshed his memory. "Oh yeah," he muttered. "Did you have to hit me *so hard?*"

Without saying a word, the big man leaned over and picked up the short sword that Savin had dropped on his short trip to the wall.

"Oh, yeah," the thief mumbled again, allowing his head to sink into his open hands.

"Now continue," said the big man, turning his suspicious eyes back to the sorcerer.

"We are going to split this evenly," said the caster without preamble, looking the big man straight in the eye, or rather where his eyes should be.

"I do not think—"

"That was a statement, not a question," Sordaak interrupted, his tone leaving no room for discussion. "Anyway, I will do the thinking from now on." Sordaak paused to see what, if any, would be the reply.

The big man started to protest but evidently changed his mind.

"We'll start with your name," continued Sordaak as if the matter were settled.

The big man hesitated, obviously taken aback by the spell-caster's approach and the sudden turn of events.

"Thrinndor," the big fighter said. "Most call me Thrinndor." He still seemed baffled by his loss of control.

"All right," Sordaak said as he did some mental brow-wiping. "Thrinndor it is. I'm Sordaak, and the damaged one over there is Savinhand." He paused to further collect his thoughts. "The three of us I feel will prove insufficient, however. We need another, maybe two. A healer would do nicely, and possibly another sword."

"A healer, huh?" mused Thrinndor. "I know where we can lay our hands on some potions that would help along those lines, but not a healer—not around here anyway." His voice trailed off. "However, if you can handle the hocus-pocus stuff, I can handle the sword play." With that, there was a flash of movement and, as if by magic, a huge sword appeared in the fighter's monstrous fist. "And my training in the Paladinhood has given me some small amount of knowledge in the craft of healing. Small, mind you," he added hastily. "Now, can we have some light in here?"

Sordaak leaned forward, but even squinting did not help him see the man's face. He nudged Savinhand, who left the room still shaking his head. Presently, he returned with a smoking oil lantern.

The first real look at the paladin proved he was even more formidable in the light. He towered head and shoulders above the caster, wore a voluminous black cloak over some type of armor. Sordaak thought he could make out some sort of chain underneath. The sword he held in his hand was almost as long as Sordaak was tall, its edge glinting in the flicker of the lamp.

As Sordaak watched, Thrinndor reached back and placed the blade on a hook behind his cloak, its pommel still visible over his left shoulder, obviously ready for a rapid draw. The man had an aura about him, something that was hard to pin down, but it was there. The sheer size and power of him made Sordaak uncomfortable. Yet there was something in the big fighter's eyes that inspired trust.

"Savinhand here should be able to help in the muscle area, as well. I've seen him swing a fairly competent blade a time or two," said the sorcerer.

"Gee thanks, boss," the rogue said sarcastically. In a flash, both hands dove beneath his tunic and returned with two long, curved blades. He grinned to demonstrate that he was just showing off. His hands flashed again, and the blades were gone.

He bowed before the giant. "Savinhand: rogue, locksmith, trap finder/disabler and all around great guy, at your service."

Thrinndor started to return the bow, but he spun on the caster instead, suddenly remembering why he was here. "Enough of this crap! Get on with the tale!" His eyes narrowed menacingly. "And remember, this had better be good."

Sordaak cleared his throat and poured himself a cup of water from an urn on the table. He drank the entire cup. His mouth remained dry, something that recent events had failed to improve upon. Clearing his throat again, he began. "According to the legends and tomes I've unearthed in my research, the High Wizard Dragma set up his kingdom in a keep just a few leagues from a great sea."

"You want us to go chasing all over only the gods know where, looking for these jewels on the basis of a clue like that?" Thrinndor interrupted, his anger returning.

"Put a cork in it and sit back down!" Sordaak snapped, an edge to his voice.

After the big paladin reluctantly complied, Sordaak steeled himself for what was to come. One slip and this brute would probably carry out his threat to snuff out both him and his thief friend.

The extra time also allowed Sordaak to dredge up from his memory what few details he could recall of this ancient legend, in which there were more than a few holes. He would have to fill them in as he went along.

"Very well, you have my attention," Thrinndor said. "But I truly hope for your sake there is more than that. A lot more." The big paladin glared menacingly at the caster.

Quickly, Sordaak continued. "He included in his building of the keep a secret tunnel that went down to a hidden boat dock, which was actually a cavern that had been hollowed out by the waves and which opens out to the great sea."

"Now look here!" Thrinndor bellowed as he leaned forward, reaching for the caster's neck.

"No, wait!" Sordaak said quickly, his hands coming up to protect his exposed throat. "I have located the cavern!"

It took Thrinndor a moment or two, during which Sordaak was fairly certain his heart stopped beating, to digest this information. A look of doubt crossed the paladin's face. "You have?"

"Would I lie to you?" asked the caster matter-of-factly.

Thrinndor's face regained its menacing look. "I do not know. Would you?"

"You know," Sordaak said, annoyance creeping into his voice, "if we're going to have to work together, you're going to have to learn to trust me." After an eyebrow inched higher on Thrinndor's skeptical face, he added, "Look, as I see it, you have a couple of options here. You can choke the shit out of me now, and I am certain that would make you feel better for the time being." A nod was the only response he got. "Or you can go along with my plan and see what comes of it. If I am unable to produce the keep, and the jewels therein, you just choke the shit out of me at that point." The mage folded his arms across his chest. "What have you got to lose?"

Time seemed to stand still for Sordaak while the big man pondered. "Very well," Thrinndor said finally. "You have my undivided attention." When Sordaak started to protest he added, "And my tentative trust. Tentative, remember. Try to skip out on me, or double-cross me in any way." He paused for effect. "Well, I think we all know what will happen."

Sordaak eyed the brute for a moment, trying to determine how far he could push him. He decided not very far was the best option.

"Very well," the mage said, mimicking Thrinndor's formal tone. "Allow me to amend my earlier statement: I have found *a* cavern." Quickly the caster continued when he noted the red starting to creep up the big man's neck. "However, it does have a tunnel that was dug out by hand leading inland."

"Then you have found the Keep."

"Umm, not exactly." Again the eyebrow started the short journey toward the paladin's hairline. Sordaak rushed on. "The tunnel has caved in, but I am certain this is the right place. I've been searching for this—these—jewels off and on for almost two years. Now I've found them. They're waiting for me, I mean us. I can feel it in my bones."

"So why have you not retrieved the jewels?" Thrinndor asked.

"Remember the cave-in? There is no getting past that. It goes back in for a long ways. I've been unable to tell exactly how far, but it is safe to say we're not getting in from *that* direction," the sorcerer said. "I've not been able to locate the entrance from the other end, either. Too damn many orcs. The old part of the keep has been occupied by a group of orcs that use it as their home base to raid the surrounding countryside." He paused while considering his next move.

"Orcs?" snorted Thrinndor. "Mere scum!" He patted the haft of his sword, which loomed over his shoulder. "I can handle that part of the excursion."

"Two-hundred?" replied Sordaak in his best I-don't-think-so tone. "There are said to be at least that many operating out of there—maybe twice that number."

"Hmmm," mused the paladin. "Two-hundred *is* a lot of scum." He paused to put a big smile on his face. "Still, if you could arrange it such that only three or four could get at me at a time, I think I can handle them!" A bigger grin, now.

It was Sordaak's turn to have an eyebrow climb his forehead. A disgusted look crossed his face. He reached down to curl up the edges of his robe—getting it up off the floor.

After a few moments of this, Thrinndor couldn't restrain himself. "What, pray tell, are you doing?"

"He's rolling up his robe because it's getting pretty deep in here," said Savinhand, finally joining the conversation. At the confused look that crossed the big man's face, Savin continued, "He doesn't want any of that shit you're talking to get on his best robe!"

The look on Thrinndor's face went from confusion to understanding to disbelief to rage to laughter in the span of about three heartbeats. Soon, all three were laughing heartily.

"Ok," Thrinndor said, "I guess I deserved that. I might need a bit of help with that many orcs, at that." Still chortling, he added, "I do know of an unemployed dwarf who just might be available for the right price."

"Well," Sordaak answered, the mirth still in his voice, "another sword would certainly be useful. However, I have a plan that should ensure the upper keep will be all but deserted for a few days. The few that remain will be all yours." His smile broadened. "However, I will do what I can to ensure no more than three jump you at once!"

He laughed again.

"Ha, ha," mocked Thrinndor, grinning widely. Then his face took on a more serious look. "You do realize, of course, that Dragma was a member of Valdaar's high council? He was thought to have fallen in the final battle with his master, but his body was never found. Centuries passed before it was discovered he had lived to set up a base, still in the service of his lord..." His voice trailed off ominously.

"Service? Bah!" spat Sordaak. "How can anyone 'serve' a god who's dead?"

Thrinndor hesitated, obviously holding something back. "Dead in the physical walking, breathing sense," he said. "But his spirit is kept alive by those that remain in service to him."

"Bah," repeated the caster, even more vehemently.

"Legend has it," the paladin went on as if he had not been interrupted, "that one day he will return to rule the land that is rightfully his. But first the path must be prepared for him. His disciples must join together and set up a kingdom worthy of his rule. His sword—*Valdaar's Fist*—must be found and the power contained within must be released. Only then—"

Sordaak took in a deep breath to protest yet again, but Savinhand cut him off. "No," the rogue said. "I have heard parts of this, as well. Something about after the power in the sword is released, Valdaar will walk among men for a time, returning those who serve him to power before assuming his rightful place among the gods."

Looking from the rogue to the paladin, Sordaak said, "Look, you mental midgets! Both of you put together don't know half as much as I have learned during my search for this old windbag! So do not try to spook me! He's dead—D-E-A-D, *dead!*"

Taken aback by the passion with which Sordaak spoke, Thrinndor was silent for a moment. "Yes, his physical presence no longer walks among us." Another pause. "However, explain please, Dragma's long life? He reportedly lived for five or more centuries *after* the death of his lord. Such power can only come from…"

Sordaak interrupted. "Ah-ha! There I have you! No god kept that old sorcerer alive. That is what I am really after, not the damn jewels. I am after *Pendromar,* Dragma's staff! The power contained within…" His voice trailed off wistfully. "Well, long life is only *part of* what is contained therein."

"I too," said the big man impassively, "am after something other than the jewels."

Sordaak gave him an inquisitive, sidelong look.

"The sword," Thrinndor said simply. "Dragma was the last living being to see my lord alive and thus his sword, *Valdaar's Fist.* It is my hope finding the wizard's final resting place will lead me to the blade."

Nothing was said for a few moments.

"Ahem," Savinhand broke the silence, clearing his throat and raising his hand. "I'll take the jewels."

They all looked from one to the other, and again the gravity of the moment evaporated in a burst of laughter.

When the levity subsided, Sordaak continued. "Very well, it is decided. We can depart from here, but first there are some things we need. And…" he paused ominously, "…there is something I need to take care of. It may require a couple of days, and there are some components I will need from the local apothecary, as well as a few other things we will need from town," he said. "And as my and Savin's presence there might cause some, ugh…Well, let's just say it might be frowned upon—"

"Let's just say it might be frowned upon," Thrinndor mocked under his breath.

Sordaak gave him a stare that would have withered an ogre, but Thrinndor just sat there smiling. "As I was about to say," the magicuser continued icily, "that elects you to do some shopping. Let's work out a list of what we will need."

*

When Thrinndor came riding back from town, he was accompanied by a dwarf—walking, of course—and both of Savinhand's mules laden with supplies.

Sordaak and Savinhand heard them coming from inside the farmer's house and walked out to meet them at the gate.

The dwarf looked the pair over without expression and glanced around the place with a dubious eye.

"Sordaak, Savinhand," said Thrinndor without preamble, pointing at the dwarf, "this is Vorgath. Vorgath, these are our new companions." He pointed to the caster. "That is Sordaak, and the other is Savinhand, otherwise known as Thumbs."

"Vorgath Shieldsunder, son of Morroth of the Dragaar Clan of the Silver Hills at your service," said the dwarf formally. His voice sounded as if it were coming from inside a barrel.

Sordaak bowed at the waist as is the custom, and said, "I am Sordaak, sorcerer extraordinaire at yours."

Savinhand bowed in turn. "And I am Savinhand, Rogue, Locksmith, Trap Finder/Disabler and all around—"

"Scoundrel," Thrinndor broke in with a grin.

"At your service," said the rogue, a large smile on his face.

"Yeah, yeah, yeah," said Sordaak. "Did you get the components I asked for from the apothecary?"

"Of course," said Thrinndor. "However, I had some trouble getting that particular incense. The old man at the shop did not want to give any up. It cost three times what you expected, and even then I had to convince him it was in his best interest to hand it over." He flexed his right arm.

"Three times!" exclaimed Sordaak. "You should not have paid it! Why, even the three gold I told you it should cost—figuring in a mark-up for this remote village—was too high! I can get it for less than two back in Hargstead!"

"Well, you are not in Hargstead! Nor were you there," Thrinndor said. "He was also asking questions as to why I needed this stuff! Questions that were *much* better not answered! I paid him what he asked under the condition of no questions asked, or answered."

"I see your point," mumbled the caster.

"All the same," continued Thrinndor, "I think we should be on the road as soon as possible. I do not trust that old man, and I am certain it will not take the townspeople long to figure out who needed sorcerer supplies." He paused while the others considered this bit of advice. "I did all I could to disguise our trail, but three laden animals and one walking dwarf cannot be disguised very well. That, and the townsfolk are still more than a little sore at the two of you." He waved his hand at Sordaak and Savinhand.

"I would imagine so," said Sordaak. "After all, our scoundrel here tried to burn their town to the ground!"

"One small stable," Savinhand said. "At least I did not single-handedly double the size of their local graveyard, as you did!"

"Enough!" said Thrinndor. "Sorry I brought it up." He rolled his eyes as he swung down from the big black and stepped over to the first pack mule. He dug into the pack on the side nearest him and retrieved a small leather bag. "Here is the stuff you asked for." He tossed it to the caster, who bobbled it for a moment before securing it in his left hand. "I am certain I do not want to know what it is for, but that small bag cost almost as much as what the rest of this cost us," he said, sweeping his arm toward both laden mules.

"Never you mind!" Sordaak snapped. "That will become apparent soon enough." He started to walk away, but turned back to face the fighter. "Did you do as I asked at the tavern?"

"Yes," answered the big man. "But I am not sure that plan will work. The barkeep there did not seem anywhere near smart enough to be the information gatherer for even a band of old women, let alone the marauding orcs you have talked about."

"Worry not about that," chided Sordaak. "He will get the information to them. With the keep being two days away, we will need to leave by the day after tomorrow.

"Early," he added as he turned and headed into the woods. "That means I need to get to work immediately."

Curiosity got the better of the remaining three and they followed, leaving the animals chewing absent-mindedly on the sweet grass they had discovered next to the gate.

Sordaak stopped in a clearing not far away and turned to survey his companions who had halted a few steps away. "If you intend to watch, keep it quiet. And," he added, looking into each of their eyes in turn, "ensure I am not disturbed—for *any* reason." He paused. "Understand?" Without waiting for a reply, he abruptly sat. He crossed his legs and unceremoniously dumped the contents of the bag onto the grass before him.

Rummaging through it, he pushed around the different components and nodding his approval. He then picked up an incense cone, sniffed it and put it on the ground next to a small, delicate-looking porcelain brazier with intricate runes drawn like spider webs around the exterior. He repeated the process for the remaining incense cones, placing each in a particular place and pattern it appeared to his observers, until all were spread before him.

His companions looked at one another, shrugged and dropped to a sitting position in a rough triangle around the caster, each at least ten feet away.

Sordaak crumbled some charcoal into the brazier and removed some perishable components from their protective packaging. He then pulled out his steel and flint. With them in hand, he set about striking up a spark. After some gentle blowing, he got the charcoal smoldering. Pulling a small package from under his tunic, he loosened the tie, unwrapped it and broke off small bits of the fat inside. These he added to the brazier. A lively sizzle ensued.

Finally, he reached back and pulled his hood over his head, hiding his face and eyes.

To those watching, nothing appeared to happen for some time, time only measured by the ever-changing position of the shadows. And then, if they listened intently, they could hear a low chant emanating from under the hood. The caster reached out a steady hand and grasped a piece of incense and added it to the brazier.

Soon a sickly sweet, foreign aroma wafted out to the nostrils of Thrinndor. He wrinkled his nose, stood and moved over to stand next to Savinhand. After a few moments he dropped down none-to-quietly to sit next to the rogue

"How long is this supposed to take?" the paladin whispered.

"Shhhh!" Savin whispered back. "If this is what I think it is, it could take anywhere from a couple of hours to an entire day. That assumes the call is answered at all."

"Wonderful," groaned Thrinndor. "I am going to go unpack the mules and sort the rest of our stuff so it will be ready to travel when we are. I will return to relieve you in a bit."

After seeing he was going to get no more than a nod from the rogue; the paladin grunted, stood and clanked off in the direction of the farmhouse. Savin winced at the noise and glanced nervously at the caster, but Sordaak seemed too deep into his trance to take notice.

Savinhand got quietly to his feet and, careful to make no more than a whisper of sound, walked to the edge of the trees and leaned against one.

Vorgath raised an eyebrow but remained where he was.

Savin peered up at the late morning sun, squinting as he did so. He also wondered idly how long his friend was going to be, and then shrugged as he reflected on the events that had brought him to this point.

He'd been working the local towns along the northern edge of the desert known as the Sunburnt Sea when he'd happened across Sordaak. He'd been gathering information for Shardmoor about yet another sect gaining popularity in the region—this time a sect serving a dead god known as Valdaar. This lead certainly looked promising.

The afternoon dragged on and morphed into the evening. The three took turns watching over the caster lest he need anything. The night passed without incident. Indeed, the only thing that marred the silence was the endless chanting coming from Sordaak. The stillness was broken only when he moved his hand out to place another piece of incense in the burner.

Morning found them pretty much the same way, with Thrinndor snoring softly under an old oak, Vorgath apparently asleep where he sat, and Thumbs staring with red-rimmed eyes at nothing.

By mid-morning, however, something had changed. It took Savin a few moments to notice, but he was sure the chanting had increased in volume and pace. He shook off the effects of standing in one place for hours on end and attempted to step in the direction of the slumbering paladin but fell flat on his face with a thud. He might have been diligent in his effort to ward his mind from sleep, but both legs had most definitely succumbed.

He thrashed about in the tall grass, biting off the moans and curses as the blood rushed back into his legs with the associated pins and needles for emphasis. Finally, the pain subsided and he could stand again. Savin stumbled his way over to the sleeping fighter, whereupon he kicked him in the side.

"Wha…" the big man moaned as he woke with a start.

"Shhhh!" hissed the thief. "Something is up. His incantations have changed. I think this might be it."

"Be what?" the paladin said, still shaking his head and rubbing his side.

"His spell, stupid," whispered the thief. "The culmination of his summoning. I think this is it." He started in the direction of the spell-caster.

The warrior climbed slowly to his feet and followed the rogue, still probing his side gently. "Why did you kick me?" he whispered.

"It seemed like the thing to do at the time," replied Savin. "Reaching down to shake you by the shoulder seemed like a poor choice, so…" Savin's voice trailed off. "Now watch closely." He turned back to the caster, who was now only a few steps away. "Oh my god!" he exclaimed as he took a wary step back, his eyes locked onto a figure perched on the caster's shoulder.

The big man started to speak but evidently thought better of it and stepped around the rogue to get a look at what had drawn Savinhand's awe.

It didn't take him long to figure it out, because what was sitting on the caster's shoulder was an ugly sight indeed.

About a foot-and-a-half in height, the creature had two spiraling horns extending upward from the top of its head. The eyes were deeply sunken, almost invisible, and its small nose perched precariously over a hideous mouth. The claws on the tips of its long fingers looked sharp, and a long tail with a flat point on the end protruded from between its scrawny legs. The monster was covered in green, reptilian skin.

"It's a demon," said the thief as his hand dove under his tunic. His short sword flashed, but a massive hand locked onto his wrist, jerking his motion to an abrupt halt.

"No," said the paladin. "That is a Quasit. It has heard the call."

Vorgath walked up behind them, shaking his head in wonder. "I've never seen one, and heard that they only rarely come to answer the call of a powerful sorcerer." He paused. "I have not heard of such a summoning in several hundred years."

"It appears," mused Thrinndor quietly, "our friend may indeed be special after all."

Savinhand's eyes looked from one to the other and swiveled back to the creature staring back at him from the shoulder of the spell-caster. "May the gods have mercy on us!" he muttered.

Chapter Three

The Entrance

Peering over the ledge of their hiding place, Savinhand could see the orcs massing for a march, presumably to Treblong Pass. While the distance was still great—a couple of miles—his keen eyes could clearly discern the leaders and their attempt at order, although that was mostly wasted effort.

He glanced over at the spellcaster just a few paces away. He still seemed a bit weak—not quite up to his usual self anyway. The spell had taken a massive amount of energy. In fact, the caster had not been able to move for almost a full day. Immediately after his familiar had appeared, Sordaak had fallen over onto his brazier. Vorgath and Thrinndor had to drag his spent body back to the farmhouse, where he collapsed in his cot and did not stir. It was interesting to them all that the creature—Quasit, Thrinndor had called it—never left the mage's shoulder.

It stared with unblinking eyes at anyone who approached the caster.

In fact, Sordaak might yet be in his cot had the need for them to be on the trail not been so dire.

Again, he needed help just getting to, and then on, the mount the paladin had acquired from the farmer. Once situated in the saddle, however, he seemed to perk up noticeably, and he spent the remainder of the trip—two days—learning his new companion.

The trip had been uneventful, and now it seemed apparent that Sordaak's plan was working. The tip from Thrinndor a while back in the village indeed seemed to have been passed along to this band of orcs. For now it was obvious they were preparing to sortie out to meet the fictional caravan "laden with supplies and a king's ransom in jewels."

Treblong Pass was two days distant, at even a fast pace. That would presumably give the companions five days. The orcs would surely wait for at least a day before deciding their information had been incorrect. Not being overly blessed with intelligence, the orcs might even take longer in that assessment.

Seeing the crowd marching off to the north, Savin whispered intently, "Hey! The orcs are moving. We'd better load up."

Thrinndor and Vorgath rolled out of their bedrolls easily, but the caster had a little more trouble. Soon all three joined the rogue at the ledge, peering into the first rays of the rising sun to see a band of more than a hundred—possibly a lot more—of the vile creatures disappearing over the opposite horizon.

After watching for a short while, the caster turned back toward the camp and said, "All right, loosely stake the animals back in the trees where they can get both food and water. We may yet need them for the return trip. From here on out we will go on foot, carrying only what supplies we need on our backs."

As the group members started for their own part of the camp, the mage added, "We will take only what we need to last us one week. If we are longer than that," he paused, ensuring he had their attention, "we will not be coming back."

"That's the spirit!" grumped the rogue as he rolled his bed. "Just a bit of cheer to start the day!" He started to say more, but he could see the caster was ignoring him as he made up his own pack. Disgusted, he dumped out everything he had with him and began making two piles.

His picks he tossed into the must-take pile, not sure what he would need them for. However, visions of locked doors and laden treasure chests sprang to mind. Five flasks of oil, rags already stuffed into the top for ease of ignition. Fifty feet of rope, which he coiled about his waist under his tunic. He separated out ten iron spikes and then threw five of them back into the not-going pile, figuring he would probably need to travel light. Of course, his week's supply of rations—mostly hard biscuits and dried meats, two water skins, and one wine— would be going. An assortment of empty leather bags he tied to his belt, with the obvious hope they would not be empty long.

Then he belted his short sword over his leather tunic and stuck two sharp daggers pulled from his pack behind his belt. Finally, he rolled the pack onto his back and threw his cloak around his shoulders, tying it under his chin. He bent, stretched, did a quick draw of the daggers and sword each in turn to verify he was not overly hampered by his pack.

After some minor adjustments he was satisfied and turned to see his companions still rummaging around in their packs.

He sighed and walked back over to the ledge and peered at the scene in the distance. "Ugh-oh, looks like they left us a welcoming committee."

Presently he was joined by his companions.

"Well, we expected that," said Sordaak. "At least they just left us two."

"Only two?" said a disappointed Thrinndor.

"Out here," said Savinhand, sarcasm dripping from his voice. "But how many will be inside?"

"That we'll have to find out the hard way," said Sordaak.

Vorgath grunted agreement. "I'll take the one on the right," he said with a big grin on his face. "Then I'll help you with yours," he winked at Thrinndor.

"Ha," snorted the big man, "You never saw the day—nor are you likely to— that you could best me in anything!" He also grinned to take the edge off of his words. "Especially when it comes to combat."

"Bah!" spat Vorgath. "I can kill more orcs before you finish your dainty breakfast than you could in an entire day!"

They eyed each other for a moment, each waiting for the other to blink. Finally, they began to laugh.

"It's on, then," said the dwarf, his right eyebrow arched well above the left. "Highest count takes ten percent of the other's take?"

"Make it twenty, and you are on!" retorted the big man.

"Deal!" snapped the dwarf. "Final blow is the only one that counts. Savin here will have the final say when it comes to disputed kills." And after a quick pause, he said, "Just see that you do not try to 'steal' any kills after I get them whittled down!" His left eye almost closed during the last bit.

"Deal!" said Thrinndor, and they clasped forearms, sealing the contest.

"Give me a break," said the caster, rolling his eyes. "If you two ladies are done chatting we have some work to do." He threw his leg over the ledge and jumped to the ground below.

"Whoa there," said a concerned Savinhand. "Don't you think we should sneak up on these guys?"

"Nah," replied the caster. "I believe the direct approach will work better in this situation." He looked back over his shoulder at the two creatures who were obviously not very enthusiastic in the performance of their duties. "Well," he said after a moment's thought, pointing lazily at Thrinndor, "on second thought, maybe you should creep around behind them and I'll come up with a distraction." He winked at the big man.

"I do not creep!" said the paladin in protest.

"I think that is more in my line of work," Savin said hurriedly. "Give me a few minutes to get in position." Without waiting for a reply, he disappeared behind a promontory of rock.

The remaining three sat upon the ledge and adjusted their packs while they waited

"All right," Sordaak said abruptly, "he's had long enough. Let's get a move on." He stood, stretched, adjusted the pack on his shoulders and started off toward the entrance following a faint path through the soft grass that covered the floor of the valley.

Thrinndor stood easily and fell in step behind the caster.

Vorgath grunted as he stood, shouldered his pack, and got in step on the path with the others.

"What is the matter, old one?" chided the paladin. "That pack too heavy for you?"

"Shut it, pretty boy," retorted the barbarian. "Just you let me know if you need help with that minuscule bundle you are struggling with!"

Thrinndor snorted his derision at this but said nothing more.

The approach was much easier than expected. In fact, the guards allowed the group to approach to within a few yards before grunting some sort of command.

The trio halted, obligingly.

After a few more unintelligible grunts and some confused looks from the three in front of them, one of the orcs spoke in a halting form of common.

"Get lost, scum," the orc said to Sordaak, who was in front of the other two, and therefore the leader—at least as far as the orcs were concerned.

"Look who is calling us scum," the mage said, trying to sound hurt. He noticed that Savinhand was in position behind and above the monsters, waiting for the signal.

They did not have to wait long. As the caster lifted his left hand to brush his nose, there was a blur of motion from Thrinndor, an almost imperceptible scrape of metal on metal, immediately followed by a *whoosh*.

Sordaak just barely had time to duck as he saw the motion out of the corner of his eye. The blade of the big fighter came around in a vicious arc that decapitated the orc coming at him, splattering dark blood on the caster's robe.

The beheaded body, still holding its halberd menacingly before it, took another step forward as if to attack, then collapsed in a clatter onto the ground, where it lay twitching.

Savinhand had leapt onto the back of the other orc, and it fared no better. Vorgath's greataxe appeared in his hands as if by magic, sweeping in a wide arc that caught the beast just above the hip, cleaving deep into its flesh about the same time as the rogue's blade bit deep into the creature's spine, severing the spinal cord.

The now paralyzed orc remained upright as Savinhand landed neatly on his feet next to it. Vorgath wrenched his blade free by planting his foot on the orc's leg just above the knee, and shoved. The axe came free with a sickening slurping sound as the creature tumbled to the ground. Vorgath wasted no time in finishing the task as he whipped his blade in a high arc. It came down and neatly severed the head of this unfortunate as well.

Sordaak was rubbing ineffectually at the stains on his robe, and he glanced sidelong at Thrinndor. "Do you think you could be a little less messy, next time?" His eyes shifted back to the stains.

Thrinndor blinked a couple of times and said, "I could let you take care of the next group of 'not-so-friendlies' we run into." A wide grin spread across his face.

"Which could be sooner rather than later," Savinhand said, motioning for quiet.

"Huh?" said Sordaak.

"Shhhh!" hissed the rogue, cocking his head. He was apparently listening to something he heard from inside the cave opening. "I think we're going to have company." He ducked behind the left edge of the cave mouth.

After a quick glance at the spellcaster, Thrinndor and Vorgath quickly did the same on the right side. Sordaak bent over and started rifling through what served as pockets on the two dead orcs.

"Hey," whispered Savinhand. When he got no acknowledgment, he repeated a little louder. "Hey!"

"Shut it!" whispered the caster without turning his head. "I'll be the bait. Just make sure you don't miss!" Then under his breath he added, "moron." He rolled his eyes and continued to search the bodies.

Just then there was a shout from within, followed by the heavy thumping of several sets of feet running in their direction.

More unintelligible shouting caused the mage to lift his head in obvious surprise. "Four!" he whispered out of the side of his mouth as he spun and bolted down the path, deliberately dropping a coin or two to show that he had been looting.

Shortly the orc party appeared in the mouth of the cave. Two stopped briefly to check on the status of their fallen comrades while the remaining two took off down the path in the direction of the fleeing caster.

Seeing the chase was going to be a long one, one stopped after only a few steps, shifted his grip on his halberd and reared back to throw it spear-style.

He never let go, however, as a bolt from the crossbow mounted cleverly to the back of Thrinndor's shield caught him square between the shoulder blades. A scream ripped the air as the creature dropped the spear and spun around, clawing at the offending bolt.

Hearing the scream, the orc's companion stopped and spun just in time to catch Thrinndor's second bolt in its right arm—the aim thrown off by the sudden change of motion.

"Not fair!" shouted Vorgath, who then let out a blood-curdling yell and leapt at the remaining two with his greataxe poised high above his head for immediate action.

Savinhand, who had been sneaking up on the nearest orc, was startled by the yell from the dwarf as he jumped onto its back, a dagger in each hand. However his aim was now off, and his first thrust merely scratched the creature along the left shoulder. The orc reached back, grabbed the rogue by his tunic and flung him to the ground, where he landed flat on his back in a cloud of dust.

Momentarily stunned, Savin barely had time to roll out of the way as a halberd split the dirt where he had been lying.

The rogue surged to his feet and lashed out defensively with the dagger in his left hand, catching his opponent in the muscled area just above the left knee, which only seemed to upset the creature all the more.

The other straggler, caught by surprise at first, recovered quickly to lash out with its halberd. Savin's sudden standing caused his aim to be off, but still the ugly, thick blade cut deep into the rogue's side. Savin fell back, swinging wildly with the dagger in his right fist, narrowly missing the eyes of the orc he had stabbed in the leg.

Into this melee the dwarf charged. His first swing caught the orc whose halberd had slashed the rogue in the middle of the back. The beast fell forward under the thrust of the attack and landed on its face in the dirt with Vorgath's blade still protruding from its back and the dwarf yanked forward by the sudden motion.

The other orc, oblivious to the fate of his companion, stood over Savinhand, his halberd already beginning its descent from being raised high over his head, intent on ridding himself of this pesky human.

The rogue could just barely see through the veil of pain—but what he saw was enough to spot the blade as it began its arc toward his neck. He tried to summon the effort to move, but his limbs refused to respond. Then, as he started to close his eyes anticipating the worst, a blinding flash split the air above him, and the orc, halberd and all, simply vanished.

Savinhand blinked several times as he tried to clear his vision to see what had happened, but his vision began to fade. As he succumbed to the alluring throws of darkness that came to envelop him, he wondered just where he was headed. Death had always intrigued him. He had no use for gods; a man in his line of work seldom does, he thought as consciousness faded. But there was so much still to be done. So many places still to see. So much...

Thrinndor, who had exchanged his crossbow for the sword, followed his bolts in, sword in hand. He wanted desperately to go help the rogue, but he knew deep inside that if he did not take care of the orcs in front of him, and soon, it would not matter for his friend.

He gripped the pommel of his greatsword tightly in both hands as he raised it above his head and brought it crashing down on the nearest foe. This unfortunate creature was the one he had hit in the arm; it had reached up earlier and yanked the arrow out with its free hand, dropping it to the ground at its feet. Howling in either rage or pain, it turned just in time to see the paladin rushing at it and managed to raise its halberd in an attempt to ward off the coming blow. This proved ineffectual, however, as Thrinndor's blade easily cut through the weapon's shaft and bit deep into the creature's neck. Death was instantaneous, and the orc's eyes glazed over as it fell to the ground in a heap at the paladin's feet.

Thrinndor wrenched the blade free with a jerk and spun just as Vorgath came rushing into his field of view, his bloodlust obviously in firm control as his greataxe whirled in flashing arcs about his head. It did not take a master strategist to see the barbarian had the task well in hand, and the remaining orc was doomed. He considered telling Vorgath that he was breaking off to attend to their fallen comrade but quickly discarded the idea, knowing it would fall on deaf ears. Very little could penetrate the rage of a barbarian once invoked. Fighting down his own lust for battle, he spun and rushed to the side of his fallen ally.

He did not need the opinion of a medicine man to tell him the wound was indeed grave. Blood was rushing out of a huge gash in the rogue's side, and his skin was already ashen from lack of the life-sustaining fluid.

Ripping a piece of Savin's own tunic, he stanched the flow of blood as best he could, cleaning the wound in the process. *The orc's weapon had probably not been the cleanest of surgical instruments*, he thought absently as he worked.

After he had the wound treated as best he could, he lowered his head, closed his eyes and said a few words—obviously a prayer—working his hands over the damaged area as he spoke. Power coursed through the paladin's hands, and the wound seemed to close of its own accord, the bleeding coming almost to a stop.

After a few moments Thrinndor pushed back, a haggard look on his face. It was as if this act had taken more out of him than the battle. Sordaak and Vorgath walked up then, concern lining the caster's usually impassive face.

"How is he?" Sordaak asked.

"I cannot tell for certain," replied Thrinndor. "There may yet be internal damage. And how can one know what poisons the orcs have on their blades?" He paused to collect his thoughts. "Yet the life desire within him is strong and he is young. I have worked what lore I can for him—that may yet suffice." He looked back tiredly at the resting rogue. "Only time will tell."

"Well," muttered Sordaak, "time is the one thing we do not have an abundance of right now." He paused as if considering his next move. "We'll let him rest for a bit while we explore the entrance to ensure there are no other unfriendlies lurking about. After that, we must rouse him. A potion of Healing may be in order." He grabbed the dwarf by the arm, signaling the decision had been made. "Come on," he said roughly. "Let's go see what awaits us inside."

Vorgath looked questioningly from Savinhand to Thrinndor, hesitating to leave them.

"It is all right," said the paladin. "I will watch over him. We will be fine." Then, with a twinkle in his eye, he said, "Just do not try to pad your count in my absence!"

"Bah!" spat the dwarf as he spun on his heel, following in the footsteps of the caster who had already started in. "Three to two, me," he said over his shoulder. "No padding required."

*

Savinhand slowly became aware that he had not passed from the realm of the living. He was not exactly sure when that fact made itself clear, but it probably had something to do with his being fairly certain that in the afterlife there would not be the searing pain in his side. Or maybe it was that what clouded his vision had nothing to do with the proverbial mists that were supposed to surround the hereafter.

As the mists faded he tried to place himself. Unable to do so, he attempted to raise his head to look around, but he didn't get very far. A blinding flash of pain, starting at his side and working its way up to his head, ripped a groan through his clenched teeth. He allowed his head to fall back.

"Look who has returned from the dead," Thrinndor said as he climbed to his feet and walked over to check on the thief. He turned to the mage, who sat a short distance away. "Do you think we should give him one of the potions?"

Opening one eye Sordaak said, "If we don't, we'll be waiting here for days." Sighing heavily, he rose and picked up his knapsack. "Anyway, that is still a pretty nasty wound, and we can't afford to waste any more time sitting around here."

After fishing around in the pack for a bit, he removed a small vial and held it out to the paladin.

Thrinndor took it from him. Holding it gingerly, he removed the seal. Slowly, he knelt and slipped his massive arm behind Savinhand's shoulders and raised him to a sitting position. Then, raising the vial to his own lips he pulled out the cork with his teeth. Spitting out the cork, he put the bottle to the rogue's lips. "Here, drink this," he said. "This potion will get you back on your feet in no time."

He tilted the flask, allowing only a small amount of the precious liquid at a time to pass between the thief's lips. Little by little, he was able to administer the entire vial.

When finished, he let Savinhand's head sink gently back to his cloak.

"Wha—?" the thief began, although not much more than a croak was heard. Then, with some effort, he cleared his voice. "What happened?"

"Do not worry about it now," Thrinndor chided softly. "Just get some rest so the potion can do its work."

"No," Savinhand went on, "I mean, what happened to that orc?" His voice got stronger as he spoke. "He had me lined up dead to rights. Then a flash of light blinded me. And, well, everything is pretty much a blur from that point on."

"Yeah well," the big man started, "your conjuring friend over there took out that ONE, itty-bitty little orc with a lightning bolt." He tried—mostly unsuccessfully—to conceal a snicker.

"I had to be sure," Sordaak said defensively. "That one 'itty-bitty little orc' had more on its 'itty-bitty little mind' than small talk!"

"But a *bolt of lightning?*" The paladin was openly grinning now. "All that was left of that poor creature was a pile of ash and his boots!"

Turning back to the prone thief he said, "Oh well. Get some rest. We have to be moving out shortly." He stood up and headed back over to where he had laid out his pallet.

As Thrinndor sat down he began to think. So much had happened so fast. First his mount had been stolen. Then, when he found the men responsible, he not only did not wreak his vengeance on them, he joined up with them! And now he was running all over creation searching for that old wizard, Dragma.

High Priest Dragma, he mused thoughtfully. *I have been searching for him for the past two years—or some sign of him in this region, anyway. And now this spellcaster is leading me right to him. Fate really seems to have taken a most fortunate turn.*

Dragma was the only known survivor of the battle that saw the demise of his Lord, Valdaar. It was rumored that he had come to settle in this region, but until now there had been nothing to support that.

Dragma, the jewels, and *The Fist of Valdaar.* Yes, the sword of legend that rightfully belonged to his Lord was last reported to be in the possession of his servant, Dragma. Where else could it be? No sign of either the blade or the High Priest was ever found after that final conflict. *And now,* he said to himself, *I can almost feel its nearness. This is it, the final resting place of the High Sorcerer—and maybe even the sword. I can feel it in my bones.*

During the intensive training he had undergone, the old High Paladin had said that members of the Paladinhood of Valdaar would be able to sense the presence of others who serve their Lord, even if that person had been dead for many years.

Such a feeling had been made known to him—Dragma *was* near. *It is up to me to find him, and thereby find the sword.* Only then could the way be made ready for the return of his Lord.

With such thoughts crowding his mind, he closed his eyes and pushed them aside. He prepared for communicating with his Lord's disciples. Some called it prayer.

"Oh Great and High Lord Valdaar," he muttered silently, such that even someone sitting next to him would have heard only unintelligible mumblings, "hear my words and grant me the wisdom I need to understand your will in these strange times. Please grant forgiveness in the choices I have made in companions, as I realize they are not followers of your greatness. However, I believe them to be necessary to meet the end required of me.

"If I am to be the instrument through which you are to work your return, grant me the wisdom to see the best means to ready a kingdom for you. The final resting place of one of your High Council is near. I can feel his presence. Help me to find him so that I may find the jewels, whereby I can use that wealth to set up the kingdom needed to prepare for you. But, more importantly, aid me in finding your sword, *Valdaar's Fist.* With the sword and the jewels, nothing dare stand in our way!

"I thank you, my Lord, that I have been chosen to serve you. I am eager to do your bidding, and I am eager to further your presence here in the land."

Feeling better after this communication, he reached over and doused the light at his elbow. He tried to get comfortable, but his armor precluded that for the most part. He briefly considered removing it but dared not. There was no telling what was lurking around the next corner.

Sordaak, only slightly disgruntled over the needling he had received over the lightning bolt at the hands of that oversized, over-muscled meat shield (a term he often applied to those who were at the front of the party, there to protect the more important ones bringing up the rear). After all, he *had* to make certain. A dead thief was of no use to anyone.

That big lug had a way of growing on you, he admitted, almost grinning. *He definitely had his uses. The way he took care of those orcs—oh yeah! A couple more of him, and...*

Oh, well, they would make do. Vorgath was no slouch, either. It should be easy from here on in, he reasoned. It's doubtful the orcs left any more behind that absolutely necessary, and the entrance to the Keep proper shouldn't be that hard to find. There were only a couple more places he had not investigated.

Tired, so very tired. Those spells took a lot out of a mage. Rest. Rest so he would be ready for the morrow. Fahlred, his Quasit, would keep watch.

With that, he dozed off to sleep.

Chapter Four

Descent

Sordaak woke with a start. The hand shaking his shoulder was far from gentle. "What...who?" he managed to rasp out, his hands attempting to rub the sleep from his eyes.

"Come on," a voice urged. "We've got to get a move on! Those orcs won't stay away forever!"

The voice sounded vaguely familiar, but he could not place the owner. *Now where had...* he thought as he opened his eyes.

Savinhand stood before him, hands on his hips, a big grin displayed across his face.

"I thought you... How did you...?" stammered the mage, glancing quickly in the direction of the pallet that had held the almost-dead thief only a short time ago.

"Yep, it's me!" Savin said cheerfully. "Come on out from under there! The day is wasting!"

With that, the rogue turned his attention to the large bundle of blankets that could only be Thrinndor. He planted a swift, but not harmful, kick in the general area of a side.

The bundle of blankets transformed into the paladin rather fast as he rolled out of them and surged to his feet, sword in hand. The big man checked his swing just in time to avoid parting the thief's hair at the neck.

Savinhand jumped back in a show of fear, but a snicker escaped his lips.

"Do—not—do—that—again!" Thrinndor said slowly and distinctly. "Next time I might not look before I take your head off!" He then turned and started rolling his bedroll.

"My, my, aren't we a bit testy today?" Savinhand said, still grinning.

Next the thief sauntered over to the remaining bundle. But as he was winding up for his usual wake up call, Vorgath's voice came from within. "Don't even think about it!"

Savinhand stopped his foot short and he backed away, deciding he had better not push his luck further. "Well, let's get a move on then. We're burning daylight—not that it's going to matter where we're going." He looked over at the cave entrance, a short distance away.

Sordaak, finally having gotten his thoughts together, said, "You recovered fast. That potion seems to have done its work." He turned to put his pack together, "Anyway, you're correct. We'd better be on our way."

Savinhand moved out first, using his acute senses to search for traps and/or any lurking wannabe bad guys. The rest of the group moved out shortly thereafter, Thrinndor in the lead. Vorgath was just behind and to the left and Sordaak bringing up the rear. Fahlred was also far ahead, as he needed no light to see. When properly focused, the mage could see through his eyes. This had proved a bit unnerving to the caster at first, but he was adjusting to it.

As they moved deeper into the cave, they noted the walls became smoother. Soon it became obvious the formation of the walls was no longer natural but done by hand. The walls also closed in to where they were no more than ten feet wide, and the ceiling closed in until it was about the same distance between it and the floor.

"We are descending," Vorgath said matter-of-factly. "Slowly, though."

"How can you tell?" asked the caster in a voice that rebounded uncomfortably off of the walls.

"I am a dwarf," replied Vorgath in a tone that identified a stupid question.

"Right," Sordaak said sardonically, deciding to let it go.

They came across a few places where there were branch intersections. A cursory inspection revealed them to be sleeping quarters for the guards, all empty.

After a while they came to a set of double doors blocking their path.

"Is this it?" asked the thief, having materialized at Sordaak's side.

"Stop that!" snapped a very startled caster.

"Is this it?" repeated an amused Savinhand. "I mean, that seemed a bit too easy."

"No, this isn't it," replied Sordaak. "And that *was* too easy. This is only the entrance to the underground hideout the orcs use. But if I am right, this is also just an extension of the Keep." He slung his pack off of his back. "According to the map," he said as he rummaged around in the packs contents.

"Map?" said a suddenly interested Thrinndor. "I do not remember any mention of a map."

"That's right, and for good reason." Sordaak paused for effect. "I never mentioned a map." He paused again. "Ah, found it," he said as he withdrew an old rolled-up piece of dilapidated leather tied with leather string. "This was given to me several years ago when I was just a child. The old man was not sure of its authenticity, but everything pictured seems to fit. Unfortunately, many sections are illegible, and still others are missing altogether."

"But why did you not tell us of it?" persisted the paladin.

Sordaak was silent as he removed the tie and unrolled the piece of leather, spreading it out on the stone floor. His companions gathered around, Vorgath holding a torch close for better light. "As I said, it's not in good shape, and..." He paused as he looked squarely into each set of eyes in turn. "...until now, I was the only one alive who knew of its existence."

"But what of the old man?" asked the rogue.

"He is no longer among the living," Sordaak said simply, leaving the empty thought hanging. His companions looked from one to the other and then knelt to get a better look as the caster began again. "He was my second teacher. I had learned all I could from him, and after he gave me the map, he said it was his time. He had lived long and hard, and his health had long since failed him. So I assisted him on his final journey." Again a long pause. "He knew very little of the original story or of the origin of the map—most of that I had to piece together on my own. But, he was certain that Dragma's Keep, and the jewels, really did exist.

"He was also sure that they were here in Rhetland, but after a lifetime of searching, all he had was the map—slightly more worn than when it had been passed to him."

He paused yet again, attempting to gather his thoughts. Finally he shook his head, trying to scatter the mood that had settled on the party.

"It wasn't until I found the hollowed-out cavern by the sea that I was able to put the two together—the orcs' base camp and the keep, I mean. I stole my way in here once before, but was discovered and barely escaped with my life. But not before I had a chance to look around. I managed to eliminate a few places—those crossed off on the map—but as you can see, there is still a lot to check."

He stopped and looked up at the others, still bent over the map. "Let's get started," he said simply as he rolled the map, bound it and stuck it back in his pack.

"Savin," he said, turning toward the thief. "Have you checked out these doors?" After looking back at said doors, he added, "I doubt they are trapped or even locked, but check them nonetheless."

"Not yet," said the rogue, grabbing a torch off of a wall, and using its light to peer closely around the edges of the doors.

Soon enough his inspections got him to the latching mechanism. "I don't see anything," he said, backing away.

Thrinndor stepped forward, grabbed the pull ring and tugged. Nothing happened. Raising an eyebrow, he grabbed the ring with both hands and pulled harder, twisting it in the process. There was a screeching of metal, and then the ring snapped off in his hand.

"These doors were not so hard to open last time I was in here," said the caster. It was now his turn to raise an eyebrow.

"Hmmm," said the rogue. "They might be locked, at that." He stepped back up and looked the mechanism over again. "Yes, I can see what they have done, now." Savin pulled a pouch from his belt. Opening it, he selected a long, thin wire. He bent it in a couple of places and then he pushed this into the crack in the door, working it up and down. There was a faintly audible *click*, followed by the sound of a bolt being withdrawn.

He turned back to the paladin a bit sheepishly, who only reached forward and grabbed what remained of the pull ring. The door came open easily to reveal a landing. So far the way had been lit by an occasional torch mounted at regular intervals along the walls. But the darkness ahead was complete—not even their bull's-eye lanterns could show what lay ahead, except for a vast empty space. Steps leading down into the darkness sat off the left side of the landing.

Sordaak stepped forward and peered into the darkness below but was unable to discern anything in the void. Looking back at the others, he turned and stepped forward and down, starting down the steps into the looming darkness.

The three others looked at one another, shrugged each in turn and hurried after the caster. Thumbs scrambled to get ahead of the group, quickly disappearing into the darkness. Thrinndor brushed past the caster and assumed his position at point. Vorgath was content to follow, knowing that it was not certain they were not being followed.

The steps were wide enough, at least here near the top, for two to descend side-by-side, but they went single file.

The steps went down only a short distance, no more than thirty or forty feet, before ending at another landing, similar in size to the one above. Here they found another set of double doors blocking their path.

Savinhand, without being asked, grabbed the torch from the paladin and stepped forward to investigate.

"Check them over good," said the caster. "It makes no sense to have another set of doors here, unless they are also locked and possibly trapped." The mage then moved as far away from the doors as the landing would allow. "I would assume, also, that there will be more of a welcoming committee on the other side." Then, after some thought he muttered, "Be careful."

"Gee, thanks," replied the thief under his breath as he turned and knelt to get a closer look at the mechanism.

After a few moments he said, "Yup, they left us presents all right, unless this piece of wire turns loose the welcome mat."

He stepped back, once again withdrew the bundle containing his picks and unrolled them on the stone at his feet. Selecting a couple of tools, he moved back in. "I think you had all better move back. This can be a bit tricky."

Thrinndor looked over at Vorgath. Both shrugged and moved obediently up a few steps up from the landing.

Thumbs worked on the mechanism for a while; a thin sheen of perspiration glistening across his brow in spite of the chill in the air. After a tense period, he stepped back and said, "Ta da! That should do it." He turned toward the group gathered at the edge of the darkness. "All right Pally, your turn," he said, a smile playing across his lips.

"I do not think so," said the big man softly. "On a 'should,' you get to open your own doors." He returned the smile.

"Chicken," said the rogue as he walked back over to the doors, grasped the pull ring on the right and tugged. When nothing happened, he planted a foot on the other door for leverage. Gathering himself, he pulled again, harder.

This time the door surged open, the rusty hinges protesting with a loud screech. The sudden movement caused Savinhand to lose his balance, and he fell flat on his back. As he fell there was the sound of two dull thuds from the direction of the doors. A couple of nasty looking bolts were stuck in the wood of the door, precisely where he had been standing.

"Should," Thrinndor repeated as he came over and offered the rogue a hand, assisting him to his feet. He then grasped one of the bolts and with effort pulled it from the door. After looking it over closely, he said, "Poisoned, as I figured. It is a good thing you are clumsy."

"Clumsy!" retorted the thief as he dusted himself off. "There must have been more than one trap," he said defensively as he stepped up to look at the mechanism.

"Well, I'll be," he muttered, scratching his head. "This is not the work of any orc." Wonder had edged into his voice. "This wire was only a decoy." He traced it along the edge of the door. "See here, this is where the real trap was. No orc is this clever..."

"What are you suggesting?" asked Vorgath.

"I'm not suggesting anything," snapped a perplexed Savinhand. "These orcs are not alone. And since this work is recent and we did not see anyone—any-thing—leave with the orcs..." His voice trailed off.

"They, or it, are still here," finished the caster. "Great! If that's the case, then they probably know we are here considering all that noise you just made!" He looked accusingly at the paladin.

Thrinndor stepped forward and pulled the door the rest of the way open, the hinges again screeching loudly. "Noted," he said as he pushed his way through.

On the other side of the door was another long hallway, with doors lining both sides at regular intervals. Their way was again well lit by sconces spaced every fifteen feet or so. Savin had the distinct feeling they were expected.

Sordaak paused once he was in the hallway to again get his bearings. He pulled the map from his pack and unrolled it, spinning it in various directions in an attempt to make what was in front of them line up with what was drawn. "From what I understand of the map," he said, "what we are looking for is essentially a library." He paused to look up at the doors ahead of them. "During my last time in here, I was able to search most of the doors on the right, which, as you know, turned up nothing." He paused again to consider. "So it's either behind one of the doors on the left, or behind another set of double doors at the other end of this hall."

"What was behind the doors you checked?" asked Savinhand, his cheeks still flushed at his failure.

"Not much," replied the caster. "Mostly guest rooms converted into sleeping chambers for the orcs."

"Well," mused the thief, "since the doors seem to be regularly spaced, and the doors on the left are directly across from the doors on the right, that seems to indicate the hallway—and therefore rooms—are symmetrical, so…"

"The remaining doors on the left are also just more sleeping chambers," finished the caster. "Makes sense to me," he went on. "Very well, the double doors at the end it is, then." He rolled and retied the map, stashing it back into his pack.

Again Thrinndor took the lead. The end of the hall proved not only to have the aforementioned set of double doors but also an intersection of hallways—one each branching off to either side of the hall they were in. They could see no doors in either direction. The halls just seemed to go off into the distance.

Muttering, Sordaak said, "I didn't make it this far, but I don't believe those hallways are on the map." He sounded puzzled as he again retrieved the map.

"Well," said Thrinndor, "perhaps they are not on the map because they were deemed to be unimportant by the map's creator."

Sordaak looked up from the map and slowly raised an eyebrow. "I knew there was a reason we brought you along."

Raising an eyebrow in return, the big man performed a short bow in mock appreciation.

"The double doors it is, then," repeated the caster.

Thrinndor grabbed Savinhand by the shoulder and shoved him toward the door. "You are again up," he said shortly. "Just try not to screw it up this time!"

Vorgath chuckled as he took an exaggerated step back.

"Ha-ha," said the rogue. "Very funny!" He started eyeballing the mechanism. "You know," he said plaintively, "a little show of support would be nice."

"Get one right," growled Vorgath, "and you'll have your support."

The rogue turned his head slowly and cast a withering glare at the dwarf, who shrugged indifferently.

Mumbling, Savin turned back to the door. As he reached again for his picks, a thought struck him. "You sure you want to go in here?"

"What do you mean?" asked the caster.

"These doors are locked from the *outside*," said the thief as he stepped back for the others to see. "Look, three crossbars holding shut *iron*-reinforced doors." He pointed just in case some in the group had missed the looming doors.

"So?" said Sordaak.

"Don't you get it?" said the rogue in his best *you're a dumbass* tone. "These doors were not locked to keep someone out of that room, but something *in*!" He let that thought settle over the group.

Finally the paladin spoke up. "It matters not. That is where we must go. Can you open it?"

"Of course I can open it!" snapped Savinhand. "I was just...oh, never mind!"

After selecting an intricate-looking tool from his pack, he began to probe the inner mechanisms of the lock. A moment or so later, a distinct snap was heard from within the lock. Savinhand jumped to his feet and said, "Damn!" He then threw a now much shorter pick to the floor. He glared at the dwarf and paladin, standing together, as if daring them to say anything.

As he reached for another pick, Thrinndor stepped forward and roughly shoved the thief out of his way. "Move," he said.

"Hey," stammered Savinhand as the big man reached forward, grasped the lock and twisted. The veins in his neck bulged, and his face turned red with the effort, but there was a screech of tortured metal as the entire hasp assembly came off in his hand.

He stepped back and held it out to the rogue, who slapped it aside and moved back up to the door. "Wait," Savin said, thinking aloud. "You 'unlocked' it—you open it!" He stepped back, a triumphant grin on his face.

Again the paladin shrugged. As he reached forward he said, "Remind me again just *why* we brought you along?" Not waiting for a reply, he lifted each of the bars off in turn, grasped the door ring and pulled. Again there was more screeching as the hinges complained loudly. He continued pulling until the door was open wide.

"Smartass," snapped the rogue as he stepped forward to peer into the darkness beyond. "Torch," he called, not turning his head, instead reaching blindly behind him.

While waiting for one to be passed to him, he peered deep into the gloom, trying to adjust his eyes. *Movement!* He thought he saw movement.

"Hurry up with that torch. I think we may have company!" he said as his hand grasped the torch handed to him by Sordaak.

"What is it?" demanded the mage.

As Savinhand twisted to bring the torch to bear, it lit the room beyond just in time to see a massive greataxe slicing toward his head. Attached to it was the biggest, ugliest creature he had ever seen. It had the head of a bull—complete with horns—and the torso of a huge demi-human. The creature was as large as a small hill giant, at least eight feet tall, and its eyes burned with the hatred of the lower plains of Despair.

The rogue saw all of this in the span of a blink of the eye as he ducked and dropped to the floor. He rolled to his right and into the room beyond. As he went down, he felt the tug of the blade as it brushed the leather on his left sleeve, narrowly missing taking off his arm. Once on the ground, torch hastily tossed aside, he kept rolling, hoping his companions would distract the beast.

Thrinndor looked up just as the blade bounced off of the rogue's leather armor and clanged off of the metal on the other door. He used the time it took for the beast to right its axe to draw his own weapon, jump through the opening and slash down on the beast's exposed arm. His haste, however, caused his aim to be off, so much so he did not even scratch the hide.

The beast—Thrinndor had instantly identified it as a minotaur—roared a deep, gut wrenching cry that hurt the ears. That was followed quickly by a battle roar from the dwarf as he rushed past, his own greataxe poised for action.

Savinhand bounded to his feet once past the monster, his eyes adjusting from the bright lights in the passageway. Another blur of movement caught his eyes deeper in the back of the room, which was larger than he first thought.

"Shit!" he shouted. "Another one!" and he turned to face this new threat, dropping into a low crouch as he did. "I'm not meant for the front lines," he muttered fleetingly, and glanced hopefully at the shadows flickering at the edge of the torch light. At least this one was not quite as big at the first—it only looked like a small cabin moving toward him instead of the entire house!

As the beast approached, Savin was about to spring into action when three small bolts of light hit the minotaur square in the chest, leaving small smoldering patches. It distracted the monster, whereupon it dropped into a crouch, pawed the ground with its left hoof/foot/whatever, and charged off to Savin's left, leaving him a bit bewildered at the change of fate.

Taking the out, Savinhand melted into the shadows.

"Yikes!" shouted the caster. "Somebody stop that thing!" He realized he now had the second minotaur's full attention.

"On it," snapped Thrinndor as he spun to face this new threat, relying on his friend Vorgath to tackle the first. A quick glance revealed the obvious size difference, and he said with a smile in his voice, "Hey midget! You want to swap? I think this one is more your size!" He didn't have time to wait for the reply, however, as the beast attempted to rush past him, its attention focused on the caster. Besides, he knew the answer would involve generally unacceptable behavior with one or more members of his immediate family, and maybe the occasional farm animal.

Dwarves can be so crude!

As the monster roared past, he brought his sword crashing down on the back of its neck. And while this did have the desired effect of distracting it from the caster, it did nowhere near as much damage as he had hoped.

This was obviously going to take a while.

"Savin," he snapped, not bothering to look around. "Help Vorgath, I have this one." He brought his greatsword back to the ready position. "I think," he muttered under his breath.

This one, he noted, did not have a weapon. Instead, the creature crouched low, obviously intending to use the horns on top of its enormous head and the might of its huge arms. She—Thrinndor was almost certain it was a she—had skidded to a stop a short distance off, changed direction and was again pawing the dirt on the stone floor. The minotaur charged again, this time directly at the waiting paladin.

Thrinndor crouched, holding his sword in both hands, wrapped around above his head and behind. At the last possible second, he neatly stepped out of the beast's path and extended a leg to trip it. At the same moment he brought his blade again crashing down on the back of the creature's neck.

The force of the blow this time had the desired effect and sank deep. It also served to knock the beast off balance. That combined with the contact with the paladin's outstretched leg caused the minotaur to pitch forward onto its hands and knees.

Thrinndor, his leg smarting from the impact, spun to swing again, but the beast was incredibly agile and had rolled hard to its right. The paladin's sword clove nothing but air where only a moment before there had been a head.

The beast was on its feet far quicker than Thrinndor would have believed possible. She spun and instead of pausing to prepare again, she charged immediately. The paladin was still off balance from his earlier miss.

With Thrinndor caught completely unprepared, the beast's horns took aim on his chest, and only throwing himself back hard prevented serious injury. As it was, the horn still caught him in his left shoulder, easily penetrating the armor at that point, digging deep into the muscle tissue.

A groan escaped his lips as he launched himself to the left, jerking his arm free of the horn as the minotaur charged past. Unable to bring the blade of his sword to bear, he instead brought the pommel down hard on the back of its head, again knocking the creature to its knees.

The minotaur hesitated, momentarily dazed. It was enough, however, as Thrinndor's blade again flashed in a vicious arc toward her neck—though a small target that seemed to be, as the head seemed to be mounted directly to the massive shoulders. His aim was nonetheless true, and the blade again penetrated deep—this time to noticeable effect. The beast howled in pain as it lunged away from the blow, again surging to its feet and searching for her adversary.

She turned unsteadily to face the paladin, pain clouding her vision. But still she came on. Fast. Thrinndor easily anticipated and sidestepped the next charge, again placing his leg in the path and whipping his sword with all of his might at the again exposed neck. His aim was again true, his sword plunging deep into a wound already bleeding profusely.

There was a distinct *thud* as the blade again hit bone. The minotaur hit the floor hard, where she managed to roll over onto her back, struggling still to rise. But the effort proved too great as too much of her life force was on the floor beneath her. The monster's head fell back to the floor, her eyes glazed over, and she lay still.

Breathing hard, Thrinndor turned to check on his companions.

Vorgath had not fared as well. When the first beast turned to confront the paladin as he had leapt through the door, the dwarf swung his mighty greataxe with all his might at the chest of the beast. Something, however, forewarned the creature as it raised the haft of its own axe to block, Vorgath's blade biting deep into the shaft of the weapon instead of the intended target.

The barbarian's greataxe was nearly jerked from his hands as the creature began its counter swing. Somehow, Vorgath managed to hang on. The dwarf's blade came free, but not in time to be of assistance as the minotaur took advantage and brought its mammoth greataxe crashing down. The blade sliced through the armor on the fighter's right side, and there it cut deep.

Vorgath felt nothing as his vision was clouded with the battle fury of his rage, and he cared not whether he had been hurt. Realizing, however, that he was not going to best this brute by sheer strength, the barbarian dropped to the ground and lashed out with both feet at the creature's right knee as he fell.

He felt like he had kicked a tree stump! Still, it caused the beast to back up a step. As Vorgath rolled hard to his left, the minotaur's greataxe bit stone merely a hand's breadth from his face, causing sparks and stone fragments to splatter into the dwarf's beard.

Vorgath surged to his feet, swinging his own greataxe wildly, somehow making contact with the same knee he had just kicked. The creature howled madly but otherwise absorbed no damage. The minotaur turned to face this diminutive foe, more deliberate now.

Savinhand had been waiting for such a move, and now he leapt onto the back of the beast, his shortsword extended downward in front of him. The blade was very sharp, and it bit deep into the muscles of the monster's upper back.

Still the minotaur refused to go down. Instead, the monster lunged backward, causing Vorgath to miss badly with his next swing. The creature crashed into the wall behind it, pinning the thief.

Savinhand, minus his wind, sank to the floor when the beast surged forward again. The rogue sat there, momentarily dazed.

As the minotaur turned to deal with this pesky new foe, Vorgath seized the opening to swing his axe above his head, where it hit with a thud next to where the rogue's blade still protruded from the creature's back.

The minotaur screamed in pain, spinning yet again to face the dwarf. Vorgath's axe had bitten too deep to remove quickly, and the beast's sudden move wrenched the blade from his hand.

Sensing victory, the beast lurched forward only to be hit in the chest by three small bolts of light. This caused the minotaur to stagger back, howling in pain as it did so. The creature recovered quickly and pawed the stone as it stepped forward, low and menacing.

Sordaak's distraction had given Vorgath the chance he needed to pull a long-sword from its sheath on his side. He crouched, ready for what was to come. The minotaur rushed, and with an almost casual flick of Vorgath's wrist, the creature was bleeding from yet another spot. Now the monster's movement was beginning to slow.

The minotaur hesitated, just the move Vorgath had been waiting for and he leapt high and forward, stabbing the beast in the chest with all his might. The sword penetrated deep and the monster dropped his weapon and fell to its knees. Vorgath, sensing victory and never having relinquished his grip on the pommel of his sword, stepped in and finished the thrust with both hands, pushing his blade on through until the point protruded from the monster's back.

Still not finished, the creature surged forward with hatred burning in its eyes. In so doing, it pushed the dwarf's blade the rest of the way through until the pommel was touching its skin. The beast then reached out with its massive hands and wrapped them around Vorgath's neck and began to squeeze.

At first the dwarf tried to pry the monsters hands free from his neck, but the minotaur was simply too strong. In desperation he tried beating it about the head and face with both fists, trying to force it to drop him. The beast opened its mouth and howled again, blood now frothing at its lips, and bit down hard on the armor protecting the barbarian's left upper arm when it got too close.

Vorgath continued to pound away at the face and head of the minotaur with his remaining arm, but it soon became obvious the beast was already dead. The now even more desperate dwarf lashed out with both feet in an attempt to free his arm to no avail. He could feel himself weakening rapidly from a lack of air and blood, and managed to rasp out a feeble "Help!" as his vision clouded and his surroundings went dark.

Thrinndor, having already dispensed with his foe, heard the plea as the minotaur and dwarf crashed to the ground, locked together. He rushed to his friend's side, sword at the ready.

A quick assessment of the situation made it clear the hands around the throat were the more pressing need. With no small amount of effort he managed to pry the dead fingers away from the skin. Seeing that the dwarf began to breathe on his own in ragged gasps, he began to work on freeing the arm pinned between the beast's massive jaws.

Unable to get the jaws to budge, he looked up and spotted Savinhand, still dazed, but starting to move. "Savin!" he shouted. "Come help me get this thing's mouth open!"

The rogue shook his head as if to clear the cobwebs and got shakily to his feet. He stumbled over and grasped the jaw opposite from where the paladin was working feverishly. Together they strained with their combined strength. There was a snapping sound, and the lower half of the jaw fell away, broken at the joint.

Thrinndor carefully extracted the barbarian's arm, pulled the unconscious dwarf to the side and laid him out on his back. Satisfied he was still breathing, he began to remove the upper armor to get a better look at the arm.

This took a while, during which the caster approached and watched silently as the paladin worked. Savin too looked on somberly.

The arm under the armor was a mess. The plates protecting the bicep had to be unbent to free them so the area could be inspected. The underlying garment was soaked with blood and was difficult to remove without further damaging the tissue. Blood was pumping out way too fast from a damaged artery.

"Hold this right here," Thrinndor told the caster who was closest, indicating he put pressure on the inside of the arm where the blood was coming out the fastest.

"Oh, no!" panted Sordaak as he took a step back, his face green.

"Move," said a disgusted Savinhand. He roughly pushed past the retreating caster and placed his hand at the point indicated. This slowed but did not stop the rush of blood. "Hurry," the rogue said unnecessarily as he looked up, worry lining his face.

Without saying anything, Thrinndor tore the remains of the dwarf's undershirt into strips. Wadding up a piece of it, he tied that in place with the torn garment.

The flow of blood was at least no longer making it to the floor. But after Savin removed his hand, the cloth began to saturate quickly with the life-supporting fluid of their friend.

Clearing his mind, Thrinndor closed his eyes and began moving his hands slowly across the most damaged areas. An astonished Savinhand watched as the skin closed as if of its own accord in the worst areas, and the bleeding for the most part stopped.

"How did you...?" he began, but he stopped as the big man sagged back to a sitting position, his breathing now coming in ragged gasps.

"You're hurt!" said the thief, noticing for the first time the damaged armor on the paladin's shoulder and the blood beneath.

As though in a daze, the paladin's head slowly turned to survey his damaged shoulder. "I will be all right," he said through clenched teeth.

"Uh huh, sure you will," said Savinhand, not sounding convinced. He moved to help the paladin remove his upper plate. Once that was gone, and the blood-stained tunic underneath with it, the damage was shown to be significant. The rogue tore the tunic into small pieces and covered the rather large hole in the paladin's shoulder as best he could. He tied them in place with the remainder of the tunic and stepped back to admire his handiwork.

Savin's look of concern deepened still as he saw how short a time it took for the bandages to soak through. "Ummm...you had better work some of that healing stuff on yourself and get that flow of blood stopped."

Thrinndor shook his head weakly. "No." His voice came out among rasping breaths. "I have no energy left for that." He turned to look at the unconscious dwarf. "I put everything I had into him."

Savinhand looked dubiously at the wound. "Well, that needs more than I can do for it." He looked around for the caster, who had come up silently behind them, his face still tinted green. "We have more of that healing elixir, right?"

"Yes," replied Sordaak. "And I can see no way around using one right now." He glanced around them nervously. "We can't stay here. This area is too large to defend, and I believe we are going to find there is more than one entrance." He paused to consider. "At least I *hope* we will find another entrance...." He allowed his voice to trail off as he slung his pack off of his back and began rummaging through it.

He removed another of the small vials, which Thrinndor eyed with a mixture of hope and trepidation. "While I see the need to get me back on my feet," the paladin said, "I am concerned that if used, we will be down to but one such potion." He paused to allow that to sink in. "We have only just begun our search."

"Agreed," said the caster, "but if you don't take it, we may never be able to finish our search." After a pause, he added, "I know I am repeating myself, but we cannot remain here. We *must* get moving!" He again looked around the large chamber. "We have not even explored this room to see if there are others in here besides us. That and there has to be a reason those creatures were locked in this room."

The mage extended the vial to the fighter.

"Those creatures were minotaurs," Thrinndor said as he took the proffered flask. He removed the seal almost reverently, and with one swift motion, as if once his mind was made up there was no reason to delay he emptied the contents into his mouth. He allowed the sweet concoction to remain there for a bit and then swallowed in one gulp. Almost immediately color came back into his cheeks and Savin stared in wonder as the blood ceased to seep from the wound. He watched as the skin knitted together before his eyes.

While the wound looked much better, it was nowhere near completely healed. "Its power is limited," explained the paladin. "It can only repair so much damage. The rest will have to heal with time." He looked down at his shoulder, and flexed the muscles of his left arm, wincing. "It will be enough, for now."

After looking over at Vorgath, he added, "Sordaak is right. We must be moving. I will rouse the dwarf. You two scout around and see what else is in this chamber."

Both the mage and rogue moved off obediently, each in a different direction. Thrinndor bent to revive the dwarf.

Chapter Five

Cyrillis

Vorgath came around slowly. When he raised to a sitting position, the dwarf winced as he lifted his injured arm.

"Easy there, old one," chided Thrinndor. "You will need to take it slow on that arm for a bit."

"Old one?" spluttered the dwarf, trying to get to his feet. "I'll show you—"

"I said take it easy," Thrinndor said as he helped the shaky dwarf to stand.

"Who you callin' old?" Vorgath asked, some color coming back to his cheeks.

"You, of course," replied the paladin, smiling now. "Last time I bothered to check, you had celebrated your 150th birthday some time past."

"Well, 150 is hardly old—for a dwarf!" snapped the barbarian, now playing along with the jibe with a twinkle in his eye. "I can't help it if you humans are an inferior race!"

"Inferior?" Thrinndor responded in mock indignation. "Why we humans—"

"Hello," Savinhand said from across the room. "What have we here?" After a moment he added, "If you two old ladies can take a break from your bickering, you might want to see this."

Both fighters turned to see what had garnered the rogue's attention. He was thirty or forty feet away, his torch showing him plainly, but it also served to illuminate a figure that was hanging by outstretched arms from the ceiling in front of what appeared to be a large fireplace.

As they approached, Savin continued. "I've found several dead bodies scattered about—or rather the remains of several bodies—but I think this one might be still alive." He turned back to look at the figure hanging there. "Just barely, though, I should think." He turned and handed his torch to Vorgath. Turning to the paladin, he said, "Help me get her down."

"Her?" the caster said from a distance, now moving in their direction.

"Yes, a human female," the rogue went on. "Fairly young, I believe." How he could tell was anyone's guess. She was wearing the remains of a tattered robe that could only have been some sort of an undergarment that did not fit well. The tattered garment also served to hide any suggestions about body contours. Her hair was long but stringy and matted. It was also of an undeterminable color. Her face was dirty, streaked with blood and had bruises in several places. One eye was almost swollen shut by a welt. She was hanging limply by both wrists, her ankles also shackled.

The paladin grabbed her around the waist, easily supporting her emaciated body as the rogue cut the ropes that held her up. They carefully laid her out on the floor, cut away the ropes at her ankles and what remained of those on her wrists.

Thrinndor bent over to inspect her right eye. "This looks fresh." He pointed to the swollen area and the cuts above and below the eye that still bled.

The girl began to stir. She raised her head feebly to stare wide-eyed at the big man crouched before her. Quickly, though, her eyes narrowed and she spit in his face.

Caught unprepared, Thrinndor's face showed his surprise and then quickly mottled in rage. He drew back a fist but stopped just short. "Girl," he said through clenched teeth, "I am going to assume that you have temporarily taken leave of your senses and do not know we are trying to help you. But if you do that again, I will have just cause to make your left eye match your right."

She gathered herself to hurl another wad of spit at him and then hesitated. She allowed her head to sink back to the floor, exhaustion apparent in her motions.

"That is better," Thrinndor said, a mixture of satisfaction and concern creeping into his voice. He reached up and dried his face with a piece of cloth he removed from a pouch on his belt. "Let us start with an easy question: Who are you?"

Her eyes darted back and forth between the two men she could see, Savin and the paladin. "Who..." she finally managed to rasp out. She licked her dry, cracked lips, swallowed and tried again. "Who are you?"

She was barely audible, but the tone was unmistakably defensive.

"Forget her," said the caster as he approached. "This is obviously the room we are looking for. I can't find the other entrance, but it must be here somewhere." As he materialized out of the darkness and into the light of the torch, he added, "We don't have time for her—we *must* find the entrance before we are discovered."

"Just hold on a minute," Savinhand said as he turned back to the girl lying prone before him. "I'm Savinhand. This is Thrinndor. The grouchy one over there is Sordaak, and the dwarf hiding in the shadows is Vorgath." As he spoke, he untied the thong attaching a water skin to his belt, removed the stopper and held it out to her. "Now, who are you?"

"I'm not hiding," said the dwarf stiffly. "Merely being cautious."

"We don't *have* a minute!" Sordaak said sternly. "We've taken too long already. We must find that other entrance!"

"A few minutes will not hurt," chimed in the paladin. "If we are cutting it that close, then we are probably already doomed." He eyed the girl curiously. Something about her disturbed him. "Besides, she might have information we can use."

"I am Cyrillis," she said haltingly as she reached for the skin, put it to her mouth and took a healthy pull from it. Handing it back, she said, "Thank you. Would you have anything that might put some color back in these cheeks?"

Savinhand arched an eyebrow and silently untied a different skin. "This should do the trick," he said simply as he handed the bulging wine skin over.

She took it from him without a word, removed the cork and took a long pull from it.

"Easy there, young lady," the rogue said as the others looked on. "You surely have not had much to eat, and that stuff is potent."

It was her turn to arch an eyebrow as she pulled the skin away from her lips, color rapidly flushing its way back into her face. "Thank you," she said, her voice husky from the drink. "Something to eat would also be greatly appreciated. It has been—" She paused to consider as Savin's hands once again began their search. "—what day is this?"

"It is six days past the new moon," Thrinndor said. "Assuming we have been down here only one day. It is kind of hard to tell for sure, though."

"We were captured the day before the new moon," the girl spoke quietly.

"We?" Sordaak asked from across the room, his torch giving light to his disembodied voice. "How many of you are there? And where are they?" He made his way toward the group.

"Were," she said, sorrow filling her voice. "We were six, but I am the only one who yet lives."

"Were? Where are they? They abandoned you here?" said Savinhand, incredulity edging into his voice.

"No," she said, tears welling up. She pointed to a pile of bones barely visible at the edge of the circle of light. "There. That is all that remains. The minotaurs ate them." Silence hung heavy in the air until she continued. "While I watched— they *forced* me to watch." Revulsion threatened to choke off her words. "I was to be next," she finished, her voice a mere whisper in the large chamber.

The silence was deafening as she wiped the moisture from her eyes with an almost embarrassed wave of her hand. She then lifted her chin as she gathered herself. "So," she said, "seven days then." She looked up at the rogue as he held out some jerked meat and dried biscuits. "It seems like longer." Cyrillis eyed the food greedily. "But," she added, a pained tone creeping into her voice, "I cannot take your food. You surely did not bring extra."

"That's right," snapped Sordaak. "We didn't!"

"Relax," broke in Thrinndor, giving the caster a withering look. "At our current rate of unfortunate incidents, we will be out of healing elixir by the end of this day. At that rate we will never *make* it until our food runs out." He turned back to Cyrillis, a thoughtful look crossing his mien. "However, if I am correct, we might have no more need for elixir."

"Huh?" spluttered Sordaak. "Make sense, you big moron! Why would—"

"Silence," said Thrinndor with an impatient wave of his hand in the general direction of the caster. "Young lady, what is your profession?" His voice gave the impression he already knew the answer.

She hesitated, obviously suspicious, but could see no reason not to answer at this point. "Healer," she said, some of her strength returning. "I was progressing quickly until the death of my mentor." The look of defiance was slowly dissolving as she was unable to take her eyes off of the proffered rations in Savinhand's hand. Finally, she gave in, reached out and quickly snatched the food.

As she wolfed down the biscuits and meats, occasionally taking a pull from the water skin, Thrinndor continued, "This dead mentor thing seems to be a growing problem." He turned toward Sordaak as he spoke, but the caster had wandered off again, muttering.

"What?" she asked. "Well, my mentor was *very* old—even ancient, by human standards." Almost as an afterthought she added, "He once told me he had trained as a boy with Dragma's council."

"What?" Sordaak said. "That's impossible! Dragma and his council have been dead for at least a millennia, probably two!"

The defiance returned to her demeanor in a flash. "You doubt me?" The food and drink had obviously returned some of her strength as she surged to her feet, her face twisting in indignation. "You know not of what I speak, and you are an imbecile to speak such!"

Taken aback by her vehemence, Sordaak, who had once again been approaching the edge of the light of the torch in the paladin's hand, stopped in his tracks. "Look lady," he said as he struggled to regain his composure, "of course I—"

"Let her finish," Thrinndor said. "I think her tale will prove interesting—and possibly even helpful to our cause." A reflective eyebrow had climbed well above its accustomed location on his forehead.

Sordaak was forming a retort, but something in the big man's tone caused him to take another look at the young woman before him, her frail form standing defiantly and staring in his direction. "Very well," he said after giving the matter some thought. "Let's hear it, sister." He dropped to the ground, still outside the firelight's ring of influence. "But this had better be good!"

Her stance softened somewhat, but she did not sit down. "Sister?" she began. "I am not your sister. Nor am I inclined to continue my tale."

She crossed her arms defiantly on her chest and looked at each of them, struggling ineffectually to see into the darkness from which the dwarf's voice had come. "I do not know you—any of you. I do know that the information I have is not meant for unbelievers." With a curious glance toward the paladin she added, "I must assume that means *all* of you."

With that she sat down, searching for the remnants of the biscuit she had been working on before the recent commotion.

Silence settled into the chamber until at last the caster surged to his feet. "Hmph," he grunted. "It's as I thought, nothing of substance. Now maybe we can get on with our search?"

"You go ahead, O Great Wise One," mocked Thrinndor, his eyes following the rapidly departing caster. Turning back to Cyrillis he said, "There is more this young lady can tell us, and I, for one, want to hear it." He reached into his pack and removed a small pouch with some biscuits inside and offered her one.

She hesitated only slightly before snatching it from his hand.

"Waste of time," Sordaak's voice said from across the chamber, mocking. "You heard her, 'the information I have is not meant for unbelievers.' Whatever *that* means!"

"It means that her cause is Holy, and it is her cause, not ours," retorted Thrinndor." His eyes reverted back to the healer. "Unless," he went on quietly, cutting the caster out of the conversation, "we have a commonality we are as of yet unaware."

Cyrillis looked up quickly from her biscuit. She tried to see if she could discern the meaning of his words by looking into his eyes, but the flickering firelight cast them in deep shadow.

"Anyway," the paladin changed his tone, "maybe you can tell us how you came to be a prisoner in this room."

She contemplated her answer as she finished chewing the last of a biscuit. "Very well," she began, "I suppose you deserve at least that much for saving my life." She paused while gathering her thoughts. This had happened so fast! Just a few minutes ago she was facing her mortality as the beasts were preparing to make her last supper theirs.

"My companions and I were traversing south out of Horbalt when we were surprised by a band of orcs—a *large* band of orcs. We fought valiantly, but there were just too many. I was knocked unconscious during the latter part of the battle, and when I came to, I was suspended just as you found me." Again she paused. "As you figure, that was at least a week ago. It seems like more. Way more!

"We were brought here as best I can figure as food for what I can only assume are the orc's pets." Suddenly remembering where she was, she looked around quickly. "What happened to them?"

"Ummm," said Savinhand, underlying humor creeping into his voice. "We sort of met them, already. I hope they were not friends of yours, because Superpally here and the Mighty Midget over there sent them rather unceremoniously into the hereafter—with a *little* help from yours truly," he finished with a flourish and a mock bow.

"Very little," said the disembodied voice of the barbarian from beyond the edge of the light. "If you had stayed out of the way…"

"Oh, do shut up!" Thrinndor cut in with mock disdain. "She does not want to hear the grisly details about how both of you almost got yourselves killed!"

The three of them chuckled lightly. Cyrillis looked from one to the other, shrugged and went on. "They ate my people that were killed in battle first and then tortured the rest of us." Tears welled up in her eyes again. "As each died, they ate them, preferring their meat fresh. They made those that remained watch." She shuddered. "There were initially six of us. Three survived to be captives here." Again she looked around. "I just do not know where 'here' is."

"We came down through the orcs' lair—Sordaak and I made 'arrangements' for them to be away for several days," said the paladin.

"Well, I guess we found it after all," she muttered under her breath.

"What was that?" asked Thrinndor, leaning forward to better hear her.

"The orc lair," she said simply. "That is what we were looking for." She looked around, as if seeing the chamber for the first time. "This is just not exactly how we planned on finding it."

"Why were you looking for their lair?" Sordaak said as he stepped into the light of the torch.

Cyrillis looked up at him, and then shrugged her frail shoulders as she turned back to face the torch, staring intently as if to coax some heat from it. "That is my business," she said simply. "I will say no more as to my motives or missions."

Again the silence hung heavy in the closed air of the chamber. Sordaak fought down his desire for another sharp retort. Spinning on the ball of his foot, he grabbed the torch from Savin and headed for the nearest wall. "Well," he said, "It's obvious we'll get no more out of her. Unless you want to 'convince' her to talk," this last he said looking at the paladin. "No?" he went on, "I didn't think so. Well maybe we can just leave her be and get back to trying to find the door?"

"What door?" Cyrillis asked, confusion clouding her visage.

"We are…" began Savinhand.

"Stop!" shouted Sordaak. "Tell her *nothing*! This 'information is not meant for unbelievers' goes both ways, sister."

"I *told* you I am not your sister!"

The ensuing silence was decidedly uncomfortable. The two stared at one another over the light of the torch until Thrinndor said softly, "Sordaak is correct. She is not one of us. If she wants to leave, she should be able to make it back to the surface, assuming she is careful. But she must know nothing as to why we are here."

"But..." began the rogue.

"Unless," said Thrinndor as if he had not been interrupted, "she were to join our cause." He turned to look straight at the sorcerer.

The caster was silent, but his stance softened visibly. He appeared to ponder the situation. "Well," he mused at last, "she did say she is a healer. And we are certainly in need of one."

Thrinndor was silent also, but for a different reason. Something continued to bother him. He couldn't put a finger on it, but he felt something strange, something that was overshadowed, almost, by the presumed nearness of Dragma. But... "Who is your Lord?" he asked abruptly, turning to face her.

She hesitated, clearly taken aback by the question. "You have possibly never heard of my Lord. And even if you have, you would not understand."

"Try me," said the big man. But he already knew what she was going to say before she opened her mouth.

"I serve Valdaar."

Finally Thrinndor understood the feeling that had been gnawing at him. "Then you are welcome to join us, sister." Somehow his calling her that sounded different from when Sordaak did. It sounded...*right*. At her confused look, he explained, "I too serve Valdaar." He drew up to his full height. "I hail of the Paladinhood of Valdaar."

Stunned, Cyrillis had to put her hands out to steady herself.

She started to reply but was cut off by Sordaak. "Now wait just a damn minute!" he said. "This is my party, and *I* will say who will be welcome to join and who is not! I got us this far and—"

"You what?" interrupted an incredulous Savinhand. "You have got to be kidding! Why, if—"

Sordaak cut him off with a wave of his hand and continued. "I was about to say that she would be welcome." He turned to look at the paladin. "While your services as a stand-in healer have been appreciated, they have also been woefully inadequate." He rushed to continue as the big man started to protest. "We are down to just one elixir remaining and are obviously in no condition to continue. We also have yet to find the entrance to the Keep." He turned back to a suddenly bewildered Cyrillis.

With a formal bow, he continued. "If you would be so kind to join us, we would gladly share in the take with you." He raised an eyebrow. "However, as you are joining this expedition at this late juncture, your take will be ten percent."

Savinhand made to protest, but the caster held up his hand, forestalling him. "There will be no discussion." And he followed that proclamation with a stern look that encompassed the three others.

"I…" Cyrillis stammered into the silence that followed. "I have no need for loot!" Indignation crept into her voice. "I am here—"

"No matter," continued Sordaak. "You may give your take to your church, or we will in your name." He raised an eyebrow by way of question. "Ten percent. No more!"

Changing his tone, he added, "Now, are you well? I mean other than the obvious food and drink deprivation?"

The question caught her off-guard, and it was several moments before she could reply. The others were also stunned into silence by the abrupt change in their self-proclaimed leader's demeanor.

"I am rather weak," she began. "But, there is nothing broken. In time, food, drink and rest will restore my strength."

"I don't know whether you have been listening, but time is the one thing we are even shorter in supply of than the elixir." He paused to consider. Having reached a decision, he slung his pack off his back and pulled from it the remaining elixir. "Drink this. It will restore some of your lost energy."

Cyrillis reached for it hesitantly. Then she shook her head and dropped her hand to her side. "No," she said, "There is nothing wrong with me that time will not mend. Besides, we may still come to a circumstance when we will yet require that potion." She looked around again. "Now, if I only had my staff," she said, more to herself than for any of the others' benefit.

Sordaak shrugged and then wrapped the single remaining elixir in a piece of cloth for protection. "As you wish," he said and placed it gently back into his pack, signaling the end of discussion.

He too looked around, peering into the surrounding darkness. "Well, it's obvious we are in no shape for further encounters." His eyes settled on the rogue. "Savin, can we secure the doors we came through so that we are not surprised from that direction?"

The rogue glanced back that way, shrugged his shoulders and said, "I can try. The doors opened out, however, and securing them will difficult, at best."

"Good," said the caster, ignoring any implied difficulties. "See what you can do." Turning his attention to the paladin he said, "Thrinn, see if you can get some light in here. And Vorgy," he added as he looked in the direction of the still hidden dwarf, "see if you can find anything that will burn and start a fire in that fireplace." After a moment's pause to consider, he added, "Go easy on that at first, though, because we can't know if the chimney is blocked."

"It is clear," said Cyrillis. "The minotaurs occasionally prepared a meal there." She shuddered. "I would rather not discuss *what* they prepared, however." Her eyes took on a forlorn look. "They usually preferred their meat raw, though."

Sordaak raised an eyebrow. "Understood. However, there is something else that has been bothering me: Why is it so dark in here? I mean if these creatures actually lived in here, and had food brought to them, it goes without saying they should have had some light."

"They did," Cyrillis said. "When they heard your work at opening the door, one of them doused the torches and lights while the other knocked me unconscious—presumably to keep me from warning you."

Sordaak started to reply, but Vorgath broke in. "What's bothering me is that if these minotaurs were the prisoners, then why were they allowed weapons?" He hefted the huge greataxe recently wielded by one of the monsters to make his point.

Cyrillis paused to consider her answer. "I do not know. But I got the feeling they were more pets than prisoners. On more than one occasion they were led out—where I do not know—and they were allowed their weapons."

The chamber was beginning to brighten as the paladin lit a couple of torches along one of the walls and was moving toward still more. Vorgath had found a stack of firewood next to the hearth and was busy setting a fire. Savinhand had closed the doors and was busy rigging up a means to secure them from within the chamber.

"Now, young lady," said a thoughtful Sordaak, "a few more questions, if you don't mind."

"If you do not mind my sitting, then please, do ask," she replied pleasantly, turning so she sat cross-legged across from him.

Sordaak also sat, pondering what to say next. "Well, let's start with why exactly you are searching for Dragma's Keep."

She looked at him with a measuring eye. "I did not say we were looking for Dragma's Keep," she said slowly, gauging his reaction. "I said we were looking for the orcs' lair."

A startled caster cursed under his breath. "That you did, young lady," he tried to smooth his blunder over, thinking quickly all the while. "I was making an assumption."

Now it was her turn to raise an eyebrow.

"No mere party of six could ever hope to deal with the number of orcs that would have certainly accompanied the discovery of their lair." He did some mental brow wiping, rather pleased with his answer to her calling him out. "Ergo, you must have been looking for more than just the lair—something that was known to be in this region." He smiled in satisfaction. "Dragma's Keep!"

Considering her reply carefully, Cyrillis began. "The fabled Dragma jewels are not what one would call a secret—"

"Right," broke in the caster, impatiently. "But you have already said you are not interested in loot."

Cyrillis gave him a withering stare. "If you do not interrupt my answers, I will not interrupt your questions!"

Her eyes held him until he shifted uncomfortably. "Agreed," he muttered meekly. "I do apologize. Please continue."

Unsure as to whether he was mocking her or not, she reluctantly released him from her gaze. "Very well. I was about to add that I do not believe the jewels are even in the keep."

Sordaak started to cut in with the obvious *why* but quickly changed his mind as her stern gaze again sliced into him.

"To answer your unasked question—thank you, by the way—there have been recent reports that several gems and pieces of ancient jewelry have been showing up in vendor's shops throughout the land, jewelry that dates back several thousand years." She paused for dramatic effect, a maneuver not unnoticed by the caster. He erred on the side of wisdom and chose to say nothing—yet. "Nothing is certain, however, because it is not known what exactly composed 'Dragma's Jewels.' But let us say the periodicity and timing seem to indicate the keep has been plundered."

"But…" Sordaak blurted out. Receiving the hairy eye once again, sheepishly he said, "Sorry."

"I know. If the temple had been found, surely word of that would have leaked out, right?" she continued.

"Yes! Exactly!"

No hairy eye this time. "Well, as I said, it is only rumors—unverified reports. But, it all seems to fit. My staff—" She looked around furtively. "My staff is also from that period. It was given to me by my mentor, but he said he purchased it from a local arms vendor who saw it only as a quarterstaff with a pretty bauble." Again, she looked around the now brightening chamber. "It is old, very old—ancient even. Not much is known about it, but it is *very* powerful. My mentor had not even begun to scratch the surface of what it is capable of, I think. I have been able to discern very little more than he."

Savinhand, who had finished with the doors and was poking around the well-lit chamber, said, "Umm, looky what I found." The rogue grabbed an askew bookcase and pulled it away from the wall.

Cyrillis and Sordaak both turned to see what drew the interest of the thief as he reached behind the case. Savinhand let out a howl as he jerked his hand back, shaking it profusely. "Son of a bitch!" he shouted. He stopped shaking it to peer at the smoldering skin of his right hand. "What the…?" he said as he looked deeper into the hole moving the shelf had created.

"Oh my," Cyrillis said as she sprang to her feet and rushed to the thief's side. He was again reaching into the void, this time with a dagger in left hand to probe the area.

"Stop!" she said. "Do not touch that!"

A bewildered Savinhand quickly pulled back the offending scout. "Why? What is *that*?" he said, perhaps more harshly than intended. He figured he had earned some leeway.

"My staff," she said with a hint of affection in her voice. "None but those with the purest of intentions may grasp it." She reached into the void and withdrew a very large quarterstaff. Holding it reverently, she clutched it to her chest and cradled it, a relieved expression plain on her face.

The staff was at least as long as she was tall, maybe even longer. It was as big around as her upper arm, which is rather big for a staff. It had a metal heel that somehow looked as if it had been forged the day before, while yet appearing ages old. At the head, the wood spread out and was ornately carved to leave a hole inside which a fabulously beautiful ruby was suspended.

Initially dull in appearance, the gem immediately started glowing with a brilliance that far belied the base material of a ruby once Cyrillis touched the staff. The body of the staff was of an indeterminable type of wood, and it was covered from head to heel in intricately carved runes. The runes were so small as to be hard to decipher, yet if one fixated on a single one it appeared to grow in both size and power.

The staff appeared incredibly old, yet no blemish was discernible to the naked eye. Its shaft was polished by prolonged use, yet no wear was visible.

"*Kurril*," Thrinndor said reverently. He had approached to see what was going on. "The staff of Angra-Kahn ," he added reverently. "Tell me again how you came to be in possession of it."

"My master—" she began, but was interrupted by Sordaak.

"That is not important at this juncture," he said. "What can it do?"

She started to reply, but an irritated Thrinndor said harshly, "It *is* important—obviously more than you realize." His eyes were fixated on the staff as he continued. His voice softened, concern edging its way into it. "If that is indeed the High Priest of Valdaar's lost staff, and the jewels have indeed been appearing across the land, then…" He allowed his voice to trail off, not wanting to speak what was next.

Vorgath, who had also approached the three gathered tightly around Cyrillis finished for him. "Then the keep has already been plundered, and our efforts are wasted."

"I don't believe it!" snapped an irritated Sordaak. "Word of the keep being found would have surely leaked out." He stared down each of them, defying any to contradict. "I have heard of no such finding!"

Silence permeated the chamber for a few moments, but Thrinndor finally broke the reverie. "Not if the plundering is still in progress," he said, "and therefore kept secret."

"Bah!" said a disgruntled caster, but he now sounded like he was trying to convince himself. "Secrets like that are impossible to keep! If one was trying to keep it secret, you would not sell even a single gem that could be traced back to the keep!"

"Yes," agreed the paladin. "That logic is certainly sound." He raised an eyebrow for emphasis. "However, only if the plunderers are intelligent enough to do so. I think we may assume that whoever, whatever, is doing the looting must have stumbled on the temple by accident."

He now had everyone's attention. He went on. "Because, no one that knew of Dragma, or of the history that surrounds him, would have ever sold that staff to a vendor!" As he finished his eyes again went to the staff cradled against the breast of the healer.

Silence overtook the group for a moment while they digested what had just been said. Sordaak was the first to recover. "Then," he started, his own eyes wandering back to the staff, "all is not lost. It's possible the entire keep hasn't been plundered!"

"That is true," said Thrinndor. "However, I would not rest a lot of hope there. That staff, it would figure, should have been highly protected."

"My, aren't we the voice of gloom and doom?" said Savinhand.

"Well," said Sordaak, ignoring the thief, "we must assume they are still in the process of looting, and therefore have not removed all items of interest." After a pause, he looked around the room. "All the more reason to get moving as quickly as possible. We *must* get there before they—whoever they are—are finished and depart!" He spun back to face Cyrillis. "Now, young lady, could you please tell us where the secret door is?"

A confused look quickly clouded her face. "Secret door?" she repeated. "The only door I have seen used since my imprisonment was the one by which I assume you entered."

"Shit!" snapped a clearly agitated Sordaak. "It's here! I *know* it's here! It can be *nowhere* else." He turned to look at the haggard group around him. "I know we are weary. And I know our perimeter is relatively secure. But, we *must* not rest until we find the door!"

"Sordaak is right," agreed the paladin, shocking the caster for the moment. "If there is another door to this chamber, and we do not know its location, we cannot defend against intrusion from that quarter." As the others digested this information, he added, "This is not a large chamber. *If* the entrance is here, we will find it."

"It's here," said a confident Sordaak. "There is no other place it can be. Let's break up the chamber into sections, and each of us will search a different section. If you find nothing in the section you are in, trade with another, putting a second set of eyes on each section." After a pause, he added, "And a third or fourth, whatever it takes. It is *here*! I can feel it."

Split up they did. Sordaak gave out directions, but most of the attention was given to the bookcases, and there were plenty of those to go around.

However, after several hours of searching and trading locations a number of times, no door was found.

Finally Cyrillis was at the limits of her endurance. "You still have not told me why you think there is a secret door," she said, "and why it is in this chamber."

Sordaak had gotten cranky, and now was dealing with doubts of his own. "All right!" he snapped. "Map. I have a map."

"That is different," she said. "May I see it?"

Grumbling, the caster stumped over to where he had set his pack and opened it. He reached inside and withdrew the rolled up map. As he untied the thong, he raised an eye to Cyrillis, patiently standing before him. "You tell *no one* about this, understand?"

She made to reply, but Thrinndor spoke first, "What difference does it make?" he asked testily. "If we find the entrance, the map will be of no more use. If we do not find the entrance, the map will have proved to be useless."

Sordaak threw him a cold stare but kept silent on the issue. Instead, he turned back to Cyrillis and pointed out on the map where they had come, and where they were. She took the map in her hands, and spun it so that she could look at it from various angles.

"Well," she said finally, "I agree with your assessment that we are in the right location. I also agree that the entrance should be from in this chamber." She spun the map one last time, turning her body so she was facing the fireplace. "However, if the orientation is correct—and we have no reason to believe it should not be—the secret door will open into a passage that leads off in that direction." She indicated the fireplace.

"Give me that," said the caster, crossly. "Hmmm, I think you're correct, young lady." No one chose to point out that he was, at most, only a year or two her senior. "That would indicate that either we have to go out through that wall, or maybe the fireplace. It's that or the entrance is through either the floor or the ceiling before heading off in that direction."

They all looked up. The ceiling above them was about twenty feet away, appearing seamless from wall to wall. Solid rock. Almost in unison, they looked down at the rock under their feet. It also appeared seamless from wall to wall.

"The fireplace it is, then," Sordaak muttered. He moved in that direction.

"But we each have taken a turn looking the damned fireplace over," protested Vorgath. "There's nothing there!"

"We must have missed it!" snapped the mage. "If we all search the same area at once, with more attention given to the fact that *it must* be through there, we will find it."

"If we don't trip over one another," groused the dwarf.

"And, if it's there!" added Savinhand.

"I tell you it is there!" said the caster, biting off each word for emphasis.

Savinhand took in a breath to make a snappy reply, but a quick glance at Sordaak and the evil eye he was getting caused him to clamp his mouth shut instead.

Without another word, Sordaak marched up to the fireplace and began searching, deliberately ignoring the others.

Thrinndor scratched his head, shrugged and moved to follow. The others looked at one another, sighed and shuffled in that direction, as well.

Savinhand was the one who finally noticed the almost imperceptible scratches in the floor which moved uniformly off in one direction from the fireplace. Hardly believing what he was seeing, he brushed the dust that had accumulated aside and got down on his hands and knees for a better view.

"Hey, look at this," he said as he bent lower and blew the remaining dust away to better reveal the scratches. The others came over obediently to take a look.

After looking them over, then getting back to his feet to get a better overall view of them, Savinhand finally said, "It appears to me that this side of the hearth—the *entire thing*—swings out somehow."

After a few moments of gauging the orientation of the marks in the floor, Sordaak said, "I agree." He moved to inspect closely the side of the fireplace that was supposed to pull away from the wall.

After a few more minutes, he stepped back, disgusted. "I can't find *anything!*"

"That fireplace is too big," said Vorgath. "There has to be a counter-balance somewhere to move it." All eyes fixed on him. "And that means, somewhere there also has to be a control mechanism."

Sordaak raised an eyebrow and turned slowly back to the fireplace. "Now that makes some sense," he said. "Everyone look for buttons, levers, whatever!" He began running his hands across the once elaborate mantle. The others did the same, each pushing bricks, pulling anything they could grasp and kicking what they could not.

After a few minutes of this, an exasperated Sordaak stepped back and said tightly, "OK, that's it! Thrinn, Vorgy, grab that side there and use some of that muscle for something!"

The dwarf and the paladin looked at each other, and then looked at the fireplace dubiously. "Move *that?*" said Vorgath. "You've got to be kidding!"

"Just do it!" snapped the caster, no room for argument in his voice.

Sighing, Thrinndor moved to comply. "You grab low, and I will pull high."

"Ha-ha. Very funny!" groused the dwarf, but he moved into position as directed.

"On my mark," said Thrinndor. "One, two, three!" The last word was accompanied by a tremendous heave. Much grunting and groaning ensued as both fighters strained with all their might, veins bulging in their necks, feet sliding on the stone floor.

Nothing moved. Nothing even hinted at movement. They both stopped and stepped back, bent over at the waist. The effort had taken its toll on their already depleted reserves. "We are not going to move it that way," said a winded Thrinndor, strain apparent in his voice.

"Dammit!" yelled the caster. "Very well, I guess I'll have to do it the hard way." Both fighters looked at him as if he had taken leave of his senses. "Get out of the way." Sordaak pulled one of his ingredient pouches from beneath his sash, waving them both aside with his other arm.

He removed a small pearl from the leather pouch and held it out before him. He closed his eyes and began to chant. Soon the strain was apparent on his face as well. His arm trembled and sagged as if it were holding the weight of the fireplace in his hand instead of the pearl. He continued to chant. His breaths came in ragged gasps and he chanted louder. Still nothing happened.

And then, something did. Slowly, almost imperceptibly, the fireplace began to move. At first it was only a small crack formed along the edge. Then the crack widened into a gap. A grinding could be felt and heard deep within the walls and floor. Slowly the gap widened.

The veins bulged on the caster's neck as he strained against they knew not what. Sweat ran down his face and dripped into a gathering puddle at his feet. His knees buckled, but with a groan he forced himself erect. His arm trembled, his legs shook, yet he continued his enchantment. The gap widened further still.

Finally, a loud moan replaced the chanting and he pitched forward toward the floor. Only a quick save by the paladin, who had moved into place for such an occasion, kept him from landing flat on his face. Catching him, Thrinndor lowered the caster gently to the ground.

"Water," Thrinndor called. "Get me some water!"

Savinhand quickly slung a waterskin off of his back, removed the cork and handed it to the paladin.

"Here, drink this," the big fighter said as he held the skin to the caster's lips, allowing a few drops to trickle into his mouth.

Sordaak coughed, spluttered and opened his eyes wide. "Did I get it?" he croaked, as if speaking required as much effort as moving the hearth did.

"Yes," said Cyrillis, wonder choking her voice. "You did. I do not know how, but the passage is open."

"I do not understand," panted an exhausted Sordaak. "There must have been powerful magic holding that door closed. That spell is sufficient to smash open even locked and barred keep gates!"

He groaned and twisted to get his legs under him. "Help me up," he commanded, some strength returning to his demeanor. A grunt escaped his lips as Thrinndor pulled him easily to his feet. He stood still for a moment, shakily leaning on the big fighter.

"Thank you," he said quietly. "Now, I guess we had better see what is on the other side." With an effort, he pushed himself upright and moved toward the newly created opening between the wall and the fireplace.

Savinhand made to follow, but then abruptly spun back toward where he had found the staff. "What about the loot?" he said.

"Huh?" said the caster absent-mindedly, turning to see what the rogue was talking about. As he spotted him digging through what remained in the hole behind the case he said, "Oh, that. Leave the copper, carry what you can. We cannot burden ourselves at this point."

Savin separated the coins and looked wistfully at the copper as he put the remaining gold and silver into a large bag. As he did this, Thrinndor and Vorgath kicked around the other stuff, the fighter selecting a longsword from the pile and sliding it behind his belt, while Vorgath tested the Minotaur's greataxe for balance and sharpness. Apparently satisfied with the weapon, he tied it to a thong and slung it over his back so it would not drag the ground, because the haft was as long as he was tall.

Cyrillis had gone through the pile earlier in the hope of finding the rest of her gear, but she only found her armor—a scarred, diminutive set of banded mail that she was nevertheless glad to have back. She also had taken a cloak that was too large from the pile, but she slung it around her shoulders anyway, liking the feel of it.

Savinhand picked up the sack but had underestimated the weight. He was about to redistribute the coins into smaller bags when the paladin, who had been watching, sighed heavily and picked up the bag, tested its weight, then tied it to the back of his belt on his left side.

Sordaak, who was regaining his strength and had been watching with an impatient eye, said, "Are we ready, now?"

"Aw, zip it, spell-slinger!" snapped the dwarf in a gruff voice. He still smarted at not being able to move the fireplace. "You needed the rest, anyway!"

Sordaak opened his mouth for a quick reply, and then clamped it shut again. He didn't want to waste any more time bantering. He grabbed a torch, turned and stepped through the opening.

Chapter Six

Respite

They filed one at a time through the opening. As Cyrillis—who was last—got inside, they all heard a scraping sound coming from behind them.

They spun as one to see the opening inching shut. Thrinndor and Vorgath rushed forward and threw their weight into the stone, to no avail. Both planted their feet, grunted and groaned, but still the huge fireplace inched closed, their feet sliding on the dust-covered stone.

At the last possible moment, Savinhand jumped in and jammed the shaft of a large torch into the remaining opening. The fireplace did not even slow perceptibly. It snapped the torch into kindling. There was a booming thud as it came to rest, echoing in each of their ears. Not even a seam showed where the opening had once been.

The paladin and dwarf turned to look at one another, a grim expression clouding their faces.

"It's just as well," said Sordaak. Thrinndor fixed his gaze on the spellcaster, waiting for him to explain. "Now the orcs will think we were just a raiding party that came and left." After a moment during which the paladin's eyes did not leave the mage, Sordaak shifted uncomfortably. He continued. "Also, I don't think we'll be able to leave this way—we have been too long. By my way of thinking, the orcs will return within a couple of days, three at most."

After no one broke the uneasy silence, he added, "There is no way we can find the Temple, get what each of us is after, and get back here by then." A brief pause for effect followed—unnecessary, as he had their undivided attention. "We're committed."

Unable to stand the silence that followed that statement, Savinhand said, "But, what about the cave-in? Surely we cannot expect to get out that way."

This must have also been on each of their minds, because they waited for Sordaak to speak. He did not disappoint. "I have given that some thought. If the

Keep has indeed been plundered, or is being plundered, whoever is responsible obviously did not come this way. So, if the tunnel from the boat dock is impassable, then—"

"There must be another way in!" Thrinndor finished for him.

"What tunnel?" asked Cyrillis. "What boat dock?"

"We will explain that as we move along," said Sordaak. "Now, silence." He waved his hand in a motion asking for conformity.

"What...?" started Savinhand.

"Shhhh!" hissed the caster. "Just listen."

After a few moments a faint sound could be heard over the crackle and hiss of their torches.

"Water," said an eager Vorgath. "I hear the drip of water off in the distance!" He cocked his head to one side, attempting to gain a direction. "This way," he said, indicating the darkness before them.

"That's good," muttered the rogue. "There is only *one* direction we can go!"

A withering stare from Vorgath seemed to pin the rogue to the wall. "It is not far off," he said. "It might make a decent place to rest."

Thrinndor shrugged, took up his torch and turned toward the opening before them.

Savinhand, glad to be free of the dwarf's penetrating stare, dissolved into the darkness. "Give me a moment to let my eyes adjust," came his disembodied voice from down the path. "Then follow."

The big fighter again shrugged and turned his attention to the chamber they now occupied. It was not near as large as the chamber they had just departed, but it was by no means claustrophobic, either—maybe twenty feet by twenty feet, and the ceiling no more than ten feet above their heads. The passage down which Savinhand had disappeared was not quite ten feet wide, and the ceiling dropped low enough at that point Thrinndor could reach up and touch it.

"All right," Sordaak groused after a short pause, "let's get a move on. I'm not getting any younger!"

Thrinndor moved obediently ahead, Vorgath behind and to his right, Cyrillis next in the middle of the passage and Sordaak again bringing up the rear.

The passage immediately began a slow, gradual curve to the left and descended at a good rate. As they followed the passage, the sound of the water gradually became louder.

When they had moved carefully for several minutes, the passage began to widen perceptibly. Soon they could feel the damp coolness that the water promised. Not only that, but the farther they moved, the lighter the passage got.

"All clear, boss," said Savinhand, startling Sordaak as he materialized out of seeming thin air.

"I told you not to do that!" snapped the caster, trying to get his heart rate back down to something resembling normal. "If you do that again you'll be pulling one of my lightning bolts out of your ass!"

Knowing that his caster buddy would never waste valuable spell energy in such a manner enabled Savin to bow with a sardonic smile on his face. "Yes, sir!"

"Now," the rogue went on, still smiling. "This cavern is huge. I was not able to find the other side. There is an underground lake, or pond, here. Hence, the water noise we heard. The path we are on," he said as he turned to point off in the direction ahead of them, "continues for some distance. I followed it a bit further, but turned back as I heard you approach. I did not see an obvious ending. The light improves dramatically once you enter the main cavern. However, I have no idea where it comes from."

"Hmmm," said Sordaak as the others gathered around. "We will rest by the water's edge. Any tracks that you were able to find?"

"No," replied the rogue. "But the light was not *that* great, and I had very little time to work with. Now that the rest of you are here, I will attempt to scout around as you set up camp. If anything is around, I will know about it."

"Very well," the mage said as he walked toward the water. "I will test the water to ensure it is fit to drink." He looked up toward what he assumed must be a ceiling above their heads, but could see only a hazy light filtering from—what? "It looks like smoke will not be a problem, not with a cavern this size. If we can find something suitable to burn." He turned to look at the dwarf. "I believe a fire would be appropriate." With that, he pushed his way past the paladin and moved to stare into the steel gray of the water.

Something occurred to him as he bent to scoop up some water. He closed his eyes and held out his arm. Shortly, Fahlred appeared.

Cyrillis reached out and grasped Thrinndor's arm in alarm and hissed under her breath. "What is *that?*" she asked, pointing at the creature that had now wound his tail affectionately around the neck of his master.

"That is a quasit," the paladin said matter-of-factly, drawing only a look of confusion from Cyrillis. "It is his *familiar.*"

"Oh, I have heard of them, but have never seen one." After a moment's thought, she added, "I do not believe that I have heard of one answering the call for a long, long time."

"Indeed," Thrinndor said. "Nor have I. It has not happened for several centuries, at least, unless I have not heard of it. That is possible, I suppose. However, it is unlikely."

"Hmmm," she muttered as she dropped her grip on his arm and moved to get a better look.

Fahlred turned his black, unblinking eyes on her as she approached, but she was certain the creature was still communicating with Sordaak. She felt herself being drawn into the deep, lucid pools, but he turned back to his master and winked out of existence.

Startled she said, "Where did it…it go?"

"It is a 'he,'" answered the mage, amusement trickling into his voice. "I sent him out to see if we are alone."

"Oh," Cyrillis replied. "How long have you—"

"Just a few days now," he said, guessing her question correctly. "I still have not learned all that he—we—are capable of." With that, he turned his back to the cleric, bent down and scooped some water into a small vial he produced from a pouch at his side. Into this he sprinkled first one ingredient from a pouch, then another.

Finally he raised an eyebrow and turned back to the others who were waiting expectantly. "Looks good to me," he said. "Vorgath, dwarves have strong constitutions. You first, if you please."

Vorgath's own right eyebrow jumped, and he opened his mouth for a sharp reply and then clamped it shut. He shrugged his shoulders and stamped his way to the water's edge. He bent down, cupped his hands, scooped as much water in them as was possible, lifted them to his mouth and drank deeply without as much as a taste.

"Yup," he said crossly, "tastes good to me." With that, he turned and stomped off, presumably in search of wood.

"You could have at least washed your hands, first," said the caster lightly. "No telling where they have been!"

Vorgath continued walking as if he had not heard. "I know where they've been." He didn't turn around.

"Right," said the caster, staring off in the direction the dwarf had gone. "You heard him, should be safe enough to drink." He looked up, still trying to discern a ceiling. "Well, as much as I would like to press on, we all could use a rest. I don't know whether it is night or day on the surface."

"Day," said a voice said from the distance.

"Well, obviously dwarves have good hearing as well," the mage said stoically.

"Damn right!" the voice responded.

"Never mind him," said Thrinndor. "He is just grumpy because he is behind in the kill count."

"By one!" the voice boomed from even farther away. "And you cheated on that one! No matter, you never saw the day…" his voice faded with the distance.

Sordaak chuckled. "Day it is. No matter, we will rest. Let's try to keep it to only a few hours, OK? Fahlred will keep watch. All must rest. We don't have time for shifts!"

As one, they dropped their packs where they stood. Sordaak moved off some distance along the rocky shore and bent to wash his hands and face. He liked the sting of the cold water against his skin. He scrubbed hard as if attempting to remove the events of the past few days.

The others drug their packs away from the main group, each looking for a modicum of privacy.

Without a pack, Cyrillis moved off a short distance and sat cross-legged, put her face into her hands and was silent. It was all a lot to absorb.

She looked up and stared at her newfound companions and wondered what their stories were.

From what she could tell, Savinhand's story was easy. A rogue trailing along in search of whatever he could carry away.

She peered in the direction Vorgath had disappeared. She was certain his story would be worthy of telling. A dwarf traveling with a band of humans was uncommon enough, but one traveling with a band on a mission.... Yes, she wanted to hear that tale.

She eyed Sordaak as he rummaged around in his pack, presumably looking for something to eat. He was most certainly on a mission and seemed to be in charge of the group. There was something about him that she could not quite figure out. He was obviously after Dragma's staff, but something else, too. She felt it. Another tale for the telling. She hoped.

As her gaze shifted to Thrinndor she felt her pulse quicken. Tall, handsome to a fault and well mannered—this was an uncommon group of characteristics to be held by one man. A paladin of Valdaar on top of all that! His quiet demeanor belied the strength poised just below the surface, waiting to emerge. He was a natural leader, she was certain, but he allowed the caster that role, at least for now. What she could not figure was why he was with *this* group of individuals. That he was after something, she was certain. But...what?

Presently, Vorgath stumped back into the clearing carrying an armload of wood that was higher than his head. He dropped it unceremoniously onto the sand of the beach area and set about moving stones into place to build a fire pit.

After a few minutes he had a fire blazing. One by one each of the group approached the fire, drawn by the same promise of camaraderie that had drawn beings to similar fires for many thousands of years in many lands.

Savinhand pulled a small cook pot out of his pack and prepared a hot meal. When each had eaten, they separated out to their private areas and settled in to get some sleep.

Hearing Cyrillis toss about, Savinhand, who was having trouble getting recent events out of his head, moved toward her and whispered, "You still awake?"

"Yes," she whispered in return. "I have had not much to do but sleep the past few days." After a short pause, she added, "Rest is what I need, however. That is different. Rest and time to meditate."

"Very well, I'll leave you alone," the rogue said.

"No, that is all right. The nearness of others of my kind—who do not have plans to have me for their next meal—is very comforting. Your voice is actually helping me to rest."

"OK," he began slowly. "Well, a couple of questions, if you don't mind, then."

"Please, do ask," she said pleasantly. Already she could feel herself begin to unwind.

After a moment's hesitation, Savin said, "How is it you came to be in the service of a dead god?"

Cyrillis hesitated, forming her answer to a question she had been asked many times. "My God is not dead," she began. Then she added by way of explanation, "Gods do not die. They can be banished—or their physical presence removed—from one plane of existence, but they do not die." She paused to consider how to continue. "Valdaar's life form was slain on our plane of existence, which precludes his physical return here, at least through normal means. But those of us who follow him are able to commune with him, and he is able to continue through us." She turned toward him in the pale light. "Did that help?"

"Yes, and no," said the rogue with a chuckle. "I sort of understand the inter-planar concept, but if Valdaar does not exist on this plane, how…?"

"We, his followers, exist here for him," she tried to explain. "We must make way for his eventual return."

"Return?" mused the thief. "But you said—"

"I know," she interrupted. "It is written that through his faithful he will return to the land, and what was his will be so again."

Silence fell over the two for a bit until she thought he had drifted off to sleep. "OK," Savinhand said finally. "Let's assume I'm with you on that—which is a bit of a stretch, mind you—but I guess my real question is: Why do you choose to serve a dead *evil* god?"

"I will handle that question, if you do not mind," said Thrinndor.

"Please do," said Cyrillis.

"First, allow me to apologize. It was not my intention to eavesdrop on you, but it was impossible to *not* hear," the paladin said. He approached them from where he had set up his pallet. "Define evil," he said simply as he seated himself nearby, looking at Savinhand.

Taken aback by the reversal, Savinhand stammered, "I…ugh…" His mind raced to grasp the fleeting concept. "Well, ummm…"

"Allow me to assist you there, as well," said Thrinndor, amused by this turn. "Evil is defined by some as 'that which is morally wrong or bad,' others as 'the absence of what is good or just,' and still others as 'when those who place their own desires or dreams above those of others to the extent that life comes second, defines evil.'" The big fighter paused to let that sink in. "Praxaar and Valdaar are twin brothers. Their feud dates back many thousands of years. Both sides call the other 'evil.' To those who serve Valdaar, Praxaar cast his brother out due to jealousy, and took what was deemed rightfully his brothers by force. He even called for the slaughter of those that opposed him. To that end, is that not one of the definitions of evil? If not, more than one?"

He paused again, but when he received no response, he continued. "The followers of Praxaar made sure to point out the evil ways of the followers of Valdaar, thereby increasing their own stature among the races. In reality, both sides turned to evil as a means to an end. Both sides sought to raise the status of their followers, unfortunately sometimes through ways not normally deemed acceptable.

"These two gods brought their feud to the land, asking for the help and under-standing of all the races. Sides were chosen, battles were fought, and wars were waged. Many tens of thousands of the land's beings died before the hand of one side or the other, good men and women on both sides. Some not so good.

"Praxaar claims to want only peace for the entire land—but peace at what cost?" he continued without pausing for a reply. "His 'peace' was only acceptable if he ruled. A peace only if his brother and his followers were dead."

Nothing was said for a while. Finally the paladin again spoke. "Where is the 'good' in that?"

He stood and moved back to his semi-private area. "Enough talk. Rest. Sleep. We have a long way to go, and I fear we will need every bit of our strength if we are to prevail."

Savinhand lay with his hands folded up behind his head, going over the 'almost' answers he had just received. He had to admit that Thrinndor had a way about him. He never really answered the questions, he thought. Yet what he said made sense, sort of. You simply wanted to trust him, believe him. But Valdaar was dead, right? Yet the paladin got his powers from *somewhere*! It had to be from his god. Maybe that inner-planar mumbo-jumbo explained it. But all that stuff made his head hurt thinking about it.

He sighed as he closed his eyes and pulled his cloak, now doubling as a blanket, up to his chin. It was cool in here. Perhaps he should have made his bed closer to the fire. Those thoughts wandered through his head as he finally suc-cumbed to his fatigue.

*

Savinhand woke slowly to the sound of someone poking the coals of the fire, trying to bring the embers back to life. Presently he could make out the grim face of the paladin as some shredded material caught and flickered to life.

Sighing, he rolled out of his warm bed and soon discovered he had holes in his stockings as the bare skin came in contact with the cold, hard stone. He rolled up his pallet and sat back down on it as he hiked first one leg up, then the other to inspect his stockings with a critical eye.

Well, he mused, *there was no help for them out here*. So he stuck his feet down into his boots, shivering as he did because they had grown cold as well. *Should have left those by the fire, too*, he thought.

Savinhand stomped his way over to the now blazing fire and moved as close as he dared, trying to get warm. "Damn," he muttered, "that hard stone can suck the heat right out of your bones!"

"Agreed," said the paladin, looking and sounding refreshed.

After a few minutes dwarf sauntered up to the fire and spread his fingers, trying to absorb what warmth it had to offer.

Sordaak was next. He eyed the others through bleary eyes. "Coffee on yet?"

"Not hardly," chuckled the rogue. "Thrinn just got the fire going, again. I'll get started on it, though." He turned to move back to his pack when he noticed their number was one short. He tried to peer through the dim light ringing the fire but was only barely able to discern Cyrillis' rest area, not much else.

Deciding to take a better look, he moved in that direction. As his eyes readjusted to the gloom, he saw that her blankets were empty. "Hey," he called back to the others standing around the fire, concern creeping into his voice. "Has anyone seen Cyrillis?"

They turned as one to look in his direction, and Thrinndor spoke first. "I believe I heard her get up early and go toward the water."

Savinhand considered this information, then moved warily toward the water's edge. As he approached, he heard some splashing from up ahead. "Cyrillis," he called softly. "Is that you?" Getting no reply, he crouched down and went into sneak mode, certain that something was amiss.

He padded silently forward, but as he got to the water's edge, he neither saw nor heard anything. Confused, he scouted about, still in sneak mode, looking for prints or other sign. Now decidedly concerned, he turned back toward the water's edge just as Cyrillis surged upright from beneath the surface not ten feet from where he stood, causing him to nearly jump out of his skin.

She was wearing only the tattered undergarment they had found her in. Those garments were thin and the wet material clung to her form in all the right places in a most interesting fashion. She did not notice him standing there, his mouth agape, because she was intensely scrubbing her hair.

"Ummm," he finally managed to stammer, which caused her to jump back in surprise. She then moved to cover herself and dipped back into the water so that only her neck and head were out of it.

"Did you see what you were looking for?" she said angrily.

He averted his eyes and turned away. "Yes," he said too quickly, then "No!" as his face turned a deep crimson. "I mean," he spluttered, then, "Shit! I am very sorry, ma'am. I saw your blankets empty, and got concerned. I had no idea! I swear! I was just looking for you to make sure you were alright. I had no idea." A sudden question crossed his mind. "How do you stand that water? It is so *cold*!"

She hesitated and her tone softened. "It is not so bad once you get used to it." She paused to consider her situation. "Now, if you do not mind, would you please hand me my cloak?"

Savinhand looked for the required article of clothing, finally spotting it draped over a rock. It was wet, as well, having been recently wrung out and put there. He picked it up and started to turn, then thought better of it. He held it out at arm's length to his side, and heard the faint splash of disturbed water as she approached.

"Thank you," she said as she took the cloak and donned it, her back to him.

"Again," he said quickly, "I am very sorry. It was not my—"

"Forget about it," she interrupted. "I *mean* that," she continued, leveling a harsh stare at his demure stance.

"Yes, ma'am," he said quietly, knowing that was not likely to happen. Although the light had not been good, the image of her coming out of the water, clad as she was, was likely to be with him for a *long* time...

Realizing this as well, her face reddened, and she set her face grimly. "Now I *am* cold," she said, finally, spotting the fire in the distance. She walked stiffly in that direction.

With nothing left to do but follow her, he did.

As she approached the fire, she spun and said, "But, know this: I am reserved. No man may touch me. None!"

"I, ummm."

Without waiting for a reply, she spun again and moved to the edge of the fire, shivering from the cold and the wet clothing.

Sordaak raised an eyebrow and smiled sardonically. "Now," he began, "there surely must be a story behind *that*!"

"Shut it!" snapped Cyrillis.

"I, ummm," said a clearly befuddled Savinhand.

"You, too!" she said, sternly.

A silence settled over the group.

Savin turned and headed silently to his pack to retrieve what he had started out for what seemed like oh, so long ago! Coffee...

Chapter Seven

History 101

After a quick breakfast, they lingered around the fire, seemingly unwilling to begin the trek anew. Sordaak looked down at his empty plate and sighed. He was itching to get back on the trail, but something had been nagging at him. At first he had merely shrugged it off as being in close proximity to two lawful types. But the arrival of the second such lawful, who just so happened to serve the same god—a *dead* god—was eating at him.

"Perhaps before we continue," he began, his eyes still on his plate. He felt four pairs of eyes swivel to alight on him, and maybe even some raised eyebrows. "Perhaps we should get to know one another a little better." The mage raised his eyes to meet those of the paladin.

A heavy silence descended on the group, accentuated by the occasional popping of sap from deep within a piece of wood in the fire.

"What did you have in mind?" Thrinndor asked.

Sordaak stared at the paladin, willing him to understand and maybe even start the conversation. Thrinndor merely raised an eyebrow and returned the stare.

Irritated, the magic-user shrugged and again looked down at his plate. "I don't know!" Sordaak complained. He looked up sharply. "Yes I do! A little background on each of you, please." He got blank stares in return. "Where you're from, parents, background training, why you're here—that sort of stuff." More blank stares.

"Aw, hell!" Sordaak snapped. "I'll begin." He stared at each of them for a few seconds. "But then I want some *answers!*"

Thrinndor leaned closer to the rogue, who was sitting on the paladin's left. "Perhaps you should put on another pot of coffee." Despite his whispering, none had any trouble hearing what he was saying. "It seems our leader is a bit grouchy this morning." He winked at Savinhand, who nodded and obediently began another pot.

"Very funny!" Sordaak said. However, he waited for Savin to return from the lake with a fresh pot of water. As the rogue added the coffee and set the pot by the fire, the mage began.

"My father is Lord Fauntlaw, and I was raised as the only child to a noble in a keep in the Nomarr region. As such, I was tutored in all of the usual: arts, sciences, math, histories." Sordaak made a pained face. "And athletics." He grinned. "It seems I was better with anything having to do with this," he said, tapping his head with a finger, "than this," he flexed his skinny arm. That drew smiles from his companions.

"My father wouldn't take that for an answer, though." Sordaak shook his head. "Following the death of my mother he personally saw to my instruction in the use of swords, staves, pikes and anything else that might be used in physical combat." He again frowned. "I became proficient." He shrugged. "But in reading, math and especially the sciences, I excelled.

"My father had dabbled in the mystic arts as a teen, and sought to teach me as such. It turns out I kind of liked that." Sordaak smiled. "So much so that I quickly exceeded anything he could teach me and word was sent out that a tutor in that discipline was needed. An old man named Fizzbang answered the call, professing to be a great sorcerer that had tutored many such as I."

Sordaak paused while he considered a smoke. With a shake of his head he passed on that thought. "It turned out the old man was a fraud, and my father sent him and his very few magic tricks out the door after only a few short months. Word was again put out, this time for a *real* sorcerer. A man and his entourage answered the call, but it was required that I go to live in his keep so as to have no distractions. So I did. I was thirteen at the time." Sordaak paused while he considered how much he needed to share with these his new companions.

"This new taskmaster is a powerful sorcerer who worked me all hours of the day and night." The mage took in a ragged breath. "I loved every minute of it." He smiled again.

"He took to sending me on small errands, gathering components for powerful spells, or obtaining the finest in parchment papers for special scrolls. Sometimes he even assigned a healer and some fighter-types to go along for a particular artifact or gem. Usually short quests, but I grew in power and stature— sometimes too fast for my master, I think."

Sordaak paused to accept a cup of coffee from the rogue. He nodded his thanks as he continued. "A lot of the quests he sent me on were to gather information, nothing more. If I returned with gold and gems, he would slap them from my hands. 'Knowledge is the true reward for those such as us. *Never* forget that,' he would frequently say." The mage took a sip of his coffee.

"A couple of years ago I returned from what had been a longer trip where he had me digging for information concerning an ancient rumor. I had uncovered a tome that described the old section of Dragma's Keep in detail. My master was so excited he had danced for more than an hour as he read through the manuscript! When I asked him what was the big deal, he had clammed up and kicked me out of his chambers, and he forbade me to speak of the tome ever again." Sordaak paused while he took another sip of the coffee.

"Of course, now I had to know why that old keep interested him so. While he slept, I used some abilities he knew not that I had, snuck in and borrowed the tome. Back in my chambers I made a copy of all I could and then returned it before he woke."

"That's where the map came from?" Vorgath asked.

"I'm glad you're paying attention," Sordaak said, smiling. "But, no. The map was given to me by an old man who my father interviewed and dismissed as a crackpot. He hung around our keep while my father continued the search for a tutor. He waited for me on several occasions and taught me much. One day he told me he was too old to continue the search, but the map was authentic and I should one day take up that quest." The mage took another sip of his now tepid coffee.

"I forgot about the map until my master sent me for information concerning Dragma. He began to be gone for longer and longer periods of time, leaving me to work his holdings and study from his library. This I did, and that is where I found his references to the Keep. I became mesmerized with the tale of the old wizard. And then I discovered what it was my master wanted. He was—is—after Dragma's staff: *Pendromar, Dragon's Breath*."

Cyrillis took in a sharp breath. "Has he found it?"

Sordaak shook his head. "No, not that I am aware. But I know that he believes he is close." The magicuser paused as Savinhand refilled his cup. "Thanks," he said. "I have not seen him in almost a year. We seem to have had a parting of the ways."

"Does he know that you also seek the staff?" Thrinndor asked.

Sordaak again shook his head and shrugged. "I don't think so. He sent me to Hargstead to see what I could learn last time I saw him. He's disappeared—or at least I've been unable to find him since then."

"Who is your master?" Thrinndor asked.

Sordaak hesitated and then shrugged. "Quozak," he said.

An uncomfortable silence ensued. "Quozak?" the paladin repeated, his tone subdued. "The servant of Praxaar?"

"The one and same," Sordaak said, his voice also quiet. He had known this moment would come but had avoided it.

The paladin stood, Sordaak's eyes rose with him. "Sit down," the mage said quietly. Thrinndor shifted uncomfortably on his feet. "I said, *sit down*!"

Reluctantly, the big fighter complied.

Sordaak licked his lips. "Look. Quozak can choose to serve whoever he wants! It doesn't mean that *I* serve that god—or *any* god!" He stared belligerently into the eyes of the paladin, who also refused to look away. "I've said it once, and I'll say it again: I have no use for a god—or gods!" The mage was breathing heavily now. "I could no more serve Praxaar than that pair of minotaurs we recently dispatched." He paused as he let his vehemence pass. "In this you must believe me!"

The two pair of eyes remained locked for a few moments more, and then the paladin slowly nodded. "Very well," he said. "I will reserve judgment until such a time as I am able to verify this information."

Sordaak considered pressing his argument but decided that the paladin had the right to be suspicious, for now. He stood and walked over to stand before Thrinndor, putting his right hand out.

The paladin also stood, and the two locked forearms. Sordaak gripped Thrinndor's arm with all his might and said, "That will have to do for now." The sorcerer's eyes continued to bore into those of the paladin.

Both nodded slightly.

"Damn," Vorgath said. "You're a wordy sumbitch." All eyes turned to the barbarian as he slung the cold coffee from his cup into the fire, where it hissed briefly. "My story is *much* shorter."

Thrinndor and Sordaak released their grip and returned to their seats.

"Let us hear it then, o ancient one," Thrinndor said with a smile. "I for one find that a bit hard to believe, knowing how long you have walked the land."

"Sit down and shut up," the barbarian said. He raised his fist. "And if you interrupt me with questions like you did him, you'll get you some of this!"

Thrinndor grinned at Vorgath and sat down.

"I thought you'd come to your senses," the dwarf said with a smile. He turned his head so he faced the others. "As most of you know I am Vorgath Shieldsunder, son of Morroth of the Dragaar Clan of the Silver Hills. Morroth my father is a chieftain of the clan, and they mine the Silver Hills for the vast riches hidden far beneath the ground. I chose at an early age that digging was not my destiny. I longed for the horizon, to wander the mountains and valleys below with abandon! I longed to test my skill in battle against the land's best.

"I longed for the life of a barbarian. As such, I sailed to their lands in Pothgaard and trained with the best to be the best." He puffed out his chest. "I've fought battles. I've fought wars. And still I trained. For nearly a hundred years I tested my skill in combat against those that would see me dead." He paused as he checked the eyes of those seated. He had their attention.

"And I lived," the dwarf said, his jaw thrust forward in pride. "None could take me down, although many tried! The wars ended, the battles ceased. So I again boarded ship and set sail for Farreach. There, I sought others of my kind and tried to win a path through The Badlands to the west." He shook his head in remembrance. "For more than twenty years I led foray after foray into that accursed territory. Scores of us died, and finally I was unable to get others to follow my lead. Cowards." He spat.

"So I decided to return to the lands of my birth and try to get them to come with me. I was certain a band of stalwart dwarves could conquer The Badlands! But, they were even fatter and lazier than when I left! *Complacency* had set in! With no one to fight, they became...soft." Vorgath paused as he thought back.

"Once again I shook the dust of my homeland off of my feet lest their attitudes take root in my soul. So, I headed west to the land of men. There I found others such as myself—men whom the wanderlust hand not merely touched, it had left an indelible mark!" He turned his head and locked eyes with the paladin. "It was there I met Thrinndor." He paused as he again turned to face the others.

"I knew that damn paladin was after something! That didn't matter to me, as long as we had someplace to go. Something that needed killing! We fought evil wizards, powerful clerics, enormous elementals, minotaurs, demons, countless orcs, goblins, bugbears and various other denizens of a generally uncouth nature." He paused to wipe the mist from his eyes. "Damn! It has been a *great time!*"

The barbarian scratched his beard. "But, no dragon—yet! We'll find one! And when I do, it will be *glorious!*"

A silence settled over the companions as Vorgath and Thrinndor exchanged glances and nods.

"I'm not sure I can follow all that battle and glory," Savinhand said with a smirk, "but I'll give it a try." He poured a little coffee from the pot into his cup as a warmer, then sat the cup on a rock near the fire. It was cooler down here than one would have thought.

"I'm an orphan that was dropped off at a temple in a town I don't remember by a wandering band of gypsies that my mother may, or may not, have been a part of. I have vague remembrances of my mother, and none of my father. I was around seven or eight when the troupe unloaded me, professing some secret mission into the Sunburnt Sea that was too dangerous to take a child." Savin shook his head. "The chief priest of the temple told me my parents were dead, and that I was far better off with him than the gypsies.

"I believe my mother was an acrobat in the wandering troupe, and that she taught me much before abandoning me in that remote region. I learned many skills that came into play later in life." He smiled. "I was admitted into the local school, tested and my skills were sought after by sorcerers, priests and others. It was after I defeated the local bully who was twice my size in hand-to-hand combat that I was taken to train with the monks."

He paused as he picked up his cup and took a sip. "I trained with them, rapidly rising up through the ranks until after only a few years only the Grand

Master was my superior in combat. And yet I yearned for something—what, I did not know. However, I knew that I was not going to fight the Grand Master to attain the next rank, so I walked away."

Savin was silent for a moment as the memories came flooding back. "As an early teenager I wandered the land in search of what I knew not. Still I searched. Several years later I came across a group of adventurers who asked if I could open a lock on a chest. They had tried other ways to get it open, so the lock was in pretty bad shape. I borrowed a couple of daggers and soon had it open.

"They were exceedingly glad, gave me an equal share and bade me to join them. It was more coin than I had had my entire life! We adventured together for a couple of years, but one by one party members left the group to return to their families. Finally it was just the leader and me. He wanted to return to his mate and a child he had not seen in three years."

Savinhand put his cup to his lips, blew on the hot liquid and took another sip. "But first he introduced me to a man he thought could help me in my new profession—a rogue. Jundeer and I became fast friends, and he took me to meet with his guild, Guild Shardmoor. I was tested, given the oath and admitted." He took another sip to help hide his emotions. "I now *belonged*! For the first time in my life I had a *purpose*! I knew what I was going to do the next day, and the one after that, and the one after *that*!"

The rogue took in a ragged breath and let it out slowly. "I again rose rapidly through the ranks. In just a few short years I was among the leaders most trusted scouts and advisors." Savin smiled. "Or what passes for trust among thieves!" He winked at the sorcerer, who smiled in return.

"I was in Brasheer gathering information—"

Sordaak interrupted. "That's not *all* you were gathering!"

"Ha! There are many ways to gather information," he said. "While passing the time in a game of chance is one."

"Yeah, well," the mage said sarcastically, "there was not much of a 'chance' in it for those poor farmers!" He smiled to show he was poking fun at the rogue.

Savinhand smiled again in return. "Your way was not very conducive to information gathering, if I recall." He winked again at the caster. "Dead men don't usually talk much!"

"What were you there to gather information on?" Thrinndor asked.

Savinhand almost spilled his coffee the question startled him so much. "Umm, orcs!" he blurted out. "I was trying to gather information on the recent orc movement."

Thrinndor noted the surge in movement, the almost spilled coffee by a usually sure-handed man and the momentarily dilated pupils of his eyes. The rogue was not being entirely truthful.

An uneasy silence settled on the group.

"Very well," said the healer formally, "I suppose I will go next." She glanced over at Thrinndor, who nodded for her to do so. "My story will be even shorter than our esteemed barbarian." She smiled and nodded at Vorgath, who returned both. "If for no other reason than I know nothing of my parents, and have accomplished even less."

She took a deep breath and waded in. "Following the death of my parents in an orc raid, I was taken by my nanny, Jacinth, to a safe place. There I was trained in the ways of a cleric in the servitude of Valdaar by both Jacinth and an old man named Ytharra." Cyrillis gulped to force down the knot in her throat as she struggled to remember what she had fought to forget.

"In my fifteenth year, Jacinth went out to gather herbs and never returned." A single tear made its way down her cheek. "Three, maybe four years later, Ytharra said my training was compete and it was time to expand my horizons—he began taking me to town with him. I had not been more than a mile from the cabin where I grew up since I got there at age two."

She looked down at her cold coffee, set it aside and retrieved her staff from where she had propped it. "On one of those trips to town he found *Kurril* in a pawn shop." The cleric rubbed the staff affectionately. "That is when things got weird. He started by taking a different route back to our cabin. When we got there he put out all the lamps and closed and locked all doors and windows."

The cleric looked down at the staff in her hands. "He then proceeded to tell that the staff was very old, and once belonged to Angra-Khan, High Priest on Valdaar's Council." She was silent for a few moments, and Thrinndor began to think she was done. "Then he died."

When Cyrillis looked up, tears were freely flowing down both cheeks. "He told me the staff was named *Kurril*, that I had to unlock the secrets of the staff and that I had to find out from whence it came." She sniffed a couple of times. "And then he died."

"Interesting," Thrinndor said. "Is that all he said?"

Cyrillis nodded. "After that I could not stay at the cabin anymore, nor did I feel safe in town. The only other memories I had been of a temple to the god Set not far from a town. After some searching I found the temple. There I also found a small cadre of clerics devout to Valdaar that were tolerated by the Minions of Set. With the others of the Order of Valdaar I continued my studies and began my search."

When she did not immediately continue, Vorgath asked, "Search?"

The cleric turned her unseeing eyes on the barbarian. "For where *Kurril* came from and how to unlock its secrets."

"Oh," the dwarf said.

"I made the rounds to local villages and offered my healing services to adventuring parties." Again her eyes misted over. "I had joined up with a promising group who knew of a group of orcs that had recently been selling off items of fantastic value at the local pawns." She lowered her eyes, and the companions had to strain to hear her. "We were following one such band when we were ambushed." Her shoulders shook as she fought for control. When she raised her head, her eyes were red. "You know the rest."

All four of the men nodded. Sordaak got to his feet, dumped the coffee out of his cup and rinsed it with water from the skin leaning against the rock he had been sitting on. Then he filled the cup and walked over to the cleric and offered it to her.

Cyrillis gratefully accepted the cup and downed the cool water, quickly. "Thank you," she said and smiled. "You will have to forgive me. I am not usually a blubbering fool. I do not know what has come over me."

Sordaak nodded, returned the smile and went back to his seat by the fire.

"By comparison," Thrinndor began, "my story is much shorter than any of those yet told. I have always known what I am supposed to do and what destiny holds for me." He turned his eyes on Cyrillis.

"I am a Paladin of Valdaar because my mother is a Paladin of Valdaar and my father was one until he was slain in the service of his god. My mother raised me, and saw to my training in the Paladinhood at Khavhall, Paladin-home. It has fallen to me to find the sword of my lord, *Valdaar's Fist*. For that I have been searching since allowed to begin questing." He turned to look at Vorgath.

"It was about two years ago that I came across this barbarian." Thrinndor shrugged his shoulders. "I figured who could help me more than one who has as lived as long as he?" He smiled at the dwarf. "We had just finished an adventure when I stopped in Brasheer for the night." The paladin turned toward the sorcerer. "While there, my mount was stolen—"

"Borrowed," Sordaak corrected.

Thrinndor smiled. "Borrowed," he conceded. "And I believe the rest is known to everyone here." He got several nods in return.

Thrinndor looked across the fire and caught the eye of Savinhand and winked as he turned back to the dwarf. "You know, old one," he began, mirth dripping from each word. "Mayhap you are just past your prime." The paladin shook his head.

"Prime?" spluttered Vorgath. "I am still a hundred years *from* my prime!" His right eyebrow was nearly in contact with his hairline. "And, when I *am* a hundred years past my prime, I could still whoop your narrow ass any day of the week!"

"Oh, really?" Thrinndor asked.

"And I told you not to call me old!" The dwarf surged to his feet and leapt across the fire, catching the big fighter square in the chest with his bull rush. The air left Thrinndor's lungs in a rush as both tumbled over the rock the paladin had been sitting on.

The barbarian rolled with the contact and was first to regain his feet. He swung a heavy boot that caught Thrinndor on his right side, sending him tumbling yet again. Vorgath leapt after to press his advantage.

Thrinndor knew what was coming, however, and kept rolling, giving him a chance to recover. He sprang to his feet just as a ham-like fist whisked by his nose uncomfortably close. The paladin grabbed the wrist as it flew past and jerked. This pulled the dwarf off balance. As he fell forward, the paladin stuck out his leg, tripping the barbarian. Clasping both hands together, Thrinndor brought them crashing down on the unprotected neck of the dwarf, who went down hard.

Vorgath got to his hands and knees slowly, shaking his head from side to side to clear the cobwebs. From that position, he launched himself with unexpected quickness at the fighter, again catching the paladin off guard. Both tumbled to the ground once more, grappling for an advantage that was obviously tough to gain.

Cyrillis watched the proceedings with a look of horror. Finally, she regained some sense of composure. As she made to rise, words formed on her lips.

Sordaak, who had been sitting next to her, put his hand on her arm, restraining her. "No," he said, "let them go." Cyrillis leveled a look of disbelief at him and tried to rise anyway. Sordaak held the cleric's arm, preventing her from getting involved. "They're stretching." The disbelief gave way to confusion. "It is how they shake the tightness off after a rest period and get the blood flowing in their muscles. Call it morning calisthenics!" he said with a wink.

"You mean," she started, turning back to see the dwarf land a right cross to the paladin's chin, sending him reeling. "You have got to be kidding me!" she added, unable to take her eyes off of the spectacle. Thrinndor leg-whipped the dwarf as he was falling to the ground, taking Vorgath with him.

Both surged to their feet, less quickly this time, their chests heaving with the effort to suck in enough air for their expended muscles. They circled each other warily, looking for an opening.

Having had enough, Cyrillis was unable to restrain herself any longer. "If you heathens are finished perhaps you can save some of that for our common enemies."

Both stopped their circling mid-step, and looked at this new adversary. Thrinndor, a small rivulet of blood trickling down his chin from a cut lip, said curtly, "Not finished!" as he swung a right roundhouse that would have surely ended the match had it connected squarely.

Vorgath, however, suspected such a maneuver. As he caught the motion out of the corner of his eye, he flung himself back and to his left, grabbing the big man's wrist as it flashed by his head and twisted hard. This, combined with Thrinndor's own momentum caused him to be drawn off balance.

The dwarf continued the twist, spinning the paladin's arm around his back and up between his shoulder blades. A quick placement of the boot neatly tripped the bigger man, and Thrinndor sprawled face first toward the stone floor. Only a quick save from his left arm kept him from serious injury due to a face plant. However, that pinned his left arm under him as the dwarf followed through with the trip, ending up with his knee firmly in the middle of Thrinndor's back, effectively pinning him to the hard surface.

Vorgath twisted toward the remainder of the party, a triumphant grin splitting his face. "Now we are fin—" He never got the last word out as Thrinndor used all of his remaining strength to buck hard, sending the much lighter dwarf sailing through the air toward the water, where he landed with a splash.

He came up coughing and spluttering but otherwise stood where he had landed in the waist-deep water. He was a sorry sight, his hair plastered to his head and water dripping from his now tangled beard.

Thrinndor was laughing hard as he turned to the rogue. "Hey Savinhand, give our diminutive friend some soap so he can get his weekly bath out of the way!"

"Bah!" said Vorgath, still not moving. "Why, I had a bath just…" his voice trailed off as he cocked his head to one side and considered. "What day is today?" he asked finally, a big grin now splitting his usually impassive face. "Hmm, I might need one, at that," he said as he caught the cake of soap Savin had tossed his way.

"I might as well get the monthly laundry done, as well," he said, his eyes shining with humor. "No sense getting my clothes wet for nothing!" He turned to stump off out around a bend in the shore. "No peeking!" he tossed over his shoulder as he splashed his way out of their sight.

"You know," said an exasperated Sordaak loud enough to ensure he was heard by even the departing dwarf, "I would like to get moving *sometime* today!"

"Aw, keep your pants on!" snapped Savinhand. Then after a quick glance at the caster, he added, "Sorry. I forgot you don't *wear* pants." He got a cross look from the caster, but he just grinned to take any misread sour feeling out of what he had said. "A few more minutes here and there won't change what we find when we finally get where we are headed."

"But," Sordaak started.

"Not to mention the fact," cut in the paladin loudly, "that if a dwarf finally agrees to take a bath, one should definitely not discourage him!"

"I heard that!" said the dwarf amid much splashing. "When was the last time *you* had a bath?"

Thrinndor, his mouth open as he had been about to say something else, stopped and turned his head to one side, pondering the question. With a sigh, he sat down and began removing his armor, all the while muttering under his breath. "Do not use all the soap!" he said at last as he splashed his way in the direction his friend had gone.

"Just you keep your distance," groused the dwarf good-naturedly. "Here." He tossed the soap in the direction of the splashing coming his way.

A grumpy Sordaak glared at the two remaining companions across the fire. "Anyone else feel the need to bathe?" he said crossly. "If so, let's get it done now!"

"I cleaned up last night," said the rogue, hastily turning to peer at Cyrillis.

"I do not need to be reminded in matters concerning personal hygiene from a group of unkempt *males*!" she said haughtily. The water still dripping from her hair gave emphasis to this point.

Sordaak cleared his throat and opened his mouth to speak, but Savinhand beat him to it.

"What about you?" he asked.

"Don't you worry about me!" snapped the caster. "I took care of all that while you all were chatting the night away!"

He slumped back down silently to the rock he had warmed up and began poking a stick into the fire absentmindedly.

Chapter Eight

From the Depths

Ablutions taken care of, packs redistributed—at Cyrillis' insistence, not that it took much, as it was apparent to all that their supplies were rapidly diminishing—they climbed somberly to their feet and prepared to travel.

Vorgath approached the dying embers of their fire and kicked dirt over them. He slung his pack over one shoulder, glanced around one last time and stepped out without preamble.

The others fell into their places in the line, with Savinhand moving off of the path and melting into the background, their direction having been determined before the rest period while sitting around the fire.

The scouting by Savinhand and the quasit revealed that the underground lake would not be that large on the surface, but here below ground it appeared enormous. As was the cavern the lake was in. They had been able to determine that some sort of luminous moss was responsible for the subdued lighting, but none had ever encountered its like.

The companions set off at a good pace and had traveled about an hour, circling the lake to the right of the tunnel they had emerged from, when the path came to an abrupt halt. The path had approached the water's edge and was lost in the soft sand nearby. The wall of the cavern had also closed in to the point where it intersected the shoreline abruptly. The caverns wall rose sheer as high as their eyes could see—which was not really all that far because of a mist that seemed to enshroud what they assumed to be the ceiling of the cavern, thirty or forty feet above their heads.

Savinhand joined them as there was no other place to be. He looked confused. "I followed the cavern wall, and it is without a break as far as I was able to determine."

Thrinndor walked up to the wall to give it a closer inspection. It did not take long. "Well, I do not believe the path continues *that* way." He craned his neck in an attempt to see what might be over their heads.

Sordaak called his familiar and sent him up to see if they were missing anything. The report was negative.

"Well," said the paladin, turning to look at the water's edge, "if the path comes this far and it does not go up, it stands to reason that it must go down."

They all walked to where the water lapped silently at the sand. They peered across the impenetrable distance.

"Or across," said the dwarf somberly, pointing to some subtle markings in the sand and rock. Markings that might have been made by a boat or skiff pulled up onto the shoreline.

"That's not good," said Savinhand quietly. "I have seen no sign of a craft, nor any other means of crossing."

"We must have gone the wrong way," said Cyrillis. "We can go no further, here."

"No," snapped Sordaak. "The other way had no path and ended in a similar wall much sooner." He looked around defiantly, and then added, "It *has* to be this way. There is no other."

Thrinndor looked at the caster, raised an eyebrow and said, "Very well. If it is not up, and we have no means to go over, then the only remaining possibility is down." He turned back to the water, trying to penetrate the depths with his eyes.

"Huh?" said Vorgath, incredulity dripping from his voice. "You must be out of your rock-pickin' mind!"

"No," said Sordaak, also staring into the water. "It stands to reason. There must be an underwater tunnel or entrance."

Cyrillis turned to look at the creature sitting idly on the caster's shoulder. "Can that thing swim?"

Sordaak started to make a sharp reply but changed his mind and turned to look into Fahlred's eyes. There was a moment of obvious communication, then Sordaak turned back to Cyrillis. "No."

Without another word, Thrinndor sat down in the sand and began removing his armor. Finished, he stood and waded out into the water. Before his head went under, he turned back the party. "I should be gone no longer than two minutes."

Savinhand shifted uncomfortably. "And if you are longer?"

"Find another way," the paladin said. He took a deep breath and ducked his head under the surface.

The rest of the party stood expectantly at the water's edge. One minute passed. A second...

"This ain't good," muttered the rogue.

"Just give him a minute," said the dwarf confidently. "He'll be back. He's a powerful swimmer." Still, he eyed the water intently, as if imploring it to return his friend.

After what had been well over three minutes, Vorgath said, "Shit!" and plopped his bulk onto the ground and quickly removed his boots and the remainder of his armor. "Always have to be saving his ass." He swore under his breath as he put his foot into the cold water.

Just as the barbarian was about to go under, the paladin's head broke the surface of the water with a rush. He gulped air into his starved lungs and heaved himself onto the beach where he knelt, head down as he gasped for air.

"Well?" said Sordaak.

Thrinndor turned to eye the impudent caster. "I believe I found another cavern, or tunnel, but the light does not penetrate the water, and it is impossible to tell."

Sordaak raised an eye. He then reached into his pack, removed a silver coin and began chanting.

Meanwhile Vorgath climbed out of the water with mock disgust etching his face. "Two baths in one day." He began drying off with his cloak, shaking his head all the while.

Thrinndor turned to look at his friend, a gleam in his eye. Between gasps he said, "Getting a little worried, were you?"

A look of disdain rippled across the barbarian's eyes, and he opened his mouth for a sharp retort but was cut off by an angry Cyrillis, "Of course we were!" she snapped. "You said two minutes! Yet you were gone more than three!"

"Was I?" said Thrinndor, feigning ignorance. "I did not know I had been…" His voice trailed off as the caster ceased chanting. Sordaak then he reached out to hand the paladin the coin, which now shone brightly in his hand.

"What did you do?" queried the big man. "How long will it last?"

"Continual Light is the spell," answered Sordaak. "Apprentice crap—and I don't know. It kind of depends on several factors. But it will last more than long enough for what you need." He reached under his cloak and removed a small piece of leather, made stiff by some means. "Here, wrap this around the coin like this," he said as he rolled the leather around the coin edge-wise and tied it there with a thong. "There," he said. "That way it will not blind you as you use it to see what is in front of you."

A bewildered paladin took the proffered device and put his hand in front of it. His palm was illuminated brightly by the device. His right eyebrow arched toward his soaked hairline.

"Just point it at what you want to illuminate!" said Sordaak. "Here, let me show you." He reached out to take it back.

Thrinndor pulled it out of his reach, "I think I can figure it out! After all, it is not Astrological Science!"

"Well," said the caster, amusement crowding his voice, "its range is limited, so you will have to get close for it to do you any good."

"Got it," said the big fighter as he turned back to the water and waded in. "I will be back in…whatever. I will be back when I get back." He again inhaled deeply and disappeared below the surface.

He was gone less than two minutes this time. He climbed out of the water, puddles forming at his feet. "There is a cavern on the other side," he gasped out. "It is at the end of a short tunnel." He glanced around the group, "All should have no trouble making the swim."

"What's there?" asked Savinhand.

Thrinndor turned to face him, "A large pool with stone steps leading out of it. Where they go, I did not take time to ascertain." He paused as he considered. "It does not matter. They lead to where we need to go. There is no other option."

The paladin looked around. "While the swim should not pose a problem, each of you should put anything heavy in this pack." With that, he built a make-shift sled out of his armor. He then placed sacks of coin, various weapons, and everyone's armor into the sled.

Everyone's, that is, except Vorgath. "You never know what lurks in those depths," the dwarf said stubbornly. "For a 'short' swim, I keep my armor on." He crossed his arms on his chest.

No amount of discussion was going to change his mind, so Thrinndor read-ied the pack by tying two lengths of rope to it. "I will go through first with this rope," he said, holding up the end of one of the ropes. He tied it to his belt. "When I am on the other side, I will pull the sled through." He turned to the thief. "Savinhand, if you would be so kind as to come along first and guide the sled into the opening." The thief gave him a brief nod. "Vorgath, if you would anchor this end of the rope, then bring it through with you when you come." Another nod.

"We do not want to keep a rope anchored here in the event we have to return?" asked Cyrillis.

"No," said Sordaak brusquely. "We won't be returning." All eyes turned to the caster. "Not this way, anyway."

Into the brief silence that followed that revelation the paladin said, "Right. Each of you follow in turn. Just hand-over-hand the rope, and pull yourself through. It will take you less than one minute to get through. It will be dark, so do not panic. I will have light on the other side."

With that said, he turned and splashed unceremoniously into the water. He took a deep breath and disappeared into the murky depths. For a short distance his makeshift light allowed them to track his progress, but even that soon van-ished as he approached the wall of rock.

When the sled started moving, Savinhand jumped in and guided it as requested. The others followed, and soon the entire party was standing on the landing, water dripping into puddles at their feet. Each dried off, put on armor, reslung weapons, tightened belts and distributed packs.

As whatever had provided light behind them was not in evidence here, Thrinndor removed a couple of torches from their protective wax covering and worked to get them going. As they spluttered to life, he handed one to Vorgath and took the other to scout around.

The steps led up from the water's edge to a ledge about 10 feet above. The steps had obviously been cut into the rock by tools. The shelf was large enough that the walls of the cavern could not be seen from the steps by torchlight.

Vorgath went to the right, Thrinndor to the left.

Soon both fighters met up at the same point, having reached the edge of the shelf and having to move along a wall of rock across from the water.

Where they met, they found a door, or rather a set of doors. There were sconces in insets on either side of the doors. With a shrug, the paladin lit first one and then the other.

As the area brightened, the others came to see what they had found. The steps to the water were no more than fifty feet away. Savinhand moved up for the usual inspection as Thrinndor stepped aside.

"While he's looking the doors over, let's take a few minutes to eat and rest," announced Sordaak. "Something tells me it might be a while before we again get the chance."

"There is some writing here I can't figure out," said the rogue. He turned to face the caster. "Runes, I think."

Sordaak moved to get a closer look. "Yup," he said after a cursory inspection, "runes. They say, 'Turn back, fools. Death's messenger waits beyond these doors. Opening them will trigger a curse you of which you can never be rid.'" Into the silence that followed, he added, "The usual warning." He waved an arm of dismissal as he turned back to his pack and sat down. "Then it gets nasty."

"You mean there's more?" Savinhand sounded decidedly unhappy.

"Yes," mumbled the caster, his mouth full of biscuit. "But the rest is the aforementioned curse. I don't believe I'll read that aloud."

"Gotcha," said the thief quickly as he stepped back in to continue his search.

Vorgath plopped down and promptly stretched out. He tilted his helm over his eyes and said, "Wake me when we're ready to move on." Within moments he was snoring deeply.

"I wish I could fall asleep like that!" groused Sordaak.

"Yeah, well," said Thrinndor, "you obviously have too much on your mind." He reclined against the wall and closed his eyes as well.

Sordaak glared at the paladin, thought about making a sharp reply but decided against it. Muttering, he leaned against his pack and pulled out his map. After turning it every which way, he decided that whoever had drawn it hadn't been this far—or didn't come this way. He rolled the map up and returned it to his pack.

Finally, he turned a lazy eye to the rogue, who was still inspecting the doors. "Well?" he said.

Savinhand turned to face the caster, scratching his head, perplexed. "I don't see…" He was cut off by a shrill scream.

"Help!" Cyrillis screamed from the direction of the water.

Vorgath and Thrinndor surged to their feet in the same instant, weapons at the ready. Sordaak was only a blink of the eye behind them as he rolled over hard and fast, coming to a crouch and poised to cast. Two daggers appeared as if by magic in Savin's hands as he broke into a run in the direction of the screams.

Vorgath turned to look at the paladin and said, "'Bout damn time we got some action! I was getting bored!" He turned, let out one of his blood-curdling yells and ran after the rapidly disappearing rogue. Sordaak was close on his heels.

Thrinndor grabbed a torch and joined the pursuit. He got to the water's edge only to see Savinhand staring intently at the bare rock. Cyrillis was nowhere to be seen.

He looked up at the approach of the torch. "Someone—some*thing* has taken her!" he shouted. He turned and plunged headlong into the water.

Vorgath never slowed as he got to the edge of the shelf. He leapt over the edge and dove in with a tremendous splash.

Thrinndor hesitated as he handed the torch to the caster. "Wait here in the event she returns!"

As the paladin turned to follow the others, Sordaak grabbed his arm. "Wait! Take this." He pressed the makeshift light he had made earlier into the fighter's empty left hand.

"Thank you," said Thrinndor as he plunged into the water.

"I'll wait here," muttered the caster as the paladin disappeared below the surface. "Someone's got to hold down the fort!" He peered into the water, trying to will his friends to reappear.

Finally a disturbance broke the surface and Cyrillis appeared. A long tentacle was wrapped tightly around her body, the other end still in the water. She gasped for air as she struggled to free herself, but she had no time as she was pulled below the surface once more.

This all happened too fast for Sordaak to do anything. Frustrated, he stared at the ripples that marked where she had been and withdrew a dagger from beneath his tunic. He readied it for throwing, should she appear again.

Vorgath was next to break the surface, also encompassed by a tentacle. With one short swing of his axe he severed it and was dumped unceremoniously back into the water. He kicked hard and dove back below the surface.

Again Cyrillis broke the surface. Sordaak shouted, "Here!" Without waiting for a reply, he tossed the blade spinning in her direction. Cyrillis heard the shout and was able to snatch the blade out of the air with her right hand. Immediately she stabbed at the appendage that gripped her.

Sordaak pointed his finger and three darts leapt from it and flew unerringly to strike at the tentacle where it came out of the water. It was the best he dared to do for fear of hitting the cleric.

A large disturbance in the water gave way to the main body of the monster as it rose from the depths. The monster fixed its single eye on Sordaak, and another tentacle shot out of the water in his direction.

He dropped to the ground as it shot past and rolled hard to his right. The tentacle was too quick, however. The long thin appendage wrapped around his ankle and dragged him toward the water.

At first the mage clawed at the ground, trying to find a grip. He quickly realized the futility of this and changed tactics. Sordaak readied a spell as he twisted his body and grasped the offending tentacle with both hands. He hit the water and was pulled under in the same instant that he released the energy for the spell. Electric impulses surged through his fingers and into the tentacle. Sordaak didn't have time to contemplate the effect water might have on the spell, and he felt some of the energy coursing along his arms. He did not relinquish his grasp, however, and continued to pour energy through his fingers.

The tentacle, now charred and burnt, released its grip and Sordaak swam back to the surface. There he gulped air into his starved lungs as he quickly swam toward the steps.

He reached the steps and was climbing out of the water, when yet another tentacle lashed out at him and encircled his waist. Frustrated, he spun and located the monster's eye. The sorcerer cut loose with his most powerful spell, a ball of fire.

A small ball engulfed in flames leapt from the end of his pointed finger and sped toward the body of the monster, still visible above the surface of the water. As the ball neared, it exploded in a cacophony of flames and sound.

This had the desired effect. The monster's tentacles released him, and he turned to see Cyrillis dropped into the water, as well. He could not see where the other three were. The creature's head disappeared below the surface, and Sordaak jumped into the water to help a floundering Cyrillis.

The tentacles obviously released some sort of toxin; he could feel the deadness in his ankle. One of the tentacles had been in contact with the healer for much longer, and the mage could see she was in trouble. As he approached, her eyes rolled back in her head and she slipped below the surface.

In desperation, Sordaak kicked hard while diving to where she should be. He immediately collided with the cleric as she slowly sank. His quick grasp netted only hair, but he decided that would have to do. He kicked his way toward the surface, dragging her dead weight with him.

A powerful swimmer he was not. Through no small amount of effort he got back to the surface. Sordaak changed his grip to get her under her arms as he glanced about wildly, trying to locate the steps.

There! Fortunately, they were not far away and he kicked with all of his remaining strength toward them, all the while trying to keep Cyrillis' head above water.

As he reached the steps, unseen hands reached out. One set pulled the healer from his grasp. Another grabbed him by his robe and hauled him out of the water.

The mage was dumped unceremoniously on the ledge, where he fell to his hands and knees, gasping for air. A quick glance showed it was the rogue who had pulled him from the water, and that the paladin was bent over Cyrillis' limp form.

"Where's...Vorgath?" Sordaak said between heaving breaths.

A brief look of confusion from Thrinndor was all Sordaak needed to know that the barbarian had not been accounted for. Further confirmation of that came immediately from Savinhand.

"Shit!" the thief shouted as he headed back down the steps to the water's edge. Just as he was about to fling himself back in to the frigid murk, the missing companion lurched out of the water, dragging something behind him. Gasping with effort to get oxygen into his starved lungs, the barbarian turned to look at the monster that was now mostly out of the water. Satisfied, he turned back to face the party and said, "Even!" A glance showed serious faces in return. "Cyrillis?"

The rogue turned to look to where the paladin was bent over her limp form. "Thrinndor has her." He paused, looking for words to say but finally opted for "I don't know."

Leaving the barbarian to his own ends, Savinhand stumbled back up the steps. He stood next to the paladin and stared down at Cyrillis. Seeing she was not breathing, he said quietly, "Is she..." His mind refused to carry forward with the thought.

Thrinndor did not even glance his way. "I do not know," he said, strain apparent in his voice. "Leave us."

Savinhand stood his ground stubbornly, wanting to help.

The big man shrugged and reached down and put his hands together, palms down, in the center of her chest between her breasts. He pushed down, none to gently.

"What are you doing?" protested the rogue, indignation crowding his voice.

"Be silent," snapped the paladin, concentration wrinkling his forehead. "Or leave us." His hands left her chest, went to her head and tilted it back. What transpired next surprised Savin even more: The paladin bent down and put his lips on hers.

"What...?" was all Savinhand managed to get out before Thrinndor's arm shot out, his mouth still poised over Cyrillis', pointing back toward the way they had come.

Savinhand stifled the words caught in this throat. He remained where he was, his jaw set in consternation.

Soon it became obvious that the paladin was forcing air into the healer's mouth. Both sets of cheeks puffed out and her chest rose slightly with each breath.

After an uncounted few of these, her eyes fluttered open, and she began coughing violently. Water spewed from her mouth as Thrinndor rolled her onto her side, seeking to ease the coughing wracking her body. Next he closed his eyes and Savinhand could feel the air charge with power as the paladin poured his healing into a gagging Cyrillis.

Once the coughing subsided she tried to rise.

"No," chided Thrinndor. "Not yet. Lie still and let the healing do its work."

Dumbfounded, the rogue just stood there, his eyes roaming from one to the other. "How...?" he finally managed to stammer, seeing color slowly begin to come back into her cheeks.

"It is something we are taught at the beginning of our training," Thrinndor said. "The lungs need air. That air can be put there by another, if done correctly." His eyes never left his patient. "Once began, the injured will sometimes start breathing on one's own, as in this case."

"But..." said a bewildered rogue as Cyrillis struggled to rise. This time, Thrinndor moved to assist her.

Now sitting, she looked toward the paladin. Questions clouded her gaze. But, instead of asking, she closed her eyes and mumbled the words to a spell. Once again Savinhand felt the air charge with power as she released a healing spell on herself.

The effects were apparent immediately. Her back straightened, and her neck flushed with renewed vigor. She put her hand on the big man's shoulder and said, "Thank you." She pushed herself to her feet, where she stood shakily. There the cleric clung to the paladin, who had risen with her.

"Now," she said, looking around the group. "Are there any others that require my ministration?"

Sordaak mutely lifted the bottom of his robe to show swelling on his right ankle. He winced as he tried to put weight on it, but shrugged it off. "It will heal on its own, I believe," he said. He didn't sound convinced.

"Nonsense," said Cyrillis as she knelt to inspect the ankle. She uttered the words to a spell and waved her hand over the area. The swelling diminished instantly, and the redness faded.

Sordaak tested the ankle. "Ah, yes," he said. "It's much better now. Thank you."

"You are welcome," she said simply. "Anyone else?" She eyed each of them in turn.

Thrinndor grinned as he turned to look at Vorgath. "Not unless you can do something for brain damage!"

"I'll show you!" grated the barbarian as he turned toward the paladin and dropped into a low crouch.

"Enough!" snapped Cyrillis. "We have no time—or energy—for that! We must move away from this area in the event there are others."

"There are no others," mumbled Vorgath. "I believe this beast must have been trapped here to protect this entrance. The pool there is not that large, and this thing is way too big to come in the way we did. There's no telling how long it's been here."

"Or how many victims it has slain," said Cyrillis quietly.

Vorgath walked over and kicked what had been the head of the monster, which alone was almost as big as he was. "It won't kill anymore," he said. As he spun to face the paladin, a big grin split his face, "We are now even! I claim this one," he said, defying with his tone any to contradict.

Sordaak sauntered up, and with no small effort rolled the head to the side. "No, this one is mine!" he said triumphantly.

"What?" roared the dwarf. "The final blow was mine!"

"Look at the head," said Sordaak, indicating the charred area that had once been its eye. "I did that."

"Right," said Vorgath belligerently. "But I did *that*!" He kicked some tentacles out of the way to show a huge gash in the beast's underside, through which hung much of the monster's inner workings.

"Ugh!" said the caster as he turned away sharply. "You win!"

Vorgath chuckled loudly. "A bit squeamish, huh?" Gagging noises from Sordaak was all he got for an answer. "Well," the barbarian said as he turned to look at where the water was lapping against the rock ledge with a knowing look in his eyes, "if that monster has been here for untold years protecting this entrance..."

"Then it stands to reason it could have collected a large hoard in its lair," finished the rogue.

"We don't have time for that!" Sordaak had his voice back.

"Well," said the paladin as he looked at the water, "it might stand to reason that if the Keep has indeed been plundered, then some might have tried to escape this way. Therefore, some of Dragma's loot could await us down there."

"But," stammered Sordaak. "Aw, hell!" His gaze went from the paladin to the barbarian and back. "You go look! I'm not going down there!"

Thrinndor chuckled as he pulled the makeshift light out and verified it still worked. "I guess I am elected," he said with a mock sigh.

"I suppose we can trust you," said Savinhand.

There was a sharp intake of breath from Cyrillis as the paladin focused a withering stare at the rogue, but Vorgath spoke first. "This coming from a thief?" Savin started to protest, but the barbarian continued as Thrinndor quickly went to the edge of the pool and dove in. "Never," snapped Vorgath, "*ever* question the integrity—in any way—of a paladin, even in jest!"

"Why, I…ummm" stammered the rogue, forced to back up a step as Vorgath got in his face.

"Shut up and listen," grated the dwarf. "A paladin is incapable of falsehood. He could no more lie to, or steal from, any of us than he could pull the moons from the sky! He's *incapable* of such behavior!"

Seeing an opening, Sordaak interrupted. "A paladin also will never back down from a fight. He generally won't pick one, either. But, once began, he's in it until it's decided, one way or the other."

"Sheesh," muttered Savinhand. "Sorry, I didn't know. I was only kidding, anyway!"

"Again," said the dwarf menacingly, "not even in *jest!*"

"Enough, already!" interrupted Cyrillis, trying to diffuse the situation. "Live and learn."

"Die and don't," finished Vorgath as he turned and walked to where the water slapped against the rock edge. He peered morosely into it.

Savinhand looked from one to the other. He started to say something, but a look from Cyrillis and he thought better of it. Instead, he turned to his pack and rearranged items in it to keep his hands busy.

A short time later the surface of the water parted and Thrinndor returned, dragging his cloak behind him. He had obviously used it to wrap around several items he had been unable to carry.

"It appears our former friend there was pretty busy," he said, casting a glance at the dead creature. He dumped the contents of his makeshift pack onto the hard rock at the feet of the party, who had all gathered to see what he brought.

"My armor!" shrieked Cyrillis as she bent to retrieve some soggy chain mail. The metal was still shiny despite its time in the depths. "And my potion bag!" Loosening the tie on the leather bag, she peered inside. "Yes! Everything appears to be here and intact!" She turned to look at the paladin, who stood quietly nearby. "Thank you," she said. After a quick glance at the pile, she added, "Did you happen to see a wand case?"

"I forgot," he said, as he pulled a long, thick wood tube from behind his belt and handed it to her.

"Thank you!" she repeated as she snatched the case from his hands. Before he could react, she threw her arms around the suddenly red fighter and gave him a big hug.

Releasing him, she spun, picked up her items, and disappeared out of the light from the torches. "I will be right back," she said over her shoulder.

"Don't wander off too far," said Savinhand. "You know what happened *last* time!"

"I will not be far. I just need a few minutes."

The others poked around at the remaining items. Thrinndor said, "There is more down there, but I grabbed as much as I could. I do not think anything that remains is worth the effort."

The paladin reached down and grasped the pommel of a longsword and withdrew it from its sheath. The blade burst into flames, and a huge grin broke out across the fighter's face.

"A flamer!" said the rogue wistfully. "Very nice!"

"Yes," said the big fighter as he swung it about his head, the flames flickering mightily. "This should come in handy." He sheathed the weapon and tied it to his belt.

Savinhand bent and picked up a shortsword, also sheathed, and withdrew the blade with a hopeful expression. The expression turned to disappointment as nothing happened. The blade's edge, however, appeared unusual to him. He held it closer to a torch to get a better look at it. "What the...?" he said as he tested the edge and jerked his hand back bleeding from a deep cut. "Wow! That is *sharp!*"

A suddenly interested dwarf said, "Lemme see that." He plucked it from the thief's hands.

"Hey!" protested Savinhand. "Give that back!"

"Just a minute!" snapped Vorgath, as he held the blade closer to the firelight. "Something is written here." He bent to peer closely at the blade.

"Where?" said Savin. "I didn't see anything."

"That's because you weren't looking, stupid!" grumbled the dwarf. His tone robbed the comment of any malice.

"Hey," protested the rogue, "I resemble that remark."

Vorgath chuckled. His tone then took on a somber air. "This blade is called *Soriin.* I'm not sure, but I believe it's a Vorpal weapon."

"*Vorpal?*" said Sordaak incredulously. "What would that be doing here?"

"For that matter," said Thrinndor into the silence that followed, "what were Cyrillis' things doing here?"

That threw a hush over the group. "Shit!" said the caster suddenly. "That means all of our assumptions to this point are *wrong!*"

"What's a *Vorpal* weapon?" asked Savin as he reached out and snatched the shortsword back.

"What?" asked the paladin. His mind was already working on a different problem.

Vorgath answered for him. "It's an extremely sharp blade that has been enchanted to cut off the head of your foe with the proper swing."

"Ohhhh, sweet!" said the rogue as he looked at the blade with renewed interest. "*Soriin,* huh?" He took a few practice swings to test the blade's balance and then placed it back in the sheath. He secured it to an easily accessible place on his belt, one that corresponded to favored weapon status.

As the rest of the group sorted through the remaining looted items—a ball of fire wand for Sordaak and miscellaneous gems—the discussion continued. "There *must* be another way into this cavern," said Sordaak, thinking aloud. "I'm fairly certain no one had used that secret entrance we found behind the hearth."

"Hmmm?" said Savinhand, rejoining the conversation. He had finished rearranging his weapons. "No. No one had used that secret door in many years."

"Then there must either be another way in to that main cavern, or into this one," mused the caster.

"Remember the marks on the shoreline?" said the paladin to no one in particular. Sordaak turned his eyes on him, waiting for more. "Those were the marks of some kind of boat."

"So?" said the rogue, not understanding the significance of what the paladin was saying.

"A boat for what? To where?" said Cyrillis. She had changed into her armor and rejoined the men.

"Precisely," said Thrinndor. "A boat is used to go from one place to another. If there are markings on the shore there, then it stands to reason there is a second location for the boat to go to, and the boat is currently at that place."

"But where?" said Savinhand. "We followed the water's edge both directions from the entrance we used, and both ended in a cliff wall!"

"Yes," said the big fighter. "But we did not *cross* the water. There must be something on the other side."

"The boat dock," said Sordaak suddenly.

"But you said the entrance had collapsed," said the rogue.

"Yes," replied the caster. "The tunnel I assume led to the underground entrance to Dragma's Keep was indeed collapsed. Yet there was a dock—with a boat—inside that cavern!"

In the silence that followed, the water could be heard lapping softly against the steps along with the hiss of the torches.

Finally Cyrillis broke the silence. "For a secret keep, there sure seem to be a lot of entrances!"

"It is doubtful," Thrinndor said, "that this is the main entrance. So it stands to reason that there is still one other."

Sordaak continued the thought. "And that this entrance was discovered by some of those looting the keep. But they must have not figured on the sentry squid."

"We must assume," said the paladin softly, "that this entrance—or escape, as the case may be—has been used more than once."

"And that it will be used again," murmured Savinhand, mimicking Thrinndor's tone.

They all looked around uncomfortably. Finally Sordaak said, "That seals it. Break is over. I know we could use some recovery time, but we've got to assume we will have company—from either direction, and soon!" He looked at each. "So grab a bite to eat and shoulder your packs. We go in ten minutes." The mage turned to the rogue. "Savin, when you have packed and eaten, please continue your search of the doors."

"Sure, boss," the thief said.

Chapter Nine

Welcoming Committee

The members of the party reluctantly climbed to their feet, weariness apparent in everyone's eyes.

Savinhand moved obediently to the doors as the others stood back and waited. "I still don't find any traps," he said. "But they are locked."

No one said anything; they just stood there wearily. He muttered some curses under his breath and turned back to the doors. Removing his pick pouch from its place at his belt, he selected one and began probing the mechanism.

Sweat beads formed on his furrowed brow as he worked the lock as carefully as he possibly could, the curse weighing utmost on his mind. Finally the pick found its mark and a distinct click could be heard as the mechanism gave way. He stepped back, a smile of satisfaction playing across his lips. "Your turn," he said to the paladin, relief plain in his voice.

Thrinndor raised an eyebrow and moved forward, slid the bolt back, grasped the pull ring, set his feet and pulled. The doors opened easily and noiselessly on well-oiled hinges. However, as the paladin turned to face the party, the sound of voices broke the silence.

"Fools!" they said. "You have chosen to ignore the warnings given you. So be it!" The voices alternately came from two mouths that had appeared in the wall on each side of the doors. "After the slow and tortuous deaths you will incur within, your souls will be certain to enjoy the afterlife as they are sent to the Planes of Despair, where they are hereby condemned to wander for eternity!"

The members of the group all turned to look at Sordaak. "Magic Mouths," he said with a shrug and a dismissive wave. "Lightweight stuff, intended to ward off wimps."

Thrinndor opened the doors the rest of the way, pulled his flaming sword and peered inside.

What could be seen was seen as through a haze. It was a hallway, branching out to the right and left. It was well lit by sconces placed at regular intervals on both sides of the hall. The haze seemed to take the place of the doors.

"It's the back side of an illusion," explained Sordaak. "My guess is that from the other side, it will appear as if there are no doors at all."

The paladin hesitated only briefly and stepped through, the others right behind him. As Sordaak stepped in, last as usual, there was a whoosh as the doors slammed shut with a clang. Two more magic mouths appeared and began to laugh hideously. The volume of the laughter built almost to a shriek, and then cut off suddenly, leaving a deathly silence.

Sordaak looked quickly around. Sure enough, Savinhand had the look of a cornered rat in his eyes—crouched and ready to bolt at the slightest move or sound.

"Thrinndor!" the mage whispered as intensely as possible, trying to avoid spooking the rogue. "Grab Savin, *now!*"

The paladin hesitated for just a moment, unsure of the caster's motives. The hesitation was long enough, because when the rogue heard his name, he spun and bolted down the corridor to their left.

Cyrillis and Thrinndor dove after him, and the priestess managed to catch an ankle, enough to trip him up. The fighter grappled with him, but it wasn't easy holding on because Savinhand fought to free himself with the strength and intensity of a man who has seen his own death and knows it awaits him.

Sordaak rushed over. "Savin!" he shouted into the rogue's face. "Snap out of it!" When the thief just hissed at him in return, the caster slapped him hard across his face, trying to break the spell.

"That will do no good," said Cyrillis as she moved to his side. "It is a curse. Hold him still. I believe I can remove the fear that grips his heart." She closed her eyes and began to chant. Savinhand continued to struggle.

After a moment, she opened her eyes and reached out to touch the forehead of the trembling rogue. When she made contact, he let out a blood-curdling scream and shouted, "Doomed! Doomed! You are all doomed! Before this day is out, your souls will be mine!" He then began to laugh hideously, sounding rather like the recent laughter of the magic mouths. Finally he fell silent and went limp in the paladin's grip, his eyes closed.

Startled, Cyrillis reached out and shook him lightly until he began to stir. "It is not supposed to work that way," she mumbled. "That was a demon speaking. I fear we are in grave danger."

"Demon? What demon?" Savinhand questioned, trying to figure out why everyone was staring.

As Cyrillis explained his eyes went wide. Finally, he disentangled himself from Thrinndor's grip. "Nobody mentioned *demons!*" he said. That wasn't part of the deal!" He looked around quickly, trying to place where he was. "We have got to get out of here!"

"How?" asked Sordaak, sarcasm putting and edge to his voice.

Realization came to all at about the same time as they turned to look where the doors had been. Try as they might, they could find no sign of the portal.

"It matters not," Sordaak went on. "We've come this far, and I am not leaving without Dragma's staff!" He glared at each of them, daring them to contradict. "We'll just have to be more careful," he added, trying to make it sound simple. "I can handle the spooks."

"But *demons?*" said Savinhand.

"Don't worry about demons!" the caster snapped irritably. "They don't have time for the likes of us. Besides, we have a demon of our own." He held out his right arm, and his quasit appeared obediently. "Fahlred will warn us if any approach."

"And then what?" began the rogue, but he was interrupted.

"End of conversation," Sordaak said flatly.

"I'm not sure I want to know, anyway," muttered the rogue.

Ignoring him for the moment, Sordaak turned and looked down the hall. "We will worry about that if and when the time comes. For now, we should worry about the welcoming committee that is approaching from down that hallway!"

"I should not wonder why, with all the noise we just made!" said Cyrillis. They all turned and drew weapons as Fahlred winked back out of existence.

"Some help he is," mumbled the thief, crouched low with a dagger in his left hand and his new vorpal sword in his right.

Sordaak started to reply but instead closed his eyes. When he opened them he said matter-of-factly, "Orcs. There are more than ten of them, and they are approaching from down that branch hallway." He pointed, indicating a hallway that opened into the one they were in about forty feet away.

"Former comment retracted," said Savinhand, and he melded into the shadows. Try as he might, Sordaak could detect *no* shadows.

Thrinndor turned and sped down the hallway, Vorgath right behind him. Sordaak moved into a better position in a more leisurely fashion in order to unleash his spells. Cyrillis moved so that she could reach any who needed her services quickly. She also threw her cloak back over her shoulders, freeing her arms in the event direct conflict with her staff became necessary.

The paladin stopped short of the edge of the branch hallway and peered around the corner, exposing as little of his head as possible. Hearing the clatter the approaching group was making, the barbarian hesitated only briefly and rushed past his friend, screaming out one of his battle cries in the process.

The suddenness and proximity of the yell startled Thrinndor, causing him to jump, his heart in his throat. He turned to chastise his companion but realized the futility of trying to reason with an enraged barbarian. Besides, his friend had sprinted past him, past the opening, and instead of turning down the hall toward the hoard, he continued down the hall, *away* from the orc party, still yelling at the top of his lungs.

Confusion gripped the paladin at first, but the advancing group took the bait, let out a howl of their own and gave chase. They did not even look down the hall-way from which the dwarf had come. *No one has ever accused orcs of being all that bright,* Thrinndor thought as he watched the last of the group round the corner.

He counted thirteen in all, with a couple in the back of the group being some type of spell caster, either healers or sorcerers—or both.

Vorgath continued perhaps twenty paces down the hallway, then abruptly spun and charged back into the group, his greataxe swinging in huge arcs. His change in tactics caught the orcs by surprise, and the barbarian's first swing nearly cut one of them in two. "Four!" he shouted, spinning to face one trying to get behind him.

Thrinndor chuckled as he launched himself at what he figured to be the healer and slew him with one thrust of his sword before the beast even knew there were others around.

Savinhand appeared out of nowhere, and his new shortsword neatly remov-ing the head of the magic using orc as it wound up to cast. "Sweet!" he said, taking a moment to eye the edge of the blade before turning his attention to the orc who had heard the thud of the head hitting the ground behind him and had whirled to attack.

Cyrillis, realizing the barbarian was out of her range, tried to sneak along a wall to get into position to be able reach him and still be in range of the oth-ers behind her. She was successful, until one of the orcs backed up suddenly to avoid being hit by one of his mates and bumped into her. She let out a started yelp and brought her staff up into a defensive stance as the monster turned to face this new foe.

The beast smiled in anticipation of an easy kill with this female in front of him. The orc raised its sword and shield and lunged. Ready for the attack, Cyrillis slapped the brandished weapon aside with the head of her staff and swept his legs out from under him with the heel. This exposed the orc's head for an instant, and she smacked it hard with a resounding crack from the head of the staff. The creature lay still, unconscious—or dead. Now was not the appropriate time to find out.

A quick glance revealed Vorgath to be under attack from all sides. An orc stabbed him from behind. The dwarf shouted "five!" pain obvious in his voice as he ripped the creature in front of him from his left shoulder to his lower right side. He then spun to face the offending foe, obviously favoring his left side, where he had been stabbed.

Cyrillis said a few quick words and pointed at the barbarian, thereby releasing the healing energy. Doing it this way without direct contact used more of her precious energy, but that was more often than not unavoidable in times of battle. The bleeding visibly slowed, and she could immediately tell her spell gave needed vitality to the barbarian. A glance revealed Thrinndor was similarly surrounded but undamaged.

Somewhere along about there, Sordaak joined the fray. He briefly waved his arms, pointed his index finger at one of the orcs in the middle of the pack and muttered a couple of arcane words. The creature immediately spun and hammered a blow to its nearest ally, causing much confusion amongst the pack.

Laughing, the mage repeated the spell, selecting yet another victim somewhat removed from the first. The effect was the same. A general uproar ensued. One of the orcs recognized his efforts and flung a spear in the caster's direction, which he barely dodged.

"Yikes!" he yelped and ducked into the hallway from which the orcs had come to get out of their line of sight. The offending creature made to follow, but the paladin stepped in front of him and quickly dispatched the creature.

Still surrounded, Vorgath could not know that one of them was now an ally, the dwarf screamed in rage and spun in a circle, his axe cutting a deadly swath around him. He caught one creature completely unaware as the blade cut across its abdomen, spilling its guts to the floor. One of the new allies, its back to the dwarf, was injured slightly as the blade whisked past. Yet another orc who had ducked an earlier blow caught the blade square in the side of the head.

Prying his greataxe from the orcs skull, he shouted, "Six!" A quick glance at the disemboweled creature—which had pitched face forward into the mess at its feet—and he added, "Seven!"

Savinhand had no difficulty with the one who had turned on him. As suddenly as the melee began, it was down to the four orcs fighting one another. Two of them bled from various wounds.

One of the temporary allies suddenly looked around, confusion contorting its face. He lunged suddenly at Thrinndor, who happened to be closest. The paladin neatly side-stepped and brought his blade crashing down on the exposed neck of the beast, nearly severing the head. The creature dropped to the floor and lay still.

The two remaining enemies decided quickly this had not gone as planned, and tried to bolt back the way they had come. Vorgath hefted his greataxe and, with massive effort, hurled it at the nearest. The axe caught it between the shoulder blades and stuck there. The force of the blow knocked the orc off of its feet, and it pitched face first onto the cold, gray stone floor and lay still. "Eight!" said an enormously satisfied dwarf.

Sordaak tripped the other as it tried to run past, and Thrinndor's blade finished the task.

Remembering the orc at her feet, Cyrillis knelt to determine its status, only to find the side of his head stove in. That orc would not be bothering anyone anymore.

The one remaining orc, still under Sordaak's spell, stood in the middle of the carnage, unsure what to do next. Finally, it moved to be near its new 'friend', Sordaak.

"Keep that thing away from me!" snarled the caster.

Thrinndor raised an eyebrow and with amusement tinting his voice said, "What? You do not trust him? He is your new pal."

"Yeah, well, we don't know how long that spell will last," growled Vorgath. "I'll take care of the critter." After retrieving his greataxe, he moved toward it menacingly.

"No, wait!" said Sordaak. "Bind him. He may be able to tell us what's going on down here and how many others there are."

The dwarf reluctantly lowered his axe as Savinhand did as directed, tying the confused beasts hands behind its back. Vorgath leaned heavily on the axe, now used as a crutch. His blood lust was sated, and exhaustion took its place.

"Feet, too," said the caster, looking on with a critical eye. "We don't want it running off to warn any that are still out there."

"Right," said the rogue, kneeling to bind the orc's ankles together.

Cyrillis approached the group, stepping around the dead bodies. "Anyone hurt?" she said, looking over each with a critical eye.

Vorgath tried to crane his neck around to get a look at his back but was unable to see much. Blood was everywhere, but there did not seem to be much pain. "Thank you," he said. Weariness of battle was obvious in his voice. "I think I will yet live."

"I will be the judge of that that," she said as she bent over to peer closer at the hole in his armor. "Yes, you will live. But, this will help you heal much faster." She muttered a few words and worked her hands over the wounded area. The skin neatly knitted together, leaving a nasty scar. "I am afraid you will always have a scar, however."

"Another one," Vorgath said proudly. "Proof of battle and badge of honor!"

"Yeah, well, we will have to keep an eye on it," the healer said. "There is no telling what might have been on their blades." She looked into his weary eyes and said, "Here, this will restore a spring to your step." She closed her eyes and cast yet another spell.

Vorgath straightened visibly and hefted his greataxe in one hand. "Oh, yeah! I feel much better now!" he said, a huge smile playing across his lips. "Let's go finish what we've started!"

He made to move down the hall in the direction from which the orcs had come, but Thrinndor clamped a halt on that. "Hold on there, o diminutive one!" he said. "*You* might feel much better, but there are others in this party!"

"Thrinndor is correct," said the caster, formally. "We will take a few minutes to assess our battle readiness and let our thief…"

"Rogue."

"Whatever," replied Sordaak. "We'll give our *rogue* some time to determine if these orcs were carrying anything of value." Then to Vorgath, who seemed decidedly less than pleased with the delay, he said, "Vorgath, if you would be so kind as to see if our new found friend here has any information of value."

The dwarf brightened visibly. "Got it!" he said as he moved menacingly toward the prisoner.

"Just don't kill it," Sordaak said. At the dwarf's disappointed look he added, "Yet."

A nasty look played across the barbarian's face as he reached for the orc. The creature surprised them all by saying, "Yeah. No kill." Vorgath hesitated for an instant, then grasped the beast by the shoulder and hauled the orc to its feet, where he teetered unsteadily on bound ankles. "Me help," he said, wincing in pain at the dwarf's none-too-gentle grip.

Just then the spell must have worn off, because it snapped at Vorgath's hand, narrowly missing the barbarian's fingers with its jagged, nasty teeth.

Without hesitation, Vorgath backhanded the beast, knocking it back to the stone floor in a heap. "Sure you will," snarled the dwarf. "Now, tell me how many are you?"

With its hands and feet tied, the orc struggled to sit up. He looked at the dwarf warily with pain-filled eyes. "One," it said finally, a confused look on its misshapen face.

"No, you idiot!" the dwarf said. "How many orcs are in your party?"

Still confused, the orc looked around at his dead kindred being searched and dragged into a pile lining one wall. "One," it repeated hesitantly.

"Argh," huffed the dwarf, as he raised his fist to strike the beast.

"Wait," said Cyrillis. "Let me try."

Vorgath glared at her, irritated at the interruption. "Very well," he said, lowering his fist. "But make it quick. We don't have time for tea!" He remained within easy striking distance.

The cleric returned the glare for a moment. After the dwarf looked away uncomfortably, she turned her attention to the prone orc. "OK," she said slowly, "Listen carefully." At the beast's hesitant nod, she pointed at the piled-up bodies and said, "Many orc." Then she pointed down the hall in the direction they had come from and said, "Many more orc?"

At first she got a confused look, but then his face brightened considerably. "Yes," he said in guttural common. "Very many more orc!" He was obviously pleased at being able to answer a question without the threat of being struck.

Cyrillis turned to glare at the dwarf again, but he was pointedly looking a different direction. "There!" she said triumphantly and started to move away, but she then stopped. "Wait," she said, tuning back to the orc. "Are there any other races with the orcs?" The beast obviously understood because there was no look of confusion. Instead, it clamped its mouth shut and looked away.

Her lips pursed into a grimace of disapproval as she clubbed him with the end of her staff, knocking the beast from his sitting position to lying flat out. "Moron!" she spat and walked away, shaking her head.

"My, my," chortled Vorgath, mirth hiding none too delicately in his voice. "Aren't we a bit testy?"

"Shut it!" Cyrillis snapped, her eyes flashing. "Anyway, I did better than you!"

"That you did, lassie," the barbarian said. "Now let's just see if that knot on the head has loosened his tongue any." He reached down and jerked the creature back to a sitting position and recommenced his interrogation.

The rest of the group settled in to tend wounds, repair armor, and sharpen blades—the usual stuff after a minor skirmish.

Savinhand had piled anything he deemed of value in the middle of the floor and was searching the orc caster when suddenly he straightened and held up a finely crafted necklace, encrusted with jewels. "Hello, there," he said loud enough for all to hear, still looking at the item inquisitively. "What have we here?"

Sordaak looked up wearily at the proffered necklace. He did a double-take and said, "Let me see that!" The mage surged to his feet and snatched it from a bewildered Savinhand.

"Hey!" said the thief.

"Damn!" whispered the caster, reverently. "Where could he have gotten this?" He looked sidelong at the orc caster, Sordaak's right eyebrow threatening to leave his forehead entirely.

"What is it?" said the rogue.

"It's Dragma's necklace of the magi!" Sordaak had a wondrous tone to his voice. "It was rumored lost in the final battle."

"There seem to be a lot of things that were rumored lost in the final battle turning up recently," mused Thrinndor. "It is becoming obvious that they were not lost, but sequestered away by those that served Valdaar." Into the silence that followed, he added, "Lost, but now found."

"Right," said the rogue, clearly not all that interested in legends and so forth. "What's it do?" His eyes never left the necklace.

"Hmmm?" said the caster. "Oh, the necklace? I don't know—not exactly, anyway. Its name is Borophat, and it grants the user additional spell power. Beyond that, I don't know. Its power is beyond me. But, not for long. Not for long…"

Disinterested, Vorgath turned and was staring at the pile of bodies. "Five," he said. "I killed five." He turned and looked at the paladin. "How about you?"

Thrinndor looked around and counted in his head. "Four. I got four."

"You?" the barbarian said, his attention now on the rogue.

"Two," Savinhand said.

The barbarian did some quick math in his head and said, "That's eleven. There are twelve dead." He looked around at Sordaak. "You get one?" he asked.

"Ummm.... no," said the caster. "I just caused the confusion in the middle of the pack, befriending two of them."

"Well somebody killed it!" Vorgath did a recount in his head.

"I did," said Cyrillis softly, distaste apparent in her tone.

Vorgath's head snapped around, "*You?*" he asked.

"Yes, *me!*" she said.

"Bah!" snorted the barbarian. "I don't believe it. I must have killed it by accident."

"Why do you find it so hard to believe?" asked Cyrillis, her voice low and menacing—at least as menacing as she could manage.

"You?" repeated the dwarf. "You don't have the skills required."

Cyrillis glared at the dwarf. "Release him," she said with a nod of her head toward the bound orc.

"*What?*"

"You heard me," the cleric said. "Release him."

"I do not think that is a good..." started Thrinndor.

Cyrillis interrupted him without even a glance in his direction. "Stay out of this." Her eyes narrowed. "Release him," she repeated.

Vorgath stared at her for a moment longer, then bent to undo the bindings on the orc. "Very well, it's your funeral."

The orc stood when told. He rubbed at his wrists to get the blood flowing again and looked around, confused.

"Give him his shield and weapon," Cyrillis said in a tone that left no doubt what she intended.

"But..." began the barbarian.

"Just do it!" she said.

Vorgath reluctantly did as directed as the others gathered around. With a shrug, Thrinndor turned to look at the orc and began making guttural noises, pointing to indicate the cleric. At first the beast merely shook his head and took a step back. Thrinndor said something else, and the beast smiled and nodded.

The orc then clanged his sword against his shield, dropped into a fighting stance and advanced on the cleric.

"I didn't know you spoke in the tongue of orc!" said the dwarf, trying hard to appear unconcerned with what was about to unfold.

"There are a few things you do not yet know about me, old one," replied Thrinndor. His eyes never left the orc, however.

Vorgath started to reply, then shook his head and turned back to the action. Despite his apparent indifference, he didn't want to miss anything.

Cyrillis remained as she was. She stood without apparent concern, leaning on her staff.

When the orc got close enough, he jumped at her, swinging his sword in a broad arc at her upper torso.

Cyrillis snapped into action faster than those watching would have believed. She whipped her staff around and knocked the blade aside. Continuing the swing, she brought the heel of the staff in line with the creatures head and jabbed. The heel hit him squarely on the nose, smashing it in a torrent of blood. This also caused the orc's eyes to water uncontrollably, and he swung his blade around blindly.

Cyrillis spun the staff in a short, quick stroke that brought the heel up between the creature's legs and sharply into his groin. This brought a collective *ugh* from the men watching the events, along with several sets of knees knocking together simultaneously. The orc's eyes crossed, and he dropped his sword as he clutched his groin. Cyrillis brought the head of her staff crashing down on the back of his head. He pitched forward onto his face, out before he hit the floor.

Into the stunned silence that followed Vorgath said, "You didn't kill him, did you? I still had some questions to ask."

Cyrillis glanced dismissively at the prone beast, "No, I did not kill him." She looked at Thrinndor, an accusing look in her eyes. "What did you tell him?"

The paladin hesitated, but only slightly. "I told him that if he kills you, I would release him," he said with a shrug.

"*What?*" said the rogue. "Certainly you would not have…"

"You are going to have to learn to quit questioning my integrity," said the paladin. "Of course I would have released him if he had accomplished his task." After a short pause for effect, he smiled hugely and said, "Of course, he never would have gotten that far." He tilted his shield over to reveal the crossbow hidden there, a bolt loaded and ready.

Vorgath turned to look at Thrinndor, who raised an eyebrow in question. "OK, that's it!" he said. "Remind me not to mess with her!"

"What?" the paladin said, his tone confused at the sudden change.

"That staff," explained the dwarf. "If she were to smack me in the nuts like that with that thing, they'd rattle around down there for a week!"

Thrinndor's eyes bulged out with the effort to keep from laughing, at which he was mostly successful. All that escaped was a gagging sound. He covered his mouth with his left hand to hide the effort.

"From now on, it's 'yes, ma'am' and 'no, ma'am'!" said the dwarf, raising an appreciative eye in the direction of their healer.

"Ha, ha," said Cyrillis. "Very funny. Your faith in me is touching." Her tone could have withered old boot leather.

"Know this," she went on before she could be interrupted. "I am not a battle cleric. However, I have had *some* training in the art of self-defense. I can—and will—defend myself, if need be."

"So it would seem," muttered Savinhand, also working hard to keep from laughing.

"My primary duty," she went on, "is to the party. As distasteful as it might become, my job is to keep each of you alive. If you are dead or dying, we cannot complete the mission and you cannot protect me.

"However," she added, sarcasm dripping from her voice, "if you 'Meat Shields' are unable to keep up your end of the mission, I will protect myself."

"Hey!" said the caster. "That's *my* line!"

"What?" said Cyrillis, trying to refocus her attention away from the conversation that had obviously deteriorated from where she had intended it to go.

"'Meat Shield'—I'm pretty sure I coined that phrase!"

The cleric looked at the mage uncomprehending. She then blinked a couple of times and started to laugh. Soon all were laughing as the tension washed out of the air. Even Thrinndor was unable to hold it in any longer; he guffawed with the rest.

"All right," said Sordaak, wiping the tears from his eyes, "enough of the levity shit! Remember where we are and why we are here!" He moved his eyes to take in the bodies of the orcs. "The rest of the orc party will be missing this group any time and send more to investigate."

The sorcerer looked at the unmoving orc. "Kill him," he said simply, drawing a gasp of protest from Cyrillis. "Contrary to our contrary dwarf, we have all the information out of him we're likely to get." His tone left no room for discussion. "If we leave him alive, he will find a way to warn others we are here."

Vorgath nodded agreement, then whipped his axe around and removed the beasts head with one swing. "I will not count that one," he said, a grim expression on his face.

"Was that *really* necessary?" asked Cyrillis.

"Would you have liked to cross paths with him again?" asked Sordaak. Cyrillis merely shook her head. "I didn't think so. I doubt your deftly applied staff work would be appropriately appreciated if you did."

"Well…" she began.

"Enough," the caster said. "It's done! Let's get a move on." He turned to look down the passage from which the orc party had come. "That way is as good as any," he said. "They had to come from *somewhere*. And presumably, that somewhere is where we want to be!"

Chapter Ten

The Keep Proper

Once again the members of the party reluctantly climbed to their feet, adrenaline from the battle having washed away any lingering weariness.

Sordaak called his familiar and sent him on ahead as they took up their positions.

Vorgath stretched and tested his newly healed area. Finding it satisfactory, he bowed to the cleric. "Thank you," he said.

"No thanks required," she said. "It is all in the job description." Cyrillis winked at the dwarf.

The diminutive barbarian blinked twice and muttered "whatever" under his breath and marched off, still shaking his head.

She chuckled and then fell into her place at the back of the troop.

The hallway they entered was long and well lit. Someone had taken care to ensure that any approach would not be under the cover of darkness.

Before they had gone more than a few steps Sordaak announced, "Company coming! I guess that last group was missed after all." He closed his eyes and said matter-of-factly, "This group is larger, at least twenty in number. And there is at least one human among them."

Just then several orcs rounded a bend in the hallway ahead of them.

"Didn't we just *leave* this party?" moaned Savinhand as he dropped into a crouch, slung his cloak around him and melted into the background.

Vorgath let out one of his shouts and burst into motion, his greataxe gripped tightly in both hands and held high above his head. Thrinndor pulled his new flaming sword from its sheath slowly and readied for the onslaught.

"Gimme a second here, guys," Sordaak said quickly. "I want to try something." He started his windup and said, "Gimme room!" as he pointed down the hall and released his spell.

A filament shot forth from his finger, hitting the floor in front of the first of the orcs, who had broken into a run. Once the filament hit the floor, it exploded into what appeared to be a giant spider web. The first orc got past it, but the ones behind him were trapped in the sticky, gooey substance.

This effectively blocked the hallway. The trapped orcs, and the ones behind them, started hacking at the web with whatever weapon they had in their hands.

That first orc, unaware of what was going on behind him, made the mistake of taking on the charging barbarian head on. Vorgath, instead of going for the head or body, swung low and hard, cutting the legs out from under the onrushing beast. Once down, the dwarf whirled his blade and it bit deep into the torso of the orc.

The orc thrashed for a short time and then was still. "Nine!" shouted the barbarian as he turned to continue his assault.

"No, wait!" shouted the caster, loud enough that it caused the dwarf to hesitate slightly. But it was enough as Sordaak pointed his recently acquired wand and said a single word.

A now familiar ball burst from the end of the wand and sped down the hall toward the helpless orcs. The ball exploded upon reaching them, and shouts of pain and surprise went up as the web-like substance immediately caught fire and burned with a ferocity that belied its size.

The orcs immediately went into disarray as they tried to put the fires out. If they were not in flames themselves, then on a companion.

Into this screaming melee charged Vorgath, Thrinndor right behind him.

"Ten," shouted the barbarian as his blade flashed about him, quickly turning dark with the black blood of the orcs. "Eleven!"

The paladin surged through the morass of bodies, hacking his way ever closer to the back of the pack, trying to get to the human. He lost count of those who succumbed to his blade as he finally pushed his way out of the pack.

"Twelve! Thirteen!" came the call from behind him as the paladin glanced left and right. There, rounding the bend to his right he spotted a figure in colorful robes fleeing with several others—not all orc, not all human.

He was considering giving chase when he felt a sharp pain in his side as an orc stabbed him low and deep. He spun, swinging the flaming sword in a broad arc that severed the shield arm of the offending orc, who screamed and again stabbed at his foe with his remaining arm.

Again the orc's aim was true, because the fighter felt the thin, dagger-like blade pierce him just above the belt in his right side, slipping in under his over-committed swing.

Thrinndor howled in pain, and his vision blurred as he brought his blade crashing down on the top of the beast's head, splitting it nearly in two from front to back.

The pain was sharp in his side as he reached down and applied pressure to the new wound and mumbled the words to a spell. He felt the power surge through his hand.

"Fourteen!" the dwarf shouted again, drawing ever nearer.

"You are slowing down, old one!" Thrinndor shouted through gritted teeth above the din of battle. The wound still pained him greatly; the orc's blade must have been poisoned. But it had closed, and he was able to straighten to meet the attack of yet another of the monsters.

"Bah!" came the instant reply. "You had better get you a couple before I kill them all!" After a grunt of effort, Thrinndor heard, "Fifteen!"

Thrinndor chuckled, but that was all he had time for, because he now had not one, but two of the unruly beasts to deal with, and they were less than pleased.

"Savinhand!" he shouted. "You can join the battle at any time!"

The rogue materialized out of seeming thin air as his shortsword stabbed hard and deep into the back of the orc to Thrinndor's left. The orc slumped to its knees, pitched forward onto its face and lay still.

"Let me explain how this works," said the rogue formally as he turned to face an orc who had stepped up to replace the dead one. "You get their attention," … block, thrust, stab… "and I sneak up and dispose of them from behind!" After parrying a couple of ineffective swings from the offending animal, he dispatched it with a slash of his shortsword across its neck. He turned to look at the paladin with a mock questioning look on his face. "Questions?"

Thrinndor started to answer but realized his friend had vanished again. "No," he muttered, "got it." He finished off the remaining orc in front of him with a stab through the monster's heart.

Once again, as quickly as it had begun, the battle was over. The paladin stood still, his sword hissing violently at the orc blood that was dripping off of it onto the floor, where it formed a smoldering puddle. He looked around wearily. Finding himself unable to stand without assistance, he leaned against the wall.

"You are hurt!" said Cyrillis as she rushed to his side.

"Yes," he said through clenched teeth. He pointed to indicate both injuries. "Twice. Poison, I believe." He sank slowly to his knees.

He showed the wound on his front. "I worked some of my healing on this one, and it closed, but already it seems to be festering. Faster than would normally be possible, I fear."

His voice trailed off to where Cyrillis had to bend close to hear his words. She quickly withdrew her potion pouch, and searched briefly through its contents. "Here," she said, removing a small glass vial containing an emerald green fluid. She removed its seal and held it to the fighter's lips. "Drink this—just a small amount, please. It is *very* potent." She tilted his head back and allowed him to sip the contents.

He did as directed, and at first nothing visible happened. The others had gathered around and stood solemnly as the healer worked her arts. She eased her patient to where he was sitting comfortably and began probing the injured areas.

"Yes," she murmured. "This must be the work of poison. It should not be possible for an infection to grow this quickly." Without looking up, she said, "Savinhand, see if you can find the weapon used against him. It might help to know what type of poison this is."

"On it," said the rogue, who quickly retraced the path of the paladin, knowing which orc had done the damage.

"I am fairly certain," she went on, more for her own benefit; as the others could barely hear what she was saying as she bent close to inspect the wounds, "the potion will counteract this devilish device."

The wounds seemed to grow less red. She said, "Yes. I believe the potion is working. My healing spells will now function."

She lowered her head, closed her eyes and allowed her hands to caress softly and slowly both injured areas as she chanted a prayer. Immediately the skin lost its redness and the wounds seemed to heal before the eyes of the onlookers. Thrinndor's breathing became noticeably less labored.

Satisfied with her workings, she pulled back and sat down. She brushed a wayward tendril of hair that had strayed from the tied mass at her neck. "Now he must rest," she announced.

"Are you daft, woman?" cried Sordaak. "Do you remember where we *are*?"

The healer looked up and stared unflinching into the eyes of the caster. "I said," she said deliberately, biting off each word with emphasis, "he *must* rest."

Sordaak shifted uncomfortably under her unwavering gaze, but he did not back up. Instead, he met her stare with one of his own and said, "Impossible!" He continued to meet her unblinking stare with one of his own. "A small group— including the human I saw through Fahlred—broke off from this group of orcs." He waved his arm around to indicate the mass of bodies arrayed around them. "They are certain to return with reinforcements any minute!"

Her only reaction was to look around. She remained silent.

"Either you work some of that restorative mumbo jumbo and get him on his feet," he went on, his own assurance in his being right bolstering his confidence, "or we will have to continue without him! Because we can't remain..."

"I am fine," said Thrinndor not too convincingly through clenched teeth. He had struggled back to his feet unnoticed by the two during their heated argument.

Turning back to see the paladin leaning heavily against the wall, Cyrillis said quickly, "You should not be on your feet!" She threw a dagger-laced look at the caster.

"Good," said Sordaak. "Because I think we are going to have company any minute now."

Savinhand approached them carrying a nasty looking dagger with a snake-like wiggle to its blade. "I think I found the weapon used," he announced.

Thrinndor looked at the proffered weapon and said, "Yes, that is the dagger the orc used." Pain still darkened his visage, but he remained on his feet through sheer will.

"Well," continued the rogue, "this is not 'normal' poison. I don't know *what* exactly it is. I've never seen it before." He turned to stare back down the hallway the direction he had come. "I think that he might've been an assassin."

"An assassin?" asked Sordaak. "*Here?*"

"This keeps getting better and better," muttered Vorgath, his bloodlust again having worn off. He sounded even wearier than before.

"An *orc assassin*, no less," said Savinhand, knowing this bit of information would be cause for even more concern. "I can't even remember ever hearing of an orc assassin."

"I know of no such combination, either," said Thrinndor. "Orcs are generally neither smart *nor* physically dexterous enough to satisfy the guild requirements for training in such skill sets."

Savinhand spoke into the stillness that followed. "Where there is an assassin, there will be someone willing to pay for his or her services."

More silence.

"Whatever!" snapped the mage. "All this chatter isn't getting us any closer to our goal!"

"No," said the paladin. He was feeling somewhat better. "But it is helping us to understand better what we are up against."

Sordaak opened and closed his mouth as he bit off a harsh reply.

"Anyway," continued Thrinndor, "if that group that departed so hastily had intentions to return, I should have thought we would have seen them by now." Sordaak set his jaw stubbornly but said nothing as the big fighter continued. "Maybe we should take a few minutes to gather ourselves before we follow them."

The caster started to protest, but the paladin held up a hand to ward him off as he continued, weariness in his voice. "I will continue if it is deemed necessary," the big fighter said. He cocked his head to allow his gaze to settle on the barbarian, who was leaning on the haft of his greataxe. "However, I will be of little use to the party as a whole unless I am restored in some way." A hint of the old twinkle came to his eyes. "And the old one over there would be of only slightly more use!"

"Old one?" snapped the dwarf. "Why I could..."

"Silence!" Sordaak cut him off. He turned to face Cyrillis. "Very well, we will 'gather' ourselves. Do you have anything that could speed up the 'restorative' process for these weaklings?"

Both Thrinndor and Vorgath spluttered as if to make protest, but Cyrillis jumped in before they had a chance to get on a roll. "Yes," she said as she removed her wand case. "There are precious few charges remaining on this." She withdrew from it a withered, crooked looking piece of gnarled wood. She hesitated only slightly, grimly set her lips into a thin line and waved the wand at the paladin.

There was a slight sound as if a swarm of bees were nearby as the energy was released. Thrinndor's back straightened slightly. She waited a few blinks of the eye and then repeated the gesture. The big fighter stood noticeably taller now, and she made to cast yet again, but he forestalled her.

"No," he said, vigor returned to his voice. "That will be sufficient. Save some of that for later and administer to…"

"Don't say it!" growled Vorgath.

"He is undamaged," said the healer, who had fixed her gaze upon the dwarf. "Only his expended bloodlust wears on him. Each time he uses it without resting, the effects of its using wear more than the last." She clucked her tongue disapprovingly. "A simple restore will return the color to his cheeks." She closed her eyes and waved her hand in the general direction of the barbarian.

The dwarf's back also straightened and a sparkle immediately returned to his eyes. "Thank you," he said. "Now, did someone mention we still have some critters about that need killing?" A playful smile wriggled its way onto his lips, only faintly visible through his beard.

"Chill out there, old-timer!" chided the paladin. "Let us give the wiggle-fingers a chance to catch their breath and figure out what they still have available." His smile removed any harm from his words. "You can use the time to figure out where we stand on our wager. That will require you to remove your boots, I am certain." His smile broadened.

"Bah!" snorted the dwarf. "No toes required." His smile now touched his eyes. "Fifteen to…" he paused to consider. "Let me see…three, I think!"

"Ha!" retorted Thrinndor. "I figured you would try to steal a few. Twelve—for you, that is! I think I am more in the twenty range!"

Vorgath was apoplectic. "Twenty!" he nearly shouted. "Why, whatever happened to that famed 'gotta tell the truth' crap? You can't even be in double digits!"

"Of course I am!" snapped the paladin in mock indignation. "You know what they say: The memory is the second thing to go!"

"Bah!" repeated the dwarf. He turned to the rogue. "Savinhand, you were appointed mediator and official scorekeeper. Where does the count stand?"

Savin did not hesitate, "Little ugly: Fifteen. Big ugly: Twelve."

"Little ugly?"

"Big ugly?"

Silence fell upon the group while the three stared at one another. Finally, Thrinndor could hold back no more and burst out in laughter. He was soon followed by the other two, and then the remainder of the group, erasing—momentarily—the tension of battle.

"My, aren't we a jovial group?" Sordaak said, again wiping the mirth from his eyes. He pushed himself wearily to his feet. "All right, I think we have given these orcs enough of a break." He called for his familiar, who appeared almost instantly. "Shall we?"

The two communicated silently for a moment and then the quasit blinked out of sight. The mage turned to continue down the passage the way they had been going.

With a sigh the remainder of the party followed suit, each taking his or her now familiar position.

"Savinhand," said the caster, "did you find anything of value among the carcasses?"

"Not really. Just that pair of daggers from that assassin, which I wrapped carefully for later examination."

"That is interesting, in and of itself," mused Thrinndor.

"Why's that?" queried Savinhand.

"Well," said the big fighter, "all along now we have found artifacts that are presumably looted from the treasure of Dragma. But in this group, none? That does not make sense."

"Which brings up an obvious point," intoned Vorgath. "Why is it we are trusting a *thief* to check for loot?" His tone belied any hint of malice, however.

"Rogue," Savin said. "And because the two of you are too busy counting bodies and getting healed to be concerned with loot!"

The barbarian considered a rejoinder but ultimately decided he didn't have the energy for it. So he shook his head in silence and took his place in the group as they set out down the hall.

Thrinndor, feeling much better as the potion had countered the effects of the poison, said from the head of the group as they neared the bend he had seen earlier. "I saw a group break off from the rest and take off around that bend. I lost them when I got distracted by that assassin."

"Could you tell how many?" asked the mage.

"No," replied the big fighter. "More than two or three, though. I also believe there to be more than one human among them."

After going a short distance, the hallway branched to their right. That branch went only a few feet and ended in a barred door. The path they were on continued around another bend.

"Well?" asked Thrinndor.

"Locked and barred," said Savinhand, who had checked it out without having been asked. "I saw no traps."

"If it is locked and barred," said Cyrillis, "then they obviously do not want us in there."

"Which is good enough reason for me to knock down the door!" said Vorgath, who promptly started toward the door, hefting his weapon menacingly in his right fist.

"Wait," said Sordaak, his brow furrowed deep in thought. "If it is locked and barred from *this* side, then it is doubtful they could have gone this way. They would not have taken the time to do so. They had to assume we were right on their heels."

"True," mused Thrinndor quietly. "However, do we want to leave unopened doors behind us?"

The caster sighed the heavy sigh of someone who knows the answer but does not like it. "Very well, you make a good point. We can't afford to leave any possible avenues of escape not checked." He looked longingly down the hall. "So, if for no other reason than fear of having to come back this way, we must investigate." He sighed again.

"Savin," he continued, waving a weary hand in the direction of the door, "please unlock the door."

The rogue also looked down the hall as if he was certain that was the way they should be going. He nodded resignedly and moved as directed.

After less than a minute of probing there was a distinct *click* as the lock opened. Savinhand stepped back, a smile of self-satisfaction showing across his visage.

"Either you are getting better…" said Thrinndor, stepping up to remove the bars.

"Or the locks are getting easier," finished Vorgath.

"Humph!" snorted the rogue. He otherwise remained silent as the bolts were slid back by the paladin. When the big fighter pulled the door open, Savinhand stepped up to get a look at what was inside.

At first he saw nothing in the room beyond, but spying movement to his left, he quickly shifted his gaze that way. His eyes locked with another pair in an enormous head.

Thrinndor saw the rogue's demeanor relax from being tensed for battle. Savin then turned and walked back the way they had come, a serene look on his face.

"What the…" said Sordaak as the rogue passed him as if he weren't even there. "Savin! Get back here" he shouted as the thief rounded the corner, not hearing or not caring.

"Shit," the sorcerer said as he leapt after the retreating rogue.

"Wait," Cyrillis said.

"What?" said Thrinndor, who had pushed the door closed and was listening intently with his ear pressed to the wood.

"Too late," he breathed. "We are going to have company!"

"Did you see anything?" queried the caster, now at the corner watching Savinhand, still trying to keep up with what was going on behind him.

"No," was all the big fighter got out before the door was ripped off its hinges with a tremendous crash.

A glance is all it required for Sordaak to understand. The creature responsible filled the door frame—an Umberhulk! "Don't look into its eyes!" he shouted as he prepared a spell.

Thrinndor was knocked back into the hallway. He almost tripped over Vorgath as he struggled to regain his balance. He swung his sword in reflex but missed badly, the blade biting deep into the frame of the door.

This took him off to one side. Sordaak, seeing an opening, cut loose with his spell. The air crackled and split with a blinding flash as a bolt of lightning ripped through the air, narrowly missing the paladin. The bolt caught the unsuspecting monster square in the chest, knocking it back into the room. It roared loud enough to shake the walls.

Thrinndor recovered quickly, and as he jerked his sword free of the door frame he threw a nasty look at the caster and leapt into the doorway.

"I missed you!" said the caster in reflex. Quickly he prepared another spell.

Cyrillis hesitated, unsure where she was needed most. A quick glance revealed the rogue just standing still admiring a tapestry on the wall. She decided he would be alright for the time being and jumped into the room, right behind the barbarian. Vorgath shouted his war cry and barreled through the open door, his greataxe poised high above his head and ready to strike.

Realizing although the beast was huge, there was no room for her to get into the action with both the barbarian and the fighter swinging away with abandon. She stood in the shattered door frame and prepared a healing spell in the event her ministrations were needed fast.

They were.

Thrinndor approached with his shield held high to block the eyes of the monster, his sword darting back and forth. He and the beast traded blows, the paladin being knocked back into the wall, the umberhulk bleeding from a deep gash in its muscular forearm.

Vorgath saw an opening and buried his greataxe into one of the monster's legs. His axe rang and he felt like he was chopping into the base of an ironwood tree. The umberhulk roared and turned to face this new adversary. The creature reached down and, before the dwarf could react, grasped the barbarian by his upper torso. The beast lifted Vorgath high into the air and sent him flying across the room, where he crashed through a massive table to land on the floor. He did not move.

Cyrillis rushed across the room to his side, the spell already crossing her lips. She could sense that he was not seriously injured—no broken bones, anyway. But he was going to have one hell of a headache when he came to; there was an already burgeoning knot on his forehead. She was fairly certain that was what that made contact with the table first. *It is a good thing dwarves are hard-headed*, she thought.

She turned her attention back to the battle raging behind her. Thrinndor was able to hold the beast off, but only just barely. He was not in the best of shape from his recent wounds.

The umberhulk was bleeding from several cuts about its arms and upper torso, but the healer could see the paladin was going to succumb to his wounds far sooner than the beast was if she did not step in and assist.

She surged to her feet and charged in, her staff whirling above her head, gaining momentum for the strike. Oh her way in she tossed a restorative spell at the paladin and saw his back straighten slightly.

In four quick steps she was in position. She swung her staff, now held in both hands, with all of her might. As she did, she heard a cry from the paladin. "Cyrillis, no!"

But he was too late. She was really just trying to distract the monster so Thrinndor could get in a killing blow, but she was unprepared for the mass of the beast. Her staff connected solidly on the back of its head, but she was certain she was dealt more damage by the blow than the umberhulk was. It felt like she had struck a column of solid marble with all her might. The staff rang as if it was about to shatter, vibrating so badly she almost lost her grip. Her hands and forearms immediately went numb from the blow, and she stepped back, stunned at her ineffectiveness.

She was successful in her distraction, however, as the beast whirled and flung its massive left arm in a sweep that caught her still stunned. Its elbow smashed into her chest, knocking the wind out of her and launched her backward into the wall. There she slid down and lay motionless in a heap on the floor.

Seeing an opening, in one motion Thrinndor dropped his shield and whipped his sword around with both hands, using all of his remaining strength. The blade bit deep into the monster's neck. The umberhulk howled.

But still the beast came on. The blow wrenched the sword from the fighter's grip. Thrinndor dropped to the ground and rolled hard to his left away from the prone healer, pulling his trusty greatsword from its clip behind his neck as he did. He continued his roll, surging back to his feet just as the beast wrenched the sword from its neck and flung it at the paladin.

Thrinndor easily dodged the blade and set his feet as the monster rushed in, obviously intending to finish the battle by crushing him into the wall. Pain and loss of blood were making the umberhulk desperate.

The human fighter would normally have been able to easily handle such a creature, especially in its current state, but several things were combining to work against him: His recent poisoning, normal weariness from several battles in succession, and his inability to look into his opponent's eyes to judge where the next attack was coming from.

Thrinndor waited until the last possible second to side-step the rush, but the creature was obviously more intelligent than he had given it credit for, because it anticipated the move, and even guessed correctly which direction the paladin was going to move. The air left his lungs in a rush as the monster hit him square in the chest, knocking him backward into the wall. Only an intentional quick buckling of his knees kept him from being crushed there.

He tried to roll away and simultaneously bring his sword to bear, but the beast saw that coming as well. The umberhulk reached down, grabbed the paladin by the front of his armor and lifted him high over his head in preparation of a final, crushing blow.

Which never came. Sordaak burst into the chamber just then, Savinhand in tow, and quickly surveyed the situation. Not willing to risk the use of ball of fire to the dangling paladin, and not enough energy remaining for the lightning bolt he badly wanted to launch, he pointed his finger and released instead a series of darts. Then he yelled at the top of his lungs.

The darts unerringly hit the beast in the back of the head. The monster howled in pain and rage, turned and flung the paladin in the direction of this new threat.

The caster and rogue pair half caught, half got knocked over by the flying fighter. As they worked to disentangle from one another, the umberhulk roared and charged.

Thrinndor, now weaponless, spotted his recently relinquished longsword against the wall a short distance away. He dove in that direction and rolled along the floor until he reached it. Grasping the pommel, he surged to his feet and spun to locate his quarry.

Savinhand, still out of sorts from the recent confusion spell, caught the full brunt of the umberhulk's charge square in the chest and was knocked flying into the wall behind him. He crumpled to the floor and lay still.

Sordaak still had the monster's full attention, and the beast whirled to confront the caster, who was now attempting to flee. Knowing his friends relied on him to at least distract the creature while they pulled themselves together, he launched another barrage of magic darts to ensure he had its *undivided* attention.

The darts hit the beast square in the chest, and in its severely damaged state the effect was more pronounced than usual as the umberhulk was knocked back a step. The monster looked around in dazed confusion, then roared and charged after the departing caster.

"Sordaak!" shouted Thrinndor, "this way!" He moved to give chase, fearing the beast would catch the frail, unprotected Sordaak before he could re-engage.

The mage obediently spun and raced past the umberhulk at an oblique angle to give the paladin some time to shake the cobwebs from his befuddled mind.

Thrinndor cast about for his shield, but it was too far away to be of any use, so he dropped into a defensive stance and prepared to meet the monster head on.

The beast in its state of pain and rage did not even see the fighter as the caster sped by. The umberhulk lurched forward, its attention solely on the sorcerer.

As the umberhulk passed, Thrinndor grasped the haft of his sword again with both hands. He whirled hard to his right, again whipping the blade around with all of his remaining strength. He aimed for the area where he had already scored hits twice—where he assumed its neck was—and felt the blade strike home. It sank deeper this time, the paladin feeling the crunch of bone.

Still unbelievably quick, the umberhulk pivoted and again knocked the paladin sprawling with its tree-trunk-like right arm. Hurt beyond comprehension, however, it stopped and looked around, unable to figure which opponent to attack next.

Again darts—fewer this time however, as Sordaak was critically low on energy—hit the beast in the torso. Again it staggered from the impact. The monster turned sluggishly in a feeble attempt to see if it could determine where this pesky attack came from, but its eyes were clouded with pain.

Thrinndor struggled back to his feet and again whipped his blade around at the unprotected neck. He felt the blade grate on bone again as it bit deep.

The monster tried to turn but fell to its knees, instead. With its last vestige of life, the umberhulk lurched forward as it tried to grasp the paladin in its massive hands.

Too weary to dodge, Thrinndor was knocked down by the beast, which fell on top of him and lay still.

"Thirteen," he gasped. And then everything faded to black.

Chapter Eleven

Respite Revisited

Thrinndor opened his eyes slowly. Confused, he tried to place his surroundings. A vast weight seemed to be trying to crush him into the floor, which made even the act of breathing difficult and painful. He tried to shift so he could push the weight off, but the effort brought a groan to his lips and he fell back without success.

"Hold on just a damn minute!" snapped Sordaak, weariness plain in his voice. "I couldn't get that thing off of you by myself, so I'm trying to revive some help." The paladin could hear him slapping someone repeatedly some distance off. He heard the caster say, "C'mon, midget! Wake up!"

Finally, a flurry of movement indicated success. "Who're you calling..." He heard the grating voice of the barbarian.

"We don't have time for that!" snapped Sordaak. "Your pally buddy is being crushed to death over there by the umberhulk!"

"Why didn't you say so?" groused the barbarian as he climbed shakily to his feet.

"I, uh...never mind!" the mage said as he turned his attention to the cleric.

Another flurry of movement, and soon he could feel the pressure ease slightly as the dwarf tried to drag the monster away. Thrinndor twisted one way, then the other, freeing one arm at a time. Together, he and Vorgath managed to push the umberhulk aside.

"Thanks," panted the paladin, still on his hands and knees.

"Yeah, well," muttered the dwarf, "you wouldn't be of much use to us under there!"

Thrinndor turned his head so he could eye the barbarian and raised a questioning eyebrow. He smiled at the obvious feigned lack of concern from his friend. "Well, I would not have *been under there* had you not been sleeping on the job!"

"Sleeping?" roared Vorgath. "Why, that monster got in a lucky shot…"

"Lucky?" interrupted the paladin, mirth dripping from his voice. "He tossed you like a sack of potatoes! One shot, and you were out!"

"Yeah, well," repeated the dwarf, but further replies were cut off as his help was needed to get Cyrillis to her feet.

"Anything broken?" Sordaak was asking, his arm under hers and around her waist.

"No," she said weakly. "I do not believe so." She looked around. "How about the others?"

"I managed to bring the two fighter types back from the brink of death…" started the caster.

"What?"

"Huh?"

"…but I think they'll live," he went on quickly. "I have not had time to check the thief."

"Rogue." They all turned to peer as a raspy voice came from the corner of the room. "We prefer to be called 'rogues,'" Savin said as he sat up slowly, holding his head in his hands.

"Whatever," muttered the mage. "Do you have enough healing energy left to get everyone back to some semblance of battle readiness?"

Cyrillis looked at each, studied their injuries and weighed each in her mind as to what would be required.

"No," she said flatly. "Not even close." She again looked at the party, a touch of sorrow clouding her eyes. "I can ease the pain of recent events, but it has been too long since a proper rest. I am still too weak from captivity." She implored each with her eyes not to judge. "I am sorry." She bowed her head.

An uncomfortable silence ensued. Sordaak cleared his throat. "Ahem, not your fault." He glared at Vorgath and Thrinndor. "If these *meat-shields*," he spat the words out, "had done *their* job…"

"Now hold on there!" An argument immediately started as to who should have done what, and who should not have done whatever.

"Enough!" snapped the mage, raising his voice to be heard over the others. "This is pointless. When we have time we will debrief the battles to determine what we might do different next time." His piercing stare probed each in turn. "In the meantime, we must rest."

"Rest?" groused the dwarf. "Here?"

"You know of a better place?" asked the caster. His voice took on a softer tone. "Cyrillis, do what you can for each of them. Start with the *rogue*. I am unharmed."

"That's because you hid in the hallway," said the dwarf, sotto-voice.

"I heard that!" snapped Sordaak. "I would hardly call two lightning bolts and three sets of darts hiding!"

"Whatever!" said the dwarf. He said nothing else.

"Never mind him," chided the paladin. "He is just pissed because he slept through the whole battle!"

"Slept!" roared Vorgath. He stood up quickly. Then just as quickly he sat back down, his head in his hands. "Never mind," he said, his voice much quieter now. "We'll settle this some other time."

Sordaak raised an eyebrow and looked at Savinhand, his head still in his hands, as well. "Savin, can you lock that door and pin it so it can only be opened from in here?"

The rogue trained his bleary eyes first on the caster, then on the door. "If someone puts it back on the hinges, yes," he said. "Just give me a few minutes." He again rested his head in his hands.

"Take all the time you need," replied the mage. "We're not going anywhere anytime soon. And when you get done with that, please verify that is the only entrance into this room."

"Sure, boss," came the muffled reply.

"Cyrillis, could you please see what you can do to get him back on his feet?" he implored the cleric. "I'm going to be a bit nervous until we get this room more secure."

The healer moved obediently to check Savinhand, while the caster turned his attention to the room. It appeared to have been used as some sort of a storage chamber long ago. Shelves lined most of the walls, some toppled because of age, others because of the recent occupant. The chamber was not a large room, perhaps twenty feet by thirty.

He moved to get a better look at what was on the nearest shelf when he was interrupted by the dwarf. "What are we going to do with this?" A loud clank accompanied the question as the dwarf, obviously feeling better after some attention from the healer, planted a swift kick in the side of the umberhulk's head.

"Don't look into its eyes," said the mage quickly. "Even in death its gaze can grasp your mind."

Vorgath jumped back quickly, averting his eyes. Searching the shelves nearby, he spied a tattered blanket. He grasped it and flung it open and over the head of the offending creature. "There, that should keep the damn umberhulk's evil glare at bay!"

"Good," said Sordaak. "As to what to do with it, drag it out into the hallway, please."

"A better question might be," mused Thrinndor quietly, "how did it come to be here in the first place?"

"Hmmm?" said Sordaak, still deep in his own thoughts as he rummaged through the shelves.

"That umberhulk has only been in here a short period—perhaps only a few minutes, even," Thrinndor said. "So how did it come to be in here?"

The caster turned to look first at the paladin, and then at the beast as Vorgath struggled to drag it through the door. Thrinndor sighed heavily as he pushed himself to his feet and moved to help.

"I've got this!" snapped the dwarf.

"Like hell you..."

"It was a pet," said the caster. That pronouncement drew surprised glances from both fighters.

"A *pet?*" said the dwarf.

"It's the only answer," Sordaak replied.

"But a *pet? Here?*"

"Summoned, you imbecile!" At the angry look he got in reply, he added quickly, "Pets. We call them pets. It's a creature summoned by a high wizard to fight for him." He turned to look at the creature. "However," he said so quietly the others had to strain to hear him, "I have never heard of an umberhulk being summoned."

"That don't sound good," said Savinhand, obviously feeling better after some help from Cyrillis. "How high a wizard are you talking about?"

"I don't know," replied the mage after giving it some thought. "I doubt even my mentor has the ability to summon such a creature."

A hushed silence settled upon the troop as they digested the information and scouted around the chamber.

The door secured, they pulled shelving and other items together into the center of the room as make-shift seating.

"Pool together all that we have remaining to eat and drink," said Sordaak to the assembled group. "One way or the other, this will probably be our last meal down here." The others eyed him solemnly. He went on, "And our last rest period. So let's make the best of it."

Vorgath looked at Thrinndor as he dug through his bag. "Such a cheerful guy. Where did you say you dug him up?"

"It is a long story," replied the paladin. "Someday over a flask I will relate it to you." A twinkle appeared in his eyes. "It is most certainly worthy of the telling."

"And when he's done twisting the tale to his satisfaction," said the caster, "I'll tell you how it really went!"

"It is a good thing I know you are jesting," Thrinndor said quietly, "lest I have to part your hair at the neck for continuing to besmirch my integrity."

"You know, this 'integrity' thing is starting to get old." At the glowering look Sordaak got, he added quickly, "And yes, I was just teasing. Sheesh!"

The pile of food they managed to gather was barely enough for a good meal for one of them.

"Well," said the mage, "it will have to do." He reached into his pouch to remove a small capped urn. He removed the cap and sniffed tentatively at the contents. His nose wrinkled in disgust, and added it to the pile.

"That's a magical urn," he started by way of explanation. "Once a day that fills up with a substance that provides sustenance." At the doubtful looks he got, he said, "It doesn't taste all that great, but it fills you up and provides energy." No one moved. "Go ahead!" he snapped. "I promise it won't kill you, and each of you—each of us—is definitely in need of the nourishment it provides!

"Here," he added when still they hesitated, "I'll go first!" He dipped his wooden spoon into the mixture and ladled a small portion into his mouth.

His face scrunched up, his mouth twisted as he forced a smile. "Mmmm... tastes like chicken!" he said in his best Vorgath impersonation.

"Ha, ha!" snorted the dwarf. "Gimme that!" He snatched the spoon from the mage.

"Well," Sordaak continued as the barbarian sampled the mush from the container, "compared to starvation, this'll be like the King's Cuisine!"

"Hardly 'King's Cuisine,'" pronounced the barbarian as he dipped the spoon back into the mixture, "but I don't think it is going to kill us, either." His eyes twinkled as he added, "And it *don't* taste like chicken!"

"Hey!" said the rogue, mock concern lacing his voice, "save some for the rest of us!"

"Oh," said the dwarf indignantly, "so *now* you want some after verifying I survived the sample?"

The banter went on like that until the last morsel had been devoured. They sat back and looked at one another in the light of the torches.

Finally Thrinndor broke the silence. "So why the change of heart?" he said, looking at the mage.

Sordaak, whose gaze had been far away, returned to the conversation reluctantly. "Huh?"

"The rest," the fighter explained patiently. "Before you were adamant we keep going, certain we must get to the keep before it was plundered. But now you insist we rest. Please explain."

"Well," began the caster reluctantly. "I'll explain if each of you takes that time to get comfortable and prepare to rest. I don't want to be in here *that* long!" His gaze took in each, one at a time.

Getting a nod from each companion, he continued. "Very well," he said. "That we are dealing with a high sorcerer of some sort has become obvious—nothing else can explain the orcs banding together to work for a human." He paused to gather his thoughts. "That, and now there is this issue of the 'pet.'" Again he was silent as he pondered.

Finally he went on, "That summoning spell only lasts a short period of time. He *must* have done the summoning and placed the monster in here assuming we would not be able to pass up a locked door so he could make his escape."

"Why would this supposedly high wizard want to escape?" asked the dwarf in the silence that followed.

Sordaak, who had been staring into the light of one of the torches, his mind elsewhere while he spoke, shook his head as he broke from his reverie. His gaze fixed on the dwarf as if seeing him for the first time.

"'Escape' was a poor choice of words," he said. "Departed with his loot might have been more correct."

"But still," persisted Vorgath, "why leave us behind? He must assume we will come after him if left alive. Why not finish us while he had the chance?"

"Because," said the paladin, interjecting his own thought process, "he could not know our strength. We had just seriously depleted his workforce—whether army or hired hands remains to be determined—so he had to assume us to be a serious threat."

"That still does not explain this called rest period," said Cyrillis.

The mage considered laying a withering stare on her but was unable to bring himself to do so. He stuck with layered sarcasm in his tone. "It would if I can be allowed to finish!" No one else ventured to speak, so he went on. "The way I see it, there are three possibilities. First of all, we must assume we are up against a powerful wizard. And this wizard put the umberhulk here to slow us, or possibly to weaken us." He paused again to collect his thoughts. The others were settling into their makeshift beds but still listening intently. "First possibility is that he set the trap to slow us down so he could evacuate and thereby make off with what loot he has gathered. I consider this the most likely of the three, by-the-way.

"The second possibility is he set this trap to weaken us so that when we caught up with him, we would be able to provide little or no resistance to him and his forces."

"So," said Savinhand, tentatively, "If he set *one* such trap to weaken us, can we expect more?"

"Well," explained Sordaak patiently, "doubtful. As stated earlier, the summoned creature will only stay 'summoned' for a brief period of time—longer the more powerful the wizard is, of course. And only one such creature can be summoned at a time. So a rest period will negate any further pet callings."

Again he paused, this time deliberately to wait for the question that was sure to come next. He was not disappointed. Vorgath grated into the silence that followed. "And the third?"

"I thought you would never ask," said the caster around a forced smile. "Third possibility is similar to the second, in that the monster was put here to weaken us, but different in that the wizard doesn't plan on waiting for us to come to him." An ominous silence followed. When he continued, he did in a very quiet voice indeed. "He plans to attack us while we rest."

"Great!" moaned the rogue. "That is going to make me rest easier!"

"Well," said the mage, "number one, I believe that to be the least likely of the three. I think he has vacated the premises and is long gone by now with what loot he can carry. I doubt he would chance that we are weakened enough to try a straight up attack."

"That's good," muttered Savinhand, somewhat mollified.

"And," Sordaak went on, "I will put Fahlred on the outside of the door. He will remain invisible, and *nothing* will be able to approach him without my knowing about it!"

"Sounding better all the time," said Vorgath. He immediately pulled his helm over his eyes and was snoring loudly almost instantly.

Sordaak raised an eyebrow while staring thoughtfully at the dwarf, "Anyway, we are spent. If we even came upon a small band of orcs in our current state, it is doubtful we would survive. Rest is a requirement we cannot ignore. I must meditate to regain some spell energy for what is to come."

"Wait," said Thrinndor quietly so as not to disturb his slumbering friend, "if you believe this high sorcerer to have fled, presumably with his entourage, what is still to come?"

Sordaak hesitated. "Well," he began slowly, "I said *most likely*. He could still be waiting for us. But even if he has left, he will be back." Again he paused. "I doubt seriously that he found what he was after..."

"How could you possibly know that?" queried the paladin.

The caster was silent for so long that Thrinndor thought he may have dozed off in the absolute darkness after the torches had been doused. But finally the mage spoke. "I don't. But if he had found what he was after, he would have left already."

The paladin was silent for a while. "Do you know what he is after, then?"

"Of course," replied Sordaak. "The same thing I'm after. He is a sorcerer, after all. Jewelry, gems and coin mean nothing to us except as a way to get more *power*." He was silent for a moment. When he resumed speaking, a wistful tone crowded his voice. "Power is the very reason for our existence."

This pausing for effect was starting to wear on Thrinndor's nerves. "Go on," he said after a bit.

"He is after *Pendromar, Dragon's Breath*. Dragma's staff of power."

"But that was destroyed in the final conflict," the paladin snorted.

A smile crept into the caster's voice. "Was it?" he said. "Along with your precious sword?"

"That is different!"

"Is it? Why?"

"Well," began the fighter, but he bit off any further reply, knowing this was an argument he would not win.

"Rest," chided Sordaak. "There are yet other reasons I believe he has not found what he is after, but I will not speak of them at this time. Rest. There is yet much for us to accomplish."

Thrinndor started to ask what he meant by that but decided against it. Presently he heard the breathing of the caster change over to the regular breathing of one who has fallen asleep.

There was something here he did not understand, Thrinndor mused quietly, and that bothered him. Yet his beliefs reassured him that all would be made clear to him when it was required that he know.

He cleared his head for communication with Valdaar, but fatigue got the best of him and soon he was asleep, too.

*

Sordaak ran, his companions close on his heels. The passageway was dimly lit, and a mist obscured the floor. They ran along the hall as fast as they could manage, and he knew not why.

There! A pair of eyes following—no, chasing—them! Blood red in color, hideous beyond imagination. Just one pair. Still they fled.

The passage was curving ever to the left. Tighter and tighter the curve became, until...A trap! They were following a spiral passage that was sure to end soon! He looked quickly back, and the eyes were still there! No closer, but surely no farther back, either. But now there was laughter. The laughter of lunacy, or....

Sordaak awoke with a start. Panic clawed at him as he looked about wildly. Unable to see anything in the complete darkness that engulfed him, he thrashed about noisily, waking those nearest.

"What is it?" said Thrinndor. He was instantly awake, but his voice thick with sleep. He pulled the enchanted coin from behind his belt and he used it to illuminate the immediate vicinity. Time had worked its own magic, however, as the coin was much dimmer than before, even in the total darkness of the chamber.

However, the light served to calm the caster somewhat. Sordaak, his heart still in his throat, wrapped his arms around his chest. "Nothing," he said weakly. "Bad dream, that's all."

"A pair of red eyes chasing you?" asked a somber Cyrillis, her voice eerie from out of the darkness.

"Yes," the mage said too quickly. "How did you know?"

"I had the same dream," she said simply.

"Me too," said Vorgath.

"I think we all did," said Thrinndor. "What could that possibly mean?"

"It has to be the nearness to the Keep, and those that have protected it across the millennia," said Cyrillis.

"Huh?" said Sordaak, sarcasm—and something else—tainting his voice. "That's mumbo-jumbo! Bad dreams, that's all!"

"Do not discount the dead," said the paladin. "Death does not always release a being from his or her geas."

"What *geas*?" snapped the caster, obviously this conversation was making him uncomfortable.

"Those that were put here, or remained here, to protect the keep from plundering," the healer responded, her voice reverent.

"That worked really well!" said Sordaak.

"We do not yet know how well it worked," said Thrinndor. "And we will not until we get there."

"Cyrillis' staff is proof enough that the keep has been compromised," said Vorgath, entering the conversation for the first time.

"No," said Sordaak, surprising them all, "it's not. The staff may have been wielded by the protectors, and therefore not part of the treasure."

Thrinndor's right eyebrow arched higher, "What is it that you are not telling us?"

"I said I will not talk about it yet," snapped the caster.

"Did I miss something?" asked Vorgath as he rolled his blankets.

"No!" said the mage.

"Yes," said the paladin. "While you were snoring so loudly as to wake the dead, our caster friend here indicated he has reason to believe the main treasure room has yet to be plundered." He turned to face Sordaak. "But he declined to say just what it was that caused him to believe so."

"Really," said the dwarf, eyeing the mage. "Well maybe we can *convince* him to talk about it!"

"That won't be necessary," replied the sorcerer. "And I wouldn't recommend such an approach." He got into a staredown with the dwarf, who shifted uncomfortably under Sordaak's gaze.

As the others gathered their things, the caster again pulled the urn from his pack. Sure enough, upon opening it he discovered it was again full. "Here," he said putting the urn on their makeshift table. "Divide this among you. It will provide a small amount of energy for each of us. It's not much, but it will have to do."

Grumbling, the dwarf nonetheless dipped his spoon in first, but passed on any more. The others followed suit, each getting a couple of mouthfuls of the tasteless, odorless mush.

"Anyway," said the caster as he retrieved the now empty bowl, "we are almost there. Our undisturbed rest leads me to believe we will encounter no further resistance." He looked up from storing the urn in his sack. "At least for the time being."

"You know," complained the paladin, "you keep putting out bits of information, obviously intending to show your superior knowledge of the situation, but then refuse to elaborate. This is getting tiresome."

"Relax," said the caster. "As I said, we will know soon enough. But to finish that last thought, while I believe the wizard and what remains of his raiding party to have left, I don't believe they will be gone long."

"Huh?" said Vorgath. "Why?"

"Again," Sordaak said archly, "I don't believe he got what he was here for."

"And what would that be?" said Savinhand.

"He thinks," said Thrinndor, an edge of sarcasm creeping into his tone, "they were after Dragma's Staff."

"What?" said the dwarf. "It was destroyed."

"I tried that reasoning, as well," interrupted the paladin. "But he is convinced the artifacts of our lord's council survived the final conflict intact."

"Preposterous!" railed the dwarf.

"Is it?" said the caster, a menacing tone underlying the simple phrase. He surged to his feet. "Regardless, we won't find out sitting around here talking about it!"

As he moved toward the door, he spun and jabbed an index finger at the dwarf. "Mark my words," he said, "that sorcerer will be back for what he was unable to find and he won't be playing nice anymore!"

"That was *nice?*" asked Savinhand.

"Yes," said Sordaak, "any sorcerer that can summon an umberhulk to his call is a powerful one, indeed." He eyed each as he stood silently for a moment. "He is only toying with us. The real question is: Why?"

"You are certain of this?" asked the paladin into the stunned silence that followed.

"Of course not!" the mage said. "I'm making this up as I go along!" He threw a withering look Thrinndor's way, daring him to speak again. The paladin waited, certain there was more.

"But, it all fits," the mage continued. His stance softened somewhat before going on. "I worked on this while you all rested. And I've discounted most other possibilities."

Now the pause for dramatic effect had the desired effect, as the companions leaned toward the caster, hanging on his every word. Finally, sure he could milk no more from them without drawing their ire, he continued. Slowly emphasizing each word, he said, "He knows who we are. He knows why we are here. And he plans to let us find the staff for him. Then he plans on taking it from us."

Again silence filled the void following his revelation—silence that grew unbearable, until all of them started speaking at once.

"What?" said the rogue.

"How could you possibly know this?" said the dwarf.

"Interesting," the paladin said.

"How does he know us?" said the healer.

Sordaak held up both hands, palms toward them, and waited for the din to pass. Once again the tension was almost palpable in the chamber.

"OK," the mage said. "Look at it this way. He has obviously been down here for quite some time—Cyrillis' staff is evidence of that. He could have only gotten that staff from down here, and that staff was purchased from a vendor some time ago, correct?" He looked at the healer and got a mute nod in return.

"Second, he is—or was—still here. He would not be had he found what he was looking for, that is a given."

"But..." started Savinhand, but the look he got from the caster caused him to smother the rest of the question.

"That was the easy part to figure out. The rest is...less certain."

Again the rogue opened his mouth to speak but thought better of it and clammed up.

"He—the sorcerer—has to assume we are here for the same reason he is, right? After all, what else could we be doing down here? There is no way we are just a wandering troop passing through." He paused, this time not for effect but to carefully consider his next words.

Vorgath could not stand the silence, however. "Some of that could actually be possible. But how do you figure he knows who we are?"

Sordaak turned his gaze on the dwarf, but his mind was elsewhere. "I don't," he said simply. "But....it's a feeling I'm getting. Like I should *know* this guy, because he obviously knows *me*!"

Once again they all started speaking at once, except the paladin. Thrinndor only raised an eyebrow and stood waiting for what was to come next.

Sordaak again raised his hands, asking for silence. Presently it was granted. "Like I said, I don't *know* this...It's just a feeling. There are no casters in these parts capable of what he has done—at least none that I know of. And since we casters tend to keep track of one another, I have to assume he knows who *I* am."

His voice trailed off, and there were obviously many more questions on the minds of his companions. But the mage forestalled them with his raised hand and said simply, "We won't find out who *he is* sitting here." He silenced any further discussion as he turned toward the door.

"Savin, if you would be so kind as to let us out of here."

The rogue just shrugged and moved obediently ahead of the group.

"Wait," said Cyrillis sternly. "I would like to check each of you before we move out." Sordaak started to complain, but she cut him off. "I have my full complement of healing available, and I do not think it wise to continue without being at 100 percent."

Realizing it would be futile to argue with her and that she was probably right, Sordaak said, "Very well," and sat back down.

She moved to each and used here innate health sense to probe recent cuts, bruises and other injuries. She mumbled a prayer where indicated, and soon all were feeling ready to take on whatever dared cross their path.

Last was Vorgath. "Save your ministrations for those who need it," he said gruffly.

Without saying a word, she reached out and placed her hand gently on the massive contusion on the side of his forehead. She again mumbled her prayers, and the knot visibly reduced in size and became less purple.

Finished, she lowered her hand and eyed the dwarf for further signs of damage. He stood quickly and spoke formally. "That was not necessary, but I thank you just the same."

She bowed slightly, muttered "Dwarves!" under her breath, and turned to face Sordaak. "I have done all that I can at this juncture." A smile pursed her lips as she nodded toward the barbarian. "Brain damage I can do nothing about!"

"Ha," snorted Vorgath. "Very funny!"

"You cannot be faulted," said the paladin, a smile playing across his lips as well. "You cannot fix what is not there!"

"A jester!" said the dwarf, loudly. "We have us a court jester!"

"OK, OK," said the mage, his smile in his eyes. "Can we *finally* get a move on?"

They all climbed back to their feet, their weariness now mostly gone. Still some groaned loudly, others muttered silent curses.

"Heavens, yes," said the barbarian. "I hope you are wrong about the orcs, though. I signed on to mash me some orcs, and I don't count fifteen as anywhere near 'some.'" He grabbed his greataxe and headed for the door.

"*That* I wouldn't worry about," said the caster as he moved to follow. "I'm sure there are many more where those paltry few came from, and I fear our friend will be bringing all of them back when he returns!"

"Thank you," the dwarf grated. "That brightens my day!"

"Speak for yourself, o diminutive one!" said Savinhand. "I'm just hoping for a decent meal!"

The party bickered like that as they got in their places for the march into who knew what. Sordaak stuck out his arm and silently called for Fahlred, who winked into being almost immediately. They communicated in their way for a moment, and the quasit winked back out again.

Chapter Twelve

The Temple

The door open, Savinhand disappeared silently into the passage ahead. Thrinndor gave him a few moments to get into position, and led the remainder of the party out into the hallway.

Some shuffling ensued as they spread out into their usual positions. The hallway was still lit by sconces spaced evenly along their path.

"Nice of them to leave the lights on," groused Vorgath good-naturedly.

Thrinndor only went fifty or so feet and stopped at an intersection that branched to their left. "This is where I saw them go." He indicated the empty passage. At the end was a door. A lit brazier was on each side of it.

Sordaak peered farther down the passage ahead of them, and then at the door, set back about ten feet off of the main passage. "Am I mistaken," he asked of no one in particular, "or is the passage ahead curving slightly to the left?"

Vorgath peered obediently in the direction indicated, then turned and looked back the way they came. "Yes," he said, "I believe you are correct." He looked back ahead of them and added, "I don't understand why I hadn't noticed it before, though…"

"Well, through that door is where we want to go then," said the caster, and he turned that way as if there should be no discussion.

Thrinndor looked at the mage and raised his eyebrow in question but said nothing.

However, the dwarf voiced the question that all wanted to ask. "How could you possibly know that?"

Sordaak took a step toward the door but changed his mind. "I'll gladly explain once I am proven correct." He looked around for Savinhand, who was nowhere to be seen as usual. "However, until then could we please get these doors checked for the usual?" He appeared to speak to no one, assuming he would be heard by the rogue.

Savinhand materialized next to the caster and said, "Of course!"

"You know," the mage grumped, "one of these times you are going to sneak up on me at the wrong time, and I'll part your hair with a lightning bolt!"

"Yeah, yeah, yeah," said the rogue, a huge smile splitting his face. "Whatever!" He moved ahead to inspect the doors. After a few moments he stepped back and said, "Humph."

"What?" asked Cyrillis.

"Well," said the thief, "I would have expected some not-so-friendly leavings by our not-so-friendly predecessors." He continued to search all around the door. "But, I can find nothing. The door is not even locked. In fact, I can't even find a way for it to *be* locked!"

"That's because you don't usually lock doors to a temple," the mage said solemnly.

Thrinndor's eyebrow again made the trek up his forehead. He remained silent as he grasped the pull ring and heaved. The door opened toward them noiselessly.

The hallway continued beyond the door, still illuminated at regular intervals along the way. It was not a long hallway, however. After thirty or forty feet, it ended in another door. There were also two doors on either side of the hallway. All were closed.

The paladin turned to peer at the caster. "Well?"

"Those side doors will be ante-chambers—prep rooms, if you will. The door at the end will lead into the temple proper."

Now there were several sets of raised eyebrows. "Prep rooms for what?" asked Savinhand, who was already approaching the first one on the left and was checking it over.

"How the hell should I know?" snapped the caster. "Whatever these holy types do in prep rooms outside of their temples!"

"Well," said the rogue cautiously, "you seem to know everything else about this place."

Sordaak eyed him sardonically. "Assumptions, that's all. I am assuming that is the temple ahead. Again, I will explain if that proves to be correct."

"Depending on who the temple is dedicated to," said Cyrillis, "they could be used for sacrifice preparation." All eyes turned to look at her. "Or maybe a confessional or two before the temple. Maybe both."

Savinhand turned to look at the caster, questions apparent on his face.

"No, they won't be locked," said Sordaak. "And I doubt they'll be trapped, either."

"I'm not going to even ask," muttered the rogue as he moved to open the door in front of him.

"And yes," continued the mage as if he hadn't been interrupted, "you should check all of them. However, I doubt we'll find anything. I just want to be sure there is nothing behind us."

The paladin still had not moved, and he had a thoughtful look in his eyes as he started toward the door opposite the one Savinhand had just opened. "If the door ahead is indeed the temple," he said, "you are going to have some serious explaining to do."

Sordaak just folded his arms across his chest and waited for them to complete the inspections.

All four rooms turned out to be identical. A smallish chamber with a stone slab about six feet by two feet and about three feet off of the stone floor. There were grooves cut into either side of the slab that ran across the top lengthwise. These grooves fed into a single hole in the end and led to a small chamber underneath. There was a dust-filled bowl in the small chamber.

"I guess that tells us what these were used for," said Cyrillis, who had walked up behind the rogue.

"Huh?" he said. "I don't understand."

"Those grooves," she said, pointing to the sloped furrows cut into the top, "are to collect the blood of whatever is being sacrificed. It runs along here to that bowl."

Savinhand, who had just picked up the bowl in question to inspect it more closely, set it back down quickly.

"Oh, yucko!" he said and stood up quickly wiping his hands on the leather of leggings.

Having completed their search, they all gathered in the hall outside the door opposite the one they had first come through.

Savinhand moved to inspect the door as Sordaak said, "I doubt you will find anything."

The rogue turned slowly to peer at the caster.

"But," said the mage, "by all means, go ahead and check—I could be wrong."

Savinhand muttered, "Thank you," and went back to searching.

After a few minutes, no longer able to contain himself, Sordaak pushed his way past the rogue and shoved on the door. It swung noiselessly inward to reveal a vast chamber. "Behold," he said triumphantly, "The Temple for the Keep of Dragma!" He stood aside as the others filed in silently and spread out into the aisle on the other side of the door.

The temple was enormous, at least 250 feet deep and maybe 300 across. It was circular in shape, with doors spaced regularly around its perimeter. The aisles from each door sloped down toward the middle, where a vast cauldron sat on a raised dais.

The cauldron was lit, illuminating the area around the dais. There were torches that flamed at regular intervals along the upper wall, providing more than ample light to see everything. Everything but the ceiling, which sloped up from where they stood. Upward into the impenetrable darkness above.

After the initial shock of what they were seeing wore off, everyone turned to look at Sordaak. Finally, Thrinndor broke the silence. "I think it is time for you to explain."

"Very well," said the caster. "I suppose I owe each of you that." He sat down on one of the stone hewn benches spaced regularly throughout the interior and withdrew a dagger from its scabbard. Lifting the hem of his robe, he felt around until, apparently satisfied, he used the dagger to slice away a few stitches.

Reaching inside with his fingers, he pulled out a small tube made of what appeared to be a piece of bone, darkly stained with what was probably blood. He looked at the ruined hem of his garment and then tossed it aside. "I won't need this old robe much longer, anyway."

Next, he removed a seal on the end of the tube and shook it gently to remove the contents. What fell out was a neatly rolled piece of parchment. He grasped it by an edge and unrolled it as slowly and gently as he could. He placed it on the bench next to him while he attempted to smooth it out. Finally, he leaned back from his efforts, allowing the others who had crowded around to see what he was showing them.

The piece of parchment was little larger than an open hand and was obviously part of a larger document, as one edge of it was torn away. It appeared incredibly old. Neatly drawn on it was a circle than nearly filled the sheet, with spokes at regular intervals branching off it. The spokes continued through the outside circle to yet another one in the middle.

It was an accurate rendition of the chamber in which they now stood.

Thrinndor looked up from the drawing and into the eyes of the mage. "How long have you had this? And, more importantly, why did you keep it from us?"

Sordaak met his unwavering gaze with one of his own. "Several years," he said. "The second answer should be obvious." He was silent for a while. "A more pertinent question might be: Where did I get it?"

Vorgath, who had had just about enough of the dramatic pauses, blurted out, "Very well, how did you come to be in possession of this map?"

The mage turned his gaze upon the dwarf, who shifted uncomfortably under his penetrating stare.

"It was 'given' to me by a very crazy, very old man who claimed to have been inside this temple."

"Parothenticas," said the paladin, derisively.

"Yes," said the caster. "I see you have heard of him."

"He cannot be trusted! He is stark raving mad," said the fighter.

"Was he?" said Sordaak, turning back to the map. "His mind was destroyed by all the torture he endured over the years." He looked again at the paladin. "Torture he endured by those trying to pry the secrets of where he had been out of him!"

"Yeah, well, crazed nonetheless," retorted the big man as he turned away. He then spun back to face the caster. "Wait. You are telling me that he *gave* you this map? Why you, and not the countless others that had come before you?"

"There," said Sordaak, satisfaction in his voice. "Finally the appropriate question." He paused to ensure he had their undivided attention. He needn't have bothered. "I promised to release him from his lunacy, and he believed me. I did."

"But, how?" said Cyrillis. "I too know his story. Many powerful clerics of my, and many other, orders attempted to relieve his insanity. None were successful."

"That is because it could not be relieved," said the caster smugly.

"But you said…"

"I said *release* him, not *relieve* him," said the sorcerer. "Everyone always wanted to 'relieve' him so he could divulge the secrets locked away beneath the layers of insanity. That was the wrong approach."

"Go on," said a suddenly wary Thrinndor after yet another pause.

"Parothenticas did not want to be 'relieved', and there was only one way to 'release' him," said the caster. "And that was by death."

A stunned silence followed.

"But," stammered the healer, "dead, he cannot speak."

"Really?" said the caster, sarcastically. "Actually, that is true in most respects. But, the act of dying was enough to return lucidity to the old man. As he was bleeding to death, he thanked me effusively and gave me this." With that pronouncement, he carefully rolled up the map, inserted it into the tube and stuffed it into his pack.

Again, stunned silence hung over the party.

"Bleeding to death?" queried Cyrillis. "How so?" She was afraid of the answer.

"From the gash at his throat, of course," said Sordaak as if he was talking about the weather.

"But…"

"No," cut in the mage, "you listen." He looked sternly at the healer. "I know this might be hard to understand, but that old man had lived far longer than he was supposed to—far longer than he *wanted* to." He took in a deep breath. He was telling this tale for the first time. "Knowing some of what he knew, I worked with him for more than a year trying to get the rest. As he grew accustomed to my presence, he began to trust me. The more he trusted, the more lucid he became."

He was silent for a while, and none dared say anything for fear he would stop his tale. "Finally one day he asked me to release him from his geas. When I asked him how that was possible, he looked deep into my eyes—into my very soul, even—and handed me this knife." He pulled the dagger from behind his sash with a serpentine blade. "He told me then in the most lucid voice he had ever spoken to me with, 'Only then may I pass on the information to you which you seek.'"

Again Sordaak fell silent, his head down staring at the bone map case. When finally he spoke it was in a mere whisper, such that all leaned forward to hear what he said. "Still I hesitated. I wanted to find another way. He was beyond old," he looked up suddenly, silently imploring those around him to not judge. "He had lived more than a thousand years—far too long. I tried to reason with him, but his insanity returned and even grew worse, if that was possible.

"Only when I realized what it was that he really wanted, and held the blade against his throat did his sanity return. He begged me to do it, and when I acquiesced and slowly drew the blade across his throat, he began to sing."

Sordaak choked up then, and he seemed to be unable to go on. But, swallowing hard, he pushed on. "I will carry his words with me to my own end, but I have no voice for song, so I will not sing it here. Suffice it to say that I was convinced."

Choked up, he was unable to continue. When finally he was, he merely said, "I will speak of this no further."

He bowed his head and the others could see the muscles of his jaw clench in effort. Finally he threw his head back and drew the sleeve of his robe across his eyes, emotion in his voice making it rougher than intended. He held up the map case. "This came out of the slit in his throat," he said. "I have no idea how long it had been there. I believe it is what kept him alive."

"And allowed him to die," whispered Cyrillis. "May I see it?"

Sordaak obediently handed it over. She inspected it reverently, not removing the cap. "This is from Dragma's own body," she said with certainty.

"How can you be sure?" asked Thrinndor, even as he knew her to be correct.

Without answering, she continued, "It is said only a bone removed willingly from a living High Priest can be used as such to maintain the life of its host."

"Wait," said Sordaak, "That means the old man was alive when Dragma still lived!"

She looked at him as if seeing him for the first time. "Correct. And the old man is—or was—a messenger from Dragma!"

"So," said the paladin, "it has indeed begun."

"*What* has begun?" asked a very confused Savinhand.

"Our Lord will soon return," Cyrillis said simply. She turned to stare at Sordaak. "You have been chosen as messenger," she said with wonder in her voice. She bowed low, arms outstretched to either side, palms forward, honoring the one before her.

"Now hold on just a minute!" snapped the caster. "I am no one's *messenger*! I am here for *Pendromar*!"

She stood and raised herself to her full height and said with her eyes flaring. "Not all servants are *willing* servants! But they serve just the same!"

"Let's get this straight, sister—*I serve no one!*" Sordaak spat each word for emphasis. "And certainly not a *dead god!*"

She started to retort, but Thrinndor interrupted before she could speak. "Nevertheless, you have brought us here," he spread his arms and slowly spun to encompass the chamber. "Why you were chosen we may never know. But chosen you were." He turned back to face the caster, and bowed in the same manner as the healer before him. "For that, we will always be in your debt. Thank you."

"Now cut that out!" shouted Sordaak.

A beaming Savinhand looked around him in wonder. "Well, boss, just the same, looks like you *did* get us here. And it seems certain—at least to these two—that it was no accident."

"Indeed," said Thrinndor formally as he straightened and looked about the temple. "Now we just have to find this hidden chamber a High Wizard was unable to locate."

"Piece of cake," said Sordaak, smugness returning to his voice.

"Right," said Vorgath. "Either there is still more you have not revealed to us, or—more likely—you are full of shit." He grinned to remove any hint of malice—well, almost any hint.

The mage smiled in return. "You don't really think I drug you guys down here without knowing where it is we are going, do you?"

The group, which was still gathered around him, waited patiently at first.

After a few moments the rogue again spoke for all of them, "You know, O Great Leader of Ours," he said. "This habit of yours where we have to drag every bit of information out of you is really starting to wear thin on my patience."

Sordaak raised an eyebrow and breathed a deep sigh. "Very well," he said. "Even I grow weary of my own theatrics!" He turned to look down the aisle toward the cauldron. "There. The hidden chamber lies there."

Yet another stunned silence descended upon the group. Finally, Thrinndor asked, "I suppose it is pointless to ask just how you know this?"

"Yes," said the caster, "it is. That source I will not reveal." He started down the steps toward the dais and tossed a "sorry" over his shoulder.

The others looked at one another, doubt plain upon their faces.

After a moment, the paladin shrugged and moved to follow the mage, the others right behind.

When Sordaak reached the flat floor area surrounding the cauldron, he dropped his pack to the front bench and moved toward the immense brazier.

As he approached, he could feel the heat from the flames wash over his unprotected skin. "Hmmm," he said as he stopped to ponder, his hand rubbing his chin absent-mindedly.

"Hmmm, what?" asked Savinhand.

Sordaak ignored him. Instead of answering, he dropped to his hands and knees. It was much cooler down near the granite, and he crawled closer to the base of the cauldron. In this fashion, he was able to reach where the floor joined seamlessly to the base. The heat was barely tolerable, and he soon began to sweat heavily.

Still the mage endured, and he crawled thus on his hand and knees around the base, apparently looking for something. The others stood back and watched.

After the mage had made two complete circuits around the dais, Vorgath could contain himself no longer. "Is there something we can help you find?"

Without answering, Sordaak continued with his third trip around the dais, slowing even more for a careful inspection this time.

By now, everyone had dropped their packs to the ground and seated themselves on the nearest bench.

His third circumference complete, Sordaak beat a hasty retreat from the dais back to where the others were sitting. He was sweating profusely, and his soaked robe clung to his body as he stood. There was a confused look clouding his face.

"I don't understand," he began. "I didn't expect it to be found easily, but I *know* that is the entrance to the hidden burial chamber of Dragma, Angra-Kahn and his host." He looked back the way he had come. "But I can find no sign of it."

Thrinndor raised an eyebrow in his all-too-familiar sign of question. "Perhaps if you will not divulge how you came to be in possession of this information, you could maybe tell us what it is that you know so that we could help you in your search?"

The casters face twisted in indecision. "Oh, very well," he blurted out. "He told me!" With that, he spun to turn his agitated gaze upon the cauldron.

Into the again stunned silence that fell upon the group Cyrillis said, "Was that really so hard? You must know that we have no choice but to believe you at this point. And that while our goal may not be one and the same, it at least provides some commonality?"

"It's not that," said the caster, a pleading tone new to his voice. "That's it. It's all I have." He spun back to face the others. "Whether you believe or not matters not at this point. But now you know all that I do. There *is* no more!"

Thrinndor turned an inquisitive eye on the cauldron and said quietly, "Could you please relate exactly what it was that he told you? Perhaps there is a clue in the wording."

"Certainly," said the caster, "but it will do you no good." He looked at the others, then closed his eyes and recited, "Look beneath the undying flame for that for which you seek."

"That is all?" said the paladin. "You are certain?"

"Yes!" snapped the caster. "He barely got those words out as his life ebbed from his wound and the map case made itself known."

He paused to consider, struggling to remember something on the edge of his memory. "Well..." he added.

"What?" said Thrinndor and Savinhand in unison.

"Well," the caster repeated, "there was something else—something he said after I thought he had passed." His brow furrowed as he struggled to remember. "After I had removed the case from his throat, he said 'that contains all you will need.' He said nothing more."

"Let me see the map again, please," said paladin.

Sordaak walked to his pack, removed the case and handed it over. Thrinndor removed the cap reverently and shook the map out. Gently he unfurled it and spread the map on one of the benches for all to see.

They each took turns inspecting the ancient diagram. And each in turn stepped back to let another look, shaking his or her head in frustration.

"There's nothing there!" groused the dwarf. He spun on his heel and approached the cauldron, ignoring the blazing heat it gave off.

After two complete circuits of his own, he moved back to be with the party, again shaking his head, his beard smoldering. He patted it absentmindedly and said, "We dwarves have considerable lore in the art of stone work—indeed , this place shows signs of having been carved by kin of mine—yet I can find no hint of any hidden doors or chambers."

"It's there!" said Sordaak, his voice unwavering.

"I do not doubt it," said the paladin, his stalwart gaze still upon the brazier. "However, it may be beyond our ken to cause it to open." He turned slowly to peer at the caster. "Is it possible for you to open it by use of your magic?"

Sordaak turned to fix his stare upon the offending stone. "No. I too thought of that. But for the spell to work, I have to be able to 'grasp' the door or opening with my mind, and 'force' it open with summoned power."

Thrinndor was silent.

The rogue said, "How about your familiar?" He turned to look at the mage. "Can you send him in....there?" he pointed the flaming mass before them all.

"No," said the caster, "it doesn't work that way, either. I have to be able to envision where it is that I send him, which means that I have to have been there. I have to be able to *see* it in order for him to *see* it to go there."

"Damn," muttered Savinhand, his shoulders sagging.

"Sorry," said the caster.

"Wait!" said Thrinndor, a glimmer of hope edging into his voice. He pointed again at the drawing. "Look."

"What?" asked Vorgath. "I have looked at it until my eyes are beginning to cross."

"Yes," said the big fighter, "you are looking, but you are not seeing!"

"Huh?" said the dwarf. "Don't *you* start speaking in riddles like this confounded wiggle-finger!"

"See these spots marked on the outside of the drawing?" Thrinndor explained. "They appear to correspond to the sconces that line the outer wall of this chamber."

They all looked again at the parchment, then up at the braziers dotting the upper reaches of the chamber.

"So?" grumped the dwarf. "I see a total of sixteen dots on the map, and while I agree there are sixteen sconces, of what possible significance could that be?"

"You still are not *seeing*!" said Thrinndor.

"Would you please be so kind to explain just what it is that you see?" said the caster.

"It is not the 'dots' themselves," said the paladin, "but the markings around some of them. Look again."

They again obediently crowded around the unfurled drawing on the bench.

"What?" said the dwarf. "These smudge marks? They can't possibly indicate anything!"

"No?" said the paladin, still using his best, most gentle teaching voice. "Look at the detail. While the map is indeed old beyond our understanding, it is very well preserved. I see no other 'smudges' anywhere on it—except for those around some of the sconces."

The dwarf looked harder at the map, and then he looked up at his friend. "You're daft!" he said finally. He stepped back and folded his arms across his chest, defying anyone to argue.

"Am I?" said Thrinndor, the challenge in his voice apparent.

Vorgath opened his mouth to reply, but Sordaak got there first.

"No, wait," he said. "I think he has something." He leaned even closer, and rubbed his eyes to help clear them. "Not only are these markings intentional, they are not all the same!"

"Right," said the paladin. "Now we just have to figure out what exactly those markings mean."

"It's a puzzle," said the caster, excitement in his voice. "It could mean that some of the braziers are supposed to be out, the others lit."

"Could be," said Cyrillis, "but that would not explain the differences in the markings."

"Huh?" said the caster. His voice grew more excited as he realized she was correct. "Very good. Well, maybe the sconces can be moved—pulled or turned."

They looked at one another, then as one they rushed back up the steps they had so recently descended and gathered around the closest one.

"Ummm....now what?" said Savinhand.

"Let me look at it first," said Sordaak. "They might be enchanted in some way." The others moved back to give him room.

The mage stepped up hesitantly and began his inspection. Finding nothing, he reached out, grasped the sconce and pulled.

It did not budge.

"Let me try," said the paladin, undaunted.

Sordaak stepped back and swept his arm in a mock elegant bow, "By all means."

Thrinndor stepped up, grasped the sconce, set his feet and pulled. The muscles in his neck bulged and beads of sweat popped out on his forehead.

Again nothing happened.

"Don't break it off!" said the caster.

The paladin released the brazier with a gasp and turned to the caster. "All yours!" It was his turn to step back with a flourish.

Sordaak brushed by him with a huff, moving back in for a better look. Presently, he reached up and grasped it again, but instead of pulling, he twisted it. It moved slowly but easily, turning to his right.

"Well, that settles that," he muttered under his breath. He righted it back to its original position and stepped back. He turned to face the others, excitement in his eyes.

"Let me see that map!"

Thrinndor handed the map over and Sordaak peered over it, eagerly.

Finally, he looked up, concern lines now etching his face.

"What?" said Cyrillis.

"Well," breathed the caster, "if we are to assume these markings indicate the amount each brazier is to be turned from straight up," he looked again at the map, turning it upside down, then sideways in his hands. "What point of reference do we use to begin?"

"Sixteen possible solutions!" griped the rogue.

"Gimme that!" groused the dwarf as he stepped up and none too gently took the map from the caster.

"Hey," said the mage, "be careful with that!"

"Aw, don't get your undergarments in a bunch!" said the dwarf. "We dwarves revere all maps—especially old ones!" He glared at the caster, daring him to continue his protest.

When none was forthcoming he turned an inquisitive eye to the map and handed it back to the caster. "Simple," he said as he turned to peer at the cauldron, but said no more.

After a few moments, Sordaak said, "Now look at who has developed a penchant for the dramatic! Would you care to enlighten us less enlightened folk?"

"Certainly," said the dwarf smugly as he turned back to the group. He then reached out and delicately grasped the map in Sordaak's hands. "If I may," he said pleasantly. He turned the map about ninety degrees and handed it back. "All maps have a north." Before anyone could say anything he added, "All *good* maps, anyway."

The mage looked at the map, then up at the dwarf and back down at the map. "Right," he said, "but I do not see any sign that north is indicated on this map—good or otherwise."

"It's implied," said Vorgath matter-of-factly.

Into the silence that followed, Sordaak said sarcastically, "It's implied." Not a question.

The barbarian made a show of rolling his eyes. "The top of any *good* map will be north—it's just the way they are drawn. Since there are no markings, you must assume north to be here," he said, pointing to the top edge of the map.

Not sure whether he was the brunt of yet another joke or not, Sordaak said, "OK, let's assume you know what you are talking about—of which there is in no small amount of doubt, by the way—and this is indeed 'north' on the map... Which way is north?"

The dwarf looked at him as if he had gone mad. Finally, realizing he had to explain, he reached out and shoved the caster so he was facing to their right. Another small push and he said, "That way!" He then backed off a couple of steps. "Dumbass!" he muttered under his breath.

The mage bit off a snippy reply and instead held the map up in front of him.

Finally he said, "We will again assume for the time being that you know what you are talking about—if for no other reason because we *really* have few..."

"None," said the dwarf, satisfaction plain in his voice.

"Other options," continued the caster. "Now all I have to do is figure out how far to turn each of these that need to be turned." He looked again at the map. "I'm going to assume for the moment that the size of these additional markings means something, and turn the sconces accordingly.

"Meanwhile," he added, looking up from the map at Thrinndor, "I suggest each of you get ready down on the dais in the event this all works, and an opening is revealed."

"Ready for what?" asked Savinhand.

"I have no idea," said the caster. "But, we should probably be ready in the event there are still more deterrents in our path."

"Right," said Thrinndor. "We will leave the puzzle in your hands, and we will prepare ourselves for...whatever deterrents come our way."

"Thank you," muttered the caster as he stepped back up to the brazier he had already moved once. He looked at it, and back down at the map. "This one stays as is." He walked around the perimeter to the next one. The others took the steps back down into the bowl of the temple.

After shouldering his pack, Savinhand walked over to the paladin. "Hey," he said, looking up at the caster, who had finished moving the second sconce. "That's going to take him a while. I'm going to take a look around, if you don't mind."

"Certainly," said the big fighter. "Just do not wander off too far. I have a feeling we are not yet finished with our swords."

"Gotcha," said the rogue as he headed off away from the group, his curiosity piqued by some tracks in the otherwise centuries-old dust on the floor that led up and out on the opposite side of where they had come in.

The tracks led out the door diametrically opposite of the one through which they had come. As he approached the door, he scouted right and left, trying to glean additional information before actually going through.

What he found intrigued him. There were more than twenty sets of tracks. Some booted, some not. Missing toes, trimmed and worn nails, cuts on pads and/or toes, et cetera. But, there were also some tracks he was certain were human—more than one set. He could discern at least three distinct sets. There was more than just the one human, after all!

He started to go back to give this information to the others, but changed his mind when he saw Sordaak scratching his head while working on his third sconce and the others searching the area of the dais.

He shrugged and turned his attention instead to the door. A cursory glance revealed it was identical to the others he had already inspected. It was hinged such that it swung in and out. More important, he could see no trap mechanisms.

He silently withdrew his shortsword, dropped into his stealth mode and passed quietly through the door. Once through, he paused briefly to let his eyes adjust. While lit, the hallway was not as brightly so as the chamber from which he had just come.

The passage beyond was identical in every respect to the one they had entered the temple through. Deciding to first inspect the intersection at the end of the hall, he moved silently in that direction, using any natural shadows to conceal his movements.

When he got to the intersection, he cautiously looked both directions and saw nothing. He told himself he was being overly cautious, and that there was no one left down here for him to worry about. But the hair on the back of his neck was standing on end for some reason, and he had learned long ago not to ignore such indications.

He checked the tracks again, but here the dust had been trampled by too many feet, and over too long a period. Individual tracks were indiscernible.

He started to return to the two doors in the side passageway when something caught his eye, a set of tracks apart from the rest. They ran close to the wall away from him and down the hall to his left. He peered at them closely, trying to figure out just what it was about them that had attracted his attention.

He again started to turn away when his head snapped back around. It was not so much that the tracks were apart from the others, he realized, but that *they were fresh*! Within the past few hours, he estimated.

They were being watched! Of that he was now certain.

He checked both directions at the intersection again. Unsure as to what he should do, he decided he must get this information to the others immediately. He moved back down the side passage—again as silently as he could—back to the door he had come through.

As his hand reached for the door, his senses alert for anything out of the ordinary, he heard the *whap* of something as it sped through the air. He threw himself hard and to his right but felt a sharp pain in his left shoulder where his leather was penetrated right at the joint to the upper arm.

Instinctively, realizing that only a split second separated him from certain death, his hand whipped up and dislodged the dart from his arm as he rolled back to his feet, shortsword in his right hand, a long, curved dagger in his left.

Fear caused his pulse to race. No one should have been able to detect him. No one! Except possibly those trained as he was, or...*an assassin!*

Without moving, his eyes searched wildly about, knowing if that if indeed he was up against an assassin, the dart had probably been poisoned and he had little time remaining.

At first he failed to see anything, but...there! That shadow moved!

Savin dove toward his assailant. He tumbled his way toward the shadow and heard another *whap* as a dart shot past his head. In less time than it takes to blink, Savinhand was at the feet of his attacker. Unable to bring the sword to bear, he instead stabbed up and hard with his dagger as he surged to his feet. He felt the blade encounter the soft tissue of the lower abdomen and he pushed it with all his might, using his legs to wedge himself back to his feet.

This move lifted his assailant clear of his feet. The assassin stifled a scream and threw himself back, away from Savin. The move jerked the handle of the dagger from the rogue's hand. The would-be assassin fell back through one of the ante-chamber doors and out of Savin's immediate sight.

Certain the wound was mortal, Savinhand followed swiftly to be sure.

He opened the door to see his attacker struggling to rise, brandishing a nasty-looking dagger in his right hand. His face was covered in the shadow of a cowl that covered his head, but Savin could see his teeth bared in a grimace of pure hatred. He lunged clumsily at Savin, but the rogue easily slapped the blade aside and brought his sword down on the exposed neck.

The assassin crashed to the floor and struggled to rise. Unable to do so, he rolled over on his back. Savin had to take a step back because of the malice that spewed from his assailant's eyes.

"Fool!" He? The voice was female—a Halfling by the lilt of her accent. "I am but one of many!" She struggled to rise again but fell back, her breathing coming in ragged gasps. "You shall *never* gain access to the treasure!" Her words were coming slower and weaker now. "My master will..." Her voice trailed off, and she was silent. For a time her eyes remained virulent, but they soon glazed over.

Savinhand took another step back but was unable to maintain his balance. He tripped over some unseen object and fell to the stone floor. He struggled to rise, but a mist clouded his vision and his limbs felt like lead. Poison! He tried to crawl back to the door, but everything faded and consciousness slipped from him.

Chapter Thirteen

Beneath

Sordaak, having moved all of the sconces save one, wearily descended the steps to join the others. He looked at the companions gathered there and asked, "Where's Savin?"

Thrinndor looked up from some scratches he had noticed on the floor surrounding the cauldron. "What?"

Irritable from lack of food, Sordaak said, "It was not meant to be a trick question. Where's Savin?"

The paladin looked around quickly, and his tone suddenly turned worried. "He said he wanted to look around, and I told him not to wander too far off."

The mage sighed. "How long ago was that?"

"Right after we came back down here," said the fighter softly.

Suddenly interested, Vorgath answered the unasked question and pointed across the cauldron. "He went that way."

The caster looked over the brazier at the door indicated. "Shit," he said under his breath. "Do I have to do *everything*?" He started around the dais, shaking his head.

The others dropped whatever they were doing and fell in behind the mage.

Sordaak took the steps two at a time, rushing against he knew not what. He approached the door and reached out to push it open but was stopped by Thrinndor.

"Wait," said the paladin. "Better let me go first."

Sordaak raised an eyebrow and dropped his arm to his side. "Get on with it, then," he said, stepping aside.

The big fighter brushed past him without a reply, but Cyrillis was not willing to let it drop. She took in a sharp breath to reply but was interrupted brusquely by Thrinndor. "Do not," the paladin cautioned as he pushed the door open and stepped through.

She let out the breath noisily but said nothing. The look she threw Sordaak, however, as she moved through the door behind the paladin would have withered stone.

The caster merely shrugged and waited for the barbarian to precede him and then stepped through as well. Once through, he could see that Thrinndor had moved rapidly to the intersection and was looking both directions.

"Nothing here," the paladin said, his voice laden with concern. He immediately headed down the passage to the left, and Cyrillis started right when they were both stopped by the voice of the barbarian.

"Found him," they heard from the door to the ante-chamber he was holding open. "Don't look good," he added, staring down at something on the floor.

Cyrillis rushed back down the hall and pushed her way past the barbarian. First she saw the female assassin and was about to say so, but then her eyes fell upon the rogue, his supine form blocking the area behind the door, his accusing eyes staring unseeing at the ceiling.

"Oh, no!" she moaned and quickly knelt at his side. After a quick examination she said, "He is not breathing!"

"Ummm…" said Vorgath, "I think it's because he's dead!"

She was getting better at the withering looks, because the one she threw the barbarian caused him to throw up his hands and take a step back. "Hey," he said quickly, "I just call it like I see it." He stepped back out into the hall to avoid further punishment, allowing the door to swing shut behind him.

"I will thank you to leave the diagnosis to those competent to do so!" the healer snapped after the receding figure.

"Yes ma'am," was the muffled reply from the hallway.

Unable to devote any more attention to the dwarf, she began the process of seeing what, if anything, she could do.

His flesh was still warm, so it had not been long. She could see no visible wounds, but the rogue's lips were blue.

Thrinndor stepped in just then, and threw the dart he had found in the hallway onto the prone thief's chest. She looked up and he said, "I found that in the hall. There is a substance on the tip. Probably—"

"Thank you," she said icily. "I will take it from here." When he did not move, she added, "Some privacy, please."

Thrinndor raised his eyebrow but obediently left the room, allowing the door to close behind him.

Cyrillis turned her attention back to Savinhand. She quickly removed her potion bag and withdrew a vial from it. In unaccustomed haste, she removed the protective rag and ripped off the seal. Next she propped him up so that his head and shoulders were in her lap. Then she pried his mouth open and let a small amount of the liquid from the vial trickle in. She massaged his throat to work it into his system. Knowing this potion of poison neutralization would not revive him, it would be necessary to be in him if she were to able find a way to do so.

She lowered his head back to the cold stone and moved to kneel by his side. Placing her hands on his chest, she began to massage his heart as she had been taught to aid those whose heart had stopped. This, she had been told, was necessary in the event the prayer/healing process took longer than expected.

Next she mouthed the words to her most potent healing spell, hoping against hope that it would shock his heart into beating on its own. When that failed, she raised her face to the ceiling, a tear running down her cheek, and prayed out loud: *"Hear me, O Valdaar. Hear the cry of this your humble servant."* All the while, she continued to massage his heart. *"This one's time is not done. He has served you well—albeit mostly unwittingly. We still have need of his services, and he is vital to the path of your return. Hear me O Lord, and return this one to us that we may make those preparations."*

She bowed her head and closed her eyes. Tears now flowed freely down her smudged cheeks. She stopped her work on his chest and held her breath as she opened her eyes.

At first she could discern nothing and feared she had failed. But after a moment, she noticed his pupils narrowing. Then his body wracked in a cough, spewing much of what she had forced into him all over the nearby wall.

At first she was too stunned to move. But her training took over and returned her to herself. She again mouthed the words to her most powerful healing spell. She touched him on the shoulder and released that energy into him. Knowing the poison might still be lurking to destroy the work she had accomplished, she again held the vial to his lips.

"Drink!" she almost shouted the word. "Quickly!"

His eyes focused on her hesitantly, but he took the offered potion and downed it immediately.

"Good," she breathed deeply, not realizing she had been holding her breath for some time now.

When he tried to rise, she said, "No, not yet. Do not move until that potion has worked its wonder. The poison is deep within your system, and we do not want it to get back to your heart before it is neutralized."

He lay back obediently and focused his eyes on hers.

"Thank you," he said, his voice hoarse from the elixir. "I had been greeted by the wraiths of my kindred and they were leading me away when this really big, especially ugly one—"

"Show some respect for he who has enabled your return!" Cyrillis snapped.

"Err," stammered Savinhand, the color returning to his face as it went from very pale right through to crimson. "Sorry, no disrespect intended."

He pushed his way up to his elbows, then climbed shakily to his feet where he tottered unsteadily. Cyrillis put out a hand to steady him. "Still, he—it—should probably work on his—its—charismatic approach," Savin said, his voice getting stronger. "It was in my mind to refuse him, but I found myself unable to do so." He cocked an inquisitive eye at the healer, wet tracks still staining her smudged cheeks.

"*He* is a *God*!" she said as she scrubbed at the moisture on her face. "*Of course* you were unable to refuse him, you idiot!" The look on her face belied anger, however.

Savin turned to face the door as it swung open, but his voice was still directed at her. "Well thank you, all the same."

"I *thought* I heard your voice," said Thrinndor from the open door. He looked past the grinning rogue to Cyrillis. "It would seem I have underestimated your prowess as a priestess." The paladin bowed deeply.

"It was not..." she started, not wanting to take credit for the resurrection, but she was cut off by Savinhand.

"As have I," he said. He threw her a wink with a smile as he also bowed deeply at the waist.

Flustered, she returned, "Lord Valdaar obviously determined you could still be of some use to him." Then with a wink and a smile of her own as she pushed her way past the rogue into the hall, she added, "Though what that could possibly be eludes me!"

"Amen!" snorted the dwarf brusquely. "Now, if our thief is done with his nap, we should push on before I starve to death!" With that, he spun and pushed his way through the door back into the temple.

"Happy to see you, too," muttered Savinhand.

"Well, I for one am glad to see your spirit reunited with its body," said Thrinndor, trying unsuccessfully to hide a grin. "I do not want to be the one to have to discover any further traps!"

"Wow," said Savin, "you can just feel the love in the room! It's almost dripping from the very air!" His grin still worked to take the sting out of his voice. A sudden thought occurred to him, "Wait!" he called after the backs of those in front of him.

Thrinndor turned to look at him inquisitively.

"I think I had better share what I have found before we go any further," said the rogue. The door opened yet again and Vorgath stood there waiting. He held the door open in obvious impatience.

"Found?" said the caster.

"Well," said Savinhand, meekly. "*Found* might be a bit strong of a word..." Vorgath turned to once again start down the steps. "Tracks...lots of tracks...."

"Yes," grumped the dwarf, "that usually goes with lots of orcs!" He took another step, allowing the door to swing shut behind him.

"Not just orcs," said the rogue. "Humans."

There was a pause, and the door opened again, framing a now agitated dwarf. "Humans?" he said. "As in multiple human?"

"Yes," Savin replied. "At least three, possibly more.

"Well," said Sordaak, "there is now one less." He nodded his head in the direction of the closed door behind which lay the dead assassin.

"No," said the thief. "She was a Halfling—I did not count her." He turned and moved toward the intersection and pointed at several of the tracks in the dust. "There, a booted human." He then pointed to the left. "And another here, a different style of boots. See the difference in the heel?" He looked at the paladin, who was staring intently at the indicated marks on the floor for confirmation.

"Yes," said Thrinndor. "I do now."

"Over here," said Savinhand, excited to be showing part of his craft, "still another print. This one with leather footings."

The fighter looked intently at the third print and said, "I believe that could be the print of the first assassin we came across."

The rogue did a double take and said softly, "Nice work! I believe you are correct! I hadn't noticed that, before."

"But," said Cyrillis, who had come up behind them to see what all the fuss was about, "that other assassin was an orc, wasn't it?" She couldn't see even a single track in the dust.

Savinhand looked at her quickly. "Yes, you are correct," he said. "However, it was an orc with leather footings!" Realization came rushing back to him. "I remember noting that as odd at the time, but didn't pursue it."

"Where do all these tracks lead?" asked Vorgath.

"Presumably to another exit," said the big fighter. "If we stick with our earlier conclusion that the wizard escaped…"

"Or went for reinforcements," put in the sorcerer.

"Either way," said Thrinndor, "he more than likely did not go far if he expects to return to relieve us of any bounty we might gather."

"So," mused Cyrillis, "why exactly are we concerned with this group?"

"Food," said Savinhand, simply.

"Say again," said the dwarf, suddenly interested.

"Food," repeated the rogue.

"I heard that part!" snapped the barbarian. "What about food?"

"A group as large as they maintained, at least until you buffoons whittled them down some, must have a supply of food around here, somewhere," said the rogue.

"*Orc food?*" said the paladin. "No thanks!"

"By my count, there are at least three humans," said Savinhand, patiently. "And at least one Halfling." He again indicated the door leading to the assassin. "They had to eat, too."

The idea obviously took hold slowly among the group, but it took hold nonetheless.

Thrinndor looked both ways down the hall and said, "Presumably you can follow the tracks, right?" He got a nod from the thief. "They should lead us right to the cache."

"Or," put in the barbarian, "I can just follow my nose."

Now it was Cyrillis' turn for the eyebrow treatment, "You can *smell* the food at whatever distance?" she said, disbelief obvious in her voice.

"No," admitted the dwarf with a sidelong glance in her direction. "But I can the wine." His face broke into a broad grin. "Both the orcs and the humans like their wine, so there should be plenty."

"Yeah, right!" said the healer.

"Ummm…" said Thrinndor. "In that it would not be wise to doubt him. Where wine is concerned, a bloodhound would surely lose the scent before our diminutive party member would."

Vorgath bowed formally and said, "Thank you."

Thrinndor nodded in return, "My pleasure," a smile playing across his lips.

"Could we *please* get started?" snapped the caster. "One way or the other, let's look for their food, or continue as we were. Either way, let's get a move on!"

Feigning damaged pride, Vorgath obediently stuck his nose out and, with no small exaggeration, sampled the air from both directions. After a second sample, he turned and pointed down the hall to their right. "That way," he said simply, and he started walking down the passage.

Savinhand checked the tracks in the dust and said, "I agree. There is most definitely more traffic in that direction."

Cyrillis rolled her eyes back in her head as she fell in behind the men. "Whatever!" she muttered under her breath. But, she had to admit the prospect of something to eat had its appeal—it seemed like weeks, months—since she had last eaten her fill.

Vorgath stopped at the next intersection and again tested the air down each path ahead of them. He shook his head mutely and continued down the way they had been moving.

At the next branch to their left, he again paused. This time he said, "We're getting close." He moved in the direction of the temple, stopping between the two doors presumably leading to the antechambers.

He made a show of drawing in a deep breath from the direction of each door. He said matter-of-factly, "Wine there," and pointed to the door on his left, "and food there," pointing to the one on the right.

"I thought you couldn't smell the food," said the cleric.

"I can when it's this close," he said, turning his knowing eyes upon her. "Even *you* should be able to smell *that!*"

"I do not—" she started.

"Son-of-a-*bitch*!" Sordaak snapped as he pushed his way past the fighters in front of them. "Can we just get on with it?" He shoved the door open to their right and disappeared inside.

Vorgath shook his head and said, "My, my, aren't we a bit testy!" He made for the door to the left. Then he added to no one in particular, "Lack of drink can do that to a man. I'll just be in here, if anyone needs me." He winked at the healer.

"You just go easy on the wine, old one," teased the paladin, a smirk on his face. "I am certain we are not done with our weapons."

The barbarian stopped short of the door, narrowed his eyes and turned his head to peer at the big fighter. He said slowly, "In the admittedly brief time you have known me, have you *ever* known me to partake of too much wine while still on a mission?"

Thrinndor cocked his head. "No," he said finally. "But I am fairly certain that may have been due in no small part to the fact that the quantity of wine available was in limited supply!"

The dwarf's eyes narrowed further, and then his face broke into a wide grin as he said, "You know, that may well be the case. However, I will ensure you only partake of a glass—or two, at most—since your capacity for the drink is so limited." With that, he pushed his way through the door before more could be said.

Thrinndor shook his head in mock sadness, but his grin gave him away. He turned and followed the caster into the door on the right, still shaking his head.

He soon found that the antechamber had indeed been converted into a makeshift store room. Shelves had been brought in from somewhere, and they were laden with supplies. There must be a regular restocking trip, he reasoned, because there was no way there could be this much food if they had been down here for more than a few days—not with the number of Orcs, humans and whatever they had encountered.

*

Having eaten their fill and replenished their food bags and skins, the companions took a short respite to let their food settle. Afterward, they once again gathered in the hall to continue their assault on the temple.

Their spirits now riding high, they went through the door closest to them into the temple proper.

They descended the steps to the bottom, where they once again gathered around the dais and looked at one another expectantly.

Savinhand cleared his throat and broke the silence. "Well, I still don't see an opening!"

Sordaak replied sharply, "We got distracted by a missing party member." He paused to eye the thief. "Some idjit wandered off."

"Well," retorted the rogue, "I was on my way back to warn you when I got 'distracted' myself!"

"Warn us about what?" said a suddenly interested Thrinndor.

"That we are—or were, I don't know for sure—being watched," said Savinhand, the humor gone from his voice.

"What?" said Vorgath. "How do you know that?"

"Tracks," said the thief, simply. "Lots of tracks. Some fresh—within the past couple of hours, anyway," he added. "I think I found the one responsible for the most recent ones, however…"

"Or, she found you," muttered the dwarf, drawing a cross look from the rogue.

"Be that as it may," said Savinhand sharply, "I took care of that particular issue."

"Whatever," interrupted the caster. "Are there any more?"

Savinhand took in a deep breath before answering. "I don't think so—at least not in the immediate vicinity."

"What makes you think so?" said the paladin.

"Well," the rogue said, pausing to consider, "it's really not much more than a feeling." He held up his hands to forestall what he knew to be forthcoming protests. "However, the only recent tracks I could find matched the assassin who surprised me. It stands to reason the recently departed wiz-weenie would leave behind someone to keep an eye on us, and bring word to him once we've succeeded in entering the vault."

"*If* we succeed in entering the vault," groused the dwarf.

Ignoring him, Sordaak said, "Wiz-weenie?" with an arched eyebrow. Before the rogue could reply, he added, "One sconce yet to turn. I was just coming down to ensure all were ready when I discovered 'all' were not present."

"Yeah, well…" started the rogue.

"Never mind," broke in Sordaak. "Just don't wander off again without letting me know!" His penetrating stare successfully warded off further protest. "Make yourselves ready. I will set this last sconce." He spun on his heel and moved back up the steps.

There was the whisper of metal against metal as weapons were unsheathed or slid from behind leather belts. Thrinndor motioned for the rogue and the barbarian to spread out, and then to Cyrillis to get her to back off a couple of steps behind him.

At last, satisfied each was in position, he turned and nodded to the waiting Sordaak, who turned his attention to the brazier in front of him.

He looked down at the map in his left hand to reassure himself, took a deep breath and reached out with his right hand to grasp the sconce. Twisting it to the right, he was prepared to leap back.

As it moved into what he figured was the correct position, he released it and stepped back. Instinctively, he dropped into a crouch and waited warily.

For…nothing. Nothing happened. He raised back up to his full height, reached up and scratched his head through the cloth of his hat, causing it to bob back and forth in a comical fashion. He looked about confused, allowing his gaze to settle on the group below who were now watching him with interest.

"Well?" said Vorgath, his tone grating.

"Well, what?" snapped Sordaak. "I'm not the moron who pretended to point to north like a compass!" He waved his left arm in exasperation, indicating the direction he had been pointed earlier.

"Pretended?" said the barbarian in a low, menacing voice. "There was no 'pretended.' North is as I indicated. You must have screwed up your 'puzzle!'"

"Horseshit!" bellowed the caster as he waved the map at the recalcitrant dwarf. But before he could go further, reason seemed to sink in, and he brought the map up close to his eyes. "Oh, what the hell, I'll check each sconce again!"

"Thank you," said the paladin, trying to keep the sarcasm out of his voice lest he set the caster on another tirade.

Unable to restrain himself, Vorgath said, "We'll wait here."

Sordaak threw the dwarf a withering stare but said nothing as he stomped his way back to the first sconce he had dealt with. The lack of sleep served to keep his ire close to the surface.

"This one still requires no movement," he muttered under his breath. He moved to the next and reached up to make an almost imperceptible adjustment, moving it back slightly toward vertical.

Again, he stepped back and waited, holding his breath. He released the breath in an expletive. "Shit!" he said as he stomped on to the next.

In this manner he moved around the upper portion of the chamber until there were only two sconces remaining. At the next to last one he peered at the map, then reached up to make a minuscule adjustment to the offending brazier, but stopped. He again held the map up, peering at it. Seeing something he had not seen before, he tilted it so that the light from the brazier hit it at an angle.

"Shit!" he breathed as he again reached out and grasped the brazier. Twisting further to the right, he did not stop until the he had gone past 180 degrees from vertical, and on around another 90.

As he released the sconce and withdrew his hand, there was an audible click followed by a rumble that he could feel through his leather-soled boots.

He stepped back and dropped into his wary crouch, ready to spring in any direction that seemed indicated. "What the—" he said as the others scrambled from where they had seated themselves wearily, hastily readying their weapons.

The rumbling increased in both volume and intensity as Sordaak could feel the floor tremble beneath his feet. He turned at a gasp from the cleric to see what had drawn her attention. She was staring at the cauldron in the center of the chamber.

The dais, it was *rising!* Slowly, almost imperceptibly at first, it began to lift free of the floor. The whole damn thing! Rising to reveal...what?

Before he could wrap his mind around what was happening, there was yet another sound.

A whisper—a whisper that should not have been audible over the rumble of the rising dais, yet it was. Voices—he heard voices in the whispers...

"Wraiths!" shouted Cyrillis. "Ward yourselves!"

Sordaak shouted his new favorite word, "Shit!" and bounded down the steps two at a time to get closer to the group—but not *too* close, readying a spell as he went.

Chapter Fourteen

Puzzles

Sordaak loosed a magic dart at the nearest wraith. The creature was bobbing and weaving all over the place, and he thought it was a damn good thing those darts unerringly hit what he aimed for, because there was no way he could track one long enough for any other attack.

The creature wailed even louder (at least it *seemed* like it did), and made a bee-line for the caster. "Yikes!" he shouted as he ducked, dropped to the floor and rolled to his right. He loosed another set of darts at the same wraith as he surged back to his feet. He knew from experience that he was harming the creature, but his eyes could discern no damage.

The wraith came at him again, but his third set of darts caught it on the way in and there was a faint pop. The wraith dissipated into thin air before it got to the mage.

Vorgath was flailing away at a wraith that was buzzing around his head to no avail. "Hold still, damn you!" he shouted as it darted just out of range of his greataxe yet again.

Anticipating the creature's next move, he finally made contact, but the blade of his greataxe passed right through, doing no damage that he could see. "What the—" he shouted as the wraith danced close enough for the monster to put its ghostlike hands on him. Vorgath felt a shiver run through him at its touch.

"Silver or ghost touch weapons only," shouted Thrinndor, who was busy with a wraith of his own. Actually, he seemed to have attracted the attention of two of the creatures. *Lucky me*, he thought as he brought his greatsword to bear again.

"Damn!" shouted the barbarian. "That would have been good information a couple of minutes ago," he added as he dropped his axe to the floor and hastily drew a shortsword from some hidden place on his body. Having only one such weapon, he also reached over his shoulder and whipped his shield around so he could make use of it.

Changing weapons took just a blink of the eye. Just as quickly he was looking around for the offending creature. "Come get me now, you little ghost fart!" He needn't have asked as he felt the chill touch of the undead from behind. The barbarian whirled, whipping his new blade in a vicious arc that passed right though the wraith. He knew he scored, however, when its wail went up a notch.

He smiled broadly as he set his feet to do real battle. "Now we're cookin'," he said as he again slashed at the creature when it got close enough.

Thrinndor had issues of his own. While his greatsword was silver, it was unwieldy against the darting wraiths. That two of them were focused on him didn't help matters. He felt their icy touch several times, and that that was starting to affect his ability to thrust and parry before he finally managed to kill one of them.

Cyrillis was having no problem keeping the two whose attention she had somehow snagged at bay with her staff. However, that same staff was also too cumbersome to be effective against the fleet creatures. She contented herself with a defensive posture for now, which also allowed her to keep tabs on the health of the rest of the party.

Seeing the barbarian and the paladin weakened by the chill touch damage these creatures inflicted, she abruptly changed tactics. Cyrillis threw up her hands and shouted "Be gone!" This allowed her to throw her given undead turning abilities into her voice. While she doubted her abilities were sufficient to turn these wraiths, she just needed to affect them and give them pause while she tended to the others.

It worked. While they were indeed not turned, they were knocked back by the ferocity of her command. This gave her ample time to sling a restorative spell at Thrinndor and Vorgath. Savinhand, she could not see. She made the quick assumption that his dexterity would serve him well here. Sordaak was ducking and dodging still another of the creatures and appeared undamaged. So she turned her attention back to the two that had targeted her. Cyrillis hoped someone would come to her aid quickly. Her arms were tiring of whirling her staff in defense.

Having dispatched the lone wraith that had been bothering him, Vorgath saw her plight and bellowed to get his rage up, then he charged in. "Leave our healer alone!" His shout again caused the creatures to pause. With the wraiths already weakened by the attempts to turn them by the cleric, it required only a single blow from his blade to send one of them back to the netherworld. Cyrillis took out the other with a thrust from her staff while it was distracted with the dwarf.

"Thank you," she panted as she used the staff for support while she regained some modicum of strength.

Enraged, the barbarian appeared not to have heard her. Instead, he ran off in search of something else to fight.

She stared at his receding figure mutely, shook her head and turned her attention to more pressing matters. Finding the rogue was utmost on her mind.

But try as she might, she could not locate him. A quick glance showed the barbarian, caster and paladin had the wraith situation well in hand and the few remaining offending creatures would soon be sent back from whence they came. It was apparent they would not need her ministrations any time soon.

So she moved to look at the pillar that had risen from the floor, taking the burning cauldron with it. Assuming Savinhand had gone this way, she circled the pillar, looking for the entrance—stairs, ladder, *anything* to allow her into the chamber below.

Having circled it twice, she looked up perplexed as her companions joined her. Thrinndor immediately noticed her concern and said, "What is wrong, sister?"

Cyrillis looked his way, but her gaze seemed to pass right through him. It was obvious her mind was elsewhere. She turned to look back at the stone on which the cauldron sat. "I cannot find an opening," she said quietly. "And Savinhand is missing, again."

"Huh?" asked a weary Vorgath. "Now where did that damn rogue wander off to this time?"

Hearing the strain in his voice, Cyrillis absentmindedly tossed another restorative spell his way without turning away from the pillar.

The dwarf sounded better when he said, "If he has wandered off again, I am going to break him in half with—"

"Who?" said the rogue, who was suddenly standing next to the barbarian.

If Vorgath was startled, he didn't show it. Instead, he turned his head slowly to face Savinhand. "You, you marble-headed moron!" His tone was low and menacing.

Savinhand hastily took a step back.

"You know, one day you are going to do that to the wrong person. You *may* live to regret it," Sordaak said with his eyebrow arched way up.

"May," agreed the dwarf.

"Hey now," stuttered the rogue. "No need to get nasty!" He took another step back, giving him room to move quickly should the need arise.

He continued in his best placating voice. "If I caused any consternation, I apologize. It wasn't my intent."

Attempting to defuse the situation, Cyrillis interrupted. "Where were you?"

Quickly seizing on the distraction, Savinhand answered, "I had no weapons that could harm them." His wary eyes never left the dwarf. "So I thought I would go into stealth mode and see if I could figure out where the wraiths came from."

"Well?" asked Thrinndor.

Startled, the rogue looked at the big fighter. "Huh?"

The paladin rolled his eyes in exasperation. "Did you find where they came from?"

"They did not come from under there," said Cyrillis. She pointed at the solid marble pillar supporting the cauldron.

"The doors," said the rogue. "They came through the doors."

"I never saw any doors move," said Sordaak.

"No," said the rogue patiently. "They came *through* the doors!"

The cleric explained. "Wraiths do not require doors as we do." Her tone was almost reverent. "They can pass right through even some stone walls."

"OK," said Sordaak. "That part I'll go along with. But the question becomes: Where did they come from if not from underneath the dais?" Before anyone could answer he added, "Why now, and not before?"

The paladin and the cleric looked at one another and shrugged simultaneously. "That we may never know," he said. Thrinndor turned to grin at Vorgath. "Unless 'Wraith Slayer' here left any alive for us to question?"

"Alive?" The dwarf turned a deep red. "They were never alive—"

"Yes they were!" Cyrillis interrupted. Several pairs of eyes turned to look at her. "It may have been long ago, but those were wraiths of living, breathing *beings* at one time! They were imprisoned here among the living by some—"

"What*ever!*" bellowed the dwarf. "If you wanted me to keep one of those…" His stare bored into the cleric, and the barbarian waved his arms to emphasis his point, "…*alive*, then you are outta your *holier-than-thou* minds!" His eyes darted back and forth between the healer and the paladin.

Obviously worked up, he was breathing hard. "I mean," he went on after a brief pause, "number one: How do you capture a *wraith*?" Seeing no answer was immediately forthcoming, he raged on. "Number two: You obviously were not 'touched' by one of those critters bec—"

"I was," interrupted the paladin.

"As was I," said Cyrillis.

"Me, too," said the rogue.

"Missed me," said Sordaak. "But that is because I have been 'touched' by them before, and I made damn sure they didn't get close enough to do so this time!"

Vorgath's eyes were bulging. He looked from one to the other. "Whatever!" he shouted again. "If you wanted one *alive*, YOU should have captured one! Their touch chilled me to my very bones, and I wanted no part of them!" He glared at each, daring them to argue further.

Thrinndor cleared his throat uncomfortably and said, "Well, I doubt it possible to actually 'capture' a wraith. And, if one was captured, it does not seem likely they could be made to divulge any secrets." He smiled broadly. "I merely wanted to jerk your chain a bit."

Vorgath, at a loss for words, flushed an even deeper hue of red. Sordaak took a step back. But, slowly the red lessened and a smile appeared on the dwarf's face.

"You know," Vorgath said, "it's a damn good thing I like you."

Sordaak snorted as he pushed his way past them on his way to the pedestal. "If you guys are finished with your little love-fest, we still have work to do!"

"Work?" Vorgath made a face. "Who's he talking to?"

"Certainly not you, Old one," said the paladin, the grin still on his face. "You have never worked a day in your life!"

"Ha!" retorted the dwarf. "I could define the word for you, draw you a picture you still wouldn't get it!"

Thrinndor made as if to reply, but Sordaak cut in. "Ladies, please!" His eyes darted back and forth between the two and his tone left no doubt he'd had enough banter. "Could we *please* get on with what we came down here for?" His voice was almost pleading. "I have a sinking feeling that we will soon have visitors."

"Feeling?" said Savinhand, sarcasm exuding from his tone. "What kind of feeling? It certainly wasn't from that monkey on your shoulder!" The caster turned slowly to face him. "I mean, a little notice on those wraiths would have been nice!"

Fahlred, perched lithely on Sordaak's shoulder, bowed its neck and made a noise that sounded a lot like a hiss. The mage's face turned red, and he opened his mouth for a reply, but he never got it out.

The quasit winked out of existence and reappeared on Savin's back, its long tail whipping instantly around his neck.

Savin's eyes began to immediately bulge and his hands shot up to try to wrench the tail free. It looked to be a battle he was not going to win.

"*Enough!*" Cyrillis' voice rang with command. "*Stop this, NOW!*"

Fahlred looked up from his precarious hold on the rogue's back and loosed his tail ever so slightly.

"I just facilitated his return to life, and I will not have that undone!" Her inflection was scathing and left no room for options.

The quasit released its hold, disappeared and then reappeared on Sordaak's shoulder, winding its tail, delicately this time, around the caster's neck. He crouched behind Sordaak's head, trying in vain to avoid the penetrating stare of the angry healer.

Savinhand dropped to his knees, his chest heaving as he tried to pull air into his starved lungs. He turned to peer hatefully at the offending creature, but any thought of vengeance was immediately snuffed out by the continuing rant of the healer.

"Each one of you listen, and listen *good!*" she began. "This petty bickering and infighting ends *NOW!*" She glared at each of them. "It wastes both time and valuable resources, neither of which do we have in abundance! We are all on the same *team*. Each one of us has one—some more than one—specific purpose that is valuable to the team. You do not have to like one another, but, so help me Valdaar, you *do* have to work together. You *will* respect one another and accord to each that respect as is due." Now *she* was breathing heavy.

All eyes were either on the incensed healer or staring at their feet. That was the case with Vorgath, who was certain he saw something worthy of his attention down there, as he was pushing that something around with a toe.

"Am I clear enough?" she barked. "Do you understand?" She drew each word out as if speaking to schoolchildren. "Or do I need to draw you a picture? Because I most certainly will!" Again, her angry stare pinned each of them to some imaginary wall. She held her gaze on them one at a time until she had the acknowledgment she wanted.

Finally she got a nod of the head from the barbarian, who had regrettably cheated a look at the healer during the prolonged silence. "Good. Just see that you do!"

Into the cavernous silence that followed, Cyrillis decided to try to lighten it up some. "Listen, I know we have been down here a long time—me longer than you, allow me to remind you—and I know this journey has been arduous." She took in a deep breath before continuing. "But our goal is *in sight*. We must not lose sight of that now." She again looked at each of them. "We are *so close*! I can feel it! Surely you can, as well."

Silence again hung over the party like a dark cloud until Thrinndor cleared his throat. "Cyrillis makes a good point." His tone was both stern and light as he tried to get the group working as one. "The end is indeed close at hand—I too feel it. We must stick together, for I also feel the toughest part of this quest is yet to come."

Sordaak's head snapped around, his attention suddenly riveted on the paladin. "What is it you sense?" He had learned to trust the instincts of this big fighter.

Thrinndor cocked his head slightly to the right, almost as if testing the air around him. His mien was thoughtful. He sighed loudly and said, "I know not." He held up a hand to forestall the objections he knew to be coming. "However, there is something out there—something that was awakened by our arrival." No one said anything. "Something that either does not like our presence or does not like being awakened."

"Or both," said Savinhand lightly. "Whatever!" He looked from the caster to the paladin. "Either we whup this something's ass, or it whoops ours. Standing around here talking about it ain't gonna get it done!"

Thrinndor stared at the rogue, his right eyebrow almost hidden under his shock of dark hair. After a moment he chuckled and said, "I believe our light-fingered friend is correct." He shook his head as he again laughed softly. "I doubt we will ever be more ready or…" He stole a quick glance at the healer. "…more healthy than in our current state."

Sordaak looked from one to the other and said, "Very well. Now all we have to do is figure out just where it is this something is that needs its ass whupped!"

All eyes turned to the caster and waited.

It took a minute for the mage to realize they were waiting on him for something. "What?" he said.

His voice laden with sarcasm, Vorgath spoke what each was thinking. "You're the one with the maps."

"Dude!" said an exasperated mage. "I got us *this* far!" His reproachful glare went from one to another. "Like I told you before, that's it! You've seen all I've got. I have *no more!*"

Thrinndor's eyebrow practically did a back flip, but he remained silent.

"*WHAT?*" yelled the caster, aware all were openly staring at him now.

"*Dude?*" said the paladin, a half smile twisting his lips.

"Huh?" said the caster, confusion evident on his face. Then, realizing what he had said, he added, "Oh, that." Now it was his turn for the half-smile. "My therapist says that she believes I occasionally channel beings from another time, or perhaps another dimension."

Now it was Savinhand's turn for eyebrow acrobatics. "Therapist?"

"Yeah, well," began the mage. "Occasionally those of us of superior intellect—"

"But—" interrupted Vorgath.

"Zip it, meat shield!" snapped the caster. He glared at the dwarf, whose mouth worked open and closed a couple of times, but nothing came out. "That's better," he said smugly. "Now, where was I? Oh, yes—those of us of superior intellect occasionally require discussion with professional concerning incidents in our past. There might also be discussions to discover why it is I…" He cleared his throat, "I mean we, sometimes like burning things a bit too much…" His face was deep crimson.

"Or maybe 'shoving lighting bolts' in inappropriate places?" interjected Thrinndor.

"If the need arises," Sordaak said icily. He waited to see if there was further comment. "If we are through delving into my personal matters, perhaps we can get back to what we are here for before the end of time?"

"But—" began Savinhand.

"No," interrupted the paladin. "Sordaak is correct. We must get moving. We have delayed far too long." He looked thoughtfully at the doors to the chamber. "I fear that sorcerer, with a host of other unseemly denizens, will soon return." Everyone turned to look at the doors, as well. "I also fear he will not be so easily defeated this second time around."

"Gotcha," said the rogue, his tone more somber than his words. "So, what's next then?"

"Well," said Thrinndor, turning back to face the cauldron now being supported by the column of granite, "first we find the entrance to the chamber beneath." He moved to the stone edifice and began studying it without waiting for a response from the others.

"But, I've..." said the thief. "Aw, never mind!" He turned his back on the group, and began ascending the steps to one of the doors. The others were too busy searching the granite for an opening to notice his departure. He pushed the door open and stopped abruptly. "Hmmm," he said. "That's interesting." He stepped through.

A quick search confirmed his suspicions. He spun quickly and pushed the door back open and called to the rest of the group. "Hey," he said, concern showing plainly in his voice. "Come take a look at this." He now had everyone's attention. "It doesn't make any sense," he said as he motioned for them to come and see what he'd found.

"What doesn't?" snapped the caster.

"Our footprints are gone." He received only blank stares. "Just come take a look, dammit!"

Vorgath was the first to start up the steps. "Just as well," he said. "There ain't nothing to find down here."

The rest fell in step behind the dwarf as he ascended the steps. They all picked up the pace once they started moving in anticipation of...something.

When Sordaak reached the open door, he looked around quickly. "What? I don't see anything."

"That's because you're not looking," said Savinhand. "That and you don't know what to look for."

The caster started to say something, but Thrinndor spoke before he had the chance. "I see what you are talking about," he said, puzzlement tainting his voice. "Were we not here a short time ago?"

"Yes," said the rogue. "Through this door I had my encounter with the assassin." He looked down the passage to the antechamber doors. "But, I don't believe we'll find her behind that door—which is where we left her."

"Nor I," said the paladin. "Look at the dust on the floor—it has not been disturbed for centuries."

"Are you sure this is the correct door?" said a bewildered Sordaak. "You must be mistaken."

Savinhand looked back down at the cauldron, glanced left and right. "No, this is the door. Of that I'm certain."

"Then," said the caster as he pushed his way past the rogue, "you must be mistaken about the footprints. Some dust must have settled during all that rattling around when the cauldron was raised." He reached the antechamber door and pushed it open. After a moment he stepped back into the hall, a puzzled look on his face. "She's not here," he said as he looked up and down the hallway.

"Maybe her companions came to claim her," said Cyrillis, although her tone said she did not believe that to be true.

There was the hiss of metal against leather as weapons were drawn or otherwise made ready.

"No," said Savinhand, still scouring the floor with a practiced eye. "No one has set foot on this floor in many, *many* years."

"Then you *must* be mistaken on the door," said the mage irritably.

"For the last time," snapped the rogue, "*that* is the door we re-entered the temple through!"

"OK, OK," said the mage. "Then…Hell, I don't know what is *then*!"

"Perhaps," said Vorgath, "the cauldron didn't rise." He paused when the others turned to stare at him. "Perhaps the temple descended."

"Preposterous!" said the caster.

"That's not possible," agreed Savinhand.

"Yes, it is," said Thrinndor. "I have seen similar mechanisms—although admittedly on a much smaller scale."

"It *would* require some considerable engineering, but it is most definitely possible," said the dwarf. "My kindred have been building such devices for thousands of years. But…not on such a grand scale. Not to my knowledge anyway!"

"You guys have been hitting the humus pipe a little hard, don't you think?" said Sordaak.

"Well," said Vorgath, "you're going to have to come around to this sooner or later, because it's the only explanation that makes sense."

While the mage was still trying to wrap his brain around that bit of information, Thrinndor said, "It matters not, I suppose." Sordaak looked at the paladin, not sure what was coming next. "We have been unable to find a way out of the temple, and," he waved his hand at the undisturbed dust on the floor, "we have obviously not been this way. So, I say we proceed with caution."

The big fighter started down the hallway toward the intersection, knowing the others would follow. Sordaak shrugged and fell into his place in line.

Thrinndor added, "The presence I detected earlier is assuredly closer."

Fahlred hissed as if he agreed.

The paladin paused at the intersection. He looked first to his right, then to the left. He stepped confidently down the hall to the right, the others warily following.

"I have a question," said the rogue as they marched along. "How do we get back out of here?"

Sordaak looked at Savinhand, the wheels in his mind obviously turning. "Well," he said, "I doubt we can raise the temple back up—*if* indeed it descended—so it won't be that way." After some further thought, he added, "There has to be another way in here, one must assume. Right?"

"I sure as the Seven Hells hope so," said Vorgath from up front.

In silence they continued their march. The passage was identical to the one they had recently followed that led them to the temple. The walls were lit as before with sconces at regular intervals. And the same intersecting branch hallways that led first to the antechambers and then the temple. Only the thick layer of dust on the floor and a dank, moist odor told them they were not where they had been.

The passage bent almost imperceptibly around to the right, forming the same circular path around the temple. However, after passing one of the branch hallways to their right they could see another intersection ahead—this one to the *left*.

When they got to the intersection, Thrinndor waited for the others to approach. He pointed down the new passage. "I believe we have arrived at our destination."

"Finally," said Sordaak, peering down the new hallway.

He did not have to look far. Perhaps twenty feet down that hall was a set of doors that took up the entire breadth of the hall and from floor to ceiling, as well.

The doors appeared to be made of the purest of gold.

They were inscribed and etched on their entire surface. They were also incredibly beautiful.

On the walls just prior to the doors were two ornate sconces, also apparently made of gold. The flickering light from them played across the golden surface of the doors in an almost hypnotic pattern.

Sordaak sucked in an incredulous breath and whispered "Wow!" It was a sentiment they all seemed to share, as no one else said anything for a moment that seemed to stretch on for an eternity.

Finally, Savinhand snapped the reverie by turning back to the group. He said, "Am I going out on a limb here by saying that it is probably a good assumption that these are going to be trapped?"

Sordaak shook free of the trance placed on him by the doors. "I think you can count on that." He turned back to gaze at the doors. "Probably more than one."

Savinhand, who had started warily toward the doors, stopped and slowly turned to face the caster, "Gee, thanks, boss. You sure know how to ease any apprehensions I might have been harboring!"

"Just be careful," said the mage. "I wouldn't want to see those doors damaged in any way!" A half smile appeared on his lips.

The rogue turned back toward the doors. He removed his tool pouch from its accustomed place and went over the doors in small sections, nodding to himself occasionally. Finally, without turning, he said, "You are correct. I find three traps, each progressively more difficult to detect." He paused as he selected a couple of items from his pouch. "There is something else here. Something I have not seen before." He craned his neck to peer over his shoulder at the caster. "I believe it is an enchanted trap—that one I will leave to you."

"Gee, thanks," mocked the mage. "You get your nasties taken care of first and I'll come take a look."

"Got it," said Savinhand. "A couple of these are going to test my skills—"

"Oh, shit!" said the dwarf. "I'm moving back into this other hall, then!"

The thief gave a pained look. "That's confidence-building," he said. He smiled at the others still standing there. "That's actually not a bad idea."

"Moving," said the paladin.

"You don't have to warn me twice," said Sordaak as he disappeared around the corner. "I'm suddenly reminded of that nickname you were saddled with…"

"Ha-ha!" said the rogue. "Very funny!"

"What nickname would that be?" asked the paladin.

"Thumbs," said the caster with a wink.

"Thumbs?" said the barbarian. "As in 'all thumbs'?" He shook his head. "Let me just move a bit further down this passage."

"Comedians!" snorted Savinhand. "You all missed your calling. I hear there is an opening for 'Court Jester' at the palace!"

Cyrillis was feeling a bit left out. "Just focus on your work, please. I doubt my lord would be as understanding a second time around."

"There's the confidence-builder I was looking for," said the rogue as he turned back to the doors.

No one else said anything, so he concentrated on his work. Off and on he muttered good-naturedly under his breath.

Soon he was sweating profusely. The cool dank air was suddenly less cool. He paused to wipe his hands frequently on his tunic.

After what seemed an interminable time, Vorgath said, "Are we there yet?"

"No," snapped Savinhand. "Don't rush me. The technician who put these here was *very* good." He cocked an eyebrow and muttered under his breath. "Maybe *too* good!"

He finished tying off a piece of thin wire and anchored it to a pin he had driven into the frame of the door for the purpose. "That's two," he said for the benefit of the audience. "Now," he said quietly, "it's this third one that has me worried!"

Savin took in a deep breath, wiped his hands yet again and reached for the trigger mechanism only he would have been able to detect. That was when he noted his hand shaking ever so slightly.

The rogue pulled his hand back and allowed both hands to drop to his sides. He then closed his eyes and raised his face toward the stone ceiling above. He took in several deep breaths, the pause between each longer as he went.

Finally, he put his hand out for inspection and held it still. After verifying it no longer shook, he moved back in to resume his work.

"Well?" said the dwarf.

Savin appeared not to hear as he grasped the mechanism with the index finger and thumb of his left hand. Next he inserted a small appliance selected for the purpose into the almost imperceptible gap revealed with his right. As he released his grip, he realized he had been holding his breath. He let it out noisily.

Next he selected another tool and applied pressure to his wedged item, ensuring it did not wiggle free. He stepped back gingerly and stood upright.

Walking to the intersection, he located Sordaak and said simply, "Your turn." He continued down the hall to the left, crouched down on his haunches, rested his head against cool wall behind him and allowed himself a sigh of relief.

Sordaak moved into the vacated hallway and glanced over the doors briefly. "Where did you see this anomaly?"

Without opening his eyes or moving, Savin said, "Right door, just to the left of the handle. You will see a smudge."

The mage looked in the directed area. After a second—and a third—look he finally saw what the rogue had seen. "Got it," said the caster. He moved his face closer still to get a better look.

Unable to figure out what he was looking at, he leaned closer to get his nose as close as he dared and sniffed at it. There! He could detect the faintest scent of bat guano—very old bat guano. However, he had not heard whether there was a shelf life on the stuff.

"That woulda hurt," he muttered to himself. He slung his vial pouch from his shoulder, slipped the leather thong off of the opening and rummaged through the contents of the bag. Finally selecting one that looked identical to every other vial in the pouch, he retied the thong and slung the pouch back in place.

Next he removed the seal, pried out the cork and held it up to his nose for verification. Satisfied, he placed a finger over the opening and inverted the bottle, then righted it. He pulled his finger away, inspected the substance on his finger, and decided it was not sufficient for the task. He repeated the process until the end of his finger was damp and a droplet of the solution threatened to roll off.

He took in a deep breath and reached out with the finger slowly. He had to keep rolling his hand back-and-forth so the droplet did not fall off. As the liquid came in contact with the smudge on the door, there was a faint sizzling sound and a light vapor wafted up and away from his finger.

He allowed his shoulders to relax as he stepped back. Not satisfied, he repeated the process. He got a second, smaller reaction for his efforts.

Satisfied, he again stepped back. He threw a quick, cursory glance at the doors but saw nothing else of note.

"OK," he said, relief obvious in his voice. "That should take care of it."

"Finally!" said the dwarf, who moved toward the doors.

"Wait!" said Savinhand

Vorgath stopped mid-step and snapped, "Now what?"

"Better let me take one more look," the rogue said.

The barbarian rolled his eyes but obediently stepped aside and made a sweeping bow with his left hand and arm. "By all means!" he griped. "After all, it's not like we are going to starve to death anytime soon!" He reached into the sack tied at his belt and removed a piece of stale bread and chomped at it. "However," he said around a mouthful, spitting crumbs as he spoke, "I would like to get out of here *before* arthritis sets in!"

Now Savinhand made the sweeping gesture. "By all means," he said, "go right ahead." He turned and headed back the way he had come, "I'll just wait back here while you open the doors."

"Oh, all right," stammered the dwarf. "I apologize! Sheesh! Just get on with it."

Savinhand raised an eyebrow, but did not move.

"Please," growled the barbarian. "Dammit!"

"Well," said the rogue, a smile touching his eyes, "since you asked so nicely." He moved back toward the doors, brushing past the dwarf as he did.

Again Savin turned his full attention to the doors. He searched for several minutes but was unable to find anything else of concern. "OK," he said. "That's it. You were right." He threw the dwarf a huge smile.

With a huff, the dwarf stomped his way down the hall.

"Wait," said the caster, meekly.

"Aw, come on!" bellowed the dwarf. "What could you possibly want now?"

"Ummm…Well, I have one more thing I'd like to try…just in case." Vorgath's eyes were bulging. "It won't take but a minute."

The dwarf angrily stepped aside, leaned against the wall and folded his arms. "Get on with it, then," he growled.

"Thank you," said the caster as he again approached the doors. "I just want to see if there is any more magic we might have missed."

As he got to the doors he spoke a few arcane words and waved his arms in such a manner that he encompassed all of both doors with a single motion.

There was a brief sound like very faint wind chimes and both doors started to glow a very faint blue.

"I was afraid of that," said the caster.

"What?" said the dwarf.

"Well," said Sordaak, sotto-voice, "there *is* still magic here, but it doesn't appear to be anything specific. Perhaps something to do with the doors themselves."

"Great!" said the dwarf. "Now what?"

"Well," said Savinhand, "I believe all that is remaining is for me to unlock them." He stepped back up to the doors. He then said under his breath, "That is, assuming they are locked…" He looked over the mechanism once again. At last he stepped back and said, "Nope, not locked—why? I haven't a clue, but… well, we are back to you opening the doors, I'm afraid." He stepped back to make room—again with the sweeping motion.

Vorgath started to make an angry reply but clamped his mouth shut instead and marched up to the doors. "'Bout damn time," he groused as he reached up to the door, grasped the ornate pull-ring and heaved.

The door moved easily, to his surprise. In fact, both doors opened fully at once with a sound of air rushing past them, as if the chamber beyond had been in some sort of a vacuum.

Chapter Fifteen

Chamber of Summoning

Vorgath released the pull-ring and said, "Ugh-oh," as he stepped back into the hallway to ready his weapon.

A deep, booming voice filled the hallway before they could advance. This voice was far different from those previous. "Fools! You have chosen to ignore the warnings given you." The words resonated and reverberated clear through to the spines of each party member. "Very well, enter if you must, for there is no turning back now." There was a sound that sounded almost like a snicker as the booming voice continued. "Your wraiths are hereby condemned to haunt this keep for the next thousand years!"

Sordaak rolled his eyes and cringed, expecting the inevitable laughter. But it never came.

"What?" he said. "That's it? That's all you've got?" He raised an eyebrow, still expecting more theatrics. "Come on, gentlemen—and ladies!" He turned to bow formally to Cyrillis. "Our treasure awaits!"

"I think we know where the wraiths came from," mumbled Savin with a shake of his head.

"You're damn ri—" said Vorgath as he strode purposefully into the chamber beyond the doors. He didn't get far before he stopped mid-step; his entire body, weapons and all, had been turned to stone!

"What the—" said Sordaak, his head spinning from side to side, looking for an assailant.

Thrinndor rushed in and immediately stepped to his left, sword and shield in hand. He too was looking for something to swing at.

Savinhand did his disappearing act and vanished.

Cyrillis did a quick once-over on Vorgath, keeping a wary eye out for anything that might come her direction. "He yet lives, but I know not how to help him."

"Spell," Sordaak said quickly. "Flesh-to-stone." His eyes scanned the chamber for a source of whatever cast the spell on the barbarian. "I can take care of it, but I would sure like to know where that spell came from."

He removed a component from the small pouch tied to his wrist, intoned a brief incantation and waved his hand in the direction of the dwarf. Vorgath's stony appearance melted back to flesh.

"—ght," continued the barbarian. He stopped, bewildered for a moment. "What in the Seven Hells was that?" he asked. He shook his head to remove the feeling that something was terribly wrong.

"Spell," the paladin said with a smirk on his face. "You were briefly more hard-headed than usual."

"Huh?" said the barbarian.

"Skin-to-stone," said the caster, worried. "Someone—something—zapped you and turned you to stone."

Realization came to the dwarf in a rush. He growled from deep in his chest. "Show yourself!" he shouted as he glared around the chamber. "Throw any more of that wiggle-finger shit at me and I'll send you back to meet your maker!"

"Or un-maker," whispered the caster.

"Whatever!"

When nothing immediately happened, Sordaak straightened from his crouch and took time to inspect the chamber.

It was large. But not near as large as the temple they had left so recently, perhaps forty or fifty feet across. The shape was unusual, but he couldn't pin down exactly what made it unusual. Five sides! "Shit!" he whispered, loudly. "Pentagonal! The chamber is pentagonal!"

"So?" snapped the dwarf, who nevertheless did not move any deeper into the room.

"It's a chamber of summoning!" said Cyrillis, fear just below the cresting point in her voice. She too was whispering.

"Summoning what?" said the barbarian, shivers suddenly running up and down his spine.

"Good question," intoned the paladin, lowering his sword and shield somewhat, but keeping them at the ready.

Cyrillis looked around quickly. "Where is Savin?"

"Don't you worry your pretty head about him," said Sordaak, still bewildered by the lack of an assault. "He will make himself available should the need arise." He too lowered his guard, but his senses were on high alert. "What you need to worry about is where that damn spell came from!"

The chamber was indeed in the shape of a pentagram, with the companions coming through the only set of doors in its base. Like the passages they had just come from and the temple above, the room was already well lit. Burning braziers lined the walls, and a smaller cauldron threw light from a heat-less flame in the center of the floor.

The cauldron was also shaped in the form of a pentagram. There were stone benches—black, like the walls, floor and ceiling—placed in symmetric order out from the flaming cauldron.

"Where's the treasure?" said the barbarian.

"I don't think we're done with the tests," Sordaak answered.

"Tests?" Thrinndor's right eyebrow made the trek up his forehead.

"What tests?" snapped the dwarf.

"Remember the song of the old man—"

"Parothenticas," said Cyrillis

"Whatever," said the caster, who continued as if he had not been interrupted. "His song mentioned several tests, the final of which will daunt even the most stalwart."

"You never sang or recited for us the song," reminded the paladin.

"I didn't? Well, for good reason: You don't want to hear me sing."

"You could recite the words."

"Not *now!*"

"You don't think we've passed all these tests?" asked the barbarian.

"No," replied the caster. "I'm now certain there is at least one more." His eyes traveled over the walls again. "Possibly more…"

Thrinndor's eyebrow twitched and climbed further up his forehead. "Do you yet withhold information that may prove useful?"

"NO!" snapped the caster. "I just feel this has been all too easy thus far. There *has* to be more!"

"Too *easy?*" said the dwarf.

"Yes," retorted the mage. "While we have had to deal with wraiths, orcs, a giant squid and other sundry undesirables, that does not explain why no one has been this far—at least not in many centuries." His tone left no doubt. "After all, we all yet live."

"Oh," the healer said acidly. "So that is it." Her penetrating stare fixed the caster uncomfortably. "One—or more—of us must die to accomplish this task?"

"No, no," replied Sordaak hastily. "That's *not* it." He thought for a moment. "It's just that this temple and the treasure chamber herein—"

"Assuming there *is* a treasure," grumbled the barbarian.

"There is," snapped the mage. "Trust me." He held up his hands to forestall any objections to that remark. "You saw the undisturbed dust with your own eyes, didn't you?" It was his turn to fix a harsh stare elsewhere.

Vorgath remained silent as Sordaak continued. "There can have been no others to this point. The treasure remains."

"All right," said the dwarf. "Where is it?"

The caster rolled his eyes. "I told you. We have not completed the tests."

"Again," said the paladin, "what tests?"

"I don't *know*," said the caster, exasperated. "If I did I would tell you!" He looked around at his companions. "Right now I just wish I knew what—or who—stoned our diminutive friend here."

"It might have been still another trap," said the rogue. He appeared at Sordaak's elbow.

"I told you," began the mage, his heart pounding ferociously in his chest. "Oh, hell, never mind!"

"What do you mean *another* trap?" said the dwarf, who took a step toward the thief menacingly.

Savinhand held up both hands. "Inside the doors," he said hastily.

Sordaak added, "That might explain the magic energy I detected prior to our entry."

Vorgath stopped in his tracks, raised an eyebrow of his own and allowed his gaze to go from one to the other. "All right, then," he growled, his attention back on the mage. "What's next?"

"Well," said the caster, his eyes making another trip around the chamber, "wherever it is we are going, it's through this chamber." His eyes stopped on the paladin. "I say we need to investigate further."

He started to push past the paladin, but Thrinndor held out his arm to stop him. Without a word, the paladin stepped into the aisle and started down the steps.

"All right," said the mage, "battle formation." He got no arguments from the others as they took up their positions. He turned to speak with Savinhand, but the rogue had already disappeared. "Damn him," he muttered.

One step at a time the big fighter descended toward the cauldron, stopping at each to wait. Vorgath was behind him and slightly to his right.

When Thrinndor came off of the last step and his foot touched the floor of the chamber the voice returned. "You are indeed a persistent bunch. Very well, my servant will entertain you until I get there!" With that, the flames exploded in the cauldron and they appeared to writhe and grow before their eyes.

Whatever it was grew until it was more than half-again as tall as the paladin. A pair of malevolent eyes opened near what must be its head and a huge mouth split open to reveal a nasty pair of yellow fangs!

"Shit!" shouted the caster. "Fire elemental!" He turned to Cyrillis. "Fire resistance for the fighters—hurry!" He loosed a volley of his magic darts in an attempt to distract it while the cleric did her thing.

The darts flew straight and true and the beast was indeed influenced. The elemental turned and hurled a ball of fire in the direction of the offending caster. Sordaak had been ready for that; he dropped to the ground and rolled hard to his right to escape the brunt of the blast he knew to be coming. Behind him he could hear Cyrillis hurriedly placing the requested Resist Fire spells on both Vorgath and Thrinndor.

The ball erupted behind Sordaak, sending a blast of fire that singed his robe and burned the hairs off of his legs below the knees. "Better yet," he shouted as he rolled a second time, "resists all around, please!"

He quickly readied a second spell. This time he had more up his sleeve than the hastily fired dart. When his incantation ended, he pointed an index his finger at the raging monster and a cone-shaped blast of frozen particles emanated from his fingertip, catching the creature square in what the caster hoped was its chest.

It howled in both rage and pain as it unleashed yet another ball of fire at the caster. This time Sordaak was not so lucky. The ball detonated not an arm's length away. Although the healer's fire resistance spell absorbed some of the energy, the resulting blast knocked him backward. He tripped over the bench behind him, hitting his head on the way down. He sprawled onto the floor behind the bench and did not move, his robe smoldering in several places.

"Caster down!" shouted Thrinndor. He had witnessed the events while swapping out his recently acquired flaming sword for his two-hander, a feat that required him also to shed his shield. He knew the flamer would be little or no use against the elemental.

Vorgath was under no such restraints, but he needed to step around and to the right of the paladin, who had followed the pre-arranged step to his left while switching weapons. He released one of his blood-curdling battle cries as he charged past. As a result of his extra steps, both he and the paladin struck at the same time.

Their weapons made a strange hiss as they made "contact." Only because the creature howled in what the paladin hoped was pain did he know they had done damage. That and the living ball of fire's attention turned to the barbarian.

Seeing this, Thrinndor stepped further to his left, trying to get behind the monster where he figured it would be more vulnerable. Hoped…

Cyrillis ran to check on the caster. She found his hands and face were bright red and already beginning to blister. She brushed her hands across the most damaged areas while mouthing the words to her most potent spell of healing. The results were immediate, but the caster remained unconscious. Seeing the knot on the back of his head, she pieced together what had happened. She followed the heal spell with a restorative one, but Sordaak remained unresponsive. Knowing he yet lived and that she could do no more for him while the battle raged, she stood to check on the status of the others.

Vorgath still had the attention of the monster. As he hacked again with his greataxe, he felt a fiery blast as the creature reached out and slapped him with an extremity. The barbarian's face blistered and the ends of his beard began to smoke. He bellowed in rage again and swung his weapon in a great arc. However the creature had obviously learned the sting of that particular weapon and deftly twisted its torso such that the blade missed.

Now in place behind and to the left of the elemental, Thrinndor cut lose with a slash of his own that passed through the main body of the creature. The elemental screamed again and whirled to take on the paladin.

Savinhand materialized next to the fighter—also behind the creature—and unleashed an attack with weapons in both hands, both hitting their mark.

Howling continuously, the beast unleashed a ball of fire at close range that exploded instantaneously, encompassing both the rogue and the paladin, knocking them back a step.

The resist spell again absorbed some of the energy, but not all. The creature made a huge, sweeping arc with one of its arms. Flames and the force of the blow caught both Thrinndor and the thief unprepared.

Savinhand screamed in pain as he leapt back, his leather armor blackened and with serious burns to his face, hands and arms. Most of the damage was superficial, yet painful.

Vorgath recovered from his over-swing, leapt up onto the cauldron and waded in, swinging hard and fast at the unprotected back of the monster.

Thrinndor ignored the pain of his wounds and leaned into a thrust with all of his might. He felt his blade hit home this time, but he was unable to determine what exactly he hit and if any damage had been done.

All three of the men were swinging away and if the increased screaming by the elemental was any indication, they were definitely doing some damage. Savinhand darted left and right in an attempt to stay behind the creature and thus out of arm's length, his blades slashing mercilessly at the unprotected flank of the elemental.

Cyrillis tried to assess the damage to her friends as best she could from a distance, but she quickly decided that all three of them were taking damage—too damn much damage—and threw her healing energy first to one, then another as quickly as she could get the spells off. That was not the most efficient way of doing things, but she hadn't time to consider efficiency as she worked.

Again the beast released a close-in ball of fire that detonated instantly, this time catching the paladin and the barbarian within the ball of flame. Both were knocked back, but Thrinndor managed to twist his body in a way that the back of his right shoulder deflected the majority of the energy, protecting his hands and face.

Now the braided ends of Vorgath's beard were on fire, but he seemed not to notice as he surged forward, flailing away with his greataxe in yet another blow that seemed to rock the elemental to its core.

The monster swept its arm again, this time knocking the paladin from his feet, and also succeeded in pushing the dwarf back a couple of steps. Both were badly burned. Cyrillis was doing her best, pouring spells into them as fast as she could. She discovered that she could speed up the process if she alternated between her spells and using the power of the staff. This tactic, however, was rapidly depleting her reserves. She deemed there was no help for it. The lives of the entire party were held in the balance by her ability to keep the three men on their feet.

Knowing he was badly hurt, Thrinndor used his lay-on-hands healing ability on himself; the dwarf was far too distant for the paladin to be able to help him. He had to assume the cleric would keep his friend alive. He knew that if they did not vanquish this elemental soon, none of them would survive.

Indeed, seeing the paladin heal himself, Cyrillis concentrated her efforts on the barbarian. She prayed silently that Thrinndor's efforts would be enough to keep him alive, because Vorgath was taking enormous amounts of damage.

Savinhand again slashed with both blades and the beast whirled on him, knocking him from his feet with a single swipe of a monstrous arm. The rogue crashed to the ground behind a bench and lay still. Satisfied it had dealt with that threat, the elemental turned again to the pesky dwarf who had connected with a painful blow on its flank.

Just as the elemental stepped forward for an all-out attack on the dwarf, there was a whisper from across the room. A cone of frozen energy hit the creature in the side. There was a hiss as the energies collided.

The elemental raised a final wail to the ceiling and vanished.

Cyrillis quickly verified the mage, dwarf and paladin were not needing of her immediate attention and rushed to where the rogue had fallen.

Upon reaching Savinhand, a quick check showed that he was still breathing but was badly hurt. His face and hands were charred to the point the smell made her sick to her stomach. She forced the bile down and brushed her hands gently across his face and hands while pouring her healing energy into the crumpled figure lying on the floor.

The effects were immediate and his skin regained some of its color. Next she removed a container from her bag and opened it. She rubbed the salve it contained onto the areas damaged most and nodded as the restorative effect took place as she watched.

Savinhand's eyes fluttered weakly open, and he did his best to smile. He had to work had to regain some moisture in his mouth. "It seems," he finally managed to croak out, "I am again indebted to you."

"Lie still," she instructed. "I must go attend to the others." She smiled in return. "I deem you will yet live."

"Thank you," he said as he obligingly laid his head back onto the cold stone. When she had walked away, however, he struggled first to a sitting position and groaned as he climbed to his feet.

Vorgath was patting distractedly at his still smoldering beard. "Damn!" he cursed. "Son of a dragon bitch! I've worked nearly a hundred years on this beard!"

"If that is all you have to complain about," the healer admonished as she checked him over, "then you should be grateful!"

"I am grateful," he said. "Did I not sound so?" He smiled at the cleric. "To have survived the wrath of a fire elemental, I feel *truly* grateful!"

"That was no ordinary fire elemental," said Thrinndor, who was sitting on the bench closest the dais. His face was bright red and devoid of facial hair.

"That I would tend to believe," agreed Vorgath as he continued to inspect his beard.

"Huh?" queried Savinhand as he hobbled over to join the others.

"I have some experience with elementals," said Thrinndor. "That one was indeed special—much more powerful than any I have dealt with!"

"Yeah, well, it's he—or it—that is certainly the worse for wear for the encounter!" said the barbarian. Noticing the paladin's appearance for the first time, he said, "You are certainly no longer a 'pretty-boy!'" He smiled as best he could.

"What?" said the paladin as he wearily put his hands to his face. He brushed away the ashes that were the remnants of his eyebrows. "That is not even funny, o ancient one!" But he too smiled.

"You two," chastised the healer, clucking her tongue in her best mother-hen fashion. "I do not know whether to give you aid or let you stew in your own suffering!" She looked from one to the other. "Lucky for both of you it goes against my training to allow suffering!"

She applied some of the cream first to the paladin as he seemed in the most pain and then moved over to do the same for the barbarian. Their pain quickly diminished. She also applied a little of her remaining healing to each, and soon both were back on their feet.

Sordaak moved to join them, rubbing absently at the nasty bump on the back of his head.

"Nice timing on that icy blast," said Thrinndor. "I don't think we would have survived another of that elemental's fireballs."

Before Sordaak could reply, the disembodied voice spoke again. "I see that you have dispatched my servant." This time, however, there was a figure to go with the voice! They all surged to their feet at once, bringing their weapons to bear.

"I have little or no spell energy remaining!" Cyrillis shouted as she dropped into a defensive posture with her staff. "Beware!"

"Me, either!" groaned the caster, who dodged to his right. "You meat shields are on your own!"

The figure stood in the center of the extinguished cauldron. It was the figure of a human—a very old human. More accurately, the specter of a very old human. "Put down your weapons," the figure said tiredly. "I do not have the energy to do battle with you. I am Dragma." There was a sharp intake of breath from both Cyrillis and Thrinndor. "You have passed the tests, and I deem you worthy."

Silence pervaded the host for a long moment.

"Was it necessary to try to kill us to pass these tests?" snapped Sordaak.

"Yes," replied the specter. "Any lesser beings would not have proved themselves worthy." He said it as if that should end all discussion.

"Yeah, but—"

"Silence!" Dragma shouted. "I am not summoned here to quarrel with you!" A fierce stare from the specter silenced further objections from the caster. "Rather, I have waited for more than a thousand years for this moment." He paused, and seemed to lean even more heavily onto the staff he gripped in his right hand. "I can finally pass on what was given to me to hold and protect."

With that, there was a rumble in the floor, and the cauldron slowly started to rise.

"Not again!" moaned the rogue.

However, this time there was an opening underneath—an opening that revealed a winding staircase that led into a lit passage below.

"This is not the end of your journeys, however," Dragma continued.

"What?" said Vorgath. "There's more?"

"Be silent. My time is ending, and I will not be able to remain with you much longer." His voice indeed got weaker with each word. "The treasure is surely here. My scrolls, my jewels, coin uncounted for millennia as well as a few other items to help you in your search—all await you below."

"Then what—" blurted out Cyrillis, but Dragma silenced her with a wave of his free hand.

"The sword," said Thrinndor resolutely, his shoulders sagging.

"Correct, my son," said the specter, weakly. "*Valdaar's Fist* was taken, along with my staff…"

"Damn!" muttered the caster.

"…long, long ago," continued the wraith. "Even before I built this fortress. They were stolen by forces that have remained a mystery to me, even over these many years."

Silence held the companions still while Dragma gathered the effort to continue. "Not long after the battle that saw our Lord slain, we were betrayed by some of his followers who thought that with the reign of Valdaar over, they could split the remaining treasure."

With another pause, the specter before them was fading. He would surely not last much longer. "They made off with sword, my staff and *Kurril*—which I see has been found. That is good." He bowed his head, raising it again with no small effort. "We searched in vain for centuries for them all. If they were not together, then…"

"This much I do know, they remain in this plane—they cannot be removed from it." He turned to face Thrinndor. "You must continue the search," he said, pulling strength from somewhere. "*You* must find both *Valdaar's Fist* and *Pendromar,* for you are the only remaining survivor of the line of our lord." Cyrillis gasped and looked at Thrinndor with confusion in her eyes. Suddenly she dropped to her knees before the paladin and bowed her head.

"Do not," said Thrinndor.

"Allow me to finish," said the specter. "Trust in your senses young man, they will lead you to the blade. Only with it *and* the two staves can our Lord be returned to this plane. Only through you will that be possible."

He turned his attention to Sordaak. "You must aid him, my son, if you are to wield my staff." Dragma's image was now barely visible. "Now, go quickly." His voice was scarcely above a whisper. "He who searched for this chamber in vain returns. He will try to take what is not meant for him."

After a time, they were sure Dragma had passed from their presence. "You must not let him!" Again the specter of the ancient sorcerer appeared stronger. "However, he is very powerful and has brought with him a large host. He means not to be denied again!" The image faded, flickering in and out for a few moments. "There is another exit—a one-way portal. You will find it below when you are ready. It will return you to the surface, but I fear this one is aware of where it will lead and set a trap for you there. Rest below to regain your strength. While he will try, he cannot gain access to this place. But you must depart when you are able.

"Beware!"

Dragma's specter faded for the final time, leaving the party staring at one another in stunned silence.

"Well," said the barbarian, "that's a downer."

"Cyrillis," Thrinndor said gently as he stooped to grasp her arm, "stand. Do not prostrate yourself so."

"My lord," she said.

"Valdaar's blood does indeed run in my veins," said Thrinndor. "However, I have earned nothing, so please rise. When I have found *Valdaar's Fist* and returned our lord to his rightful place among us, then perhaps some humility might be warranted. Until then…"

"Very well," she said as she regained her feet.

"Can we FINALLY see what we have been fighting for?" pleaded the dwarf.

"I believe that is warranted," said Thrinndor. He followed the dwarf as he headed for the stairs beneath the dais.

"Wait!" said Sordaak. Everyone turned to look at the caster whose face was a mask of puzzlement. "Kin of a God?" he said. "That throws a new twist on things, don't you think?"

"No," said the paladin. "I have suspected for some time—although only now have my suspicions been realized." He again started for the stairs. "This changes nothing."

"Well," said the mage, "it does for me! This will take some digesting."

"Not for me," said Vorgath gruffly as he started down the steps. "Still just a pretty boy human!"

"Silence, peon!" snapped the paladin in his best commanding tone at the back of the rapidly receding dwarf.

"Whatever!" boomed Vorgath. His voice echoed off of the walls before reaching those that remained above.

Chapter Sixteen

Treasure

Vorgath wound his way down the circular stairs. Dank, musty air wafted up from below, obviously air from an area long uninhabited.

At the bottom he found a landing with a passage that led off to what he knew to be north. He paused there, waiting for the others to join him before venturing further, recent events forcing him to err on the side of caution, something he was most certainly not accustomed to.

The passage was well lit. The barbarian briefly wondered how the sconces stayed lit for *centuries*, but he let it pass. The promise of gold, silver, gems and loot in general distracted him *almost* to the point when nothing else mattered. Almost.

He waited. "Could we maybe speed it up a bit?" he asked of those still on the stairs.

"Aw," said a disembodied voice—Sordaak's—from somewhere up out of sight. "Don't get your undies in a bunch! The treasure is not going anywhere!"

A rumbling started from deep in Vorgath's chest and grew to the point that it was audible to Thrinndor, second off of the staircase. However, the dwarf said nothing. Somehow, he knew it wouldn't help.

Finally, when Cyrillis, last on the steps, was but three or four steps from the bottom, Vorgath could wait no more. He stomped off down the hallway, Savinhand right behind him.

"My, my," said the caster, shaking his head. "A bit impatient, aren't we?"

Thrinndor stole a sideways glance at his rapidly receding friend and said, "You do not want to get between a dwarf and gold." At the mage's raised eyebrow, he added, "It would not be pretty."

"No it wouldn't," snapped the barbarian as he rounded a corner, taking him out of their sight.

"Shall we go see what all of this fuss is about?" asked the paladin, sweeping his arm in a gesture for Sordaak to precede him.

"Yes, let's," replied the caster. A smile played briefly across his lips as he trudged leisurely down the hall in pursuit. He wanted desperately to run, but did not want to give the dwarf the satisfaction of seeing him in any sort of hurry.

As the sorcerer rounded the bend in the hall, he saw the dwarf up ahead standing at the entrance to a small chamber.

As he moved up behind the dwarf, he could make out more of the room beyond. It was roughly circular in shape, perhaps twenty-five or thirty feet in diameter. The lit sconces were spaced evenly around the circumference, providing ample lighting for what the chamber contained.

What the chamber contained was three chests—one very large one with two of lesser size on either side. Chests made from the finest of lacquered woods and trimmed in gold and silver. The scroll work on each of them was exquisite.

Seeing the others approach, Vorgath started into the room but was held back by a single word from the rogue. "Wait."

The barbarian's head rotated slowly on his shoulders until his eyes met those of the thief. "You can't possibly believe these are trapped?" The barbarian's voice left no doubt what he thought of the idea.

"I don't," said Savin with a shrug. Vorgath started to turn away, but Savin wasn't done. "But I wouldn't bet *my* life on it." Crimson started climbing up the dwarf's neck. "However," continued the rogue, bowing and making the now standard sweeping gesture with his left arm, "you go right ahead!"

A hush settled over the room as the remaining party members held their breath, waiting for the inevitable explosion to come.

"Get on with it then!" growled the barbarian, biting off each word menacingly.

Savinhand stood upright and allowed an eyebrow to minutely inch its way up his forehead. He had expected some theatrics, as well. "Well," he said, "if you insist!"

When the barbarian just glowered at him, Savinhand shrugged and sauntered slowly over to the chest on the left.

The others gathered at the entrance—a discreet distance—and whispered among themselves while the rogue worked.

The first chest, Savin noted, was a smallish one, probably set aside for jewels of some sort. He had to shake his head to shove aside the visions of jewels that popped into his mind, returning his attention to the task at hand.

Curious, he mused, that this chest doesn't even appear to be locked! Scratching his head idly, he moved past the large chest in the middle to the other smallish one on the right.

This chest was slightly larger than the previously inspected version, but otherwise identical. It too did not appear to have a locking mechanism.

Finally, he moved over to stand before the large chest in the middle. It had been crafted of similar materials and was made to match the other two, but it was several times their size. More than six feet in length, three feet across and at least four feet in depth it was large enough for…

What? Puzzled, he could think of nothing large enough that would require a chest of this size.

This one *was* locked, however. A large, ornate padlock hung from a just as ornate hasp.

He moved in for a closer look when he felt his blood turn cold. Out of the corner of his eye he saw the makings of a rudimentary trap.

A sharp intake of breath accompanied the required closer inspection. Not only was the trap rudimentary, Savin was certain it was *meant* to be found!

His blood dropped another couple of degrees. That meant the trap was just a decoy! He immediately started to sweat. "Uh oh," he muttered loud enough for the others to hear.

"What?" asked Sordaak. "What have you found?"

The rogue did not even glance their way. He began circling the chest, looking for other clues as he moved. "The two smaller chests are not trapped—or even locked." He continued to search while talking. "But this one…this one is most definitely locked, and now I've found a trap. So far just the one."

"Can you remove it?" growled the barbarian.

"Of course," said Savinhand as he got back to inspecting the only trap he had found. "But that's not the problem. The problem is that this trap is *easy*! Much too easy! I could have found and disabled it blindfolded!"

"So?" said Vorgath.

"*Nothing* to this point has been this easy!" said the rogue. He was still eyeing both ends of the wire. He turned to peer at the obvious indicators he had seen, his mind grasping at possibilities. "It makes no sense," he mused. "It's as if whoever placed it here *wants* it to be found."

"OK," said the mage, his mind also grinding over the possibilities and probabilities. "Agreed, that does make no sense." His brow furrowed in thought. "What if there is a trap on the trap?"

"That also crossed my mind," said the thief. "But I don't see anything that would indicate that." His eyes once again traced both ends of the wire.

"Well," grumbled the dwarf, "can you disable it, or not?"

"Again, of course I can disable it," snapped a clearly agitated Savinhand. "It's just—"

"Get on with it then!" said the barbarian.

"You're starting to annoy me, little—" said the rogue with a sidelong glance.

"You're starting to annoy *me*," Vorgath interrupted. "And I would not recommend that as a normally healthy course of action. Either disable it, or get... out...of...the...way!"

The barbarian took a step and was about to brush past the rogue, but Savinhand held up a hand to stop him. "Very well," he said with an exaggerated sigh. "But I would give me some room!"

Vorgath allowed himself to be stopped. He glared at the rogue and repeated, "Get on with it, then!" He turned and stumped back toward the stairs, the others moving back with him.

Savinhand retrieved his tools from their pouch and went through the process of selecting what he would need.

As he reached for the trip wire, he was annoyed to find that he was again sweating despite the cool, dank air in the chamber. Seeing his hands shake he dropped them to his side, closed his eyes and took in a slow, deep breath. He held it for a few heartbeats and let it back out even slower.

"Before we die of old age!" griped the dwarf.

Savin ignored him and went about the task in front of him. Calm now, he quickly secured the wire and inspected the rest of the mechanism. Finding nothing out of the ordinary, he turned his attention to the padlock.

It was *old!* Ancient, even. He had seen locks such as this back in his training sessions but never since. He shrugged and selected the proper pick from his pouch. In quick order the lock too was disabled. He removed it and put it in one of his many pouches—he wanted to be able to show the lock to his guild-mates.

Next, he lifted the hasp, placed his hands apart on the lid and set his feet to lift. It *looked* heavy, but he needn't have bothered. The lid lifted easily and noiselessly on unseen hinges.

When he got it to about half open, Savin heard the footsteps of his companions coming up behind him and he leaned forward to peer inside. There was a *poof* that accompanied a bright flash of light that momentarily blinded him. There was also a voice that sounded like it came from inside the chest that said, "Gotcha!"

He released the lid and jerked his hands back, expecting it to drop closed. However it stayed where it was, held up by some unseen mechanism. Savinhand stumbled back, his hands going to his eyes to rub them.

"Son of a *BITCH!*"

"Ha, ha," snickered the dwarf as he stepped past the now blind rogue see what was inside the chest.

"My ears!" chided Cyrillis as she too moved in for inspection.

More interested in the smaller chests, Sordaak moved initially to the one on the right and lifted its lid. He snorted in disappointment as his eyes befell the gleam of coins. A lot of coins, of course, but not what he was looking for.

So he moved to the other small chest and likewise lifted its lid. The glittering from within informed him he had probably found the fabled Dragma jewels. Still not what he was after. He allowed the lid to once again shut as he stepped up to the large chest in the middle to see what the others were *oohing* and *aahing* about.

A quick glance inside was all he needed to spot it: A smallish box, lacquered in deep ebony and its entire visible surface covered in runes was tucked neatly in the back corner opposite him. A chest within a chest.

"Yes!" he hissed as he ducked his head back out of the opening and quickly circled around behind the chest to get to where he could reach the lacquered box.

As his hands reached hungrily for it, a command from the cleric stopped him. "Not so fast, sparky!"

His hands hovered over the box while his livid stare sought out the owner of the voice that stopped him. "What?" he spat through clenched teeth.

"How do you know those scrolls are those that you seek?" Cyrillis said evenly. "And not those of Angra-Khan?"

"How do you know they're scrolls?" asked a perplexed Savinhand, his vision beginning to return.

"What?" Sordaak repeated, distracted by the two of them. He glanced down at the box. "The *runes,* you idiot!" he snapped at the rogue. He then turned his look of contempt on the healer. "Same goes for you, chick! Do these runes look like anything your precious Holy Man would dream up?"

"What?" Cyrillis said, taken aback by his vehemence.

"Chick?" said Thrinndor, attempting to defuse the situation. His right burnt-off eyebrow sprinted for his hairline.

Sordaak blinked hard several times as his eyes regained focus. He turned a confused look on the paladin. "What?" he asked.

"Chick?" repeated the big fighter. "You called her 'chick.'"

"More 'channeling'?" asked the dwarf, amusement plain on his face.

The mage shook his head as of to clear it of cobwebs and his focus returned. "Whatever," he muttered, his hands again reaching for the box. This time no one tried to stop him.

"You obviously need some quality time with that 'therapist' of yours," said the rogue, peering into the cavernous chest to see what—if anything—it held for him. Tears still ran freely from his eyes from the effects of the flash-bang.

"What's this?" asked a suddenly distracted dwarf. The barbarian was standing on the tips of his toes so he could also see inside. Roughly, he shoved aside the thief and reached greedily into the interior, his eyes gleaming in anticipation.

"Hey!" said Savinhand as he stumbled to his right. "I was…" seeing his words were having no effect, he turned his attention to the smaller chests that were being ignored by the others. "Never mind!" he said under his breath as he opened the lid to the one containing the Jewels of Dragma. "Hello, there," he breathed as his gaze became transfixed on the opulence. "I've been looking all over for *you*!"

Vorgath grunted as he had to work against both weight and leverage to withdraw what he had seen: a greataxe, one such as he had never seen before. And by the gods, it was *heavy*!

Seeing his friend struggle with getting the weapon over the edge of the chest, Thrinndor smiled and said, "Need help there, old one?"

But so complete was Vorgath's attention held by what he had in his hands that he neither heard nor responded.

The haft was made of metal, not wood. That was something he had rarely seen and certainly never managed to get his hands on. There were eldritch runes up and down the length of the shaft. But the runes appeared not to have been etched or carved into it, rather *forged* there! Impossible! Yet, try as he might—and he had considerable lore in the art of the metal craft associated with weaponry—he could discern no other explanation for what he held.

As fascinating as the haft was, it did not long hold his attention. The blade.... oh *the blade*! As he beheld it for the first time, the beauty of it caused tears to form in his eyes. First of all, it was *enormous*! The blade was half again as large as his current greataxe. And sharp? Its edge glistened as it caught light from the sconces—an edge that promised lethality with its very existence. The blade also was covered in runes, both sides. Elaborate runes that confounded his understanding, which also baffled him. He was no novice to the eldritch runes that enchanted most weapons. Yet he could not read these.

But, this greataxe was *nothing* like other weapons. It appeared to be new! No chips in the edge, no scratches marred its surface and no wear showed in the grip. Yet here his lore did not fail him, for he could read the metal and see that it was *old*! Far older than any weapon he had ever held or beheld. This blade was old a millennia ago!

The precise alloy evaded him—it was not one used in his or his father's lifetime. Probably not in his father's father's, either. Hints of adamantine *and* mithryl glinted back at him, but neither was the majority. Strange…

By the gods, it was *heavy*! And *big*! The haft alone was nearly as long as he was tall! The blade nearly as broad as his ample shoulders! There was no way he was going to be able to…Yet, when he wrapped his hands—gingerly at first—around the grip, the blade seemed to leap with….joy?

He stepped back to gain clearance and gave it a test whirl. The blade arced through the air with a resounding *whoosh*, easily. He swung it again. Very little effort on his part resulted in parries and thrusts he'd only dreamed about during his training.

Vorgath's mien was locked in deep concentration, sweat glistened on his brow, and a smile of pure satisfaction was plastered on his face as he brought the blade to a halt inches from his own eyes, as if to inspect its edge.

"Whoa," said a stunned Savinhand.

Only then did Vorgath look past the blade to the sudden realization that everyone in the chamber was staring at him, jaws agape in astonishment.

"What?" he rasped out between deep breaths, more from excitement than exertion.

The companions were silent for a moment. Typically, Thrinndor was first to recover. "That was an interesting display of swordsmanship," he said, obviously downplaying what they had just witnessed.

"*Interesting?*" said Cyrillis, not so willing to let what she had just witnessed pass. "I have *never* seen an axe of that size move with such blazing speed and alacrity!" She turned her gaze from the paladin to the dwarf. "That was *amazing!*" she added. "Does it have a name?"

"*Flinthgoor,*" Vorgath said without hesitation, "*Foe-Cleaver and Death-Dealer!*" A puzzled look briefly flashed across his face as he realized he had spoken the name without thinking.

"*Flinthgoor?*" said Sordaak, joining the conversation at last. "The Axe of Valdaar's General of Armies?" He snorted. "Impossible! That blade was destroyed by his foes after the final conflict! I have read the manuscripts that describe that in great detail!"

Vorgath's face turned crimson as he made to reply, but Thrinndor beat him to it. "The manuscripts are apparently wrong," he said. When the mage took a sharp breath in to retort, the paladin added, "Look here," he took two steps forward and pointed at the runes on the side of the blade that was visible to him. "It clearly reads: *Flinthgoor, Foe-cleaver and Death-dealer.*" His index finger traced the runes that arced across the top of the blade.

"Impossible!" repeated the caster. However, now his tone was clouded with doubt and a little awe.

The dwarf took a menacing step toward Sordaak, quickly bringing the blade to the ready position. "Maybe a quick test to prove or disprove it?"

"Try it, midget!" snapped the caster as he waved his arms, obviously readying a spell.

"Cease!" commanded Cyrillis. To Vorgath, she shouted, "Back off! You will have adequate opportunity to prove what you believe to be true shortly enough if the words of Lord Dragma come to pass!"

She whirled on the caster next, her tone scathing. "I too have read of the destruction of the Lord General's Axe. But it is not prudent to discount the words of a Paladin—especially one who is a descendant of Valdaar!"

Her ire quickly evaporated as she turned back to face the barbarian. "*Flinthgoor?* Can it be sooth?" Tears came to her eyes as the possibilities rushed to her head.

Silence pervaded the room while she came to grips with what was going on around her. "*Flinthgoor,*" she breathed. She then looked to the staff cradled in her hands. "*Kurril,*" she added reverently. The tears welled in her eyes as she turned to face Thrinndor. "And a descendent of our Lord…"

Wide-eyed, the cleric took a stumbling step back. Her companions watched in concern as she abruptly sat down, crossed her legs, buried her face in her hands and placed it between her knees.

When she looked up, tears were making small rivulets down her smudged cheeks. "It is true then," she said, her voice barely audible to her friends who had gathered around her and looked on in concern. "The time of our Lord's return is nigh…"

"Huh?" said a bewildered Savinhand.

Thrinndor cast a sidelong look at the rogue, his emotions held in check. "Have you not been listening?" he said. "According to what was written concerning Valdaar's last days, he knew that he was going to fall—it was inevitable." His visage fell upon that of the cleric, still supine on the floor. "However, he vowed that should he fall, he would once again return when the time was right."

Cyrillis finished for him, both of their countenances brightening with each word. "But first his Instruments of Power must be found and gathered together—for a purpose that has not been made known to us…"

"Yet," said the paladin, grinning openly now. "I am certain we will find that purpose when we have the instruments in hand." He paused. "*Kurril* and *Flinthgoor* are now in our possession." His voice faltered as he looked longingly at the chest. "*Valdaar's Fist* and *Pendromar* are yet to be found."

"We will find them!" announced Cyrillis, certainty resonating in her voice. "Dragma said they are still in this Plane—we *will* find them!" Silently she gathered herself and regained her feet. She then went to stand before Thrinndor and looked deep into his eyes. "We *will find them!*" she said softly.

The big fighter nodded, and mirroring the passion in the cleric's tone said, "Yes we *will.*"

He then turned to allow his gaze to take in the rest of the group. "But first," he said, "we must conclude *this* quest!"

"Right," said the Vorgath. "I believe that old man—"

"Dragma," interrupted Cyrillis helpfully.

"Whatever," replied the barbarian, his voice gruff as the emotion of the room seemed to settle in his heart as well. "I believe he promised us more action!" At the groan from the rogue, he added, "And I believe pretty boy over there needs that action as he is trailing in the kill count by two!"

"Really?" said the paladin thoughtfully, his eyes clouding as he searched his memory, obviously counting.

"Ahem," said Savinhand, clearing his throat noisily. Both fighters turned to look at him expectantly. "One," he said simply, looking from one to the other.

Vorgath started to protest, but Savin raised a hand to silence him. "You lead by one!" Then he turned and started going through the chest with the coins in it, thereby dismissing further protests.

The barbarian glowered at his back but did not argue.

"You must have been counting that poor, unconscious orc you beheaded back there," the paladin said. The hint of a teasing grin played across his lips.

"Bah!" snapped the dwarf, but his manner became thoughtful. "Well, maybe I did, at that!" Stubbornness returned to his voice quickly, however. "It matters not! It only takes one to win the day!"

"The 'day' is not yet over," said Sordaak, breaking the reverie. When both the paladin and the barbarian turned to look, he said simply. "The caster?" At the blank stares he got, he threw his hands up in exasperation. "We are not finished, yet! The caster and his army of orcs stand between us and town."

"I said that already!" agreed the dwarf. "I was merely pointing out that I was in *the lead* by two—"

"One."

Vorgath threw the thief a hairy eye. "All right, already! *One* kill." His glowering stare went from Sordaak to Thrinndor, daring either to disagree.

Thrinndor threw up both hands and backed away. "Hey, the count was not in contention as far as I was concerned." He winked at the dwarf while pointing a knowing finger at the rogue.

"You know," Savinhand started, "working with you two characters could give any self-respecting rogue a serious case of heartburn!"

"It's a good thing you are not 'self-respecting'!" said Vorgath.

"Ha-ha," replied Savinhand. "Just wait until you get my bill for keeping track of your little wager!"

Thrinndor raised an eyebrow. But Vorgath had a bit more for him. "Yeah, well that should offset my bill for keeping you alive!"

"I guess I'll get a refund on *that* bill!" Savin said smugly.

Thrinndor chuckled, but Vorgath came right back. "Hey, if you're dimwitted enough to go wandering off—"

"Ladies, ladies!" Sordaak had finally heard enough. "Can we *please* get on with the matter at hand so we can get some rest?"

The dwarf shifted his attention to the caster. "This *is* rest!"

Savinhand shook his head as he went back to counting the coins. "I ought to have my head examined!" he muttered. He then turned his gaze on the mage. "Is this therapist of yours available for those of us suffering mental anguish outside of your guild?" His lips pursed in a half-smile.

"You couldn't afford her!" Sordaak said quickly.

Savinhand, who had again turned back to the chest, said, "I can now!" The gleam of coin was in his eyes. "Wait!" he twisted back around to face the caster. "*Her*? Just what exactly is this *therapy* she offers?"

"Huh?" said the caster. Then, catching the meaning, his face turned a bright red and he said hastily. "Not *that* kind, you mental midget!"

"Hey!" said the dwarf, mock indignation in his voice.

Sordaak glared at the barbarian and bit back a sharp reply. "Oh, shut up!" he said, finally.

The sorcerer glared at each of them but studiously avoided looking in the direction of the cleric with his face still red. She was looking his direction, though, mild curiosity in her eyes. "I give up!" snapped the mage. He spun on his heel, picked up the lacquered scroll box and stepped around the chest containing the jewels. He made his way to where the walls circled behind the chests and plopped down unceremoniously to the floor.

"Just set what's mine aside and wake me when you've rested." The spellcaster glowered at them from beneath his singed eyebrows, hoping someone else would say something.

When no one did, he sat the box in his lap and said, "Until then, do *not* disturb me!" Again he glowered at his companions. "I have some scrolls to study!" With that, he opened the lid on the box and peered inside.

Cyrillis stared in his direction, obviously trying to decide whether to attend to the disgruntled mage or let him be.

Seeing the look, Savinhand laughed and said, "Don't worry about him, sister. He just hasn't had his coffee in like….five or six days!" He continued to chuckle as he deftly separated the coins into equal piles, shaking his head as he did.

Sighing, she decided to let the matter drop. Cyrillis instead turned her attention to the remaining chest, the one with the jewels.

"Holy shit!" All eyes turned to where caster was seated. "*It can't be!*" Sordaak pulled a thick book from a drawer in the bottom of the chest.

"What?" Thrinndor was first to ask.

The magicuser looked up, wonder open on his face. He held the book up for all to see. "This is Dragma's spell book."

"So?" Vorgath demanded, the fingers of his right hand gripping an emerald larger than a goose egg.

So happy was the sorcerer, he refused to rise to the bait. "Dragma's spell book will contain every spell he ever knew, and possibly even some he was working on!"

Even the barbarian understood what that could mean, at least to another magicuser. "Nice."

"Yes, nice," Sordaak whispered as he held the book tightly to his chest and scrunched his eyes shut.

In this manner, the companions sorted through the three chests. The bounty was placed into a pile in the middle of the floor for each of them check and see if use could be made of a particular item.

Savinhand got a pouch with what he said were special thieves tools, his share of the coins—a mixture of platinum, gold, silver and even a few coppers and a few of the gems.

Vorgath only took the greataxe, his share of the coins and a few gems. He only had eyes for *Flinthgoor*.

Thrinndor found a shield that he said he was certain was part of the original armor of Valdaar's set. It was deep black in color, but not glossy. In fact, it appeared to absorb all light, giving nothing in return. Not even the light of the sconces reflected from its surface. He took that and his share of the coins and gems.

Cyrillis found nothing that would be of use to her, saying the return of her staff and armor was adequate reward for her. She continued to eye the Dragma Jewels, however, as she placed her share of the coins and gems in a pouch.

After each had stored his or her share of the bounty, they gathered again in the middle of the room—all except for Sordaak, who continued to study Dragma's spell book in the back of the chamber.

They gathered around the chest containing Dragma's Jewels. That chest now stood open and the opulence within glittered and glistened in the light of the sconces.

Savinhand removed each piece delicately, as if he feared to damage whichever piece he held. He laid it out on a sheet of soft, black cloth that had also been in the chest. A necklace—amulet, really—festooned with gems up and down the chain. A pair of bracers, also adorned with runes and gems. And a ring with a massive central ruby, surrounded by diamonds, each large enough to support a ring of their own. The ring was almost garish.

An uncomfortable period passed as each of them stared at the jewels. It was Savinhand who finally spoke, voicing what each of them was thinking. "How do we split these up?" his eyes reflected with avarice what was spread before him.

Again silence hung in the air. After a slow deliberate intake of breath, Cyrillis answered. "We do not."

Vorgath looked at her as if she had lost her senses. "Huh? Come again, sister?"

She looked at him, defiance working its way into delicate features. Her voice more resolute this time, she said, "Correction: We *must* not!"

Believing he already knew what was going to come next, Thrinndor said, "Explain yourself."

"And this had better be good," said the barbarian.

"These—Dragma's Jewels—are a matched set."

Still not grasping what she was saying, Vorgath said, "So?"

"If you will allow me to finish," she said sternly.

The dwarf just crossed his massive arms on his chest, ducked his chin in stubbornness and made the loud sigh that said *I'm waiting.*

"Each piece alone," she began with her voice initially tentative. However, she gained confidence the more she spoke, "is a beautiful—no, *fabulous*—piece of jewelry." She paused to look longingly at what was spread on the sheet. "But each is also enchanted." She turned back to the dwarf. "Not only is each individual piece enchanted, they are enchanted to work as a set!"

"Go on," said Vorgath into the silence that followed.

After again taking in a deep breath, Cyrillis continued. "The necklace is said to have certain powers, granting the wearer enhanced wisdom and immunity to certain types of poison. The bracers..." She stole a glance at the items glittering at her from the black cloth. "...the bracers are said to grant the wearer enhanced powers of healing and some sort of protection."

She hesitated, but Vorgath was impatient. "Yes?"

"But when worn together..." Her eyes reflected the sparks from the gems as she spoke, her gaze now transfixed on the jewelry. She took in a deep breath, and the words tumbled out in a rush. "When worn together, additional spell power is granted the wearer, as is the ability to see all things as they truly are." She let the breath out slowly. "And it is rumored the wearer may also go invisible at will."

She turned her gaze upon her companions, trying not to appear to desire the items too much—and knowing she failed utterly.

"And the ring?" asked Savinhand, trying to figure out what fit where.

"Well," Cyrillis said uncertainly, "bear in mind that no one has seen these items for *thousands* of years!" She licked her lips; for some reason they seemed unusually dry. "There is little known about the ring. I do not know where that fits into the set—"

"That's because it doesn't." No one had seen the caster approach. In fact, no one even knew he had moved from his spot on the floor in the back of the room.

Heads turned, and all eyes fixed on the caster as he approached the loosely knit group gathered around the black cloth.

"The ring is not part of the set—it was crafted much later," he said. His attention shifted to the ornate ring, so contrasted by the stark black of the cloth on which it sat. "Little is known of its properties or powers. However, enhanced intelligence is rumored to be among them."

Into the still silence that followed, Thrinndor asked. "And how is it that you know this?"

"Because," said the caster as his eyes slowly rose from the ring to meet the gaze of the paladin, "you are not the only one among us to have descended from royal blood." He spoke softly but had no trouble being heard as everyone imperceptibly leaned forward to hear what came next. "I am of the lineage of Dragma."

Chapter Seventeen

Smoke Wars

Everyone stared slackjawed at the caster as if he were a ghost—everyone, that is, except Thrinndor. His face was split by a knowing grin. "So," he said simply, "you are the one."

"Yup," the mage said with a shrug and a wry smile. "That would be me!"

Sordaak's attention immediately shifted to take in everyone in the party. "I therefore claim the ring!" he said quickly. The sorcerer reached out and snagged the ring off of the cloth.

Before anyone could protest, he turned and smiled. "While an enhanced intelligence would be of no small boon to some of you—" at this, he looked pointedly at the dwarf, who growled deep within his chest but said nothing. "—it would surely enhance my casting abilities and powers!"

"Wait!" said an obviously befuddled rogue. His head bobbed back and forth between the caster and the paladin. Finally, it settled on Thrinndor. "The one *what*? What did you mean by 'you are the one'?"

The big fighter's eyes shifted from those of the rogue to those of the caster. He said with a twinkle in his eyes, "That is a story that could take a while."

"We have time," Vorgath said, crossing his arms on his chest.

Thrinndor looked at his friend and smiled. "Yes," he said, "I suppose we do at that." He looked around the room as if seeing it for the first time. "Let us first prepare ourselves a meal and settle in for some rest. I will explain as we do so. Just allow me a few moments to gather my thoughts so I can present them in a manner that will help you to understand."

The members of the group were silent as they went about the business of preparing a meal from the foodstuffs taken from the orc lair. By now they had a routine, and each of them had something to do. This was to be yet another cold meal as they had nothing that would burn and the sconces put out no heat, only light.

Finally each was seated with a plate of food. Vorgath, however, used the backside of the small shield he carried hidden under his cloak. He told anyone who would listen that no self-respecting barbarian ever used a shield, but carried one, just for this purpose.

Thrinndor cleared his throat by way of preamble, and said, "If you do not mind, I will speak as we eat."

"Parts of this you already know," he said. "I am a descendant of line of Valdaar." He looked pointedly at the caster, who was munching disinterestedly at a dry biscuit. "Another piece to the puzzle was just revealed: Our friend Sordaak here is of the lineage of Dragma."

His gaze shifted so he looked at each, in turn. "The part you do not know is what this puzzle is of which I speak."

"You got that right!" groused the dwarf.

Thrinndor ignored the interruption. "During his final days, Valdaar held several councils both trying to figure out ways to extend those days, and to make plans in the event he was unable to do so.

"The records kept from those councils were very detailed, but also very well guarded." He paused for a minute, obviously trying to decide how much to reveal. "Understand this: I must take care in what I say. This information is not meant for the ears of the followers of Praxaar," he looked pointedly at Sordaak, "or for those of *any* other of our numerous enemies—they would certainly long for this information. With it, those enemies could try to alter the events we know must come to pass."

He took a deep breath. "That must not happen." Again, he looked into the eyes of each of his comrades. "Vorgath I have known a few years, and I will personally vouch for him in this group."

"Yet," said Sordaak, "this has not been revealed to him." It was not a question.

"No," the paladin sighed. "He was not ready to hear it." Vorgath's gaze did not waver, nor did his mien indicate what he was thinking. "But I have no qualms in revealing it to him at this time. Others..." His voice trailed off, the implication apparent to all.

"Cyrillis," his eyes touched briefly on hers, "she is a believer—of that I have no doubt."

Next his eyes locked with those of the mage. "Sordaak, although you are of the line of Dragma—and most certainly have a part in this—it is not known to me what part that is." His eyes continued to bore into those of the caster, whose gaze never faltered. "Part of that concern lies from your lack of a god—or rather, your self-professed disdain for what the Gods can do for you. Possibly of more importance is your master's service to Praxaar."

After a few moments, unable to descry what he needed from the caster, the paladin tried the direct approach. "You remain closed to me," Thrinndor said. He dropped his eyes to his hands in his lap with a sigh.

"I suppose there may be others alive of the line of Dragma—" began the paladin tentatively.

"No," Sordaak said. "I am the only son—the only remaining living sibling *period*—from his line." He paused, then allowed a taint of sorrow to creep into his voice. "My father is dead. There were no other children. I have done no small amount of research into this once I discovered my line."

Thrinndor looked up at the caster. Suddenly his shoulders slumped and his eyes were beseeching when he continued. "Well, then it matters not whether I trust you. You must know what lies before you—before us." Again a pause while he considered. "Either you join our cause, or you condemn us to wait, perhaps another thousand years. You will join, or betray—this will not be in my hands. I will speak of this, and will trust you to…"

"Whatever it is that is so secret, it will stay with me—whether I choose to… join your cause or not," said Sordaak as if that put an end to the discussion. There was no emotion in his voice.

With a sigh of resignation, the big fighter visibly pulled himself together as he turned his attention to Savinhand. He was silent as he studied the rogue.

The thief shifted uncomfortably under the scrutiny of the paladin and threw out a plaintive "What?"

After a moment's consideration, Thrinndor said, "You, however, are *not* closed to me. I do not believe it is in my—or your—best interest to hear what I have to say."

In the strained silence that followed, you could have heard a sand flea fart at a dozen paces.

"Are you telling me I need to *leave?*" asked a stunned Savinhand when he found his voice.

"Yes," replied the paladin, his eyes never leaving those of the rogue.

"After all we have been through together—shit, I almost *died* for this cause of yours!" He stared back at the big fighter, defiance radiating from his eyes.

Thrinndor hesitated. Finally he said, "Yet you live. The key to my reluctance is in your own words: 'cause of yours.'"

Savin opened his mouth to protest, but Thrinndor raised a hand, palm outward. "You are a mercenary," he said quietly. "You are here for what loot you can carry out. You have no allegiances—"

"I do so!" snapped the rogue. "I am a member of the Guild of Shardmoor!"

"Shardmoor?" said the barbarian dubiously. "That band of thieves, cutthroats, assassins and murderers?" He snorted in derision. "That hardly lends credence to your argument!"

All eyes were now on the rogue as crimson crawled its way slowly up his neck. His mouth worked in protest, but nothing came out.

Exasperated, Savin said, "You know, I kinda liked working with you guys." He looked from one to the other. "I thought we had developed a sort of kinship—maybe even a friendship. A common goal tends to do that to a group of people." When no one said anything, he went on. "I even had the temerity to assume we would continue to quest together when we get out of here!" He continued to look from one to another, but all remained silent. "You have obviously not found everything you are looking for." His ire was met with silence. "I was hoping—no, planning—to be a part of that!"

Now it was Thrinndor's turn to fold his massive arms across his chest, but he remained quiet, as did the others, waiting for what must come next.

Savin threw his hands up in the air and said, his voice wounded, "Very well. What can I do to prove myself to you?"

There. Knowing it would come, the paladin said, "Take the Oath of Valdaar—submit your fealty to him, and..."

"What?" broke in the thief, disbelief evident in his voice. "Submit fealty to a *dead god?*" He threw his arms wide. "You have got to be out of your rock-picking mind!"

"...allow me to place a *geas* on you," Thrinndor continued as if not interrupted.

Before Savin could protest further, Cyrillis said sternly, "Did you not see *him* with your own eyes—at least your mind's eyes—when you were passing to the hereafter?"

"No!" the rogue said quickly, turning his attention to the cleric. "I mean, yes!" His eyes were defiant. "But that only proves he's *dead!*"

"No," she returned his defiance, "it does not." She thought for a moment. "His physical form has indeed been stricken from our plane. However, the very fact that he sought you out and returned you to us is proof that he is cognizant of what we do, and that his essence lives on!"

The rogue's mouth worked in exasperation, but it was some time before he could voice a reply. Finally, he managed to speak. "OK, I'll grant you the 'essence' thing." His eyes locked with those of the cleric. "But, swearing fealty to *an essence?* That alone would get me booted from my guild!"

"No loss there," muttered the dwarf.

Savin spun to stare down the offending barbarian. But then the words of the paladin apparently sunk in. "Geas?" he said, turning slowly to face the big fighter. "What *geas?*"

"If you swear fealty to Valdaar and agree to join our cause," Thrinndor said, his gaze unwavering, "even then you could divulge our secrets in a moment of weakness. For instance while drinking—"

"I don't drink," the rogue said, enunciating each word succinctly, ensuring all knew what he thought of the way this conversation had gone.

"I knew there was something about you that was not right," Vorgath said, his arms folded across his chest.

Savinhand glanced at the dwarf and started to retort, but he was interrupted by the paladin. "Silence!" he snapped. "This matter is not to be taken lightly."

He stared down the dwarf until the barbarian nodded in dissent. "The balance of power here in the material plane is at stake!"

Sordaak looked up and made as if to protest. But thought better of it, deciding he had better hear this out.

"There are other times when you might speak of this, mayhap even against your will," Thrinndor continued, his eyes now back on the rogue. "This I cannot allow and will not leave to chance."

"What you are saying is that you do not trust me." It was not a question.

"Correct." The paladin raised his hands to forestall what he knew to be the impending protest. "However, do not be offended. I would not trust my own mother with this were she not a true believer."

The ensuing silence hung in the air like the pall at a funeral.

Finally, Savinhand dropped his face to his hands and said weakly, "So let me see if I have this right." He looked up, his half-lidded stare transfixing the paladin. "It seems to me I have but three options.

"One: I swear fealty to this 'not-quite-dead' god of yours *and* submit to this *geas*. Or two: I continue to travel with this group as a free agent, so to speak. But, I will be in the dark as to whatever this secret purpose is that is the driving force for wherever it is we are and will be. Or three: After this quest is complete, I go my merry way and forget why I knew you." In silence he shifted his gaze from the fighter, to the caster, to the cleric, and finally back to the paladin. "Does that about sum it up?"

Thrinndor nodded slowly, his eyes never leaving those of the rogue.

Savinhand dropped his eyes to his hands.

"Fine!" he spat as he threw his hands in the air and spun on his heel heading for the entrance to the treasure chamber.

The others looked after him in grim silence. Except for the dwarf, who was recounting his gold and shaking his head.

As the thief reached the passageway out of the chamber, he again spun to face the group. "All right!" he shouted as his arm came up and he jabbed a finger at the paladin. "I will swear undying fealty to this god of yours AND I will submit to the geas." He paused for a moment as the others stared at him, dumbfounded by his vehemence. "However," he continued with his eyes boring into those of each of his companions before him, "I want a return promise from *you!*"

Stunned by the turn of events, the paladin stared back but remained silent.

Sordaak looked up from scroll he had been reading, happily ignoring the goings-on around him—at least until that point. "And," the sorcerer began, "what sort of promise might that be?"

The thief's eyes shifted to the caster, "Actually," he said in an even tone, "I will need a promise from *each of you.*" He jabbed his finger at the paladin again for emphasis.

The mage's eyes narrowed to mere slits. Before he could speak, however, Thrinndor beat him to it. "Go on."

"You must swear that word of this never gets out!" said Savinhand, grinding out each word.

Thrinndor's eyes widened in surprise. Then he tilted his head back and he began to laugh.

Sordaak spoke what each was thinking. "With the purported fate of the land at stake—a premise I have yet to buy into, by the way—you have the temerity to worry about your *reputation*? *You*? *A thief*?

Savinhand's response was instantaneous. "No, you moron!" his tone scathing. "Not my reputation. My *life*!" The rogue was breathing hard as he continued to speak. "If word gets back to my guild that I have joined some radical cult—which from the outside looking in you guys certainly meet that criteria—I would most certainly be expelled from said guild. That is, assuming they allow me to *live*!"

The thief's penetrating stare went from one to another until each had been touched. His mien turned thoughtful before he continued. "There is another reason," he said and fell silent.

Thrinndor arched an eyebrow. Cyrillis opened her mouth to speak, but thought better of it. Sordaak said nothing, but his eyes never left those of the thief. Vorgath merely grunted.

Seeing the group was in no mood for more theatrics, Savin said, "Shardmoor has a library." Still not getting the response he expected, he added, "An *extensive* library." His eyes fell upon those of the caster. "One that may be of use to this quest of yours—ours."

"I have heard of no such library," said the paladin, dubiously.

"I have," said the mage. He did not blink.

"How could a bunch of moldy books—no doubt stolen anyway—be of use to us?" asked the dwarf.

Savinhand turned a disdainful eye on the barbarian. "I doubt there are enough pictures in these books for them to be of any use to you! And there would be little surprise if few of these 'moldy books' were gained by purchase," he said evenly. "But the library is said to be several thousand years old!" His tone rang with satisfaction as he continued. "The Grandmaster dabbles in more than one school of magic—and he is but one of *many* who have done so over the centuries."

"Yes," said the caster, his eyes still locked onto those of the rogue. "But can you get us in?"

"No," said the thief, "not a chance."

Sordaak waved a hand. "Then your request serves me no purpose." His eyes went back to the book in his lap.

"No *outsider* has *ever* seen the 'library'!" Savinhand bristled at being dismissed so flippantly. The mage did not even look up. "Few *within* the guild even know of its existence, let alone its location!"

Now the caster slowly lifted his eyes to again meet those of the rogue. "Do you?" he said.

Savinhand was momentarily taken aback. "Do I *what?*" he asked.

Sordaak rolled his eyes. "Do you know where it is? You obviously know of its existence."

"Ummm, no…" he stammered as he realized the corner he had painted himself into. "But—"

"Then," the mage said curtly, "my assessment of your request holds to be correct."

"Now hold on there—" began the thief.

Seeing this was going nowhere, Thrinndor interrupted. "Wait, allow me."

The paladin eyed the mage first, but then allowed his gaze to drift to each of his companions. "First of all, honoring his request is simple." His eyes move back to Sordaak. "*We* will not be talking about any of this, anyway. So it will be a moot point about not telling anyone our friend here has joined our cause."

Sordaak cocked his head slightly and gave a begrudging nod of agreement. "Second?" he said, interested.

"Second," the big fighter continued, "while he might not be able to get *us* in, perhaps he can gain its location, and possibly find out if there is anything in there that might aid our cause." He placed a thoughtful eye on the rogue.

Sordaak again nodded.

"Ummm," stammered Savinhand.

But before he could go further, Vorgath jumped into the conversation—rather loudly, causing the mage to jump. "Aw, for the love of Bordin's Ale. Can we *please* just finish *this* adventure before we begin planning the next?" His belligerent stare went from one to another in the group, landing last on the rogue. "Get on with swearing fealty and getting *geas'ed* or whatever!"

Taken aback by the ferocity of the interruption, Savinhand's mouth worked, but no sound came out.

"Forgive the ancient one," Thrinndor said, eliciting a rumbling from deep within the dwarf's chest. "He gets a bit grouchy when he goes long periods without said Bordin's Ale—"

"Damn straight," said the barbarian with a twinkle in his eye. "And all this talk is keeping me longer still from that elixir of the gods!"

"Very well," said the paladin, his eyes touching those of each of the party members as he spoke. "We will do as requested and speak not of any complicity between you and our purpose." He got a nod from everyone, although Sordaak's was noticeably less enthusiastic.

"All right then," said the rogue, "just what is it I need to swear and do?"

"The swearing part is easy," began the paladin. "Simply state your desire to follow the teaching of Valdaar." He raised his eyes to lock on those of the rogue. "And pledge your support to those dedicated to returning him to his rightful place in this plane—"

"Meaning you," said Savinhand sardonically.

Thrinndor smiled. "For now," he said with a shrug.

After a moment, the thief sighed heavily and shrugged his shoulders as well. "Very well," he returned the gaze of the big fighter defiantly. "I pledge my swords, my deeds and my life—should it again become necessary—to support you, your followers, *and* Lord Valdaar."

A weighted silence hung in the air.

When Savinhand broke it, he did so with a newfound confidence in his voice. "However," he said, "know now that I do not make this pledge lightly." His eyes touched those of everyone in the room. "You are now stuck with me! For good or for ill, my fate is now tied with that of each of yours!"

"Damn," Vorgath said with a shake of his head.

"Indeed," said a solemn Thrinndor, ignoring the barbarian. Then he stepped forward and raised his right hand to clasp the shoulder of the rogue. "Our fates are certainly entwined as I felt they must be from the beginning." His voice was thick with emotion as he continued. "It is good to have you with us."

"*Pfft!*" snarled the dwarf. "Can we just *get on with it?*"

The paladin turned his head to acknowledge the barbarian. "Patience, oh ancient one!" Again his eyes twinkled. "A man has just changed his course in life." He returned his attention to the thief. "We in turn should not take this pledge lightly!"

Vorgath rolled his eyes and repeated "*Pfft!*" but said nothing more. However he too was now smiling.

"And the geas?" pressed the caster.

Cyrillis, who had to this point remained silent, finally spoke. "Is that *really* necessary?" she said.

Thrinndor turned his attention to the cleric. "Well," he began…

"Yes!" said Savinhand, his new confidence still ringing in his tone. "Absolutely it is! Now it is I that must insist."

"I do not understand," said a perplexed healer.

"Simple," said the rogue. "While I have no intention of saying anything that could possibly harm my new cause, you—we—cannot rely on that with all that is at stake."

His eyes shifted slowly back to those of the paladin. "I get that now." He paused before continuing into the stunned silence. "You *must* ensure that I do not speak of this, even if *coerced!*"

Thrinndor's already raised eyebrow threatened to merge with his hairline. "You have reason to be concerned with this?"

Savinhand again shrugged. "Thieves do not trust thieves," he said. "*Especially* those within our own guild."

"Very well," said the paladin, relief evident in his sigh. "Close your eyes and relax." The rogue complied.

Thrinndor lifted his hand from the rogue's shoulder and placed his index finger above the rogue's left eye, the middle finger just to the right of the bridge of his nose and his thumb below and to the left of the left eye. He closed his own eyes and began to chant softly in a language known to none in the chamber.

After only a few moments he opened his eyes, dropped his hand to his side and stepped back.

Slowly, Savinhand also opened his eyes. "That's it?" he said, raising the question all were thinking.

Turning his back on the group and heading for his pack, Thrinndor said, "It will suffice." He spun on his heel and abruptly dropped down to a sitting position, his legs crossed.

"Now that that matter is settled," he looked up and again allowed his gaze to encompass all of his companions. "Those that have ears let them hear."

Vorgath kicked his pack into the semblance of a seat, and unceremoniously plopped down onto it. "You know," he grumped, "at least I finally understand why you sound so pompous all the time." Thrinndor just raised an eyebrow. The barbarian explained, "This being the great-great grand-whelp of an ancient god has obviously gone to your head." He smiled.

"Old friend," began the paladin, "maybe one of these days you will show some proper respect!"

"That'll be the day!" retorted the dwarf.

"Yes," said the paladin, chuckling. "I believe that would be the case!" He waived an arm at his companions, indicating they should also sit.

After all had complied, Thrinndor took in a deep breath. "OK, now where was I?" He rolled his eyes toward the ceiling as he thought about it. "Oh yes," he said, "I was speaking of the final council." He looked down at his hands as he continued his narration. "This final council was recorded in great detail, and even the knowledge that those records existed was kept under extreme secrecy."

"Smoke 'em if ya got 'em," said Sordaak as he rummaged noisily through a bag. Finally, he looked up at his suddenly quiet companions. "What?" he said.

His right eyebrow mingling with the shock of black hair, Thrinndor replied, "Smoke 'em if ya got 'em?" There was an underlying hint of worry in his voice.

"What?" the caster repeated. His face turned thoughtful and he said, "Oh…" Now his tone got belligerent. "Well," he started, "the guild shrink did mention that the condition was probably stress related—the more stress, the more my 'flashbacks' might occur." His voice trailed off as he tamped a mixture into the bowl of his pipe.

When no one said anything, Sordaak added, "She also said that scorching things with spells seems to alleviate the symptoms somewhat—in my case, anyway." His face split in a broad grin. "I believe the phrase is meant to invite others to partake of a smoke, if one is available." He winked at the dwarf.

Noting that he still held their attention, he took his time lighting the bowl, using a flame conjured from the end of his right index finger. He puffed away slowly until he had a good head of smoke going. After a bit, he looked pointedly at the paladin. "Please continue."

Vorgath got out his own makings and quickly readied his own pipe. "Could I trouble you for a light?" he asked politely as he leaned toward the mage.

"But of course," Sordaak said, and again produced a flame on his finger.

The barbarian drew hard on the stem to get a good bowl going, then puffed contentedly and let out a sigh. "It has been a long time," he said wistfully.

Before Thrinndor could begin, the dwarf and the caster entered into a contest with their smoke rings. First the dwarf puffed out a large, almost perfect, ring. The mage arched an indolent brow, pursed his lips and sent a smaller ring out that chased down the larger ring and neatly passed completely through its opening, the sides never making contact.

The barbarian snorted, smiled knowingly and pursed his own lips in a peculiar fashion. A large smoke bird came forth that resembled a hawk, soaring on unseen currents in the chamber. He leaned back and smiled.

Now it was Sordaak's turn to snort. He pursed his lips and blew out a single, straight line of smoke that once free of the caster's mouth took the shape of an arrow. As quick as a flash of lightning, the arrow sped for the soaring hawk. As the arrow penetrated the winged apparition, the bird lost form as it seemed to explode.

Vorgath again raised his right brow—this time in obvious surprise as both apparitions faded into non-existence. Finally, he lowered his eyes to meet those of the caster and nodded his head almost imperceptibly, thereby inviting the mage to go next.

Knowing they needed the rest—and the distraction—Thrinndor settled into his makeshift seat and lowered his body down to where he was propped on one elbow. He decided to hold off on his narrative until the competition concluded. Besides, it was good to see his old friend challenged in such a manner, but he also knew the inevitable outcome.

Sordaak smiled, drew deeply on his pipe and released a huge cloud of smoke. At first its shape was indistinct, but ever so quickly it took on the shape of a large dragon. Its color deepened and its wings seemed to catch a thermal and it rose quickly toward the ceiling of the chamber. There it circled lazily as it continued to gain better form. The dragon's color deepened until it looked uncomfortably like a black dragon. As its head turned toward the puny humans below, its eyes suddenly sprang open revealing deep red orbs that caused Cyrillis to gasp.

Vorgath nodded in admiration, a thoughtful smile on his face. He drew deeply on his own pipe, its bowl glowing fiercely. The dwarf's brow furrowed in concentration as he exhaled the smoke above his head.

Like that of the mage, initially the cloud had no form. But as the barbarian continued to blow smoke into the air, it took on the shape of an armored being. More smoke, and it quickly became a dwarf in full battle armor.

The dragon's eyes glowed intently as its powerful jaws opened for a roar, but no sound came forth. Instead the beast folded its wings and the huge creature rolled over onto its side as it dropped into a silent dive clearly aimed at the still-forming figure below.

As the dwarf's form became complete, it looked skyward in anticipation. His eyes locked with those of the dragon now speeding toward the diminutive figure below and a huge greataxe appeared in his hands. The dragon again opened his maw, this time obviously intending to spray its breath weapon—a flume of black acid for this particular species.

As the gap narrowed, the expected spray of acid sped toward the dwarf. The axe flashed as it arced through the air when the dragon closed in. The blade appeared to pass right through the neck of the beast, neatly severing the head where the neck joined with the powerful shoulders just as the spray encompassed the dwarf.

The dragon crashed to the ground at the fighter's feet and immediately dissipated with a perceptible *pop*. The caster's eyes widened in astonishment.

The acid caused the dwarf to drop to one knee, his head bowing to the ground. His pain was evident.

But the dwarf struggled back to his feet and turned slowly to the mage sitting cross-legged on the ground before him, his eyes still wide. After a moment, he dropped the axe and bowed neatly before the caster.

Savinhand began applauding slowly. "Well done," he said appreciatively. "Well done!"

Her reverie broken by the rogue, Cyrillis joined in the applause—but hers was much quicker and louder.

Thrinndor raised back up to a sitting position. With a huge smile on his face, he also clapped enthusiastically. "Indeed," he said. "That was well done!"

Sordaak, surprise still written plainly on his face, looked at the bowl of his pipe, trying to discern whether he had one more in there. Sensing it was not to be, he looked up and his eyes locked with those of the dwarf. "Perhaps another time, o diminutive one?" he said indolently. He nodded acquiescence.

"Anytime trickster, anytime," the barbarian replied, a bemused smile on his face.

The mage also smiled and turned to face the paladin, who said, "If you two are finished?"

"Yup," said Vorgath.

"For now," said the mage with a wink in the general direction of the dwarf, whose eyes twinkled in delight.

"Very well," said Thrinndor, amusement in his eyes. "However, because I am tired and we must rest, I am going give you the short version."

"Wait!" interrupted Savinhand. "I swore fealty and got geas'ed for a *short* version?"

The paladin smiled. "I assure you I will leave out nothing of import to your understanding of our quest."

Not sure whether he should argue further or not, the rogue shifted on his pack but didn't speak. Quietly he nodded his approval.

Thrinndor twisted around until he brought both legs under his torso. "As I mentioned earlier, in the final days of that ill-fated battle for the material plane, Valdaar held several councils in an attempt to both forestall the impending doom and devise a plan to carry on his reign in the event he was unable to do so.

"The proceedings from these councils were meticulously recorded, and just as meticulously guarded. For Valdaar had foreseen his own demise and planned accordingly. He knew he must show no hint that he knew what was to come for fear that those who followed him might finally break under the strain that had befallen them in those final days.

"Valdaar and Dragma planned and perpetrated a ruse. With Praxaar and his army only moments away, the High Sorcerer was placed in a secret chamber—one from which he could see and hear all that happened in the temple, where the final battle was to take place. More importantly, from there he could cast spells and *appear* to actually be in the chamber, supporting his lord. A man that closely resembled Dragma—unaware of the fate decided for him—fought by Valdaar's side, instead."

Thrinndor took a deep breath. "When Praxaar's sword penetrated the heart of Valdaar, his essence—soul, if you will—was as snatched at the last instant, and..." He searched for the correct word. "Stored."

"What?" asked the caster. "How?"

"Where?" said the cleric, her voice barely above a whisper.

"One at a time," chided Thrinndor, gently. "There is a spell—a spell of the highest order. Only the most powerful of clerics—and possibly sorcerers—may know it—a spell known only as 'Trap the Soul.'"

"I have only heard of that in passing—none in the land are said to possess it," said the cleric.

"I've *never* heard of it," said Sordaak.

"And," continued Cyrillis, "from what little I *do* know, the spell would not work on *a god.*"

"Correct," said Thrinndor patiently. "Not in any *mortal* form we might hope to understand." He again drew breath before continuing. "Dragma was a sorcerer of the *highest order*—none have attained his stature in the many centuries since his death." He paused once again. "He modified the spell," he said as he again shrugged his shoulders, as if saying it was just that simple.

"He modified the spell," Cyrillis repeated, still not quite grasping what the paladin was telling them.

"Yes."

"OK," she said, her mind racing, "let us assume he was able to do as you speak. From what I know of the spell, it requires a gem of the purest type. The type required depends on the nature of the one to be trapped, for it is to be the vessel for the essence—soul, if you will."

"Correct," said Thrinndor.

"So," Savinhand finally entered the conversation, "what type of gem was it? And—the obvious question—what happened to it?"

"Black Diamond—" began the paladin.

"Of course," muttered the caster. "That figures."

Thrinndor cast a withering glance at the caster to silence him. Sordaak glared back but said no more.

"The diamond is affixed—"

"*Valdaar's Fist!*" Vorgath interrupted.

"Yes," said the paladin triumphantly as he looked over at his friend with newfound respect gleaming in his eyes.

"So," said the rogue, shaking his head as he attempted to grasp what was being said, "you're telling me that this sorcerer—who we just talked to yesterday, by the way—snatched the soul of a god and imprisoned it in a diamond mounted to a sword?"

"That pretty much sums it up," said Thrinndor.

The thief opened his mouth to speak, but no words came out.

Something finally dawned on the cleric, and her eyes widened. "But," she said, hope coming from deep inside her, "that means *he is not dead!*"

"Now you are getting it," said the paladin approvingly.

"But…" she repeated.

The rogue interrupted her before she could frame the words she wanted to speak. Tears welled in her eyes and were soon streaming down her cheeks.

"Wait," Savinhand said, "if his essence—or soul, as you put it—is in this diamond, just who, or what, was it that guided me back to my body when I was headed for the afterlife?" He crossed his arms on his chest.

"Good question," said the paladin. "One which I cannot answer." He shrugged and looked to Cyrillis.

"Hmmm…" she said, thinking as she went, as her mind was still reeling under the portent of her god being alive. "There are many servants of Valdaar who have passed into the afterlife—any one of which, I suppose, could have guided you back."

"Whatever!" groused the rogue. He was fairly certain he was not going to get a better answer, and not sure he believed the one he got.

"But," said the cleric, as her voice regained its earlier concern and she turned her attention back to the paladin. "Something else I remember about the spell: There is a limitation as to how long the soul will remain trapped." In the end her words came out in a rush, and the tears returned to her eyes.

"What do you mean?" asked Thrinndor. "What happens to it?"

"I do not know!" her voice was almost in a panic. "Something about the essence deteriorates over time and is eventually lost!"

"That cannot be," said Thrinndor. "Else we would not be here!" He sounded hopeful. "Surely Dragma knew of this limitation, and modified that contingent of the spell accordingly, as well." As he spoke, his voice once again regained its earlier confidence. "Dragma had to know that thousands of years might pass before the time would be right for the release of our Lord."

"Well," said Sordaak, "I certainly hope so!" All eyes trained on him. "Otherwise, all that you have been working on—looked for—will have been in vain."

"Yeah, well," said Cyrillis, "those of us that *believe* know that our god is still with us!"

The caster's eyes searched those of the cleric. Finally he held up has hands in submission. "I'll grant you that, sister. I'm certain you and he," he nodded in the direction of Thrinndor, "believe that he yet lives." He cocked an eye. "After all, you must get your powers from *someone!*"

"Correct," said the paladin. "In that we cannot be mistaken. Her abilities as well as my own can only be granted by a god. Therefore, he lives."

"I've already conceded that point," said Sordaak. "However, answer me this: If your god is trapped in a gem, how is it he is able to bestow said powers on you, his believers?" Now it was his turn to cross his arms matter-of-factly across his chest.

"What do you mean?" asked Thrinndor.

Sordaak rolled his eyes and said, "Try to keep up, please." He lowered his eyes back to stare penetratingly into those of the paladin, all trace of sarcasm now gone. "Your god is trapped in a rock. How is it that *he bestows your powers on you from there?*" His gaze cycled back and forth between the cleric and the paladin. "Surely Praxaar would have detected him were Valdaar *able* to accomplish that amazing feat!"

Thrinndor appeared to ponder briefly. But when he spoke, his voice belied no hint of trepidation. "As believers," he said, command returning to his voice, "*we* are the source of our god's powers. As long as we believe, he cannot die." He was silent for a moment, obviously working out in his head how he wanted to phrase what was next. "Our god *exists* so we have our powers. There is no more. There is no question."

Sordaak's eyes never left those of the paladin. "Right answer," he said. He then turned to finish unrolling his bedding.

"But—" said a now bewildered Thrinndor.

"No, no 'buts' either," said the caster as he whipped around and jabbed a finger at the big man. "I had to be certain *you* two knew that." He turned his attention to Cyrillis. "Valdaar is not granting you your powers from his prison—that's not possible. It is *your belief in him and devotion* to him—and each other—that grants you your powers." He shook his head in wonder that there were those out there who actually chose to obtain their spells that way.

Sordaak again returned his attention to his bedroll, ignoring the stupefied looks he was getting from everyone in the party—everyone save for Vorgath. The barbarian's arms were crossed on his chest and his head was cocked to one side as his eyes looked thoughtfully at the caster. Finally, he too shook his head silently, smiled and turned to get his pallet ready.

Savinhand looked around at his companions, who were still staring at the prone paladin. He shrugged his shoulders. "I'll take that as my cue as well," he said as he set his head back and twisted this way and that until he found such comfort as could be found on lumpy bedding over cold stone.

One by one the others followed suit, saying nothing. Not that they had nothing to say; they just didn't know how, and to whom, to voice their questions.

All except Vorgath. He remained in a sitting position, his arms and legs crossed before him. His eyes remained on his friend, his mien impassive, his thoughts roiling.

Finally, long after the even breathing of each of his companions informed him they were all asleep, he shrugged and muttered, "So it is *you!*" his great head wagged side to side. "Lineage of a God…" Wonder laced his voice, and his eyes misted. "Our adventures have only just begun." Saying nothing more, he rolled over and was soon snoring loudly.

Chapter Eighteen

The Final Conflict

reakfast was again a cold affair—they had no fire with which to make coffee or hot food. The companions got their packs together in sullen fashion.

As each finished with their pack, they stood and waited patiently for the others to do so. Some of them munched silently on a breakfast of a biscuit and/or some dried meats, washing it down with wine or water, each to his or her own taste.

Finally the last, Savinhand, stood up and faced the group. He chewed absentmindedly on a piece of jerked meat.

"Are you ready?" Sordaak asked.

"Yup," said the thief, grinning around the dried bread he had stuffed in his mouth.

"About damn time," groused the caster.

"My, my," said the rogue, still smiling, "aren't we a bit grumpy without our coffee?"

"Yup," Sordaak also grinned. "Maybe now we can find our way out of this place so I can get some!"

"Right," said Thrinndor, looking around as he scratched his head absently. "High Lord Dragma said there would be a portal…"

"…When we were ready, if I remember correctly," Sordaak finished the thought for him. "Well, I think we are ready!"

As if on command, an apparition appeared on the wall opposite of the entrance to the chamber.

"And behold!" said the caster.

As the rogue moved toward the apparition to study it, Sordaak said, "Remember what the old man said." His voice stopped the thief in his tracks.

"Something about those that were also searching for the keep knew of this portal and would possibly set a trap for us on the other side."

Savinhand turned from the portal to look at the mage. "So are you saying we need to go back the way we came?"

"Hell no!" snapped the caster. "I don't even think it's possible—unless you know of a way to raise that chamber back up to the original passageway."

Taken aback by the caster's tone, the rogue stammered, "Uhhh, no..."

"You're a dumbass," the caster announced. Before any protest could take shape, he continued. "What *I am* saying is that we need a plan. Just stepping through the portal assuming we are safe on the other side would likely end this quest of yours." He looked at the paladin quickly. "Ours," he amended.

Thrinndor arched an eyebrow, smiled and nodded. But he said nothing.

"Very well," said the caster, "here is what I have in mind." He looked at each to verify he had their attention.

He turned to look at Vorgath. "You go in first. I want you to go in hard and fast. Get yourself appropriately pissed off and come out swinging. Immediately step to the right and make sure you have their undivided attention."

The barbarian nodded.

Sordaak looked over at the rogue. "Savin, you're next. Do your disappearing act and try to go in unnoticed. Your main objective is to get to that spellcaster and take him out." Savinhand nodded.

Next the spellcaster looked at the cleric. "You go in immediately after Vorgy and attend to any needs they might have should the resistance prove to be extreme—and for some reason I feel that might be an understatement."

Cyrillis also nodded her assent.

Finally, he turned to look at Thrinndor, who's right brow was arched in inquisition. "You're last for a reason—a *very good* reason," Sordaak said in his best placating voice. "I will follow Cyrillis after a short delay to ensure the attention on the other side is elsewhere. I will be blasting away with area of effect spells as quickly as I can rattle them off. You must follow right on my heels and take out whoever—whatever—survives and turns their attention on me." He took a deep breath at this point. "But most important, you too need to seek out that spellcaster. I intend to distract him with whatever I can throw at him, but we know he is very powerful and may thus be able to shrug off my best efforts." He locked gazes with the paladin and withdrew a piece of rolled-up parchment from a fold in his raiment. "Get his attention somehow, because I have a surprise for him," he said as he raised the scroll in a menacing fashion.

Thrinndor nodded and said, "Sounds good." His eyes still locked on those of the caster, he added, "Just what is it you are expecting on the other side?"

Sordaak puffed his chest up with a large intake of air and let it out slowly, allowing his shoulders to sag. "Hell," he said, "I really don't *know!*" He quickly looked away from the stern gaze of the paladin. "But an educated guess says more of the same as before. *Much more!*"

He looked back at the big man who was slowly becoming a friend. "More orcs. More assassins. More whatever he could dig up, or hire, to throw at us." He paused to consider. "He means not to allow us to escape with whatever it is he has been trying to get at for months. If not *years!* We have yet to face that caster and he's probably going to sling everything he's got at us!"

Sordaak was silent for a moment, allowing what he said to sink in. "After that ass-whuppin' we put on him a few days ago, he's gonna be *pissed!*"

The group was silent for a bit. Vorgath grinned and said, "Good." He looked at the others in the group as he hefted his newfound greataxe in a menacing manner. "Let's not disappoint him!"

Thrinndor grinned at his friend, who was obviously itching to get started. "I think our friend here," he said, throwing a thumb at the caster, "is just letting you go first because you need the advantage so you can get caught up!" He broadened his grin.

"Whatever!" snorted the dwarf. "I'll see if I can leave one or two for you to mop up!"

Thrinndor chuckled and turned his attention back to the caster. "I deem your plan to be sound." He swept the room with his gaze. "Are we ready, then?"

"Let's do this!" growled the dwarf as he turned to face the portal.

"All right," said Sordaak. "The three of you go in hard, fast and one right after the other." He pulled his component bag from its fold in his robe, opened it and removed several items. "I will follow after I figure you have had enough time to get their attention." He fixed his gaze on the paladin. "With you right behind me." He shifted his gaze back to the group nearest the portal. "Most important of all, we *must* spread out so as to negate any of this mage's area-of-effect spells!"

He got nods from all. Sordaak nodded and then he startled everyone by shouting, "Go! Go! *GO!*"

Vorgath bellowed his war cry and leapt into the portal, followed only a second or two later by Savinhand. Cyrillis gripped her staff tightly and was next, stepping calmly through.

Sordaak was counting in his head as he prepared a spell.

"What of your pet?" queried Thrinndor.

Startled, Sordaak replied brusquely. "He goes through with me—he cannot go before me in this case. He has instructions to seek out the caster and distract him as well." Without another word, he turned and stepped through the portal... into utter mayhem.

The landscape was a rocky plateau, with a portal in a cliff face behind him through which he had just come. The bright light of a noonday sun momentarily blinded him—a huge contrast to the dingy torch light they had left behind. It had been days, maybe weeks, since last he had seen the sun.

Savinhand had made it through cleanly and was an agreeable distance to the left, surrounded by orcs both alive and dead, one with its head missing from its shoulders. Good old Vorpals!

However, Vorgath was busy trying to extricate himself from a web and he was also surrounded by orcs who were clearly not being fair in waiting for the dwarf to do so. They were hacking away at any exposed skin and/or armor and doing more than passing damage for their efforts.

Cyrillis worked feverishly to both free the barbarian and heal him as the number of wounds mounted. Having little effect on the web, in frustration she turned her attention to the nearest orc and stove in the side of its head with one powerful swing of her staff. This action had the undesirable effect of attracting the attention of several of its companions, and she was soon surrounded by three of the creatures. More tried to crowd in but were unable to do so.

Knowing his plan was in jeopardy, Sordaak knew a change was in order. He shouted, "Duck!" and released the fireball spell he had meant for his opposing caster, centering it on the melee surrounding the dwarf.

The cleric dropped to the ground immediately, but barbarian was still held tight by the incredibly strong sinews of the web. Guessing what was to come, he at least was able to turn his head away from the direction he had come, close his eyes and duck as best he could.

The ball of fire exploded in their midst as planned, and it had the desired effect—both burning away the barbarian's bonds as well as knocking most of the orcs in the immediate vicinity to the ground, killing at least two in the process.

But Sordaak never saw any of this. His opposite number had indeed been waiting for him and had prepared a welcoming of sorts.

First, Sordaak had to fight off a Hold Person spell, which the mage had anticipated and so was able to do. However, the effort took a fleeting moment of time—more than enough for this other mage to cut loose with another spell, this time a savage bolt of lightning.

Again Sordaak had been prepared for a second spell—and a third, for that matter. Feeling the tug at his personae with the Hold spell, he immediately dove to the ground to his right to escape whatever it was that he was to be held in place for.

Unfortunately for Thrinndor, this second spell came blasting in just as he stepped through the portal, and he took the full brunt of it square in his chest. The force drove him backward into the cliff face. It worked for him that the portal was a one-way device, or he certainly would have been driven clear back into the treasure chamber.

Any lesser being would have been seriously wounded, if not killed. But the paladin's innate skills and training allowed some of the force of the blow to be shunted off by his armor. Still, the force of the bolt and his subsequent violent contact with the rock behind him was sufficient to temporarily knock the wind from him, and he sagged to his knees.

He shook his head to clear it and—his ears ringing—gulped in air to replenish his starved lungs. He was able to surge to his feet in short order, scouting about wildly for his assailant.

Meanwhile, Vorgath had been knocked from his feet by the ball of fire from Sordaak. The spell had the desired effect of incinerating the highly flammable webs that had been holding him, and it also served to cauterize several of the open wounds that had been caused by the surrounding orcs.

Seeing nothing but red from the battle lust in his blood, he jumped to his feet and swung his greataxe wildly, spinning as he did so in a vicious arc that clove the two orcs that had been stunned by the fireball completely in two.

A back swing and the remaining orc that was set to hack at the cleric was nullified. Black blood flowed from its mouth from having its lungs pierced as the dwarfs weapon penetrated through its armor that covered its back, clear through his ribs and into the monster's heart. Wide-eyed, it fell to its knees and toppled over, its eyes glazed in death.

Oblivious to the pain of his wounds, Vorgath looked about wildly for more foes. He was not disappointed as a second wave stepped over the bodies of their fallen comrades to attack. This time, however, he was not encumbered by web, and he laid about himself most arduously with *Flinthgoor* dancing this way and that. Cyrillis climbed to her feet and attended to the barbarian's wounds with her spells from a safe distance.

Sordaak jumped to his feet, his eyes casting about for any sign of his assailant. He spotted him hiding behind a large boulder perhaps twenty feet away. Sordaak whipped his hands up and loosed the first spell that came to mind, knowing he had to act quickly.

And he was almost quick enough. Almost. As he shouted the trigger word, pointed his finger and released a volley of magic darts, flames leapt up from the ground under his feet, immediately searing his unprotected legs and scorching his robes.

Wall of Fire! The flaming wall was situated perfectly to catch both he and Thrinndor as the fighter was still shaking the cobwebs out of his head from the lightning bolt.

Sordaak screamed in pain and rage at his own stupidity for allowing himself to be caught in the wall. He dove forward to get out of the flame sand rolled twice. Wall of Fire! That was a spell he had not expected. His opponent must be a more powerful sorcerer than he had figured.

That wasn't good, he thought fleetingly.

Thrinndor also howled as he burst through the flames, instinctively moving in the opposite direction of his caster. He was determined to heed that last bit of advice to not again allow the area of effect spells to catch more than one of them at a time. Once again, his natural abilities served him well and he took little harm from the flames.

He tucked and rolled out to his left and came up in a crouch. He held his shield out front in his left arm and his flaming sword at the ready in his right fist.

His eyes darted left and right over the top of the shield, trying to locate his adversary.

Nothing. He saw nothing. Wait! Behind that boulder he spied a being waving his arms, obviously preparing a spell. But the magician's focus was elsewhere, so he did not see—or was paying no attention to—the paladin. Either way, Thrinndor knew he had little time as the caster pointed his finger and released yet another spell in the direction of Sordaak.

He heard a howl of pain that confirmed his suspicions. A blast of energy hit the enemy caster as Thrinndor watched him duck back behind the rock. At least Sordaak was still able to fight back.

But this did not deter the enemy. He pulled a wand from his voluminous robe and pointed it at Sordaak. Thrinndor had had just about enough of this. The caster was too far away for a direct attack, so he turned his shield over and pointing the loaded crossbow affixed to the back at the caster and let fly a hastily aimed bolt. He knew there was little chance he could do serious damage with the device. It was meant to be a distraction more than anything.

His aim was true enough and the bolt grazed the right arm of the caster as he pointed the wand at Sordaak. He let out a yelp that was probably more surprise than pain, causing his arm to jerk up just as the wand released its energy. The resultant lightning bolt sailed harmlessly over the head of the cringing Sordaak.

The caster as his eyes locked on this new adversary. He screamed in rage as he again raised the wand, this time in the direction of the paladin.

But Thrinndor had expected this and had already righted his shield, surged to his feet and was sprinting directly at the magicuser. For good measure, he howled loudly and held the flaming sword high above his head, ready to crash it down on any target that got within range.

The caster was faster, however, and he smiled semi-confidently as he released yet another bolt from the wand—this one striking squarely on the shield of the rapidly approaching paladin.

The shield absorbed a good portion of the energy, yet the resulting blast nearly ripped it from Thrinndor's grasp, numbing his left arm in the process. It also sent him careening off of his intended path, and he crashed noisily into the boulder, missing his target by several feet.

Sordaak used the distraction to ready the scroll. He knew it was a long shot—he did not understand all of the words written on the parchment, but he felt certain he could release the energy. He just hoped he could release it in the right direction!

Thrinndor righted himself, and as he shook off the effects of his encounter with the rock and his numb arm, he looked up to see the caster just out of arm's reach. His hands were outstretched before him, thumbs together. The paladin winced as flames leapt from the fingertips, engulfing him. He felt the searing pain as he raised his shield to block, but he was too late!

Instead of falling back, though, he surprised the caster by charging forward, his sword again raised high. The yell that came from his lips was this time more from the pain, but it was still designed to strike fear into his opponent.

Flames continued to pour forth from the caster's fingers, but now his eyes widened in worry as the paladin's blade flashed under the noonday sun. Thrinndor's flaming sword connected with the magicuser's left arm just below where it attached to the shoulder.

The blade easily sliced through the unprotected upper arm and severed the limb just below where it connected to the upper torso. The arm was completely severed at that point.

The flames ceased and the caster screamed in agony. Using his right hand to cover the remaining stump and stanch the flow of blood, he flung himself backward, narrowly avoiding the paladin's next thrust.

The enemy caster was not deterred, however, and he was most certainly not finished. Somehow he cast a spell while rolling, and the flow of blood from the severed limb was greatly reduced.

His face twisted in pain and fury as he sprang to his feet, his blood-covered right hand pointing at Thrinndor. He shouted a single arcane word and a cone of ice crystals shot from his finger tip to hit the surprised paladin square in the chest.

Thrinndor was knocked backward and his reactions were slowed by the blinding effect of the blast. He tried to duck to his right and spin his way out of the cone, but the caster's right hand followed the paladin. When the icy blast ceased, the mage cast yet another of the same spell, forcing the fighter to his knees.

Sordaak finally got the correct words in what must have been the correct sequence, the last coming as a shout as he pointed his right index finger at his opposite number.

There was a faint sound of several coughs, followed by the buzz of small balls of fire streaking at their target. The balls got larger as they approached so that when instinct forced the caster to turn his attention to see the rapidly approaching doom, they were already more than a foot in diameter and still growing.

His eyes widened in disbelief as he threw himself backwards to the ground in an attempt to avoid the orbs, but there were too many—and they followed his movement.

The orbs—which were really small comets, six in all—hit all around the mage, exploding on impact. The blasts knocked the paladin back, had just recovered from the ice spell. Flying backward and unable to protect himself, he hit his head. The darkness of unconsciousness carried him away.

But the intended target had it much worse. The comets bludgeoned him from all sides, and the explosions ripped at his robe and blasted the hair from his scalp.

Still he would not die.

Sordaak sauntered up slowly, a twisted smile upon his lips. As he did, he prepared another spell.

However, the mage's triumph was interrupted by a shout from his left. "Hey! A little help, here!"

Sordaak shook off the feeling of victory to remember they were still in a battle as he turned in the direction of the shout to see Savinhand surrounded by three orcs, with several more nipping at the heels—eight or ten, at least.

Savinhand, a blade in either hand, was availing himself rather well but was bleeding from several nicks and cuts and could certainly not prevail against such an onslaught. His attacks were best done with stealth, but this required brute force.

Without thinking, Sordaak raised his right hand, pointed his index finger at the melee, barked some arcane words and released a ball of fire. Almost as an afterthought he shouted, "Duck!"

But the rogue had seen this particular act already and was way ahead of his caster buddy. He threw himself at the legs of the orc that stood between him and the mage, covering his head as he did. Sordaak's aim was true, and he had set detonation just behind the orc at whose feet the thief now lay.

The ensuing blast knocked Savin rolling, but his dexterity prevented any serious injury. He sprang to his feet to confront any opponents that remained. Only two remained in the immediate vicinity, both stunned by the blast. He dispatched those with ease, and turned to thank his friend.

But the words died on his lips as he realized that while the blast had helped him out of his mess, it had only served to piss off several of the orcs, whose attention was now on the caster. Several had broken off their attack on the rogue to confront this new assailant.

Not only that, but, unknown to Sordaak, the other caster had somehow regained his feet and was stumbling, dagger in hand, in the direction of his friend. Sordaak was oblivious to the threat as he readied yet another spell to deal with the orcs who were approaching.

"Behind you!" shouted the rogue as he dropped the short sword in his right hand. That hand flashed to his belt, and in one fluid motion he yanked a stiletto free and sent it flying through the air to sink into the throat of the mage about to stab Sordaak from behind. The mage clawed at the weapon as he sank to his knees, and then he pitched forward onto his face and lay still.

Sordaak dared not risk turning his attention from the orcs and so missed this bit of action. Instead, he raised his hands in a familiar stance, thumbs touching, and released a sheet of flame that engulfed the approaching creatures.

The orcs screamed in agony. Those who had already taken damage from the fireball fell to the ground writhing in pain. But two pressed on, their halberds poised to deal with the menacing being who tormented them so.

Savinhand, who had recovered his sword, was able to hit one of them from behind, neatly severing the head of the unaware orc. But the other pressed his attack and brought its blade down hard on the caster, who raised his right arm to ward off the attack. Quickly, Sordaak spoke the words of another spell.

As the orc's blade touched the mage's arm, electricity arced from the point of contact, through the blade of the halberd and down the shaft into the hands of the monster that held it.

Both the caster and the orc screamed as the blade hit true, slicing deep into the right forearm of the caster and on down to cut into his right shoulder.

The orc released its grip on the halberd and stared briefly down at his mangled hands. The then slumped to his knees, fell over onto his side and lay still.

Under the weight of the attack, Sordaak sank heavily to his knees, clawing helplessly at the blade with his left hand, his right dangling uselessly at his side. Unable to remove the blade, his left shot out to break his fall as his eyes rolled back in his head and he pitched forward to the rock.

Savinhand knelt to check on his friend, but a flurry of movement to his right drew his attention, and he raised his sword just in time to block the swing of yet another halberd, swung by yet another orc. And there were more behind that one.

"Cyrillis!" he shouted as he ducked and rolled to his right, not sure where the cleric was. "Sordaak is down over here!" He regained his feet, coming up in a defensive stance and narrowly avoiding the sword of another of the creatures. He parried still a third thrust as he slowly gave ground, trying to keep the beasts from getting behind him.

Cyrillis, startled at hearing her name, checked on the barbarian, now bleeding from multiple wounds. Most were surface cuts, however, and none appeared mortal. He did not appear in any way hampered by the cuts; in fact, he seemed to feel nothing as he swung his huge axe in ever widening arcs of death. Just in case she wasn't able to return to check on him for some time, she threw a spell of healing his way as she ran toward the sound of Savinhand's voice.

As she turned, an orc blocked her path and she knocked the beast unconscious with one flick of her staff. She sprinted past the monster, not looking
back to see the outcome of her effort.

"Where's Thrinndor?" she shouted at the retreating thief as she spotted the
caster and hurried to his side.

"I'm not sure," replied the rogue as he blocked attacks, returning them as
best he could. "He was by that mage when the blasts hit, but I lost track of him
after that." He was losing ground, not faring well in his defense. One of the orcs
had managed to get behind him, and the thief was bleeding from several wounds
of his own.

He spun, tumbled, counterattacked and rolled this way and that. Still the
persistent attacks were taking their toll, and he was slowing. For every orc he
managed to fell, two stepped in to take its place. He was in trouble, and knew it.

"Cyrillis," he panted, not sure he had enough energy to be loud enough to
be heard. "Find Thrinndor. I need help, here!" His efforts resulted in yet another
beheaded orc. This caused the one behind trying to step in to reconsider his
attack. Savinhand leapt through the opening, hacking at the side of the one that
had stepped back, forcing it back further still.

In a flash he was through the opening, but he knew the respite wouldn't last
long—nor would he if he did not get some attention for his wounds. And some help.

He saw an orc poised for an attack on the unsuspecting cleric, but he was
too far away to prevent it. "Look out!" he shouted. Knowing he didn't have time
to draw a throwing dagger, he threw *Soriin* his shortsword with all of his remaining strength.

His aim was true. However, the sword was unwieldy for such an attack
and the haft—not the blade—hit the creature between its shoulder blades.
The force of the blow, combined with Cyrillis ducking at just the right
moment, was enough to cause the downward swipe of the orc's sword to go
wide of its mark.

The rogue's hand flashed to his belt as he continued running toward the
cleric, and it came up with a rapier. This blade was much better suited to the
flicking sort of attack he preferred anyway. That, and he was just too damn tired
to swing that sword anymore!

As the beast whirled to meet this new attacker, Savinhand's blade pierced
its breastplate just below his ribcage and ran all the way through its chest until
the point came out through the back. The orc's eyes widened in surprise and
then glazed over as it slumped to the ground, the rogue yanking his blade free
in the process.

"Thanks," said Cyrillis. Her eyes took on a concerned look as they automati-
cally went to his many wounds.

"Thrinndor?" he said, attempting to divert attention away from his own plight.

The cleric's brow furrowed as she quickly spoke the words of healing and threw a spell after the rapidly retreating rogue. It wasn't much, but she hadn't much left.

"I do not know," she shouted after him. "I will find him next." She looked back down at the caster supine on the rock before her. There was not much more she could do for him now. She had yanked free the blade and shoved some rolled-up, clean cloth into the wound. Having no time to properly bind it, she just tucked everything under his tunic.

Also noting his almost severed right forearm, she splinted it and wrapped it with two more clean cloths; these she tied in place with a third. She had already spent a Cure Serious spell on him, and the bleeding seemed to have stopped for now.

Deeming his wounds also not to be mortal, she used her staff to push herself to her feet. As she turned to see if she could locate the paladin, she changed her mind and knelt to cast a spell of restoration, hoping to revive the caster. He needed rest most of all, but she was certain they were going to need his powers if they were going to survive this mess.

Sordaak groaned as his eyes opened and he released a stream of vile curses as he tried to push upright with his right arm. He collapsed in a heap and rolled over onto his back, still cursing vehemently as he held his right arm to his chest tightly.

Seeing the cleric for the first time, whose face was now tinged with red, he bit off yet another curse and muttered through clenched teeth, "Sorry, sister."

"Yes…well," she stammered. "I must go find Thrinndor."

Recent events came back to him in a rush and he struggled to sit up—using his left arm this time, his right lying uselessly in his lap.

His eyes quickly searched the surrounding area. Spotting his opposite number lying face down a short distance away, he pointed in that direction. "Behind that outcropping," he said through clenched teeth as he struggled to rise.

Cyrillis grabbed his left arm and helped him to his feet. "Are you going to—"

"I'm fine." The lie was obvious, but there was little more she could do for him. "Go find pretty boy!" The pain made the words rougher than he intended, but he waved her off when she looked back at him.

"Go!" he shouted, pulling himself to his full height. When she had disappeared around the outcropping of rock, he winced as his left hand went to the patch on his shoulder and settled it better in place.

"Dammit!" he cursed as he swung a swift kick at the nearest orc lying on the ground before him. He winced as the toes on his open sandal hit armor instead of unprotected flesh, as intended. "Shit!" He moaned as he pulled a wand from a pouch and limped off after the cleric.

Cyrillis found the paladin where she had been told he would be. He was still unconscious, but his wounds did not look serious; the worst of it appeared to be an already bruising bump on the side of his head, just above the right ear.

She knelt next to him, touched the lump and incanted the words to her lightest of heal spells. As she released the energy, she kneaded the lump lightly and it diminished visibly.

He moaned and slowly opened his eyes. Catching sight of the healer bending over him, he smiled. When realization as to where he was and how he came to be there, he opened his eyes wide and surged to a sitting position.

The sudden motion caused the pain to return in a flood and another groan was ripped from his lips.

"Easy," admonished the cleric. "That is a nasty bump on the side of your head."

"Right," was all he said as he pushed himself unsteadily to his feet. When he staggered to his left, Cyrillis grabbed his arm. He looked at her briefly and then stood to his full height.

"Thank you," he said simply, bowing slightly in her direction. He scouted about briefly for his sword and shield. Spotting them not far away, he ran over to them and bent to pick them up.

"Where?" he said as the caster rounded the rock in front of him.

"This way," Sordaak said, turning on his heel. "We'd better hurry. Savinhand has his hands full! And then some!"

Without a word the big fighter broke into a run as he rounded the rock, reloading his crossbow while in full stride.

He spotted the thief a short distance away, and he indeed had his hands full. He was surrounded by several orcs who were mostly held at bay by a flashing blade. But it was obvious that Savin was about to fall. A cut on his forehead was running blood into his eyes. He was favoring his left leg, which had a deep cut high up on the thigh. And those were just the obvious wounds.

Still, he fought on.

Thrinndor tilted his shield and released a bolt at the nearest orc who went down clawing at the object suddenly caught in his throat. He next whipped the shield spinning at a second orc, who it caught square in the back. It did not have the same effect as a bolt to the neck, but it did serve to get the monster's attention, and it spun to meet this new threat just in time to see a flaming sword pierce its armor and sink to the hilt in his chest.

The creature slid to the ground as the paladin put a foot to its chest and ripped his blade free.

Savinhand used the distraction to dispatch the remaining orc when the point of his rapier entered the mouth of the creature and came out the back of its head.

He yanked his blade free and swung blindly behind him, but there was nothing there; the remaining four orcs had turned to run. He stumbled after them, but tripped over a rock and crashed to his knees.

He wiped the blood from his eyes to see them disappear behind the top of a hill, Thrinndor on their heels. He looked about warily but saw no threat in the immediate vicinity.

He was still on his knees when the healer came upon him. He looked up, exhaustion worn on his face like a mask. "Hi," he said, tilted to one side and tumbled over.

The healer caught his head before it hit the rock, cradled it in her lap as she wiped away the blood and tended his wounds. There were so many! She hesitated, unsure of where to start. Finally, she settled on the thigh wound. It was very deep, and she was sure whatever blade had done that had only been stopped by bone. She could only hope it had hit no arteries.

Knowing others would need her ministrations, she worked quickly and efficiently. Soon she had stopped the majority of the bleeding and bandaged the head wound so it would not blind him further. Her brow knotted furtively, knowing it was going to leave quite a scar. But she also knew there was nothing she could do for that. Her healing, or what was left of it, was needed elsewhere.

Once again she worked her power to wake one of her companions, fleetingly wondering how many more times she would have to do so.

Savinhand's eyes opened, and he smiled when his eyes met those of the cleric. He murmured, "A guy could get used to waking up to see that face!"

"In your dreams, *rogue*," she said in mock indignation as she dumped his had from her lap onto the rock below rather roughly.

"Ouch!" he said. "That hurt!"

'Whatever!" she snapped back. "Now get back out there and *try* to kill at least *one orc!*" She smiled as she helped him to his feet.

"*One?*" he said incredulously. "Why I've killed at least..." he pointed his rapier at first one, then another of the creatures, counting out loud as he went.

"*Whatever!*" she repeated. "Back into battle you go," she said as pushed him in the direction Thrinndor had gone. He started to protest further, but she cut him off. "No time for talk now. GO!"

Sordaak had walked up on them, snickering loudly. Both looked at him, and Cyrillis said, "You, too!"

Savinhand put his hand on the mage's good shoulder to steady his limp. "A bit bossy these days, don't you think?" he said with a wink.

"A bit," agreed the caster. "I'm going to have to pass the star to her if she keeps it up!" He walked obediently with is friend, feeling better having the two of them at his side.

Cyrillis laughed. "If you two fought as well as you talked, this skirmish would already be over!"

"Skirmish!" Sordaak said loudly. "This is what you call a *skirmish?* Shit, what the hell do you call a *battle?*" He looked at her sheepishly at allowing the expletive to get past his lips. He had been working on that, after all.

She smiled, but any reply was cut off as they topped a ridge to see their other two companions standing back to back, fighting off at least a dozen orcs.

There were more than twice that number already dead or dying, scattered across the open rock.

The rogue muttered an expletive under his breath and jerked into a stumbling run, pushing himself to the aid of the barbarian who was to his right.

Sordaak rolled his eyes and muttered, "Damn! Didn't we just *leave* this party?" He stumbled off to the left, preparing a spell as he went.

Cyrillis moved in as close as she dared to tend the wounds of the two fighters, both bleeding from multiple wounds.

"About damn time you guys got here!" groused Vorgath. "I was beginning to think I was going to have to kill all these critters myself!"

"Shut it, midget," replied the paladin between thrusts. "All of your talking is just wasting precious energy!"

"Ha!" retorted the barbarian, cleaving the skull of an orc who had wandered into the path of his arcing greataxe. "You should have plenty of energy after that nap you got!"

And so the banter continued. Savin slew a couple unsuspecting orcs as he crept up on them from behind. Sordaak caught at least ten in a web and followed that up with a fireball. Those that survived those two spells were easily slain while trying to free themselves.

After only a few minutes more, the three remaining dropped their weapons and began to run for the trees.

"Stop them!" Sordaak shouted. "None may escape to tell of this, or we will be hounded!" He pointed his finger at one of the orcs, and three darts streaked at it, hitting the creature between its shoulder blades. It pitched forward onto its face, where it lay unmoving.

Vorgath reared back and heaved his greataxe at the orc nearest him, catching the retreating creature square in the back, knocking it to the ground. The beast screamed as it crashed to the rock, clawing ineffectively at the huge axe protruding from its back. The monster writhed in pain for a few moments and then mercifully fell unconscious.

Knowing the crossbow to be empty, Thrinndor sent his shield spinning after the final retreating orc at the same time Savinhand sent two throwing daggers in rapid succession in the same direction. One dagger hit it in the back, the other in its shoulder. The beast spun to face its oppressors just as the shield got there. There was a loud *clunk* as it bounced off its forehead. The creature crossed its eyes, sank to the ground and did not move.

The paladin and the rogue looked at each other, grinned and strode silently off to retrieve their weapons.

Both were startled when Vorgath bellowed. "That it? That's all you got?" He had retrieved his *Flinthgoor* and was glaring around, daring anything to make a move. Getting no response, he sank first to one knee and then the other. He was exhausted, his blood-lust sated.

The dwarf glanced at Thrinndor, who was inspecting his shield and shaking his head silently at a new dent. The dwarf puffed out his chest and said "Twenty-eight!" Then he pitched forward onto his face and lay still.

A cry of concern escaped Cyrillis' throat as she rushed to attend to the dwarf. His wounds were too many to count, but they did not appear mortal. The loss of blood was her first concern. She stripped away his tattered armor to reveal several more deep gashes. The healer soon ran out of clean cloths and had to resort to tearing away the bottom of her cloak to make makeshift bandages.

She was exhausted, but as she looked over her handiwork she said a brief prayer and sent some energy from her staff into the prone barbarian. His face went from a pain twisted smile to just a smile almost instantly.

He opened his eyes and quickly sat up, whereupon a groan of pain escaped his lips for his effort.

"Easy," the healer chided gently. "I just got the bleeding stopped!" Her eyes swept across several bandages at once. "Well, most of it anyway!" She stood and helped the barbarian to his feet.

Thrinndor watched approvingly as the healer performed her work, and was there to grab an arm and assist the recalcitrant dwarf to his feet.

The mage was walking away from them and disappeared over the rise in the direction from which they had just come. Savinhand was following at a more leisurely pace. His interest piqued, Thrinndor turned to follow, leaving the unsteady dwarf leaning on the cleric. Vorgath was still too far gone to care, or even notice.

Thrinndor crested the rise just as Sordaak reached the facedown body of the caster that had opposed them. The mage hooked his right foot under the main torso of the dead man and, with no small effort, rolled him over.

The mage stumbled back a step at what he saw. His face turned crimson as he quickly stepped toward the body and gave a swift kick to the caster's head, causing it to flop over at an odd angle. "Bastard!" he said through clenched teeth.

He was still standing over the body, shaking his head when the paladin and rogue walked up together.

"Recognize him?" Thrinndor asked, his right eyebrow melding with the shock of black hair plastered by sweat and blood to his forehead.

"That's no way to show respect!" said the thief playfully. He backed up a step, both hands held at waist level when the caster turned a furious look in his direction.

"There was no respect intended," Sordaak grated. He softened his stance slightly as he faced the paladin. "Yes," he said simply.

When he offered no more, Thrinndor probed further. "Someone I might know? Or know of?"

The mage hesitated, and then shrugged his shoulders, wincing in pain because of the damaged one. "Doubt it," he said. He returned his attention to the man lying on the ground before continuing. "He is Quozak."

Thrinndor stifled a surprised response as he looked closer at the body. "Quozak?" he finally said. "Are you sure?" He attempted to cover the doubt in his voice.

"Yes," replied Sordaak. "I believe I'm in position to know." He looked up at the paladin. "I'm his pupil. He's my master..."

Savinhand stooped over to remove his dagger which was still lodged in the caster's throat. "Was," he corrected, wiping the dagger onto prone man's cloak. "Looks to me like you are going to have to find someone else to teach you how to wiggle your fingers!"

Sordaak glared at the rogue. Abruptly, he turned and marched off the direction he had come. "Yup," he said.

Chapter Nineteen

Post-Traumatic Relief

Sordaak walked past the barbarian and cleric on his way down the hill without as much as a glance.

Cyrillis turned to look at him after he had passed as she saw the makeshift bandage on his arm was still seeping blood. The scowl on his face discouraged her enough, however, to let him go. He would live, and she would not have been able to do much for him right now. Perhaps after they had both rested.

She shrugged and helped Vorgath get back in motion toward the other two members of the party. "What is with him?" she asked as she threw another still concerned glance over her shoulder at the receding mage.

"This dead guy *was* his master," Savinhand said simply.

Vorgath arched the stubble of an eyebrow and turned to stare in the direction the caster had gone. Too late, he had disappeared over the crest of the hill. "There's a story there, I'm sure," he said tiredly. He then turned back to the dead mage on the ground in front of him.

"Yes," mused the paladin thoughtfully. "I am sure you are correct." His eyes had not left the back of the receding magicuser, and he continued staring after him even after he had moved out of his field of vision.

Presently he shook his head as if to clear it and brought his attention to back to those standing beside him. All were looking at him now.

He quickly assessed the group, raising an eyebrow when his eyes befell the dwarf. "Twenty-eight, huh?" he said, his smile belying the concern he felt for his old friend.

Vorgath pushed the cleric aside and stood straight and to his full height. "Yes," he said, belligerence strong in his voice. "Do you doubt my count?"

"No, no," said Thrinndor, who raised his hands and backed up a step, "of course not!" A twinkle was in his eye as he continued. "Except I am not sure you can count that high without removing your boots, and I do doubt you did so during the course of the battle!"

The barbarian puffed up even more and drew in breath for what was obviously going to be a loud reply, but he started laughing instead.

Soon the four of them were laughing and the intensity of what they had just been through washed away as if by a deluge.

Thrinndor, tears still in his eyes from the mirth of the moment, said, "We will have to rest here—we are in no condition to travel." His eyes swept the bluff for the first time, trying to discern a suitable location to make camp. Finally his gaze settled upon the base of the cliff where they had emerged from the chamber. "There," he pointed. "We will set up camp there."

As he turned back to face the group the rogue said abruptly, "Any idea where 'there'—or 'here' for that matter—is?"

They had all started moving toward the indicated camp site, but Vorgath stopped and looked around as if trying to get his bearings.

"Northron Hills," he said after a few moments' consideration. "And if I am correct, the southern portion." He looked to the south. "Berehmiir Pass should be a few miles to our south." He took in a deep breath as he faced east. "The Sunbirth Sea is not far to the east—maybe ten miles," he said archly, lowered his head and continued his trek toward the cliff face.

"You've been here before?" asked the rogue.

"Never been here in my life," Vorgath said without looking up.

"But..." stammered Savinhand.

Vorgath tuned to fix the rogue with a piercing stare. "Look, *Thumbs*," he began acidly, "I don't question your abilities as—"

"Yes you do," interrupted the thief, irritated at having his nickname abused in such a manner.

The barbarian arched the remains of an eyebrow and cocked his head to one side before replying, amusement dancing in his eyes. "Very well," he said. "I might at that." His tone was now playful. "However, that will change as you get better. I have noticed some *small* improvement as our little quest has progressed."

"Thank you," said Savinhand formally.

"You're welcome," said the dwarf just as formally. His tone then took on a more ominous tenor. "However, it would be in your best interest to *not* question a dwarf about location."

Vorgath turned his attention to gathering the necessary materials to put a fire together. He glanced back at the rogue, who was staring intently at the back of this diminutive character trying to decide how much to push. He was genuinely intrigued at how Vorgath could possibly know where they were if he had never been here.

"I can explain, if you like," the dwarf said patiently.

"Please," Savinhand said. Seeing the barbarian struggle with a large rock he was trying to move into place for a fire-ring, he said, "Here, let me help you with that."

Vorgath started to protest but decided it was not worth the effort. While he was starting to feel his strength return, he was nowhere near one hundred percent.

The two of them built the fire pit and gathered enough wood for a large, hearty fire. Thrinndor scouted about to ensure they were alone, and Cyrillis fussed about all three of them as they strained and undid the effort she had spent so much energy on, keeping their bodily fluids where they were supposed to be.

"You don't have to have been somewhere to know where that somewhere is," began Vorgath. "You just have to have reference points recognizable from any angle." He grunted as he plopped down on one of the boulders ringing the wood stacked for the fire. A small tendril of smoke was coming from a small pile of shaved bark the rogue was blowing on after getting a successful spark.

"Take Yogalith's Peak there to our south," the barbarian pointed at what was the tallest mountain visible in any direction. "It is easily recognizable from any direction for almost a hundred miles on a clear day. While I have never been this far north—not in this area, anyway—I've seen the maps of the region and I recognize the peak from the time when I spent a few years working the east coast near Kahndahar."

"The little people *love* maps!" said a bemused Thrinndor, who had been listening as he inspected the edge on his flaming sword.

"You know," Vorgath said as he cocked his head in the general direction of the paladin, "I only have one nerve left and you are now officially standing on it!" His tone grated as he added, "This 'little people' shit is starting to get old!" He grunted again as he started to rise to his feet.

Thrinndor, grinning widely, said, "Relax, old one!" He raised his hands in submission. "I was just teasing!"

Vorgath hesitated and then dropped back on his laurels. "One of these days," he grumbled, "I am going to have to teach you some manners!"

"As in, 'respect for my elders'?" the paladin replied innocently.

The barbarian bit off a sharp reply. Instead, he looked at his friend and grinned. "Something like that," he said with a shake of his head.

Both were still chuckling when Cyrillis walked up. "Has anyone seen Sordaak?" the cleric asked as she approached the fire.

Thrinndor glanced about quickly, realizing he had not seen the caster since he had marched over the hill. "No," he said, the concern in his voice matching that of the cleric. "He has not come back?" He had spent considerable time scouting about and had just assumed the mage had returned but was just out of sight, attending to his own business.

"We never did see any more of those assassins, did we?" Vorgath asked, concern in his voice as well.

"No," said Savinhand. "But you wouldn't if they didn't want to be seen," he added ominously.

Now they all looked around nervously.

"My point is," said the barbarian, "didn't that Halfling assassin who almost ruined your day—"

"Life," corrected the rogue.

"—mention something about others of her kind exacting revenge, or some such bullshit?"

"Yes she did," Savin replied. His eyes searched every bush, rock and hillock for anything that might not belong. "However, paid killers expect to be paid."

"What?" asked Thrinndor.

"If there were any more assassins in the group," the rogue explained patiently, "in all probability they bailed when the person—or persons—under to whom they were contracted were sent into the afterlife." He did not sound all that convinced.

"Shit," groaned the dwarf as he pushed himself back to his feet. "We'd better go find him."

"Sordaak!" Thrinndor shouted, his voice unnaturally loud as it reflected off the cliff face behind them, causing Savin to nearly jump out of his skin.

"What?" came the caster's reply as he crested the rise from the direction he had disappeared not all that long ago. He was leading two horses and some pack mules.

"You should not wander off alone!" Cyrillis said sternly. However, she was unable to keep the relief of his reappearance out of her voice.

"Miss me?" he inquired placidly.

"No!" she snapped in return. Too quickly, her face colored slightly.

Thrinndor looked at her and arched an eyebrow but said nothing until he faced the approaching mage. "She is correct," he began. "We do not yet know if the area is secure—"

"It isn't," the caster interrupted acidly. "Or rather, it wasn't." He pointed to a figure draped loosely over one of the pack animals. "Hell, these still might not be the end of them."

"What happened?" asked the paladin, trying to make sense of what the mage was telling him.

"I—" Sordaak began, but his eyes rolled back in their sockets. Stumbling, he pitched forward first onto his knees and then onto his face.

Sticking out of his back was a dagger, surrounded by a still growing bloodstain in his robe.

"NO!" screamed Cyrillis as she pushed aside the rogue and rushed to kneel at the caster's side. She put two fingers to his neck to check for a pulse. "Alive," she breathed. "But his heart is faint."

Savinhand, who had only been a step behind the cleric, stooped and jerked the knife free and examined it. "Poison!" he spat as he turned to examine the body face down on the pack mule.

Cyrillis looked up at the approaching paladin, tears making their way down her grime-streaked face to drip unchecked from the point of her chin. "I have nothing left!" she moaned. "Can you help?"

"I believe I have enough energy left to keep him from escaping to the after-life," he said quickly as he knelt to examine the stab wound. "However, you must first deal with the poison."

"There is not time!" she almost shrieked at him. "His heart will stop within a few more beats!" Her eyes were pleading with the paladin to do something.

Thrinndor hesitated at the vehemence of her words but placed his hands obediently onto the back of the prone caster, surrounding the point of penetration with his thumbs and forefingers. "Very well," he said, "but you must be prepared to deal with the poison." His eyes locked with those of the cleric.

"*Just do it, already!*" she begged, her eyes narrowing to mere slits.

The paladin said nothing more. Instead he closed his eyes and began chanting the now familiar song of healing. Before their eyes, the wound stopped pouring forth the mage's life and indeed seemed to close as they watched.

When the chanting stopped, Thrinndor fell back onto his haunches and only just barely avoided toppling over as he caught himself.

Cyrillis held her own breath as she again applied her touch to the caster's neck. Time seemed to stand still before she felt the first beat. It was stronger, but still much weaker than it should have been.

Her eyes locked onto where the dagger had done its damage. Cyrillis noted that while the wound was closed, it remained dark from the poison—and the dark stain on his skin was *growing*!

Her eyes found the rogue as he was still looking over the presumed assassin. "Get me my pack," her voice was almost a wail. When the thief started to say something, she shouted, "*NOW!*"

Startled, Savinhand hustled off to retrieve the requested pack, not even mumbling under his breath as would usually be the case. In his haste, he nearly dropped the pack, causing the vials inside to clank together noisily. His shoulders tensed for the tongue-lashing that was sure to follow.

When said lashing was not immediately forthcoming, he risked a quick glance over his shoulder only to see the healer bent over the prone caster, her eyes closed, with tears running openly down a now familiar track on a pretty face marred by concern.

Now more concerned than he would normally be in a situation such as this, he ran the few steps back to where his friend lay with his breaths coming in ragged, tortured gasps.

Not knowing what to do, he tore open the pack and quickly fumbled around inside, trying in vain to locate the correct vial in the mess he discovered therein.

Fortunately, Cyrillis became aware of his presence—and subsequent fumbling around in her pack—and snatched it quickly from his hands, knocking two of the precious containers to the ground.

A quick glance was all it took for her to discern neither was what she was after, and her hand dove into the bag. Her eyes widened in obvious despair when her hand came to the place where the potion should have been!

"No!" she moaned again, suddenly remembering the potion had been used on Savinhand a couple of days before. In panic, she turned the pack bottom side up and shook it violently.

The contents dumped unceremoniously onto the ground before her. She quickly selected a vial, inspected it and then cast it aside, not caring whether or not it survived such harsh treatment.

Frantic, the healer was about to cast aside yet another container, but stopped. A quick glance at the few remaining vials told her there was nothing that remained that was of any use. She looked at the one in her hand again and muttered, "This will have to do," as she bent back over the unconscious caster.

That Sordaak was in a bad way was obvious to them all. His skin—already pale by most standards—was almost bleached-parchment white. His lips held a faint bluish tint, and his breathing was coming in labored gasps, as if even the act of drawing in and exhaling air hurt him.

Cyrillis said to the group that had gathered to watch, "Help me roll him over," as she ripped the protective seal off of the vial.

Vorgath bent down and grasped the caster's shoulder and roughly jerked him first upright and then on over onto his back. Cyrillis raised his head until he was almost in a sitting position and held the vial to his lips. She forced his lips aside and dumped the contents into his mouth all at once.

His shoulders contused to cough, but she clamped her hand over his mouth and pressed hard. Next she yanked his head to her chest and held him tight as his body tried to expel the foreign liquid.

"You're choking—" complained the rogue, but the savage look she threw his direction caused him to swallow further words.

Satisfied at least some of the liquid made it into his system, she dropped him, still unconscious, back to the ground and rolled him over so she had access to his back.

She tore his robe open to further expose the area and quickly surveyed the wound. The blackened skin had again opened at the entry point and was now oozing a nasty, dark, puss-like fluid. The stain had grown larger in the few moments since she had last seen it.

Her hand flashed to the thin rope cord that served as her belt and came away with a short, thin knife housed in a custom-made leather sheath. She quickly withdrew the blade and cast the sheath aside.

Cyrillis hesitated, her lips drawn into a thin line of determination, and then she leaned forward until she was hovering over the mage's prone figure.

In a sudden flurry of movement, she reached forward with the knife.

Savinhand gasped, but said nothing as she cut into the putrid-looking skin on either side of the festering wound, forming a small 'X' at as near the point of entry as she could.

Next she lowered her face to the wound, closed her eyes and put her lips on the blackened skin. The party members could hear her make a brief sucking sound and then she raised up, turned her head to the side and spat a stream of dark blood.

She repeated the process several times, with each drawing some of the poisoned blood into her mouth.

"What *is* she doing?" whispered the thief into the paladin's nearby ear.

"She is drawing the poison out."

"But," stammered Savinhand, who was unable to take his eyes off of the spectacle taking place before him, "the poison was *dry* on the blade!" He was almost pleading to be understood. "It's not in liquid form as that of a snake's venom."

"She knows," said the fighter, sadness in his voice. "But the blood in the area of the wound can be drawn out, thereby removing the poison. I hope."

The paladin turned to lock eyes with the thief. "He *must* survive!" His voice was a statement of finality, although his tone lacked its usual conviction.

"But—" argued Savinhand, "if that poison gets in her mouth, in her system…" He stopped, more than a little worried for both of his companions.

"She knows that, too." Thrinndor's voice was barely audible.

The paladin thought he could see a diminishing in the black region of the caster's back, but he acknowledged that might have been a byproduct of wishful thinking.

He *knew*, however, that the poison was having an effect on the healer. Her lips were already swollen and black, and her motions were noticeably slower now after a few passes. Her breath was now also coming in ragged gasps, matching that of Sordaak.

Finally, she looked up at the paladin, confusion in her eyes as she was obviously losing grip on herself. Her eyes managed to focus on the paladin as she struggled to speak, saying, "Take this," as she pulled a small pouch from her belt, "and bandage the wound *tightly*." Her voice was barely above a whisper, making Thrinndor lean toward her to be sure he heard correctly. She looked back at her patient. "You must care for him…"

Thrinndor was in position to catch her and ease her to the ground when her eyes rolled back in her head and her shoulders sagged.

Without saying anything, the paladin obediently retrieved the pouch and dumped some of its contents directly onto the back of the caster. Next he tore some cloth from a tunic in his pack, folded it into roughly a square and placed it over the affected area.

He tore strips from the same cloth and tied them together until he had a couple of wide strips long enough to circle the slight body of the mage.

He asked for and got help as he gently lifted the mage to an almost sitting position and tied the bandage in place. He then rolled Sordaak over onto his back, figuring the pressure of the caster's own body weight on the poultice would be good to hold it tightly to the skin.

Next he turned his attention to the cleric, who was still lying where he had deposited her moments ago. Her lips were black and swollen from the poison, and her normally alabaster skin was turning a nasty shade of blue.

His eyes cast about for the container that had held the contents of the liquid she had forced into the caster. Spying it a few feet away, he retrieved it. He poured a small amount of water from the water skin at his waist into it, swirled it around in the vial and then went back to the cleric. Her breathing was decidedly worse now.

"What was in that?" queried the thief. He was at a loss as to what he could do, but he wanted to do *something!*

Without looking up Thrinndor shrugged and said, "I am not sure. My assumption is that it is a vial of Slow Poison." Then he mumbled, *"My hope."*

He knelt and held the vial to the healer's lips and slowly dribbled its contents into her mouth, taking care not to gag her.

The vial empty, he laid her head gently back on the ground, rose to his feet, and watched to see what effect his ministrations would have.

He thought—hoped—that she was breathing easier, and her lips seemed to be losing some of the blackness that made her face look so pale.

He sighed, knowing there was nothing more he could do for her for the time being. He turned his attention back to the caster.

He rolled Sordaak on his side to check the bandage he had placed over the incisions on his back, immediately seeing it had bled through, but not badly. Already the flow of blood had seemed to diminish. *At least it was red blood,* he thought furtively, not that black stuff that had oozed out earlier. And he was most definitely breathing easier.

Shrugging, he eased the positions of both as best he could and tried to make them as comfortable as possible. Sordaak he was now sure was going to make it. *But Cyrillis…*

Solemnly the remaining three went about the business of making camp, saying nothing, each with their own thoughts.

As the afternoon sun sank toward the horizon, gradually the light began to diminish. Dusk approached with Savinhand preparing a hot meal for them using supplies taken from both their own packs and stuff he had found in the bags on the pack animals.

Darkness made its way across the small valley, and a chill crept into the air—as it usually does up in the foothills. Not cold, mind you, just cool enough to cause the rogue to pull a blanket from his pack and drape it across his shoulders. He also edged closer to the now blazing fire.

Thrinndor arched an eyebrow at the rogue's efforts, snorted and rose to begin rummaging through the collective of packs from the animals. He pulled two more blankets from them and went to check on Cyrillis and Sordaak, who lay unmoving in the darkness not far from the edge of the fire.

He put the blankets on first one and then the other, checking them as best he could with the light of the fire. The mage, he decided, looked appreciably better. Sordaak's familiar was perched on a nearby rock, and the creature fidgeted nervously as the paladin approached.

Thrinndor hesitated and then faced the creature squarely. He wasn't sure it would understand, but he had to try. "You know," he said, "if your master dies, you die as well."

Fahlred stared back at the paladin from those unfathomably dark eyes. The paladin was beginning to think he had not been understood when the creature hissed and wound its tail around the caster's neck, an unmistakably affectionate move.

"Master will not die," the creature said slowly in a serpentine voice, almost too softly to be heard. The certainty in its tone surprised the paladin, and he was about to ask how the creature knew when Sordaak's eyes fluttered open.

The mage licked his dry lips and had to try twice before he was able to speak. "Water," he finally managed to croak out.

Thrinndor undid the thong that held the water skin to his belt as he knelt beside the caster. He quickly slid his arm under the mage's head and raised him to a half-sitting position while holding the skin to his lips.

Sordaak drank greedily, and then his shoulders wracked in a spasm of coughing as he choked and sprayed water all over the front of his tunic.

"Easy," chided the big fighter. "Not too fast."

The mage cast a *'yeah, right!'* look at the paladin, raised his right hand, seized the skin and pressed it again to his lips. This time he was able to drink without choking and emptied the skin.

The mage tossed the empty skin aside, moved his hands so that he supported himself and rose to a sitting position. "Thanks," he said, his voice much stronger.

As he sat up, his eyes fell upon Cyrillis for the first time.

At first he merely assumed she was sleeping, but realization soon struck that she would not normally be doing so this close to the others in the party.

"What?" he began, panic rising up in his throat like bile. "What happened?" was all he could manage as he brushed aside all offers of assistance. Sordaak surged to his feet, took two quick steps to her side and knelt to get a closer look at the prone cleric.

Curious as to Sordaak's reaction, Thrinndor did the obligatory shrug of his shoulders and said, "She has been thus since she…" He paused while searching for an appropriate word. "…removed the poison from your body."

The mage twisted around to fix the paladin with a penetrating stare. "How?" he began, his concern deepening.

"Well," said the paladin, "she made two incisions—"

"No, you idiot," spat the caster, "how long?"

Knowing there was more afoot than simple concern for a colleague, Thrinndor chose to let the insult pass. "Six, maybe seven hours," he said.

"Seven," said the dwarf, certainty making his voice gruff. "Give or take."

"Shit!" said the caster. He had not the cleric's sight for assessing the health of a patient, but even he could tell her condition was dire. She was sweating profusely, but her skin felt cool to the touch. Her skin had lost any hint of color except for her swollen black lips, which had now spread into the surrounding tissues of her cheeks and chin. This explained how she had gotten the poison out of his body.

"No!" he moaned, his mind racing to come to grip with what he was seeing.

He leapt to his feet and immediately regretted doing so. He fought back the nausea and started to search wildly for his stuff. Finally spotting his pack a few feet away, he stumbled in that direction and dropped to his knees beside it.

He tore at the strings of his knapsack and fumbled around inside with his hand. Frustrated, he dumped the contents of the sack onto the ground and pushed the pile around, looking…

"What is it you seek?" asked Thrinndor.

Sordaak ignored him and, not finding what he was looking for, continued his wild search as he went through the remainder of his things, flinging unwanted items out of his way.

He again surged to his feet and looked about the camp, his eyes fearful and frustrated. He began to pat his hands over his loose robes. In exasperation threw his head back to look at the stars as he whipped open the left flap revealing several scroll tubes shoved in many hidden pockets.

Hastily he slid one tube after another out of its place, replacing it when discovered it was not the one he was looking for.

Finally he announced, "Got it!" as he rushed back to Cyrillis' side while tearing the seal off of the tube's cap.

He dumped its contents into the palm of his left hand and proceeded to unroll the small scroll. His eyes hurriedly scanned the lines of script.

"Dammit!" he shouted as he spun to point at the paladin, who was watching the goings-on with interest from a few feet away. "You said you have some skills in the healing arts!" His words came out sounding like an accusation.

"I do," stated Thrinndor, somewhat taken aback by this recent turn of events. "But—"

"Shut up and *read!*" Sordaak said, thrusting the sheet of parchment into the paladin's face.

"But—" protested the big fighter.

"I know you don't have the required skills to cast this spell," said the caster quickly. "But you will at least recognize the words." He took a deep breath. "Get the intonation correct and it *should* work."

Thrinndor started to protest again, but was again interrupted by the mage, who was again digging a scroll case out of his tunic. It was obvious he knew where this one was by feel, because his hand emerged without any of the previous fumbling around. "But first, let me increase your abilities with this."

When the paladin opened his mouth again, Sordaak snapped, "Shut it and *read!*" As the fighter's mouth clamped shut, the mage unrolled the other scroll in his hand and rapidly called forth the incantation written upon it.

A whisper of power surged from the words on the scroll as they illuminated and flickered, traveling down the mage's outstretched arm and flew across to the paladin.

Thrinndor's shoulders immediately squared, and he took on a more authoritative posture. His hesitation was gone as he raised the scroll to read.

"Do not fail or she dies," said the caster as he stole a quick glance at Cyrillis. He fixed the paladin with a stare to match his words. "And we can't afford to let that happen."

"No pressure," muttered Savinhand, who was looking on from across the fire.

At the paladin's raised eyebrow, Sordaak said, "I'll explain later. Now *read!*"

Nonplussed, Thrinndor first bowed his head and whispered a brief prayer to Valdaar. When he looked up he glanced through the script written on the parchment and only then did he start to read the scroll aloud, using the sing-song voice commonly used by healers.

Sordaak was unconsciously holding his breath as one by one the ancient scrawling on the even older paper flared briefly as their meaning was intoned, and then vanished in a whiff of smoke.

Finished, the paladin again bowed his head to pray. But the caster studied the healer from where he stood; trying to discern what effect the spell had on her, assuming it worked at all.

Initially he saw nothing; she showed no sign whatever that anything had been done. Sordaak was beginning to believe the spell had been a failure when her eyes flashed open. Her mouth opened in a silent scream as her body convulsed and her back arched so that only the tip of her head and her buttocks touched the ground.

Startled, the mage rushed the two short steps to her side and knelt to attempt to ease her obvious pain. But by the time he got there she had already relaxed, her eyes again closed.

Thrinndor, his head raised and his eyes now open, studied the scene from where he stood. "Was that supposed to happen?" he inquired gently.

"I don't know," replied the mage as he waited for something else to happen.

"What did you do to her?" said the rogue, accusations intertwined in his tone. "What was that *spell?*"

Without looking up from his charge Sordaak replied, "A powerful form of Restoration." Still not looking up, his voice continued in almost a wail, "It was *all I had!*"

The paladin raised an eyebrow, silently wondering where all this concern was headed. He shrugged as he stepped in and pressed the first two fingers of his right hand gently on the crease of the cleric's neck.

The caster looked up at him from where he knelt, his eyes pleading.

Thrinndor considered messing with the mage some more, but ultimately decided his newfound friend was teetering on the edge, and he did not want to be the one to provide that extra push.

He sighed and smiled wearily. "Her heart is assuredly stronger than before…"

"Then she will live?" blurted out Sordaak.

"I did not say that," chastened the paladin. "Merely that she is better off than the last time I checked. Her ordeal is far from over."

A crestfallen caster allowed his eyes to drop back to her face. Morosely, he drew in a breath to speak, but the fighter spoke first. "However," he continued as he moved his hand to her face and brushed aside a stray strand of honey-wheat-colored hair, "I feel that barring a relapse of sorts, she will indeed live to see another day."

"Thank the gods!" said the mage.

"God," corrected Thrinndor.

A confused look briefly crossed Sordaak's face. "Yes, yes," he mumbled, "of course." His attention returned to the face of the cleric. It was now clear she was breathing more easily.

"Now," began the fighter, his tone firm but gentle, "perhaps you can enlighten us as to why exactly we could not let her die—by which, I assume, you meant other than the obvious reasons: Her being a companion and party member." His right eyebrow seemed to have found a permanent resting place up near his hairline. "Not to mention a servant of Lord Valdaar."

"What?" began the caster, looking away from Cyrillis in obvious confusion. "Oh, *that*! I'm not sure I can explain…"

"But," said the paladin even more firmly, "you said you would do so." His eyebrow crawled its way down from its lofty perch to knit together with its mate sternly. "So please do."

It was not a request.

Sordaak looked at him sharply and bit off a hostile reply. Their eyes locked in a battle of will for an instant and then the caster allowed his shoulders to sag wearily as he released a deep sigh.

Looking away, he mumbled, "Very well." He pushed himself to his feet, where he teetered unsteadily. He reached out and grasped the shoulder of the paladin, steadying himself as he walked slowly to the fire.

Vorgath and Savinhand, who had watched the recent rapid-fire events with more than a passing interest, looked at one another, shrugged and moved closer to the fire as well.

Once there, all four men sat at once—the barbarian and thief on their packs, which had been drug into place for the purpose, and Thrinndor and Sordaak on a convenient rock.

Sordaak stared into the fire, gathering his thoughts. He started slightly when one of the logs suddenly burned through, releasing the branch it held up to the ground beneath with a thud and a few sparks.

"Well," he began, his eyes not leaving the burning coals, "all present know I subscribe to the theories of Chaos. Random events work together to make us who we are and guide our lives." He paused as he reached for words to explain what was bothering him.

"There is no 'preordination', no predication to determine *my* path!" Finally he looked up and locked eyes for a moment with each of the men seated with him. "*Nothing* predetermines my choice of action but *me*!" His voice rose with each word, ending in almost a shout.

His belligerent stare once again locked eyes with those seated around the fire with him. Again his shoulders sagged. "That's why this is so hard to explain." His voice was a mere whisper, barely audible above the crackle of the fire.

A deep silence followed as the caster struggled within. Finally, Savinhand could stand it no more, "*What* is so hard to explain?"

Sordaak's unfocused stare turned upon the rogue. "Cyrillis," he said flatly.

Again silence washed over the group.

"What about Cyrillis?" Thrinndor's question had a strange undertone to it, as if he were almost afraid to hear what was next.

Sordaak shifted his gaze to the paladin, but Thrinndor got the impression the mage's eyes were reaching for the horizon. "Everything," the caster said simply.

This time the fighter did not wait near as long. "Perhaps you had better explain."

"I am!" snapped the caster, his focus returning to the paladin. "Or rather, I'm trying! Look, this is *hard for me*!" He almost seemed to be begging for them to understand.

"Just *what* is it that is so hard?" queried the paladin gently.

"Cyrillis was—*is*—no accident!" Now Sordaak was shouting. At whom or what the paladin was at a loss to determine.

"I'm sure she would be glad to know that," said Vorgath.

"This is not even remotely funny!" snapped the caster, the vitriol in his voice causing the dwarf to sit up straighter. Vorgath said no more.

"What *about* Cyrillis?" Thrinndor was attempting to defuse the situation before it got out of hand. Sordaak was even closer to that edge than he had first thought.

The mage's head snapped back around, and with no small effort he focused his gaze back on the paladin. *Good*, thought Thrinndor, *at least he is back with the group.*

"It doesn't make *sense*!" The caster's words came out in a tumble, as if he were trying to voice too many thoughts at the same time. "It was no *accident* that we found her in the library!" His eyes were ablaze with the fervor of what he was trying to convey—or maybe *not* convey. "It was *no accident* we found her *when* we did!" His eyes started to lose focus. "It was *no accident* she was the only one left alive of her party!" He paused as he tried to again focus on the big fighter before him.

"*It was no accident!*" The caster's voice was shrill, almost screaming. "*It could not have been an accident!*" Abruptly he dropped his gaze to the paladin's feet, his remaining energy spent. "Yet..." he finished, his voice almost a whisper.

"Focus, Sordaak," Thrinndor said sternly. "You are making no sense." He extended an arm and put a meaty hand on the mage's shoulder. "What is it you are trying to tell us? Or perhaps not tell us?"

Sordaak raised his eyes to look deep into the pale blues of the paladin. "Think," the mage urged quietly. "I know you can figure this out. It's not *that hard*!"

The paladin returned the gaze, the wheels in his mind turning. Finally, he shook his head, wondering just what this was all about.

The mage rolled his eyes. "*And they shall be three...*" was all he said, urging the big man to figure it out on his own.

Thrinndor shook his head once, but then his eyes widened. His hand dropped from the caster's shoulder as he stumbled backward a step. In the process he tripped over his pack and landed unceremoniously on his backside. It was the only time Sordaak could remember seeing him off balance.

"*Her?*" the paladin said, uncertainty clouding his voice. He turned to look at the cleric, who still lay prone on the bed made for her.

Sordaak did not say anything, but also turned his attention in the direction of their healer.

"*She* is the one?"

Chapter Twenty

Endgame

"What?" cried Savinhand. "You guys have gone way overboard on this 'the one' shit!" The look on his face descried how he felt about this piece of news. "Don't make me come over there and slap a knot on the side of your head!"

Thrinndor snorted his derision. "That would not be advised."

"Well *someone* needs to do it," said the rogue, shaking his head in confusion.

"I'll do it!" announced Vorgath as he struggled to his feet.

The paladin pursed his lips in a wry smile and said with a twinkle in his eye, "Sit down, old one. Allow me to get to the bottom of this, please."

The dwarf gave a mock bow and said, "Yes, your high-and-mightiness!" and sat back down.

Thrinndor did not appear to even hear the jibe. Instead, he returned his attention to the caster, who quelled at the scrutiny placed back on him. "You are certain?"

"Hell no!" snapped the caster. "I'm not even certain *I* am one of these *ones*—or *you either*, for that matter!" He jutted his chin out, daring someone to say otherwise. "But it all *fits*! If your prophecy is correct about bringing this dead/dormant/whatever god back from wherever he has gotten off to, then there is just too much coincidence surrounding all of this for her *not* to be the one."

"You guys are going to have to stop saying that!" groused the rogue.

Sordaak and Thrinndor turned and said in unison, "Shut up!"

The thief gave a startled look, but said no more as he folded his arms across his chest.

"Look," said the caster, who was now pacing back and forth in front of the seated paladin. He made no attempt to rise further. "The circumstances surrounding your finding me…"

"You stole my horse," interrupted the big man.

Sordaak halted pacing for just a moment to throw the paladin a withering glare. "Borrowed," he shot back. "You got it back!" He started pacing again.

"Point is," Sordaak's attention appeared to be centered on the ground mere inches from where he was stepping, "I could have borrowed *any* horse in that barn—there were several to choose from. Yet I chose *yours*."

"He is a fine steed," interjected the fighter.

"Whatever," said the caster. "To me, a horse is a horse—a means of getting from one place to another. I needed a mount to get me out of there, fast. And I chose *yours*."

He made several more circuits before continuing. "You followed us, and if I remember correctly, you had ill intent on your mind."

"I had every intention of killing you for stealing my steed," said the paladin solemnly. "It is the way."

"Borrowed," corrected the mage, again. "Yet you did not. Instead, you joined our group."

"We had a common goal," said Thrinndor defensively.

"Right," said Sordaak. "Do you make it a normal practice to join forces with a thief…"

"Rogue," broke in Savinhand.

"…and his accomplice?"

The fighter thought about it briefly. "No," he said.

"In fact," continued the caster, as if lecturing in the classroom, "would it not be considered against the paladin way of thinking to be seen consorting with a rogue?" He looked pointedly at a grinning Savin.

"Thank you," Savin said, dipping his head in a short bow.

"And said accomplice?"

"Well," said Thrinndor, also grinning by this point, "I was kind of hoping we would never be seen together!"

Sordaak paused in his pacing long enough to throw a nasty look in the direction of the paladin. "Thanks," he muttered.

"So, let me summarize to this point," the mage said as he reversed his direction back into the light. "A sorcerer—me—by sheer accident gets involved in mayhem and murder in a seedy town bar which results in us having to flee said town—"

"And burning half of it down in the process," interjected Vorgath.

Sordaak threw another of his withering glances at the dwarf before continuing. "By appropriating your fine steed. You followed us to get it back, intent on killing one, or both, of us in retribution. Instead, you joined our little venture, bringing along a companion who just happened to be in the area.

"Next we enter Dragma's Keep and fight our way down until we come across her." The sorcerer paused to point over at the cleric, who had yet to move. "She had somehow survived an attack on her party along with one or more of her companions. Each of those companions having been subsequently eaten by the raiders—minotaurs in this case—until only she remained. Which is when we show up, slay the minotaurs and rescue her. Probably only an hour or two removed from when said beasts had planned on having her for dessert."

He stopped pacing and looked pointedly at the paladin. "Do I have it correct to this point?"

Thrinndor shifted uncomfortably under the scrutiny of the caster, shrugged and said, "I believe so."

Sordaak raised an eyebrow but did not immediately continue. When he did, it was obvious he was feeling his way from this point on. "It also just so happens she is a servant of this god of yours." He looked pointedly at the paladin. "More coincidence?" He was not looking for an answer and didn't get one.

"Just how many servants are wandering around these hills?" he asked suddenly. On this he *was* expecting an answer and was not disappointed.

"Not many," replied the fighter. "Perhaps twenty-five or thirty—if you count the Paladinhood to which I belong."

"So," Sordaak said, again spinning on his heel and walking away from the paladin, "of the thousands of residents in this portion of Khandahar, two servants of a dead god just so happen to be in the same place—a place that has been 'lost' for more than a thousand years by the way—at the same time on the same, or similar, missions?" As he turned he stopped and glared at the paladin. "Does that strike you as something that would be mere coincidence?"

If he was expecting an answer to that one, he was disappointed, because none was forthcoming.

"She *has* to be the one!" concluded the mage, his face torn between a look of satisfaction and one of pure horror.

"*What?*" said Savinhand, whose attention had started to wander, but had been snapped back to the present by this last statement.

Thrinndor held up a hand to forestall more from the thief, turned his head to stare at the cleric and said, "She is the *other* one." Wonder ran an underlying current in his voice.

"Yes," said the caster, who had also turned to look at their healer. "But how do we *prove* it?" At the startled look he got from the paladin, he added, "She told us she was raised in an orphanage—both of her parents killed while she was very young by a raiding party." When the fighter still said nothing, he said, "So, how do we prove she is indeed *the other one?*"

Finding his voice at last, Thrinndor said, "If she is indeed 'the other one,' as you suspect, there will be records. We must find—"

"What 'other one'?" Cyrillis' voice came from the edge of the firelight.

All heads turned to see her sitting up, her legs crossed beneath her and facing the fire.

"Huh?" asked the mage.

Everyone began speaking at once.

"How are you feeling?" asked the paladin.

"She's awake!" said the rogue, rising to his feet.

"How long have you been listening?" asked Sordaak.

She tried to laugh, but that resulted in a fit of coughing.

Sordaak rushed to her side, slipping his water skin from its thong on his sash as he did. He wrapped an arm around her shoulders as he pressed the skin to her lips and tilted it as he gently leaned her head back. This allowed some of the tepid water to dribble into her waiting mouth.

She tried to drink greedily but spat most of it out in another spasm of coughing.

"Easy," cautioned the caster. He again pressed the skin to her lips. "Not so fast!"

Cyrillis nodded her agreement as she raised a hand to help with the transition of water from the skin to her mouth. Together they managed to get it right this time, and she took in several mouthfuls of the much needed fluid.

Pushing it away with a shake of her head, she said simply, "Some wine, please," her voice hoarse with disuse.

"Here," said the dwarf as he rose to his feet. He pulled a skin from his belt as he did so and threw it across the short distance to the mage, who caught it deftly with one hand.

"Thanks," he said as he pulled the stopper from the skin with his teeth. He started to repeat his actions with it, but changed his mind and handed it to the healer.

She snatched it from his hand, put it to her lips and drank deeply from the contents. Her shoulders again wracked in a fit of coughing. This time however, it was from the strong drink rather than her body rejecting the water as before.

Sordaak started to tell her again to take it easy, but when her brows knitted together saying 'don't' without words, he instead clamped his mouth shut and watched with concern apparent on his face.

After a second pull from the wine skin—this time with no adverse effects—she handed the almost-empty skin back to the caster and said "thank you," her voice raw from the strong drink.

Everyone watched her anxiously as she raised her head up and spoke to each in turn. First to Thrinndor, "Better, now." Then to the rogue, "Yes." And finally to the mage, "Only long enough to hear that last bit about proving someone to be 'the other one.'"

She fixed her gaze on the closest person to her, Sordaak, and repeated her first question: "What 'other one'?"

The caster stammered before finding his tongue. "Ummm," he started. "I uh—I mean we uh…" His face turned bright red. "Aw, hell!"

"What our most esteemed caster is trying to say," said the paladin in the uncomfortable silence that followed, "is that he believes you are a descendant of Angra-Khan and the third—and final—*human* piece required to return our lord to his rightful place in this plane!"

The cleric's eyes widened in surprise, and she reached out and snatched the dangling wine skin from the caster's hand, put it to her lips and once again drank deep.

Having emptied the contents, she threw the skin aside, wiped her mouth with the back of her hand and said, "Come again?"

Sordaak spoke quickly, interrupting the paladin even before he could open his mouth. "What the blowhard over there is trying to say," he jerked his thumb in the direction of the big fighter, "is that I was just advancing a theory that I have been working on for the past few days."

"And that theory is *I* am of the line of Angra-Khan?"

Sordaak now appeared to be giving the lace on his right sandal his undivided attention. "Yes," he said meekly.

"Preposterous!" she said. "On what could you possibly base this *theory?*"

"I…ummm…" stammered the caster again.

"What our imaginative friend is trying—"

Sordaak cut him off with a scathing look, saying, "It stands to follow that if I am indeed a descendant of Dragma and the aforementioned blowhard over there is indeed of the lineage of Valdaar, we were obviously brought together at this particular point in time by something—or someone—to accomplish a task."

He softened his tone as his eyes returned to Cyrillis. "And it stands to reason that if, as our paladin friend seems to believe, this task is to return your god from wherever, it would require the third offspring of the original Triad to be involved." He took a deep breath. "If that time is indeed now, and he and I are of that lineage, then a reasonable conclusion would be that you are of the appropriate lineage, as well."

He glanced over his shoulder at the two seated by the fire, still watching the proceedings with no small interest. "I am also reasonably certain we can rule out those two as candidates. There is no record of Valdaar's high priest being a dwarf." He grinned. "And the mental midget—"

"Hey!" groused Thumbs. Then he turned to look at the barbarian, a sly grin on his face. "I wouldn't let him talk about me that way, if I were you."

"Shut it," said the dwarf without taking his attention off of the scene unfolding before him.

"—over there has already told us about his heritage, and there was no mention of a high priest in it, either." As his thoughtful gaze got back to Cyrillis, he added, "So the logical conclusion is: You."

Her perplexed look went from the caster to the paladin and back. "But I have no idea as to who my parents were, let alone many generations ago!"

"I know this is a bit much to absorb right now," said the caster soothingly. "Especially in light of your recent…ordeal." He turned his attention to the paladin, who had regained his composure and was now sitting on a rock rimming the firelight. "Thrinndor is correct on one thing: If you are indeed of the lineage of Angra-Khan, there will certainly be a record of it." He shrugged. "We simply have to find it."

Cyrillis made to speak, but Sordaak gently pressed his fingers to her lips. "Not now. Everyone must rest." He looked around at each of his companions. "Eat and rest. Take time to think about what we have learned and what has taken place these last couple of weeks." His gaze once again fell upon the cleric, his eyes soft. "Sleep on it. We will open the discussion again in the morning. But for now eat, rest and sleep."

A silence descended upon the camp as initially no one moved. Finally, Savinhand broke the reverie as he started rattling pots and pans. After a few moments, he served up a plate for Cyrillis of what he had prepared earlier.

Slowly, small talk returned to the group and they began to unwind from the tension that had held each of them at peak readiness for a fortnight.

After the hearty meal, weariness settled down on the party like a blanket. As one they began setting up their bedrolls, crawled in and were soon fast asleep.

Only Fahlred remained vigilant. The quasit walked slowly over and stared down at the cleric from his perch on a rock. "This is going to be complicated," he hissed.

Chapter Twenty-One

Revelations

Morning broke over their little camp with the fire rekindled to a hearty blaze and the smell of coffee in the air. Savinhand had awakened before the rest and had quietly gotten breakfast going.

A light frost had covered everything in sight, including the blanketed bundles containing most of the party members. It reminded Savin that it was getting late in the year, although at these higher elevations the frosts generally come early.

Some mystery meat he had discovered in the packs on the animals was sizzling noisily in the pan by the time the others were poking their heads out of their blankets. Bacon, he decided, but wasn't sure exactly which type of swine it came from—he had certainly not encountered the like before. Probably not from a standard farm animal, he decided, but rather from some wild boar or such. Probably...

They'd eat it, the rogue decided with a smile playing across his lips. And probably like it. Probably. He smiled again.

Vorgath stumbled up to the fire holding his hands out to warm them. He spied the coffee pot nestled up to some coals on the edge of the fire and cursed vehemently when he bent to pick it up.

He set it back down quickly, shaking his hand violently to cool it. He glared at Savin and dared him to say something, but the rogue just smiled and pretended not to notice as he turned the meat in the pan. The barbarian grumbled as he spotted a rag nearby that was most likely there for the purpose. He grabbed it and used that to shield his smarting hand from the heat as he poured some of the midnight black liquid into his cup.

He scowled again at the rogue and stumped over to a rock rimming the fire and sat down. *Damn the rock felt good*, he decided, as it had warmed from the blaze.

One by one the rest of the group filtered in, some mumbling greetings, others dourly pouring themselves a cup of coffee.

Cyrillis was last to approach the fire. She ignored the coffee and declined to sit. Instead she stood off to one side, arms crossed and waited.

The companions again approached the rogue to get their plate filled and retrieved a hard biscuit made not so hard by sitting on a rock next to some coals.

When each had returned to his seat, only Cyrillis had not approached for food. Savinhand looked at her and noting the still slightly discolored tone of her skin, he smiled and said, "You should eat something." He held out a plate for her to inspect. "You'll feel better."

She hesitated, and then her shoulders slumped resignedly and she stepped forward to accept the proffered plate.

"Thank you," she mumbled as she stepped away. She eyed the coffee pot on her way by but decided against it and instead fetched a water skin as she dropped to the ground cross legged within reach of the fire's warmth.

She pushed the food around on her plate, allowing it to cool and sampled some of the eggs. They were seasoned with something faintly familiar, but she was not sure exactly what it was. "This is good," she said, momentarily forgetting about the heritage issues she had been so worked up over just a few minutes ago. "Where did you learn to cook?"

Savin's face colored slightly as he shoved aside what remained on his pan with a biscuit he had pulled from the fire. "Although I am but a simple rogue," he began, "I have a taste for good food." He grinned at the other men at the fire. "And if I want good food, I must make it myself—I certainly cannot rely on *these guys* to prepare anything palatable." His smile broadened. "Over the years, I've learned if one wants something, one should be prepared to do or make it oneself! So I learned to cook and I always carry my spices with me to do so." He shrugged as he sat and began attacking the small pile of eggs remaining in his pan. He looked up at the healer over a spoonful of the mixture. "And," he said, his face coloring still darker, "thanks."

Nothing more was said as they ate. Savinhand took a moment to put on a fresh pot of coffee.

As he started cleaning up his pans, Thrinndor finally broke the silence. "Well, people," he began, unsure of just what questions would be forthcoming but knowing he had to begin somewhere. "We need to talk about what is next."

Cyrillis looked up from her empty plate—she had not realized just how hungry she had been—and said before anyone else could beat her to it, "But what about me?" she asked. It was her turn for some face reddening, "I mean—"

"We will get to that in a moment," the paladin interrupted gently. "I promise."

The cleric looked back down at her plate, "I am sorry," she began. "I am not usually so impetuous." She looked up again. "But, well, I did not sleep very well last night—all of this was weighing heavily on my mind." She now looked to be on the verge of tears. "It is all so much…" Her eyes again dropped.

"Yes," replied Thrinndor, his tone reassuring. "Of that I am certain." He set his own plate aside. "That is—those are questions we must attend to ere we continue our quest. However, each of us must also attend to training issues with our respective mentors." He paused while he considered what to discuss next. "Yet one or more of us must accompany our healer friend to assist her in discovering her history—that is also now vital to our endeavor." He turned his gaze upon Cyrillis. "If she is who we suppose, then our ultimate goal is nigh." He allowed an undercurrent of triumph to creep into his voice.

"I believe my research skills would be best suited to aid her," began Sordaak. "But my own task before me is daunting." The grim expression on his face told how much he dreaded this task. "I see now that I must turn from Chaos and embrace the conscripts of Law. This is going to set me back in my studies, perhaps months! Even if my previous master still lived, he would be of no further use to me! I must seek out a new mentor, one who can intertwine what I have already learned with this new concept—to me, anyway—of Law." His face was torn with the knowledge of what he was up against.

"Do you know of such a mentor?" suggested the paladin, trying to ease his friend's discomfort.

"Yes," said the caster, a forlorn look in his eyes. "But I don't know where to find him, or even if he yet lives."

"Who is it?" asked the fighter.

"Rheagamon." Sordaak did not look up as he said this. The name seemed to tumble from his quivering lips.

"What?" said Savinhand. "*Who?*"

Thrinndor's eyes opened wide. "He was rumored to have been killed years ago by the Frost Giants to the North".

"No," said the mage, still not looking up. "He survived and began work on building a keep somewhere in the mountains to our west." He looked up to fix his gaze on the barbarian. "But I don't know where to even *begin* looking!"

"I do," said the dwarf, his gaze unwavering. "In fact, it is not far from here." He looked in the indicated direction. "And you are correct—he does yet live."

"But," blurted out the rogue, "he is a *Drow!*" He spat the name as if it were a curse.

"A dark elf?" asked Cyrillis. "Their kind was cast out from this region centuries ago!"

"Not all," said the caster, shaking his head slowly. "A small group escaped the notice of the *purge*, hiding in the abandoned mines of Yanmar. There they flourished and practiced the dark arts of their kind. Only in recent years have they started to emerge." His eyes locked with those of the paladin. "Rheagamon is one such."

"OK," said a bewildered Savinhand, "the phrases 'exile' and 'building a keep' are not generally woven together in the same story. Not for the same people anyway!"

"Why were they chased from these lands?" Sordaak asked of the thief, whose face still held a measure of shock.

The rogue shook his head to clear whatever reverie he was in, and said, "What?" His eyes focused on the caster. "Oh, because they…ummm," he stammered and a confused look came on his face. "Because they…well—I don't know the answer to that!"

"Precisely," said the caster. "You will be hard pressed to find any recording of why exactly the purge occurred." He turned his gaze upon the cleric. "Essentially the elves decided their dark brethren were getting too powerful. Rumors were circulated about the Drow, human sacrifice and other demonic rituals. And poof! You had a purge." Sordaak was quiet for a moment. "It is said that in actuality none of the rumors were true. However, by the time the facts came out, the Drow had been in exile for several years. Much effort was spent to hide the truth—and in fact you will find little in the records related to that truth, either."

Sordaak paused to remove his pipe and tobacco from their pouches and began to build a smoke. No one said anything, knowing what was to come must be important. Vorgath, however, also removed his smoke and moved hopefully over to sit next to the caster, who obligingly lit both pipes when they had been prepared.

"Rheagamon was young during the purge," the mage said as he puffed away contentedly on his pipe. Vorgath blew a few rings, obviously hopeful of another contest, but Sordaak did not appear to notice. "But he was already very powerful. In the recluse of their exile, he had little else to do but add to those powers. He soon became their most powerful sorcerer and eventually their leader."

"But," blurted out the thief, "that was *hundreds* of years ago!"

"Yes," said the mage, ignoring the outburst. "But elves live very long lives—and the Drow are no different." A small measure of envy crept into his voice. "If left to their own, it is said they can almost be counted among the immortal." His eyes lost their faraway look, and he seemed to return to the group as he took another puff. "While at five or six hundred years he would certainly no longer be considered young, he would not be considered ancient, either."

"He's not," said the barbarian as he too took another puff.

Sordaak looked thoughtfully at the dwarf. "You seem to know a lot about the goings-on in the world of the Drow."

Vorgath merely shrugged. "You keep a certain amount of attention on those you share the underground with." At the mage's raised brow, he added, "*Share* is actually not the correct term. Although both races lived below the surface, we never comingled." With a twinkle in his eye he said, "We just wanted to make sure it stayed that way!" He shrugged again.

Sordaak nodded. "Actually, that explains a lot—and confirms some of what I've suspected." A thought occurred to him. "You said his keep is not far from here?" His tone was hopeful. "You can tell me where it is?"

"Of course," said the dwarf, who puffed at his pipe in futility, for it had gone out due to inattention. Sighing, he leaned forward and pulled a smoldering branch from the fire and relit it. After he had a full head of smoke going again, he tossed the branch back into the fire and settled back to a more comfortable position. "I will take you there." He was obviously pleased to be of such service. "It is indeed not far."

"Thank you," said Sordaak formally. "Your accompaniment would certainly be welcome!"

The barbarian nodded. "Mention it not," he replied, also formally. "For it is on the path I must take to return to my people."

Thrinndor cocked an inquisitive eyebrow at this statement, but said nothing.

"What?" said the dwarf defensively. "You said we each will require time with our trainers. Mine is there with my people. That, and I must relate how I bested the whelp offspring of a god—"

Thrinndor exploded, "There must be no mention—" He stopped, however, seeing the huge grin on his friend's face.

"You have to admit," said the grinning dwarf, "it makes a good tale."

"Well, we will have to see what we can do in the near future that would allow you to tell such a tale," said the paladin, also grinning. "Even if it is nothing more than mere fantasy and exaggeration!"

"Ha!" snorted Vorgath.

"To allow you to do that, however—tell your tales, that is—we must first complete our mission," he stopped grinning as his eyes moved back to the caster. "We must first find that sword and then return Valdaar to our realm so he can regain his rightful place among the gods."

A silence pervaded the group for a moment. Finally Sordaak shrugged his shoulders. "Then find it we must!" He grinned and shook his head, "Damn!" he said. "Now I am even starting to talk like you two!" His smiling eyes went from the paladin to the healer, and back. "See what you have done?"

Thrinndor's grin went even wider. "Well, better us than a *barbarian*, right?"

"Hey!" groused the dwarf playfully.

"You got that right!" Sordaak winked at Vorgath.

"OK, then," said Thrinndor, returning the group to the present discussion. "We have Vorgath and Sordaak going—" He raised an eyebrow at the dwarf.

"West."

"West," continued the paladin, "to work on training and truth stretching." He winked at the dwarf. "Savin," he looked at the thief, "what about you?"

"I must also spend some time with my guild," said the rogue. "I need to work on my trap skills—"

"You got that right!" said the dwarf. He got into the winking act by batting an eye at their thief.

"Yeah, well," said Savinhand, "I also need to inquire about those assassins—there should not have been that many." He shook his head as he pondered this fact. "That makes no sense. Someone needs to know." He looked over at the paladin. "I will be traveling south. Our main encampment is near Grandmere."

Suddenly Sordaak looked up to fix the thief with a penetrating stare. "Can you find out for us the location of this Library you told us about?"

"*The Library of Antiquity*?" said the rogue. "Not a chance!" The mage's stare turned to a frown. "Even if I could find this out, I could never divulge such information! I would be hunted down and killed!" After a moment he added, "Slowly." When no one said anything he added, "*Very* slowly."

"We—I—would not allow that to happen," said the caster.

Savin was obviously not convinced.

"I have a feeling," said Sordaak. "No, more than a feeling, a strong hunch, that this library you have spoken of—assuming it dates back as far as you say—will have information we will *need*." He fixed his stare on the rogue, who shifted uncomfortably. "And *soon*."

"Absolutely not!" Savin's eyes darted from Sordaak to Thrinndor, begging them to understand. "I have bowed to your wishes, and will even serve Valdaar as best I can while traveling with this group! But this is too much!" At their continued silence he said, "You don't understand!" His voice rose to where he was almost shouting. "The library is the most closely guarded secret in my guild!" His eyes darted to now encompass the healer, as well. "They would probably kill me just for *mentioning it still exists*!"

The mage raised an eyebrow. "Very well," he said, drawing surprised looks from everyone in the group—even Savinhand, who had not expected to be let off of the hook so easily.

"I will do some quiet research on my own," continued the caster. "Perhaps I will be able to discern its location without your help."

"You don't understand!" Savinhand was now sweating profusely. "You must forget you *even heard of The Library of Antiquity*!" He was again shouting. "If you begin asking questions and my association with you is even suspected, then..." he drew a single finger across his throat, "you would be in the market for a new thief."

"Rogue," corrected the caster. "Very well," Sordaak repeated, again causing heads to rotate in his direction. He waved a hand dismissively and turned to begin packing his things. "I fear I will be too engrossed in my new studies—not to mention acclimating to a new master—to worry about a few moldy tomes." He looked up at the rogue. "Forget I mentioned it," he said as he began stuffing his bedroll in its bag.

Somewhat mollified, the rogue turned to pack his belongings as well. In so doing, however, his eyes fell upon the paladin, who stood unmoving with his arms crossed. He was still looking at the thief, his brows scrunched together in a frown.

"What?" cried Savinhand. "You don't *understand!* There is *nothing I can do!*"

"Whatever," groused the dwarf as he too turned from the fire to begin gathering his things.

"You do not know that," began the fighter. "You are not willing to even—"

"No!" snapped the caster from the edge of the camp, causing all eyes to again turn his direction. "Leave him be. He's probably right—nothing can be done." His eyes locked with those of the thief. "For now."

Thrinndor's forehead showed lines of deep thought. He started to speak and then decided against it, knowing the explanation might never come. He shrugged, wondering just what was going on inside the crazy caster's head, and applied his attention to packing as well.

Cyrillis was also packing, having been distracted by the tales of drow and libraries. "Wait," she said as she dropped her sack and looked directly at Thrinndor. "What was decided about learning of my ancestry?"

The paladin looked up from his pack, thought about it and said, "Nothing." Cyrillis took in a breath to speak sharply but Thrinndor added quickly, "Yet."

She exhaled and folded her arms across her chest. Her patience was nearing its end.

The paladin stood upright and scratched his head. "I apologize," he began slowly. "We all got thrown off of the original discussion." He cocked his head as he thought. "Let us see. Sordaak needs time to acclimate to a new master and a new way of thinking." He looked at Vorgath. "Vorgy here will accompany him to meet this new master and then continue on his way to his kindred." He turned his attention to the rogue. "Savin must report in to his guild to both train and work out some answers on these assassins we have had to deal with—"

"I will also make some *discreet* inquiries about the library," said the rogue, contrition in his voice.

Sordaak stopped what he was doing, raised an eyebrow and said, "Thank you." As he bent back down to his pack, he straightened suddenly. "Be *careful.*" When all eyes turned upon him, he defensively went on. "Not only must you not get yourself killed—which is important, by the way—"

"Gee, thanks, boss," said the thief. "Your concern is touching!"

Sordaak frowned as he continued. "You must also not alert them—or anyone, for that matter—as to our *true purpose.*" He paused for a moment. "That would probably end our little quest before it really gets rolling."

"Got it," said the rogue. "Don't get myself killed, and, oh, by the way, don't let anyone know I am now supporting a group of zealots trying to return a dead god to life!" It was his turn to fold his arms across his chest. "Which would also get me killed," he added. "Does that about sum it up?"

"Yup," said the mage smugly, as he went about the task of finishing his packing.

Thrinndor smiled, shook his head and continued. "That just leaves you and me," he said as he turned to look at the cleric.

"How *convenient*," muttered the caster, *sotto voce*.

The paladin chose to ignore that remark. "But I too must spend some time with the Paladinhood. Both to train and see if anything new has come to light that might aid our quest."

Cyrillis made to speak, but Thrinndor said before she could, "You too must meet with those who have done so well thus far with your training." She nodded a silent thanks. "Surely there is more you can yet gain from their tutelage." Again she nodded but said nothing. "With which temple are you associated?"

She hesitated before answering, then shrugged and said, "Myanmoor."

"What?" said Sordaak, who stood suddenly and whipped his head around. "That temple is dedicated to the Minions of *Set*!"

Knowing the question was coming, Cyrillis had prepared her answer. "Yes, it is," she began slowly. "But it is a *loose* dedication." She held up her hand to forestall the mage as he took in a breath to speak. "They tolerate us—the servants of Valdaar—as well as servants of several other *gods*." She wrinkled her nose distastefully. "As long as the coin and gems continue to flow in, that is." Again she shrugged. "There are no known remaining temples to Valdaar. Lord Praxaar made certain of that!"

"Amen," said the paladin, showing support for what she must have had to go through working through a temple dedicated to the Minions of Set.

She lowered her eyes before continuing. "However," she began, "I have not been with them long." Her eyes looked up to meet with those of the paladin. "Most of my early training was done by a single master. In fact," she said, choosing her words carefully, a fact noticed by Thrinndor, "almost all of my training was done by this man. I have only been studying at the Temple for these past few months." She shrugged as she made busy storing the remainder of her goods.

The paladin's eyebrow was wandering up and down his forehead as he tried to decide whether to push her.

"Ytharra," Cyrillis blurted out, just as the paladin said, "Who was..."

Their eyes met, and the apprehension Cyrillis had been feeling suddenly melted and she began to laugh. Thrinndor smiled and then he followed suit.

Sordaak, however, stood straight up at the name. "Ytharra?" he asked as the laughing subsided somewhat. "I remember you mentioning the name before, but for some reason I didn't make the connection."

Both Cyrillis and Thrinndor turned to look at the caster.

"Yes," said the cleric, aforementioned apprehension returning. "Do you know him?"

"Me?" asked the caster. "No. Not personally anyway." He frowned deeply before he continued. "However, I do know *of* him."

His frown continued as he was obviously deep in thought. Finally Thrinndor could stand it no more. "What connection? Please explain."

"Yes, please," Cyrillis was almost pleading.

Sordaak's brow furrows grew deeper.

"Well," he began. "Old guy, right?" He struggled to focus his eyes on those of the cleric.

She merely nodded.

"How old?" he asked.

Taken aback, Cyrillis did not immediately reply. "Ummm," she stammered. "Why, I do not really know. He was *old* as far back as I can remember."

"Why?" asked Thrinndor. He was unsure how this all tied together but was certain that it did.

The caster turned his focus on the paladin, seeming to notice him for the first time.

"Huh?" he asked absentmindedly. He took in a deep breath and released as he carefully considered his reply. "His name came up several times during some of Parothenticas' more lucid moments." The caster again fell silent as he struggled to remember exactly what the old man had said.

"Oh?" said Thrinndor. "How so?"

"Gimme a minute!" snapped the mage.

Finally Sordaak shrugged and threw up his hands. "I don't exactly remember," he began. "However, from what I can piece together of what the old man told me, he—your Ytharra—was with Parothenticas in Dragma's Keep long, long ago."

Chapter Twenty-Two

Until We Meet Again

"What?" said the healer as she staggered back.

"How can that be?" said Thrinndor.

"How the hell do I know?" Sordaak groused. "I'm just repeating what I was told as I remember it!" He glared at the paladin from under the stubble of what remained of his eyebrows.

The caster's tone abruptly changed. "How did he die?" he asked Cyrillis, turning his attention back to her.

"What?" she asked, startled by the change of direction. "Well, I don't know exactly." Her tone was reverent. "He just lay down one day, handed me the staff and said his work was complete."

"That," she added quickly, "and he told me I had to find from whence it—the staff, that is—and I came."

She then bowed her head. When her face came back up, her eyes were closed and her cheeks were wet as tears made their way to her chin, where they dripped onto her tunic.

"Before he died, he sang to me," she whispered.

She opened her eyes and began to sing.

Sordaak, his body trembling, had been listening with every fiber of his being and knew what was coming next. Together—eyes locked, with tears streaming down both sets of cheeks—they sang a song they had only heard once, yet could never forget:

> *For those that guard*
> *Time stands still*
> *Death may not take us*
> *Til our destiny we fulfill*

Silence must be our geas
    Ere those foretold walk the land
Whence we may once again speak
    For his time will be at hand
We prepare a path
    For our lords return
'Tis our fate
    Thus our hearts yearn
For those that guard
    Time stands still
Death may not take us
    'Til our destiny we fulfill

As they sang, Savin and Vorgath joined Thrinndor as they stood before the two in reverent silence.

When the last word had been sung, silence hung over the companions until the dwarf broke the reverie. "I thought you said you couldn't sing?" he accused Sordaak, his tone somehow playful and respectful.

"That was *beautiful!*" said the rogue, tears welling up in his eyes.

"Indeed," mused the fighter, quietly.

"Bah!" groused the barbarian, his voice gruff with emotion. "A bit pitchy—but not all that bad, nonetheless!"

Sordaak just grinned, but Thrinndor reached down and popped the dwarf playfully on the back of the head. "Show some respect, O ancient one!" he said, grinning from ear to ear.

Vorgath squared around and dropped into a fighting stance. "I'll show you the meaning of the word respect, your high-and-mightiness!"

But, before he could charge, Savin said, "Let me see if I can sum this up," and he put a hand out to stop the dwarf. "We have a couple of guys who hung around with Dragma in his keep several hundred years ago—making them *very old* indeed—who both now have recently died. But only after passing on what they knew to you two." He paused to indicate Sordaak and Cyrillis with a wave of his hand. "Who also just so happen to be descendants of this Angra-Kahn guy and Dragma." He went on before he could be interrupted. "And Angra-Khan's staff—one of the artifacts of power used by a member of Valdaar's Council—has now been found, as well as *Flinthgoor*—the greataxe wielded by Mondrell, Lord General of Valdaar's Armies." He took in a deep breath. "Leaving us with still needing to find Lord Valdaar's Sword and Dragma's Staff." He focused his attention on Thrinndor. "That and to release said Lord from where his soul—"

"Essence," corrected Thrinndor

Savinhand scowled at the paladin. "Very well," he said acidly, "from where his *essence* is trapped within a gem affixed to the pommel of this sword." He looked from the fighter, to the mage, to the cleric and finally back to the paladin. "Does that sound about right?"

Thrinndor hesitated for a moment, then shrugged and said, "Essentially." He smiled at the thief, who was shaking his head. "A couple of minor points left out, but nothing that requires correction."

Abruptly the paladin clapped his hands together once and then again. His smile broadened. "Very good!" he proclaimed. "Someone *was* listening!"

Cyrillis smiled and joined in the applause, although hers was more subdued. Sordaak merely folded his arms across his chest and attempted to scrunch his face in a deep scowl, failing miserably. The lack of eyebrows with the standard pointed hat just made him look comical.

No one laughed, however.

"Like what?" asked the rogue.

Thrinndor stopped clapping but continued to smile. "It is not important at this juncture. We will talk of it again—comparing notes and stories when we again meet to continue our quest."

Somewhat mollified, Savinhand shrugged and went back to packing. "Whatever!" he mumbled.

Thrinndor continued to stare at the back of this his newest convert. Somehow he felt deep inside that in him they had gained a very important piece to the puzzle.

A silence descended upon the group once again until Thrinndor turned to Cyrillis and said, "Myanmoor is not far from where I must go. I will see you to this Temple dedicated to *Set*." He spat the name as he would a curse. He pondered for a moment. "First we must stop by where we began our descent into Drama's Keep to pick up my mount."

"What?" sneered Sordaak. "You cannot possibly believe that old nag is still picketed back there? Not a chance!"

Thrinndor chose to ignore the slight, but his voice was gruff when he spoke. "He will be there. And so will the other animals—as long as they were not fallen upon by that party of orcs returning from their sojourn."

Nettled, but not sure why, Sordaak asked, "What makes you so sure he'll be there?"

The paladin bit off a sharp reply, deciding the mage simply did not understand. "You have your bond with your familiar. You would know if he were to die. I have a similar bond with my steed." His eyes bored into those of the caster. "He lives."

Sordaak decided to let it go—partly because he understood the connection thing, and partly because there was simply no point in arguing the point. He shrugged and went back to packing.

As he put the last of his gear in its place, Thrinndor turned around and noticed that all were looking at him. He said, "OK, it is settled then," and turned first to the rogue. "Savinhand travels south to Grandmere." His eyes shifted to the caster. "Sordaak and Vorgath will go west—"

"And a little north," offered the dwarf.

"Very well," said the paladin, "north and west." He next turned his attention to the healer. "While Cyrillis and I must go east toward the coast. There we should be able to pick up the main road to Lorithom. From there it is but a short distance to the entrance we used to descend into Dragma's Keep. We'll retrieve our mounts and then I will accompany her to Myanmoor." His eyes remained on the healer.

He looked from one to the other before continuing. "Well then," he began again, "there is the matter of time." His eyes fell to the caster. "Will two weeks be sufficient for everyone?"

"No," said the mage abruptly. "I will require a month—at a minimum." His face was devoid of expression. "Probably longer."

Thrinndor raised an eyebrow, thought for a moment and repeated, "Very well. We will all take extra time with our respective masters and/or trainers and meet in five weeks' time." He looked off to the north when a slightly worried expression crossed his mien. "It is getting late in the season and I would like to continue our quest before winter settles upon the land." He again circled the company with his eyes. "If all are in agreement?"

Sordaak nodded his.

"Meeting in Brasheer is obviously out of the question," he threw a mischievous glance that encompassed the caster and the rogue.

"Half of it has burnt to the ground, anyway!" said the barbarian playfully.

"So, for lack of a better place to meet," continued the paladin, a grin on his face, "the coastal town of Farreach should suit our purposes." Getting a nod from everyone, he added. "It is but a short distance from here and should have any provisions we might need to continue our journeys."

Once again, he looked around at each of them. "So, Farreach in five weeks time it is."

Each nodded.

"After I complete my time with my masters, which should not be more than a week—two at most—I will return to Myanmoor to assist Cyrillis in seeing what can be found out as to her parents. Any questions?" When he got no reply, he turned his attention to the animals Sordaak had brought back to the camp the day before. "We seem to be one mount short."

"Huh?" said Savinhand, trying to catch up with the sudden topic change.

"Four," said the paladin. "There are only four mounts, and there are five of us."

"Easy," said the dwarf. "I'm walking." He crossed his arms.

"Very well," said Thrinndor with a smile. "That was indeed easy enough."

Nothing else was said as they finished packing the animals assigned to each of them. A distinct uneasiness settled over the companions as they were loaded.

Finally, they gathered around the smoldering fire. Savinhand began kicking dirt on it, soon followed by Vorgath and Thrinndor. In short order it was reduced to light smoke, and they stood looking at one another.

"Well," the thief said suddenly, "I am the only one headed south, so I guess I'll hit the trail." He did not move. Instead, he shifted uneasily from one foot to another.

No one said anything.

"You know," he said as he looked up, trying to encompass the entire company with his eyes, "two or three weeks ago I was merely a stray working the gambling circuit through whichever town I came to next. Loosely associated with a guild that cared not whether I lived or died—as long as they got their cut." He shifted his weight again. "Now..." His eyes moved to lock with those of the caster who was standing a short distance away, amusement playfully tainting his visage. "...now I feel like I am *part of something*." He turned his gaze upon the paladin. "I feel like I *belong!*"

No one said anything at first, and the rogue shifted uncomfortably.

Finally Vorgath cleared his throat. "Enough of this mushy shit!" he groused, sounding not nearly as gruff as he intended. "Get on with that training so you will at least be of some *use* to us." His eyes twinkled. "Or I'll have to show you how it's done!" He hefted his greataxe in his ham-like right fist, illustrating just how he thought it should be done.

Abruptly he flipped the weapon to his left hand and reached out with his right. Smiling, Savinhand also reached out and they clasped forearms as they looked into one another's eyes.

They held this stance for only a moment and then the rogue spun, leapt onto his chosen mount's back and kicked his heels to the flanks of the beast. The startled animal bolted in a cloud of dust and was soon out of sight over the ridge.

Thrinndor waited until the dust had settled and then he turned to focus on the mage. "You have a plan?" was all he said, obviously referring to the discussion that had been cut short about the Library of Antiquity.

Now it was Sordaak's turn to shift uncomfortably from foot to foot. "Yes," he said finally. "But the fewer that know about it the better its chance for success." As the paladin's eyebrow inched higher, Sordaak rolled his eyes and went on, "Look, we'll talk it over when we get back together! Not before!"

Thrinndor considered pushing the matter further—it was just *too* important! Ultimately however, he decided that he was going to have to learn to trust this odd magicuser, because if he couldn't then it didn't matter to their cause, for it would certainly be lost.

He exhaled noisily and said, "Very well," his shoulders slumped in submission.

Vorgath cocked an eyebrow of his own. "Do gods use that term 'very well' a lot?" His eyes sparkled and he smiled. "Either way, it's starting to get on my nerves!"

Thrinndor inhaled to snap off an indignant reply but smiled instead. "Silence, peon!" He waved an arm dismissively as he moved toward a rather large sorrel he had selected as his mount.

The horse rolled its eyes as the big man climbed aboard, trying to determine what chance he had of getting rid of this burden. Snorting noisily, it decided it was probably not worth the effort.

"Shall we?" Thrinndor asked as he looked at the cleric, who grabbed a fistful of scraggly mane on the ungainly looking mule she had been relegated by her size to ride and swung easily into a make-shift saddle.

"We shall," she said as she too slapped her heels to the beast's flanks. The mule, unaccustomed to such behavior, simply stood there and craned its neck to see just exactly what was going on back there.

Cyrillis was trying to decide whether cuffing the animal's ear or sweet-talking it would be the best approach when a grinning Thrinndor started his mount in a slow circle to the west. The mule recognizing the sorrel as being its traveling companion fell into step behind him.

The cleric snorted derisively as she made several attempts, to no avail, to get her mount to move up beside Thrinndor's mount.

"Damn jackass!" she muttered as the paladin turned to wave at the dwarf and the mage.

"See you guys in five weeks," he called out to them. "Try not to keep us waiting, old one!"

"You won't be waiting on *me*!" replied the barbarian. "Just you make sure you don't get lost without me!" He turned to the mage with a wink. "Damn paladin could get lost getting out of bed!" His eyes twinkled.

He did not hear Thrinndor's reply as he turned and grasped the mage on his shoulder and squeezed hard enough to make the human wince. "C'mon," he said. "It's not far. We can make it before evening if we get a move on!"

"Right," said Sordaak. He eyed the mule that had been relegated to him as well. "I think I'll walk." His tone was dubious. "For now." He grasped the make-shift reins of the beast and fell into step beside the dwarf as he headed west—and a little north.

Forthcoming in 2015...
The Valdaar's Fist Saga Continues!

Valdaar's Fist Book One – Dragma's Keep

Valdaar's Fist Book Two – The Library of Antiquity

Valdaar's Fist Book Three – Ice Homme

Valdaar's Fist Book Four – The Platinum Dragon

Acknowledgements

Thank you to the following for their contribution to this book:

My wife, for her patience, understanding and support as I often floundered in my efforts to make this book a reality.

Ken McMillian, my first Dungeon Master and the guy that helped me forge this series.

Robert Lewis, the first to read this book. And then he convinced me I needed to move forward with it

David Epstein, another with a less-than-gentle push toward publishing

Craig Lancaster, my editor. He takes my story and ideas and makes them readable.

About the Author

Vance Pumphrey traces the evolution of his high fantasy novels from his Nuclear Engineering career in the U.S. Navy—not an obvious leap. He started playing Dungeons and Dragons while in the Navy, though, and the inspiration for *Dragma's Keep* was born.

Dragma's Keep is the first book in the Valdaar's Fist quartet. A second book in the series follows soon.

Retired from the Navy, Vance lives in Seattle with his wife of thirty-plus years.

To find out when the next Valdaar's Fist book will be released, check out VancePumphrey.com.

Made in the USA
Charleston, SC
25 July 2015